"Stone demonstrates a deep understand[ing] of the divide that runs between urban worldliness and small town isolation...Her storytelling weaves together disparate threads into a vibrant canvas that kept me turning pages."

JENEVIVE DESROCHES author of *Oblong*

"A well-plotted thriller...[Stone] makes the locations of Waterton and the national park into living, pulsing characters in their own right."

A.F. LINLEY editor-in-chief *Kisreth Studio*

"[Stone] takes a complicated stew of murder, mystery, and mayhem and boils it down to its essence with lyrical writing and perfectly timed revelations."

MONTI SHALOSKY author/editor

"One heck of a Crime Thriller... The ending won't disappoint!"

S.J. PIERCE author of the *Alyx Rayer Mystery* series

THE
DARKDIVIDE

a novel by
D. K. Stone

Stonehouse Publishing
www.stonehousepublishing.ca
Alberta, Canada

THE
DARKDIVIDE

a novel by
D. K. Stone

Stonehouse Publishing
www.stonehousepublishing.ca
Alberta, Canada

Stonehouse Publishing Inc is an independent publishing house,
incorporated in 2014.

Cover design and layout by Janet King
Printed in Canada

Stonehouse Publishing would like to thank and acknowledge
the support of the Alberta Government funding for the arts,
though the Alberta Media Fund.

Government

National Library of Canada Cataloguing in Publication Data
Stone, D. K.
The Dark Divide
Novel
ISBN: 978-1-988754048 (paperback)
First Edition

"Experience is a brutal teacher, but you learn.
My god, do you learn."
C. S. Lewis

For D and the Boyotes,
my first, last, and best readers.

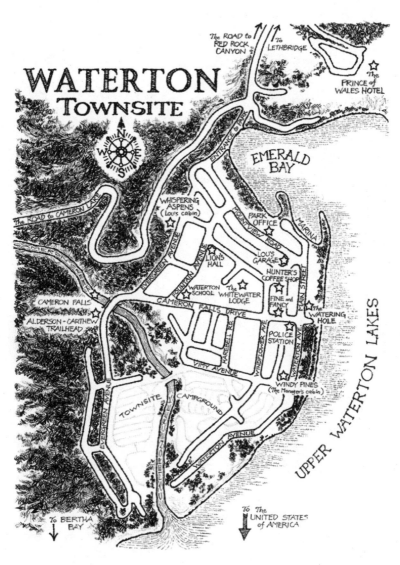

PROLOGUE: OHIO, 1970

The first hint of danger was a howl so distant, it was more a feeling than a sound.

Catherine's laughter faded uncertainly. She looked up from the firelight to focus on the screen of trees that separated the knot of students from the regal red-brick bulk of Muskingum College.

"Did you hear something?" she asked.

The boy next to her lowered his harmonica. "What?"

"I… I'm not sure. A dog, maybe?"

Around the fire, conversations hushed as the jovial atmosphere of the protest changed between one breath and the next. Catherine's gaze moved around the clearing. She took in her college friends—young men and women gathered around a fire the way they'd done any number of times since the start of the school year—and then returned to the screen of trees. Between the branches, she could see the lights of her dorm, the college a twinkling gem in the setting of New Concord. She gnawed the edge of her thumbnail. She shouldn't be out here. *Not really.* If she walked back now, perhaps she could slip past the police patrol and get back to—

A howl broke the air.

"Police dogs!" someone shouted. "They're coming for us!"

The group rose, abandoning the bonfire. Catherine struggled to follow, but her left foot had fallen asleep in the hours since they'd been in the woods. She took two uncertain steps and looked back across the flames. The woods between the college and her were no longer empty. Dots of light moved through the trees.

"Cath! Come on!"

Heart pounding, she forced herself into motion. Her leaden foot had cost Catherine time and with no firelight to guide her, she stumbled into the darkened forest, hands outstretched like a sleep-walker.

Up ragged slopes and down shallow valleys, the silhouettes of her friends disappeared into shadow, leaving her alone on the slope. Never an athlete, her speed was half theirs. A dog barked—closer now—and Catherine glanced back again. Flashlights bounced in the trees.

She rushed up the next hill. "Hold on!" she panted. "I'm coming!"

A lone figure paused at the top. "You need to hurry!"

An officer's voice on the megaphone echoed from the distant campus: "*...the use of deadly force permitted for those resisting arrest...*" Catherine had seen the videos on television: Armed troops, the bodies of protesters in the street. She *knew* what those orders meant. Panicked, she half-fell, half-ran down the nearest slope, then started up the next. A terrified voice chattered in the back of her mind: *They shot students at Kent State!*

Branches tore her hair and slashed her face. She reached the top and squinted into the darkness. All but one of her friends was gone.

Catherine caught hold of a tree trunk. "W-wait!" she gasped. "I-I can't—I can't keep up with you!" Behind her, a dog barked. She spun. "No!" Her ankle twisted and she screamed and fell to her knees. A bouncing flashlight switched direction at the sound.

"Cath!"

Crying, she threw herself back into motion. She couldn't see the officer yet, but she could hear him.

"Hurry, Cath! RUN!"

She ran and fell. Ran again. Unable to catch her breath, her vision swam. "I-I'm coming," she choked. "I—I—"

Frantic barking broke her concentration. *The dogs had picked up her scent!* Winded, Catherine lost her footing. Her ankle twisted a second time and she tumbled down the hill, the world turning end over end as her screams echoed through the glade.

She hit the bottom with a thud.

"You okay?" a voice called, impossibly far away.

She tried to answer, but her lip was split and her mouth full of blood. Twigs bit through the palms of her hands. Confused, she clambered to her feet and wavered in place. She took two more unsteady steps. *Was this the hill she'd fallen down? Or the next?* She couldn't seem to catch her breath. Couldn't see where she was supposed to go.

"Cath, hold on! I'm coming to help you. Just wait and—"

A beam of light swung across her face.

"STOP!" a voice bellowed from the shadows.

Terrified, Catherine bolted.

The valley exploded with thunder. The sound threw her backward as a white firebrand of pain tore through her chest and back. Catherine tried to scream, but her voice was gone. She slumped to the ground. The pain separated her from the night, the darkness, and the figure of the man who strode forward, his flashlight bouncing between the trees. Her legs kicked one last time as the police officer reached her side.

"Jesus Christ," he breathed. "She's just a kid."

In the forest behind him, a shadow moved.

CHAPTER ONE

It seemed to Rich Evans that his innocence was an afterthought. *Someone* would go to jail for arson, and he'd do as well as anyone else. A month after the multi-million dollar Whitewater Lodge burned to the ground, killing Amanda Sloane, Rich's preliminary hearing began.

Judge Pelletier stared at Rich over the rim of her half-moon glasses. "At this time, I would like to call back in session the preliminary hearing of the Crown versus Mr. Richard Evans, regarding the arson in the Whitewater Lodge complex in Waterton Park, Alberta..."

When Rich Evans thought back on the months since he'd arrived in Canada, it was always in terms of seasons. Spring had been coldly indifferent to his arrival in the sleepy border town, the inclement weather a match for the locals. Summer's warmth had brought with it the heat of romance with Louise Newman, the one person who understood him when no one else did. But that bright spot of happiness had been matched by a hatred that culminated in the fire that destroyed the hotel, killed one of his staff, and effectively ended Rich's career.

In the last days, fall had arrived. No longer thriving on tourist traffic, some of Waterton's businesses closed immediately, boarded windows appearing overnight. Others slowed until they were mere ghosts, the industrious summer staff replaced by weary owners. Handwritten notes on doors said: *Closed for the winter. Back next spring.* The stream of visitors slowed to a trickle.

Days were long; nights longer. The streets, empty of tourists, were replenished by returning wildlife. Bighorn sheep stood in the parking lot of Hunter's Coffee Shop and licked dirt off the hubcaps of parked cars. Deer meandered down Main Street and caused unexpected traffic jams. Even the cougars returned, slinking through night time gardens and leaving oversized paw prints in soft soil. A peaceful silence engulfed the town as the pace of life slowed to an earlier era.

Rich wondered what this new season would mean for the upheaval in his life.

"May we note for the record," the judge said, "that this hearing is *not* to judge guilt or innocence, but to assess whether there is, indeed, enough evidence for the Crown to pursue a trial. As Mr. Callaghan finished yesterday, Mr. Asharif will have the floor this morning."

After three days of testimony, Rich's hopes had all but disappeared. His lawyer, Stu Callaghan, had warned him that the prosecution would call on new witnesses today. *But who?* It was a wonder there was anyone left to defame him. The arson investigators from the Lethbridge police force had already done their damage. The staff at the Whitewater hotel hadn't helped. And Rich knew he wasn't a favorite of the locals, of course, but to put him in jail for something he hadn't done? Surely, no one hated him that much. His stomach clenched. *Did they?*

"Thank you, your Honor," Mr. Asharif said. "I'm ready to begin."

Rich frowned as the shiny-haired lawyer sauntered across the floor. Glen Asharif, crown prosecutor, knew how to twist the nuances of testimony to his favour. He'd done it endless times in the last few days.

"I'd like to thank the witnesses who've joined us here today." The lawyer cast a toothy smile toward the defense table where Rich sat. "At this time I decline the option to question Mr. Callaghan's last witness, but would prefer to call forward a new one."

Murmurs rustled through the room and Rich began to sweat in his silk suit. *This* was what Stu had warned him about.

"A new witness?" the judge said.

"Yes, your Honor. I mentioned it when I brought forward the revised list yesterday."

"Ah, yes. The prosecution may proceed."

Asharif's voice rose: "I'd like the court to recognize a server from the Prince of Wales Hotel." Rich's gaze jerked to the bench. His eyes caught a figure in the back row. A redhead. He'd missed her when he'd walked in this morning. "I call Ms. Grace Blessington to the stand."

"Grace Blessington, step forward," the foreman said.

Rich's heart sank. *The waitress from the Prince of Wales when Lou and I went for dinner.* She walked to the stand as the prosecutor organized his notes.

"Could you state your name for the record, please?" Asharif said.

"Grace," she said. "Grace Blessington."

"I'd like it noted, Ms. Blessington, though this isn't a trial, it is still a court of law. Do you promise to tell the truth, the whole truth, and nothing but the truth?"

The woman's eyes flickered anxiously to Rich. "I do."

"Excellent. Then let's begin…"

The questions started and Rich leaned in to Stu. "Did you know she'd be testifying today?"

"I saw her name on the revised list, but hoped she wouldn't be the one."

"Why didn't you tell me it was her?"

"Figured it'd rattle you if I did." Stu shrugged. "Besides, this is just a prelim. But with Grace here it seems like they might get that trial after all."

Rich sat back, light-headed.

"Yes, he came into the hotel," Grace continued.

"Which hotel was this?"

"The POW."

"Could you state the full name of the hotel for the committee?" Asharif said.

"Sorry, The Prince of Wales hotel." Grace peeked over at Rich. "Mr. Evans came in for dinner one night a few weeks ago."

"When was this?"

"August, or maybe sometime in late July. About a week before the Whitewater Lodge burned down. I, um… I can't remember the date."

"That's fine, Ms. Blessington," Asharif said. "I've called in the receipts for the week." He turned to Judge Pelletier. "The date, your Honor, is identified as July 29th, confirmed by credit card receipts." He turned back to the woman. "Now, Miss Blessington, you say Mr. Evans came into the restaurant at the Prince of Wales for dinner?"

"That's right."

"Was he alone?"

"No. He was there with his girlfriend."

"Ah, yes," Asharif said. "His girlfriend, Louise Newman, owner of Waterton's local garage. That's right." The lawyer paused next to the defense table and smirked. Rich clenched his teeth as the word 'oily' came to mind. "Tell us a little about what you heard that night," Asharif said. "You gave a statement to Constables Black Plume and Flagstone a few days later."

"I told them what he said the night he and Lou came in for dinner."

"And what was that?"

"Stuff about the Whitewater. Troubles he was having. Mr. Evans seemed pretty upset."

"Could you tell the court what he said? Keep in mind, Ms. Blessington, that you're under oath."

"Well, like I said, Mr. Evans was upset that night. He got kind of loud. He was talking about the big hotel—the Whitewater, that is—and at one point, he said it would be easier to take it down and start over."

It was like a car crash: Rich felt the impact before conscious realization of what'd occurred. The floor fell away from him. His ears rang. He *had* said something like that.

"Were those Mr. Evans' exact words?"

Rich refocused his attention on the interrogation. His neck was hot, ears burning.

"Were those his words *verbatim*?" Asharif prodded. There was no smile now. No patience.

"Um, I, uh…" She looked over at Rich. "No."

Rich released a shaky breath.

Asharif's eyes narrowed. "Do you recall what he said?"

The judge leaned forward; the entire preliminary committee hung on the young woman's words. A trickle of sweat began at Rich's temple and ran down the side of his face. He rubbed it away with the side of his hand.

Grace leaned into the mic. "Mr. Evans said he thought it'd be easier to raze the hotel to the ground and start over."

A roar of chatter drowned out the rest of Grace's words. Stu stared forward, icily controlled, while Rich's shoulders rolled inward. "*Raze it to the ground.*" There it was, the one thing that made him seem guilty above all else. He couldn't breathe, couldn't think. There was no way he'd walk away from this one, and it'd been his own damned fault. The Whitewater arson was going to trial and Rich was the one under the crosshairs.

He'd bet his life on it.

* * *

WHITEWATER ARSON TRIAL "A CERTAINTY"
by Delia Rosings, September 16, 1999
The arson trial for Richard Evans, one-time manager of the Whitewater Lodge in Waterton Park, AB, is one step closer to being announced. After a week of testimony in the preliminary hearing, an unnamed source told us that "given the current evidence, litigation for arson is nearly a certainty." If found guilty of arson, Mr. Evans will also face manslaughter charges.

At approximately 11:20 p.m. on August 4, 1999, a series of fire alarms rang throughout the multi-million dollar Whitewater Lodge. Though no smoke or fire was apparent, hotel staff evacuated guests. Sources report that around 11:30 p.m., Miss Amanda Sloane, aged 27, went back inside to reset the hotel's alarms. Shortly afterward, a massive explosion rocked the building. Ms. Sloane died in the fiery blaze. Though Waterton's volunteer fire crew attempted to control the fire, the entire structure was engulfed by the time Cardston and Pincher Creek fire crews arrived. By morning, little of the structure remained.

This tragedy comes after a string of unexplained deaths in and around the national park. Police declined to comment on the ongoing murder investigation.

* * *

Rich shoved the paper away from himself. "Goddamnit!"

Stu looked up from his coffee.

"You seen this yet?" Rich said.

"Glanced at it, yeah."

"And?"

Stu shrugged. "Don't read it if you don't want to know."

"You think she's right?"

"Who?"

"The writer. Delia Rosings." Rich nudged the paper with his finger. "You think she's right about the prelim. You think it'll go to trial?"

"What do reporters know, huh? No use worrying about it 'til it happens."

"That's not an answer, Stu."

Stu went back to his coffee.

* * *

Lou was under the hood of a recalcitrant Ford when someone knocked at the garage door. She flicked her long black hair over her shoulder and peered past the truck's mirror. Officer Sadie Black Plume, in her work uniform, waited in the doorway. She had a filing box balanced against one hip, her expression angry.

"Afternoon, Sadie," Lou said. "What can I do for you?"

"Mr. Evans around?"

A few days ago, Rich would have been, but not today. Lou had grown used to his company in the weeks since the Whitewater hotel had burned to the ground and he'd fallen into her life like he'd always been there, the patterns of his comings and goings matching hers.

"Not today," Lou said. "Rich's gone to Lethbridge."

"Ah, right. The preliminary trial's about to begin."

"It already has. The trial started Monday."

"Well, that's a nuisance," Sadie said. "Any idea when he'll get back?"

"Not tonight. He'll be a couple more days, at least."

Sadie's dark brows rose. "Days?"

"Yeah. Rich's staying in a hotel in Lethbridge until the preliminary's done. He figured it was too much driving." Lou wiped her hands on her coveralls. "Is there anything I can help you with?"

Sadie shifted the box. "Just need to return this to him."

Lou squinted. Rich's neat printing covered the label on the top of the box, though she couldn't read it from her angle. "What is it?"

"Documents from the Whitewater's office. Jim and I used them to investigate Borderline Industries. Seems like they might be important to the arson trial somehow."

"Oh?"

Sadie stepped out of the doorway and into the garage. "Yesterday, Mr. Callaghan requested a copy from the Lethbridge police, overseeing the arson. But the Lethbridge police don't have the files. We do. This morning I got a call from Captain Nelson and he told me to deliver them."

"Which is why you need to get them to Rich," Lou said.

"Exactly. But the lawyer only put in the request yesterday. Don't know how he expects I'll get 'em to Lethbridge if he and Evans aren't coming back to town each night."

Lou laughed. "Stu's from the city. Probably didn't even occur to him that it'd be an issue." She gestured to the box. "I could give them to Rich, if you want. I wasn't planning on it, but I could take a quick trip into Lethbridge tonight, drop the papers off while I'm there."

"I'm supposed to hand them over. I was going to drive into Cardston if Evans wasn't around, see if one of the squad cars could take it the rest of the way."

"But they might not get it into Lethbridge until tomorrow morning. Rich's lawyer wouldn't have time to go through the files."

Sadie muttered something under her breath before she turned back around.

"It's no problem, Sadie," Lou said. "I was looking for an excuse to go into Lethbridge anyhow." She bit back a smile. There was more truth to that than she wanted to admit. "Having me drop the papers off saves a lot of work for everyone."

"I don't know, Lou."

"Why not? I can have Rich call you when I arrive." She grinned at the thought of seeing him. "If you sent it with a courier, they'd have to do the same."

Lou put her hands on the box, but Sadie's fingers didn't loosen.

"You sure about this?" the officer said in a stern voice. "I'll take a squad car in, if needs be. I want this box to get to the lawyer tonight. He *needs* to have it. Tonight."

Lou's smile faded under the vehemence of Sadie's words. "Of course."

Sadie's fingers loosened. "Well, if you were going in anyhow, I'd appreciate it."

She handed Lou the box and her arms sagged under the weight. "I was," Lou grunted. "It's no problem."

"I'm going to need you to sign for them." Sadie pulled out a pad and pen and set them on the box. "Here. The dotted line says you're legally bound to deliver them. And I'll be waiting for Mr. Evans' call."

"Gotcha." Lou wedged the box between her ribs and the side

panel of the Ford. She scribbled her name across the line. "Sadie, I know you can't talk about ongoing cases, but I was wondering—"

"Lou, I'm not even part of the arson investigation. You have to call Lethbridge if you have questions."

Lou winced at the sharpness of her tone. "You don't actually think Rich burned the hotel down, do you?"

"That's Lethbridge's case, not ours." She tapped the box in Lou's hands. "And that's why I want to make sure Callaghan gets these. If they can help him figure out this mess, I want him to have it."

"That's kind of you."

"Just doing my job."

Sadie turned to leave and the light from the open door fell across her features. Lou's heart lurched. The officer's face was grim.

"Well, I should probably let you head off then," Sadie said. "You should get driving if—"

"You've heard something, haven't you?" Lou's voice was louder than she intended, but the words—once out—carried weight. "Something's happened."

Sadie turned back around, and light raked across her face, the mask returning. "Lou, please," she said. "You know I can't talk about any of this. Not to *you*."

"Right. I know. I just…" *What could Lou say?* That she could sense the trouble brewing. "Sorry, Sadie. I shouldn't have asked you about it."

"It's fine."

"Thanks for bringing these by."

Sadie waited in the doorway, unmoving.

"Do you need something else?" Lou asked.

"No, I—" The officer let out an angry huff, but she didn't turn back. "Evans… Rich, I mean," Sadie said. "He's got a good lawyer, doesn't he? Callaghan's smart, right?"

"Yeah. I think so. Stu seems pretty on top of things."

"Good. I'm- I'm glad."

"Sadie, there's something you're not telling me. Have you heard something about—?"

But the officer was already out the door and halfway back to the squad car before Lou finished.

* * *

Five hours after Grace Blessington's dramatic appearance, Rich stumbled into the September heat. He took a shuddering breath. Oily waves curled up from the black plane of the street and warped the image of passing cars. Hot gusts of wind tugged at his suit and tie. Rich staggered and caught his hand against a railing.

"You alright?" Stu asked.

"That was a hell of a day."

"Posturing. Trying to see how you'll react." He reached into his inside pocket, pulled out a packet of cigarettes and tapped one out. "Gotta get your game face on, my friend. Thought you were going to throw up in there." He snorted as if the thought amused him.

"So what do we do now?"

"You wait. I prepare for tomorrow." Stu lifted the cigarette and pursed his lips around it to keep it in place. "I hope those files arrive. Need them to throw a little shade on the prosecution's claims."

"Or what?"

Stu flicked his lighter. The flame danced and bobbed in the wind, the cigarette belatedly catching. "Or we'll go to trial for sure."

"Shit."

"Keep in mind, the preliminary is just to figure out whether or not the Crown has a case at all. This might be nothing like the actual trial. Might be better, but it could get a hell of a lot worse."

"So the trial," Rich said. "The real one, I mean. You think it'll take a while?"

"Given what I saw the last couple days? A few weeks at least. And that's only *if* they decide to go to trial. None of that's decided yet. But that Grace girl, she was good." There was admiration in his tone, like a card-shark who'd been one-upped in a winning hand. "Wish she was our witness," he said wistfully.

"Stu, about your fees—" Rich tried to take a deep breath, but ended up coughing. "Look man, I know you've been good about letting me do deferred payments, but my savings aren't going to last forever."

Stu's smile faded. He lifted the cigarette from his lips and angled the smoke to the side. "Rich, you can always tell me to go back to New York and get someone else to do the job. No hard feelings, buddy. You gotta do what you gotta do." He winked. "So do I."

Rich's stomach tightened. Stu was expensive, but more than that, they'd known each other since college. Rich trusted him.

"It's good. I'm sure it'll be fine. I'll figure it out."

Stu slapped him hard on the shoulder. "Good. Then let me do my job."

"And what am I supposed to do?"

Stu stubbed the cigarette out on the side of the brick wall. "You work on your poker face, buddy. You're gonna need it."

* * *

It was almost nightfall when Lou reached the outskirts of Lethbridge. Dark blue skies backdropped golden coulees and shadows of buildings stretched across roads in long, undulating bands. Rich and Stu's hotel was located in the small downtown core. It overlooked the deep river valley that sliced the city in two, a remnant of the receding glaciers, millennia earlier. Lou followed the curve of

Scenic Drive past a cemetery and urban sprawl to reach the hotel. Behind the structure, the hilly ravine and Old Man River glowed in the dying light while above them, the spindles of the High Level Bridge stitched the two sides of the city together.

Reaching the hotel's parking lot, Lou slowed the truck, and turned off the engine. The motor's rumble was replaced by gusty shudders. Outside the closed windshield, birds hovered mid-air, held aloft by the relentless breeze. Lethbridge was a prairie city, dusty and slow-moving, but it had one constant that separated it from other places on the flatland: *Wind*. Bracing for it, Lou swung the door open and caught the handle before the gusts could tear it from her hand. Black hair whipped around her face. Scents rose and swirled past, carried by the breeze. Lou breathed in sunbaked soil and sparse golden grasses, motor oil and fast food. Lethbridge wasn't *home* like the mountains were, but it held a familiar comfort. Besides, she thought, Rich was here.

Grinning, she reached one-handed across the driver's seat and pulled the box toward her. Rich's printing echoed with his voice: *Whitewater Deliveries 1997-1998, Manager: J. Chan, Coldcreek Enterprises*. Her smile wavered. Something in these hand-written notes was important enough to unnerve Sadie, but she had no idea what. Energy hummed under Lou's skin as she headed to the hotel, the unwieldy box wobbling in her arms. As excited as she was to be here, she was worried about the message she brought.

The wind shoved the door closed so fast it smacked Lou's heels. The well-coiffed desk clerk glanced up and took in Lou's stained overalls, boots and faded jean jacket. Lou fought the urge to chuckle. Yes, she looked a mess. No, she didn't care. Rich was here. Any time to stop and shower would've taken him a little further away from her.

"Can I help you, miss?" the clerk said.

"I'm here to drop off a package for a friend. He's staying in room—"

"Lou!" Rich's voice boomed and she turned to see his tall silhouette. His face was bright with joy, blond hair glinting as he jogged to her side. "What are you doing here?"

"I came to drop off some papers," she said. "Stu requested them from the police and Sadie—"

She never got out the rest. In seconds his arms wrapped around her. The box tipped on her hip as Rich's hands matched the curve of her lower back and urged her forward.

"You came to see me!" he laughed.

"I've got to go back tonight," she said. Rich's crestfallen expression hastened her next words. "But I can stay for a few hours. What do you want to do?"

"Supper first so we can catch up on news. Then maybe a drink in the lounge." His eyes drifted down her body and his smile grew wolfish. "And then… *everything*."

Lou giggled. "Everything, huh?"

"Even *more* if you think you're up for it."

In seconds his lips were against hers, and any pretense that this was only to drop off papers was gone. Lou's heart fluttered against the walls of her chest and even though she couldn't stop the kiss long enough to say it aloud, she felt the silent words hum through her body: *I love you, too.*

* * *

Sadie's shift had ended an hour ago, but she was still at her desk as she pieced together the mess of the previous summer. *The fire when Amanda died was the start of the troubles,* she thought. *When Colton terrorized the town. Things should have settled down after that, but then there was the prelim…* Her gaze lifted to the two-tone shadow of Waterton's mountains looming like a dark wall beyond the window. She frowned.

No… no, the troubles started before the fire. Back last year when the first manager of the Whitewater disappeared, and we couldn't find him. And now they had to—

Jim walked into the office and jarred her from her thoughts. "Thought you were done at nine?"

"I was," she said. "Got behind on things. You know how it is."

"That doesn't sound good."

"Nope." Sadie kicked the bottom of the desk in irritation. To-day had started off shitty and had only gotten worse. When she'd gotten back from Lou's Garage there was a message on the phone. She wasn't going to get much sleep tonight even if she left. Better to sit and mull than lay in bed and do the same. At least here she had access to files.

"You drive those papers to Lethbridge for Evans' lawyer?" Jim asked as he sat down across the desk from her. In the dimness of the office, the sprinkling of grey in his short brown hair disappeared and he seemed closer to Sadie's own age.

"No. Louise Newman offered to take them in for me. Evans' law-yer called an hour ago and confirmed they'd arrived, so don't even ask me about it."

With anyone else, Sadie's irritableness would've deterred them, but Jim gave her a broad grin. "Don't have to be so prickly. I didn't say a thing."

"Yeah, but you *thought* it, didn't you?"

"I think lots o' things. Don't judge me on that."

Sadie shook her head, black braids swinging, as the first hint of a smile reached her lips.

"Besides, I trust Lou," Jim said. "I would've done the same."

"I made her sign the forms, you know," she said. "In case you were wondering."

"I wasn't. You're the stickler for rules, not me. I'd probably forget."

"Doubt it." Sadie looked back at the papers in her hands and sighed. *Goddamn this fucking day!*

"Anything I can help with?" Jim said. "If we split the reports, paperwork will go twice as fast. I can fill in the general stuff, you do the details."

"Nah. You head home, Jimmy. I'm fine."

She expected him to leave, but as usual, Jim Flagstone did what he wanted. He toed the rolling chair around the edge of the desk and spun it sideways so they sat side by side at her desk, the way they so often did at the Watering Hole, his broad-shouldered bulk next to her lean frame.

"So what's goin' on with you, huh? This isn't just about paperwork, is it?"

"No," she said, "it isn't."

"Didn't think so." Jim put his feet up on the corner of the desk and bumped her elbow. "So what is it?"

"I'm trying to write up a report. It's a mess. Don't know how to make sense of it. 'Cause it just doesn't *make* sense."

"Can I help?"

"I was writing it up so I could give it to you tomorrow morning."

"But I'm here now. Lay it on me."

"Fine." Sadie handed him the papers. "When I came back from lunch, there was a phone message from the Zanesville Ohio Police."

"Ohio, huh? Message about what?"

"The caller didn't say. Just that they were faxing several files and making a request for further information, should we locate any."

"Information from *us*? About what? Waterton's a long way from…" He glanced at the papers. "Zanesville."

"The kicker's on page three. Take a look."

He flipped the page over. "What the hell?"

"The second print we pulled from the breaker box got a match."

"That one from the break-in at the Whitewater last summer?"

"Uh-huh. The second print no one could explain," Sadie said. "There was someone down in the basement when Rich Evans went to check on the lights. We always figured it was Colton Calhoun who knocked Rich down, but it turns out it might not have been Colt after all."

"Shit."

Sadie pushed back from the desk and stood. "And it's a hell of a time for this to arrive. The preliminary hearing is going on right now. Judge is going to be making a decision on whether to go to trial or not sometime this week."

"So call the police in Lethbridge and tell them what you got."

"I did. And they said they'd pass the information on to Evans' lawyer."

"Well, that's good, right?"

"Would be, if it was an actual trial. It'd change everything. Trouble is, this is just a prelim." She paced between the cabinet and desk, her hands fisted at her side. "If they'd only sent the goddamned thing a week ago. Would've saved us all a hell of a lot of trouble."

"Wait. Back this summer we figured the second print was one of the installers. That doesn't change a thing about Rich Evans' case. The fire at the Whitewater happened weeks later. He could still be the arsonist." Jim grinned. "Doesn't give us any extra work at all. The fire's a Lethbridge case. We're fine."

"We're *not* fine."

"Oh?"

"This isn't *just* about the fire. The Zanesville police want the person who made those prints. They want us to take him in if we can."

"But why?"

Sadie headed over to the filing cabinet where the summer's investigation files were held. She pulled out a second piece of paper—a new fax which had arrived an hour earlier—and set it on the desk before Jim.

"Here. Read this."

Jim's eyes widened as he scanned through the message: *Unidentified print matches case from Zanesville, OH, records. Print is consistent with those of a perpetrator of a murder, 1970. Cold case. Status: Unsolved.*

"A cold case," Jim breathed. "Colton Calhoun had an accomplice."

"Seems Waterton has another skeleton," Sadie said. "And it's up to us to dig it up."

CHAPTER TWO

Prischka Archer,
Coldcreek Enterprises,
23rd Floor, Flatiron Building,
175 Fifth Avenue,
New York, New York
10010

May 23, 1998

Dear Ms. Archer,

I am writing in regards to the continued construction of the East Wing of the Whitewater Lodge. Earlier this month I told you that I feared the issues from last winter would prevent us from opening in time for the summer season. I have recently reassessed the situation and am pleased to inform you that the Whitewater Lodge will, indeed, open on time.

The West Wing is complete and partially furnished. The remaining suites in the hotel will soon follow. Though funds are tight, I've recently made some lucrative business acquaintances who are inclined to help. It was with their support that the West Wing was completed.

I appreciate your patience with this project and assure you that I'm doing everything I can to bring it successfully to fruition.

Sincerely,
Jeffrey J. Chan, HRIM, Manager
Whitewater Lodge, Waterton Park, AB

Special instructions: CC

CHAPTER THREE

Lou whimpered as a dream image took root in her sleeping mind:

Terrified, she ran barefoot through the forest. Her gaze darted from the green canopy of leaves to the blue-black snarl of bark and shadows. Her tongue was swollen from thirst, feet bloody, but she didn't slow. Someone followed.

Vines tangled the path and thorns slashed her legs. Ahead an opening to a clearing appeared, glowing yellow where the tall trees of the forest thinned and let in the midday sun. Focused on it, she didn't see the exposed root that caught her foot. She slammed to the ground, losing her breath. When she staggered upright, she was no longer alone. Another had reached the glade. The sour smell of unwashed flesh filled her nostrils. Winded, she turned to face him.

It was Death himself, pale skinned and—

"No!" Lou jerked awake.

She fought her way free of the tangled sheets and fumbled for the light. The half-light of the bedroom retracted with a snap. She was here in the cabin—*her cabin*—alone. Rich was in Lethbridge for the preliminary hearing. Though it was early September, the room felt like winter; the furnace had died sometime during the night. Other than that, all was the same.

Lou took a shaky breath as the tang of sweat reached her nostrils. *The dream forest flickered in her mind.* Like the vision last year, this one was full of meaning.

She squinted at the clock, surprised to discover she'd slept through her alarm. *7:49 a.m.* Behind curtained windows, pink bands of light traced rectangles on the far wall.

If Rich had been in the cabin with her, she would have comforted herself with his nearness, but he was far from her reach. *I'm sure he's fine.* Lou dragged her fingers through tangled hair and winced as it pulled. *Unless—*

Tension filled her body. Now the dream felt like a warning.

Lou clambered out of bed and plodded down the creaking stairs to the kitchen. The uncurtained window was flooded with light, a bright day beyond the glass. With the final hours of the preliminary trial about to begin, Rich was almost certainly awake at this point.

A black rotary phone hung on the wall and she tucked the handset against her shoulder, dialing his cell phone from memory. The machine taunted her with lazy clicks.

"C'mon, c'mon…" The receiver crackled through the last digit and began to ring. Lou pressed her eyes closed. "Pick up, Rich. Please."

The connection clicked through and Louise's heart surged, only to fall as a recording began: *"You've reached Richard Evans of Coldcreek Enterprises. I can't answer the phone right now, but leave your name and a short message after the beep and I'll reply as soon as possible."*

Lou's lower lip trembled at the confident sound of his voice. She held her breath as the tone beeped down the count, waiting, uncertain until the final peal. She hung up at the last second.

"Damnit!" There was no way to warn him. And if she tried, what then? There was no way to explain her feeling to Rich, other than to say she'd had a dream. There was someone coming. Though *who* it was, Lou'd no idea.

* * *

Alistair Diarmuid had traveled the breadth of Canada in the last month and a half, but his research was incomplete. With the miles racking up on the odometer and money dwindling, he'd reached a turning point. His eyes narrowed into a scowl as he took in the pink hued mountains of Waterton. The answer felt close. *Very close.*

A pattern had emerged in the Vietnam War protesters he'd investigated: a chain of command, and an escape for those who needed one. Last spring, an interview with a middle-aged protester in Michigan had drawn his attention to the lonely border town. She'd spoken of an underground railroad that had escorted many conscientious objectors to safety in Canada. It was an angle Alistair hadn't expected.

He slowed his vehicle at the entrance gate. *Waterton is on the U.S. border. It's remote, but accessible. Hidden in plain sight.* Seeing the puzzle come together was only a matter of making the last few pieces fit. And if people were less than forthcoming. *Well,* Alistair smirked, *there were always ways to make people talk.*

A smiling attendant in a park uniform appeared in the window and Alistair put the car in park. "*Bienvenue à Waterton.* Welcome to Waterton," the woman said. "How long will you be staying?"

"Not really sure."

Her smile faltered. "Passing through?" He knew what she saw: The long dark hair, and skin tanned by the sun of five different continents.

"Oh no." He laughed. "I planned this trip."

"Are you back-country hiking?"

"Don't think so."

"Camping?"

"Nope."

"Sorry, I don't…"

"I'm here to do some research."

"For how long?"

He stared at her rather than answer. They were alone at the gate. No one to see him, or her. *I could do anything I wanted and no one would know better of it.*

The woman's smile faded as if he'd said the words aloud. "Sir?"

Alistair blinked, the dark thoughts disappearing. "What's that?"

"I asked how long will you be staying in the park."

"Oh, right. As long as it takes to find my answers. Say a month and a half at the most?"

"Ah," she said. "Then you should probably buy a season's pass."

"Alright. I'll get that."

He waited as the attendant took his information and an impression of his credit card. She was efficiency in motion, the warm smile gone. "Keep the pass hung on your rear-view mirror as long as you're in the park." She handed him a pen and the credit slip. "The wardens check for them, so make sure it's visible."

"I'll do that."

"Have you booked a hotel or campsite for your stay?"

He nodded. "The Bertha Mountain Bed and Breakfast."

"Oh! That's Ms. Varley's place," she said, her wary smile returning. "Beautiful views. Great area for bird-watching, too."

"Sounds lovely." *She's already forgotten her fear,* Alistair thought.

"There you go." She passed him a plastic admission card and pointed across the road to where a gate blocked the far lane. "Next time you come into the park, just swipe this card through the automatic gate, and it'll let you in."

"The gate. Right."

Alistair nodded and popped the car into drive. His eyes lifted to the mountains that surrounded him and he shivered, the woman at the gate forgotten. This place was so alone. So solitary. *Anything could happen here, and no one would ever know.*

While he drove, he searched for filming locations, noting them for later. In minutes, prairie flatness gave way to a shocking thrust of ragged peaks, the town site nestled in the crook of the mountain's arm. He reached the first cabins and the speed limit dropped to thirty kilometres per hour. Alistair squinted at the metric dial and slowed to a walking pace.

The town was as barren as an empty movie set, the only movement from deer that wandered the boulevards. His eyes skimmed silent streets as he searched for the bed and breakfast. A half-grown fawn, grazing near the side of the road, lifted its head and hurried off to its mother.

He crossed the heart of the town, past the one commercial Main Street, and alongside a school—shuttered and no longer in use— to a vaulting waterfall. Alistair slowed the vehicle to a crawl as he crossed the bridge. He peered through the underbrush for signs of occupation. Pine trees obscured his view. For all intents, the far side of Waterton had gone back to forest, moss-covered cabins mired in the limberlost. His smile grew into a sharp-toothed grin.

This is exactly where they'd hide. A border town with no chance of-

A flicker of yellow flashed in the green and he tapped the brakes as a brightly-colored bird burst into flight. A peeling sign appeared from behind an untrimmed hedge. *Bertha Mountain Bed and Breakfast.* The cross-timbered cabin had a quaint, storybook quality, with overhanging eaves and deeply recessed windows. Like the rest of the town, it was a place out of time, a half-step behind the busy pace of the world.

Alistair pulled the car over to the curb, his pulse racing. It was time to find the truth in the rumours.

* * *

Unnerved by her dream, Lou headed to the stairs and sat down on the bottom riser. She stared into the living room with its wooden wainscoting and faded rugs warmed by sunshine. She'd lived in this cabin her whole life, and the position reminded her of many nights when she'd sat like this, fearful of a world too full of the unknown: the night sounds and animals, her uncertainties and fears, her parents' arguments. This morning, the worry came from inside her.

She looked back at the phone that hung on the kitchen wall, but she didn't move. *Rich wouldn't believe me if I did explain.* That was the trouble with her and Rich. No matter how long things went on or how good things seemed to be, she couldn't make herself tell him the truth about who she was. She didn't understand it herself.

Lou wrapped her arms around her legs, balanced her chin on her knees, and closed her eyes. She and Rich had been dating since last spring and living together since the hotel had been destroyed by fire this summer. She tried to imagine what *else* they might have together in some uncertain future, but no answer came. *I could always look...* She shivered at the thought. Seeking a glimpse of the future wasn't something she did often; she liked the possibilities of 'not knowing'. In the wake of the nightmare, however, she felt reckless.

Just this once.

Released, her thoughts spiraled out into some distant future. She could feel Rich there, could sense him nearby, but their thread wouldn't stay still. It jumped and jerked as she forded the confusion. *Almost... almost...* Without warning, the creaking of the cabin turned into the rush of wind.

Rich stood on a mountainside, buffeted by the breeze. Her vision spread as it took in the distinct shape of the mountain chain and the lake below. It was the Crypt lake trail, Lou realized. Excited, her attention swirled in an arc, as she scanned the path behind him for a sign of herself. The trail turned into an outcrop of trees and there was movement there. She was about to push forward, when Rich lifted his gaze to the sky.

Lou paused, entranced in the hint of time's passage. The wrinkles on his face were carved deep; his body lean, tanned by sun and wind. That wasn't what held her in place. It was the great peace he carried with him, so unlike the man she knew now. It spread around him like a sail. As if hearing her, Rich smiled, and for the briefest moment Lou was certain he could see her, too—

The clamour of the telephone's ring tore the image away before she could see any more. She had no idea if she was truly *there* in this imagined future, or if—as her father had so often told her—it was *"all in her head"*. With so many secrets, she wondered if her relationship with Rich would end like all her others. She'd been alone her whole life and the future felt the same.

The phone rang a second time and with a frustrated sigh, Louise crossed the kitchen to pick it up. "Hello?"

"Lou. Hi!" Rich panted. "I was in the shower when you called. I saw your number. Why didn't you leave a message?"

She swallowed against the lump in her throat. It didn't matter how she might try to explain it, Rich would never understand these things because she didn't understand them herself.

"Nothing important," Lou said. "Just wanted to hear your voice."

* * *

It was past three before Constable Sadie Black Plume found time to sit down in front of her computer. There'd been an accident near Mountain View and she'd gone out to assist the Cardston RCMP in securing the highway. They'd diverted traffic for two hours. Any plans to check on the preliminary trial, now it its last day, had been foregone for immediate tasks. She hoped Rich Evans' lawyer had checked the updated information she'd sent.

She shuffled together her papers and glanced down at the print-out from the last police contact. Sadie's eyes grazed it without reading, the information imprinted on her memory: *The two partial prints are housed in the U.S. federal criminal database for an as-yet unidentified offender. The individual prints match those taken from a crime scene in New Concord, Ohio, in November 1970. The unsolved murder case file is located in the Ohio State police records.* Sadie's computer screen flickered as the 'new email' download bar appeared. The link she'd been waiting for *should* be in it. Pulse quickening, Sadie clicked 'open' and the email flashed to life.

Constable Black Plume,

Thank you for the enquiry regarding the Muskingum College cold case and the matching print from the Whitewater Lodge break-in. Considering our shared interest in locating this perpetrator, we'd like to stay apprised of any information you might uncover. Attached is a link for the files you requested.

Sadie groaned. External links meant more downloads. The archaic computing system was fussy at the best of times, but whenever Sadie was in a hurry, the thing was downright fractious.

Loading... Loading... Loading...

"C'mon, you sonofabitch."

Complete.

The header for the Ohio State Police appeared, complete with patriotic stars and stripes. The screen prompted her to fill in the official request for police records, open a cross-border investigation file, and provide appropriate identification. Half an hour later, she was forwarded to a secure site that housed the documents regarding the 1970 homicide.

She clicked on the pdf and waited until the grainy scan of a handwritten police report appeared. Sadie flipped through the file as images of a war protest gone wrong appeared in her mind.

On the afternoon of November 15th, 1970, a protest began on the central quad of Muskingum College. The protesters were Muskingum and Ohio State students, though public figures and civilians joined them. In light of the Kent State events in May 1970, Captain Bill Henderson ordered the protest to be broken up as quickly as possible. Thirty officers from the nearby Zanesville police force were brought in on the morning of November 16th, 1970 to enforce Henderson's orders. Small clashes occurred throughout the afternoon.

When the crowd refused to leave, Sergeant Arthur Cooper authorized the use of force. Tear gas was used and fifty-two arrests made. Most students left as night approached, but a small group of extremists moved into a forest near the campus. By 11:30 p.m., fires and property damage were reported as protesters barricaded the roads surrounding the college. Officer Randy Selburg followed two protesters up an embankment. They retreated to a wooded area. A skirmish ensued and Selburg fired on them.

Catherine LaVallee, age 18 years, was shot and killed by Selburg's weapon. An unidentified assailant attacked Officer Selburg, knocked him to the ground and shot him point-blank in the chest with his own weapon. By the time backup arrived, the perpetrator had fled on foot. Officer Selburg was unconscious at the scene and unable to provide a description of the perpetrator.

Selburg was pronounced dead on arrival at Zanesville County

Hospital.

A follow-up investigation cleared those who were near to Cath-erine LaVallee of any connection to the crime scene and suggested the perpetrator was one of the outside participants. Officer Selburg's firearm was recovered in the bushes nearby. Two sets of prints were taken from the weapon. One of them was identified as those of Officer Selberg. The other is located in this file.

Sadie leaned back from the screen, braiding her hair as she worked through the details of the police report. Somehow, between 1970 and 1999, the person who'd shot Officer Selberg had come to Waterton. Mid-summer, he'd gone down into the basement of the Whitewater Lodge alongside Colton Calhoun and cut the lights, but that attempt had been foiled when Rich Evans had stumbled into the crime scene. Weeks later, a fire had burned the Whitewater Lodge to the ground. There was no evidence on Calhoun's property to prove or deny his involvement in the arson, and no interrogation possible since Calhoun had been killed days later.

But someone *else* had been in the basement, too.

"Who *are* you?" Sadie murmured. Someone who'd known Colton, obviously. That left everyone in the town as suspects.

Her gaze flicked to the clock. From what Sadie'd heard, Judge Pelletier would make her decision on whether or not Rich Evans would stand trial for the arson at the Whitewater Lodge in the next few days. Sadie's lips tightened into an angry line. As Jim liked to point out: Evans *could* be responsible, but Sadie didn't believe it. She let go of the tight braid and it released into three loose waves. She might not know how it all came together, but she was certain of one thing.

The fingerprints on the breaker box were the key.

CHAPTER FOUR

On the far end of Main Street—one block away from the stone-work police station where Officer Black Plume sifted through the details of a three-decade old murder—the locals had gathered in Hunter's Coffee Shop for their first meeting of the off-season. One might expect the ranks to have thinned since the town's stores had closed. The opposite was true. Familiar faces, too busy in the summer to attend, now lounged in wooden chairs. They chatted about everything from the cooling weather to money troubles; the ghost of Colton Calhoun—the cause of the summer's murders—an uneasy presence in their midst. With a pot of coffee in one hand and a bowl of creamers in the other, Hunter Slate made the rounds of his friends. He laughed and joked as he refilled their mugs.

He stopped as he reached the center table. "Good to see you back again, Levi." Hunter refilled his half-full cup without asking.

"Likewise."

Levi Thompson was one of the oldest people in the Park, but he had the bearing of a much younger man. Bright blue eyes twinkled in a leathery face, a full head of white hair—creased by the brim of a cowboy hat—combed back with childlike care. He was also a bit of a recluse. Old Levi stayed out of sight all summer, but once businesses closed for the year and the tourists dwindled to a trickle, he returned.

"You bring your dogs into town with you this time?" Hunter asked.

"Of course," Levi said. "Damned hounds woulda followed me all the way to the Park gates if I hadn't. You mind if I leave 'em in your yard next time I come in?"

"Not at all," Hunter said. "The more the merrier."

"You won't be sayin' that when they dig up your whole yard."

Hunter laughed. "Believe me, it can't get any worse than the damage my dogs have already done. There's more dirt than grass these days."

"That young pup of yours still raising hell?"

"Duke? Lordy, I think he was *born* to cause trouble. Fool dog chewed off half the armrest in my truck last week."

Levi broke into a gale of rasping laughter. "You should take him hunting with you. Train him up right. Can't expect a hunting dog to sit around in town getting fat. You could come out with me, if you wanted."

"You haven't gone hunting yet?"

"Not this year, no," Levi said. "Still waiting to get my tags. You got yours yet?"

"Not yet. Hopefully in the next week or so."

"Well, give me a shout when you get 'em. I'd be happy to come along with you."

"I'll call as soon as the tags show—" His words were interrupted by the sound of the door. Another familiar face—too often absent the last few weeks—appeared in the doorway.

"Lou!" Hunter said, grinning. "Glad you could make it."

"Wouldn't miss it." She crossed the room to take the empty chair at Levi's side. "I would've been to the last meeting too, but I had to run into Lethbridge at the last second."

"Not a problem," Hunter said.

Levi's smile grew brittle and he slid his hat to the side, giving Louise ample room at the table.

"Afternoon, Levi," Lou said. "Nice to see you back in town again."

"Mmph."

"Anything new?"

Levi glared at her rather than answer.

Good friends with both of them, Hunter didn't understand Levi's prickliness toward Lou. She was a peacemaker by nature. Everyone in town loved her. (Everyone, that was, but Levi.) But, there'd been a time Hunter hadn't been too sure about Levi's feelings about *him* either. Luckily, Levi was more bark than bite, and in the time since Old Lou Newman had died, Levi Thompson had become as close to a best friend as Hunter had…barring Louise Newman, that was.

Lou turned to Levi. "We haven't seen you all summer, Levi. Things alright out at the ranch?"

"Things at the ranch are just fine."

"Heard you had a bit of cougar trouble in the spring."

Levi's eyes jumped from the table, to Lou, then to Hunter—*accusing him*—then back to Lou. "You heard that, did you?"

"I did," she said. "That's all settled down now, I hope?"

"'Course it is. The dogs ran 'em off."

"Well, I'm glad to hear it."

Hunter grabbed a chair and dragged it between the two to form a buffer. His parents had been unhappily married, and though he hadn't thought of them in years, it felt like he was reliving an unpleasant childhood memory.

"You mentioned you were in Lethbridge, Lou," Hunter said. "Picking up more supplies for the garage?"

"Not this time. Rich's preliminary hearing is this week. I thought it wouldn't come to anything—everyone assumed Colton had started the fire, after all." Her eyes flickered to Levi, and Hunter cursed himself. Levi was Colton's kin. "But it seems like the arson trial might happen."

"When does the judge decide?"

"Sometime late this week or early next," she said. "Not sure exactly."

"Well, the worst is over," Hunter said. "I'm sure Rich didn't have anything to do with the fire. And even if it goes to trial, he'll be cleared. You mark my words."

"I wish I had your confidence," Lou said. "I'm worried about Rich."

Levi made a sound that was somewhere between a chuckle and a cough.

Lou turned. "Did you say something, Levi?"

"Nope. Nothing at all."

"Levi and I were just talking about going hunting this fall," Hunter said. "Both of us are waiting to get our deer tags. Did I tell you that?"

"No, you didn't," she said.

"Gonna need some grub and a few supplies," Levi added.

"Yes," Hunter agreed. "Yes, we are."

Levi reached into the front pocket of his plaid shirt and dug out a crumpled piece of paper. He held it out to Lou between two fingers. "Here," he said gruffly. "Meant to bring the list by the garage when I came into town. Seeing as your here, might as well give it to you now."

Lou took the list and smoothed it against the table. Levi's careful handwriting—a perfect Edwardian cursive—filled the slip of paper.

"Is this dried milk or canned?" she asked.

"Dried."

"And these here are pinto beans?"

"Uh-huh. Dried ones," Levi said. "Don't want any more weight than I have to carry. Dried apricots, too. Not tinned."

Lou nodded to herself as she ran her finger down the list. "This will take me a couple days, Levi. Come in next week. I'll have it by then."

"Shall do."

Hunter felt himself relax for the first time since Lou'd sat down at Levi's side. Perhaps they could get along. As long as Levi kept his opinions to—

"So is this boy o' yours going to cut and run, same as Chan did?" Levi said.

"Levi!" Hunter choked.

"Is he going to *what*?!"

"Is he going to turn tail and take off? It's what the last manager did when things got tough."

Lou's expression tightened. "You shouldn't joke about that, Levi."

"Why the hell not? It's true, isn't it?"

"The investigation into Mr. Chan's disappearance is still open," she said. "And *Colton's* the one they think was involved."

Hunter's eyes widened as the barb hit its mark. "Lou, I don't think—"

"But Chan's not here to tell us what happened, is he?" Levi said. "And that's just mighty convenient for everyone, isn't it?"

"And how convenient, neither is your cousin," Lou said. "Guess that leaves us all in a bind. But to answer your question: *No*. Rich won't be running. Not like Colton did when—"

Levi shoved his chair back from the table and it screeched across the floor. "I don't know what happened here this summer, but I tell you one thing, all city folk are the same! That Evans boy'll up and disappear, just like Chan did." He pointed at her with a bony finger. "You mark my words, girl."

"You know *nothing* about Rich," Lou snapped.

'Don't know what you're so damned riled about," Levi said. "I heard from Hunter, this boy o' yours caused nothing but trouble this summer."

Lou turned on Hunter and he lifted his hands. "Now, Lou," Hunter said gently, "I didn't mean to hurt you, I only meant—"

"Well, I don't care if it hurts your feelings or not!" Levi said. "Town will be better off when it's back to normal. I say, good riddance."

Lou spun on him. "Back to *locals only*, isn't that what you mean? Same as it's always been. Same as you've always wanted it."

"Exactly!"

"But then I wouldn't be here," Lou said, "and neither would Hunter, or Audrika, or half the people sitting in this room."

"But that's…that's different!" Levi grabbed his hat from the table and slapped it on his head.

"Is it? I remember my mother's stories. You weren't so happy when she and my father moved to town either."

"Hardly! You don't want to hear what I'm sayin' about Evans? Don't listen." Levi walked stiff-backed to the door. He touched the brim of his cowboy hat. "Seems I came back to town a week too early, folks. Things aren't quite—" His flinty eyes paused on Lou. "—civilized yet."

The door banged shut behind him and a hubbub of excited whispers broke in its wake. Lou slid her chair closer to Hunter, her words almost inaudible. "You don't think he'd actually do anything, do you?"

Hunter turned, distracted. "Sorry, what's that?"

She leaned closer. "You don't think Old Levi'd do something to make Rich leave, do you? I mean…nothing like Colt did. Nothing dangerous. Would he?"

"Good lord, no, Lou! I'm sure Levi didn't mean anything about it at all. Levi's just… *Levi*. You know? He's ornery, but his heart's in the right place."

Lou chewed her lower lip. "I suppose."

She turned away from Hunter and in seconds was caught up in conversation. Hunter ran fingers over his stubbled jaw. He didn't think Levi would do anything, but was Hunter a good judge of character? He'd trusted Colton Calhoun too, and that'd turned sour before he'd known it. His frown deepened.

No, Hunter decided, it was different with Levi. Hunter'd worked for him when he'd first come to the Park. He'd spent months as a ranch hand on the Thompson ranch, cleaning barns and currying horses, tending the cows and shoveling manure. His fingers drummed on the table. What was it between Lou and Levi? On their own they were fine, but put them together and all hell broke loose.

Oil and water.

Lou turned, smiling sadly. "Sorry about the blow up, Hunter. I know it bothers you that we don't get along."

It was on the tip of his tongue to ask *how* she knew that, but he didn't. Lou was like her mother that way, too observant by far. "I know Levi riles you," Hunter said, "but I don't think he was part of the trouble with Colton this summer."

"You sure?"

"I'd bet on it. I mean, Colt was *your* age, Lou, and you never knew what he was like behind closed doors. Levi might be his cousin, but more than a generation divides those two men. No reason to jump to conclusions."

"You're right, of course." Lou shook her head. She looked tired and Hunter's heart twisted to see it. "It's just the stuff Levi says. It worries me."

"About outsiders?"

"Yes."

"That's just Levi," Hunter said. "Keep in mind, he doesn't like *anyone* in the park in the summertime either."

"I always figured that's because they were tourists."

Hunter winked. "True that. And I can't say I blame 'em some days."

* * *

Late Friday afternoon, Louise lay on the cement floor of the basement and fiddled with the settings on the bottom of the aging furnace. It was still early September, but the weather had dipped below freezing twice this week. The furnace wasn't cooperating. She peered into the interior, counting seconds. Her forefinger was numb from pressing the pilot light's auto-start button, but the previous times she'd released it, the flame had flickered and winked out. Now she waited. Lou figured there were three possibilities: the gas wasn't getting through, the thermo-couple was shot, or the auto-shutoff wasn't working. In any case, she had an unexpected bill to deal with. Lou had delayed putting in a new heating system for the last two years, but it seemed like this year she'd have to buckle down and replace it.

From the floor above, a door opened and footsteps crossed the floor; Lou pulled her hand back in surprise. "Rich!" The tiny flame wobbled precariously, and she held her breath. *Oh please.*

The glow stayed.

"Louise?" Rich called from a floor above. Lou closed the utility panel on the furnace, and climbed to her feet as Rich's footsteps neared. "Lou? You around?"

"In the basement!" she shouted. The door above opened and Rich appeared, backlit by the kitchen light. For a moment, the bright sunshine of the dream intruded and Lou stumbled. She wouldn't think about the vision. Not yet. Not now.

Rich jogged down the risers, his footsteps' patter as familiar as his voice.

"How was the hearing?" she asked.

"The *preliminary* hearing," he said. "I'm not gonna lie. It was hell."

"I'm sorry to hear that." Behind her, the furnace fan whined and Lou turned back to the pile of tools spread across the cement floor. "I thought this was the easy part."

"It was, and it's fine. Just not what I expected it'd be."

"Why not?"

"There's going be a trial. It's not official until the judge announces it, but…yeah. A full blown arson trial. I'd bet my pension money on it."

"Any idea when it'll take place?"

"Mid-October is Stu's guess."

Lou was caught between two emotions: excitement that Rich would be forced to stay in Waterton and fear for him. "That's not so bad, is it?"

"Yeah, but that's only half the trouble."

"There's more?"

The furnace let out one last dying rattle, then clicked off. Lou fought the urge to swear.

"It's the cost. Stu's a great lawyer, but—" Rich shook his head.

"Christ! If the trial drags on too long, I'm going to be in a hell of a bind afterward."

Lou squeezed his hand. With no heat on for most of the evening, her fingers were icy, and Rich's warmth was a welcome relief. "It'll be okay," she said. "We'll figure it out."

"Let's hope so."

"I *know* so."

Rich nodded to the cluttered floor. "So what're you doing down here anyhow? I hate basements."

"The furnace is on the fritz again. Thing hasn't been replaced since Dad put it in."

"When was that?"

"In the seventies, I think."

"That when your parents moved to Waterton?"

Lou's smile faltered. She squatted next to the furnace and opened the utility door once more. "Um... yeah. I think so."

"I remember you saying your mom came from Magrath. But where was your dad from?"

Lou clicked on the igniter, but it wouldn't catch. She knew Rich wanted her attention, but she refused to look past the tiny flame that sprang to life.

"Lou?"

"He came from the States."

Rich dropped to a crouch and leaned in so he could see her face. "Where from?"

She glanced up at him. For a heartbeat she was furious—*Rich had no right to ask about her past!*—but then, just as quickly, her calm returned. "Somewhere out East," she said. "I honestly don't know. Never asked him."

Rich frowned and stood up. The seconds ticked by as Lou waited for the pilot light to heat the auto-shutoff. From the corner of her eye, she could see Rich next to the furnace, his arms crossed on his chest. Angry.

"Why do you always do that?" he said.

"Do what?"

"*That.* You know, that thing you do where you just ignore my questions and change the subject."

"What? I'm not—"

"You *are*, Lou."

"I… I'm just a private person." Her thumb on the igniter pulsed with heartbeat.

"It's more than privacy. It's—"

"No, it's not. Why do you keep prying?"

"I'm not prying, but I have questions."

"Why?!" The word came out louder than she expected.

"Because if things are going to work, we've got to be able to talk."

"We *do* talk, Rich. I know lots about you."

"Yeah, but I want to know *you*, too."

"You do."

"I don't!"

With an angry huff, Lou let go of the igniter and stood. The fan from the furnace had begun to groan again. She'd deal with it later. She headed away from Rich before she said something she'd regret. He put a hand on her arm and stopped her before she reached the stairs.

"I just want to talk, Lou," he said. "I've waited all day—*all week*—during this fucking hearing just to talk to you, and now that I'm here, this is what I get?"

"We *do* talk. I've got a story for everything. Isn't that what you said?"

"Stories. I want to talk about you. About us."

"Rich, please. I love you but I can't…" There were too many things she wanted to explain, like the dream of danger, but none of them would come.

"Lou, if you'd just—"

She slid her arms around Rich's neck and kissed him to stem the flow of words before the conflict could spiral into something worse. For a moment he hesitated, and then he kissed her back with a desperateness that left Lou's head spinning. His lips slanted against hers, demanding. The embrace dragged on and Rich's anger shifted into want. His hands slid up to cup her breasts, the heat of his fingers warming her as he dragged her closer. Lou moaned at the feel. She loved Rich Evans so intensely it frightened her. When they broke apart, both of them were panting. Lou smiled.

Rich didn't.

He stepped out of her arms and walked up the stairs alone.

* * *

An early frost was in the air tonight. Wind whipped outside the cabin's basement windows, the last tendrils of late summer disappearing as fall took root. The dismal turn of the weather was a match for Lou's mood.

Frustrated by the argument, she'd fiddled with the furnace for another hour after Rich had stormed upstairs. In that time, the cold and damp had soaked into her limbs. Even with the furnace on full blast, her hands were numb when she put her tools away. She crept to the second floor bedroom to discover Rich sprawled across the bed, fast asleep. He was dressed; his shoes, duffel, and briefcase dumped in a pile next to the door.

"Oh, Rich," she sighed.

His face was haggard, weary lines carved into the smooth planes of his cheeks. The preliminary trial was already taking its toll, and Lou knew there'd be worse coming. She could feel it. She shrugged off her work clothes and added them to Rich's pile, then tiptoed across the bedroom. Shivering, she tried to pull the blankets out from under him, but he was far too heavy to be moved.

"Rich. Roll over so I can cover you up."

"Huh?" He jerked awake. "Lou? What—? What time is it?"

"A little after nine, but you're wiped. Let's go to bed early. Okay?"

She undid the line of buttons on his dress shirt and helped him out of his pants. In seconds they were under the covers, arms wrapped around one another. The awkwardness Lou'd expected after the argument never arrived and she was happy to put it aside. Rich stroked her long hair and ran his hands down her back. She was hovering on the edge of sleep when he spoke.

"It's funny. Now that we're in bed, I can't fall asleep."

Lou yawned. "You can't?"

"I can't relax. I have too many things on my mind."

"Thinking about them isn't going to change them."

"Yes, I know that *logically*," he said with a weary chuckle. "But my brain doesn't agree."

"Anything I can do to help?"

"Not really, unless you've paid off Judge Pelletier so she doesn't call a trial."

Lou snorted. "Knew I'd forgotten to do something or other."

Rich laughed. Outside the windows, the wind grew in intensity.

"Seriously though," he said, "there's nothing to do right now. Just got to wait for her decision. Should be soon. Stu said it'd likely be Monday."

"I hope it's good. I really do."

"Me too."

For a long time they were quiet. She knew they should talk about the disagreement they'd had—try to put things to rest—but she wasn't ready to open up any more of herself than she had. There were whole parts of who Louise Newman was that she hadn't told *anyone* about, save her mother. That separateness she'd always known was part of who she was. Laying in the dark, wrapped in Rich's arms, her eyes welled with sudden tears. *I want to tell you. I just don't know how.*

The wind off the lake grew into a steady roar; the panes in the windows rattled against their frames. Deep in the heart of the house, the furnace awoke with an unhappy groan; it puffed and grumbled for a few minutes, then released a much-needed wave of heat. Lou snuggled nearer to Rich, a half-sad smile on her lips. He was here at her side. He loved her. Surely that was enough.

Lou was starting to nod off again when Rich spoke again.

"Tell me a story, Lou."

"A story? What kind?"

"Any kind. Something—I don't know. Something about Waterton. Something you remember."

Lou rolled onto her back, though her hand stayed on Rich's chest. "Alright. Let's see… a story about Waterton." She was drowsy and warm, and her words came slowly. "A long, long time ago, there was a little girl who lived in Waterton. Her cabin was surrounded by mountains and her bedroom window overlooked the lake. Every morning she'd look out at the water, drawn to it." Lou felt Rich turn his head toward the now-dark window, as if imagining the shimmer of the bay in the darkness. "She had a few close friends," Lou said, "but not many. She was alone, but she wasn't lonely."

"Why didn't she have many friends?"

"I—She was different. She didn't see things as they did. Didn't behave the way they expected her to. Her differentness set her apart. She wasn't lonely, though."

"Why not?"

"The little girl loved to read; she lived through her stories."

"What else did she do?"

"She used to play on the shore of Bertha Bay: building castles out of stones, catching minnows in the shallows, imagining herself part of the stories she read."

Rich turned and pressed a kiss to Lou's forehead. "Is there any chance this little girl is you?"

She shrugged rather than answer.

"Now, one day this little girl was playing along the shore," Lou said, "and she found herself drawn to the color of the water. It was a bright day and the sun was glinting off the ripples: gold and black, blue and silver, a rainbow of every hue in between. For some reason on this day the play of light distracted her. She waded out into the bay, deeper and deeper, her eyelids drooping."

Lou could feel Rich, warm in bed beside her, but the room was dark and the shapes of the walls and dresser were indistinct. Shadows moved on the back of her memory.

"The rolled cuffs of her pants soaked through, then her knees, then her thighs. She could hear a voice whispering from everywhere and nowhere at once. *'Come closer, come closer,'* it called, but the girl didn't know who it was."

Rich's hand on her hair went still. "Like…she heard a *real voice* calling to her?"

"Something was. But not outside. *Inside*. And for some reason," Lou said, "she couldn't *stop* walking. It was like something needed her attention. Someone needed her to see."

"Shit." Rich let out a nervous trill of laughter.

"After a few more steps she was waist deep, the water heavy in her clothes. Around her legs, weeds swirled and danced, tickling her knees and feet, brushing her skin. And then—inexplicably—a cloud crossed the sky. The hypnotic glare of the water disappeared and for the first time, the girl could see under the surface." Lou's voice disappeared. She could remember the moment so clearly she couldn't breathe. *Had it been real?* The question terrified her. Not because she didn't know, but because she *did*.

"So what was it?" Rich asked. "What did she see in the water?"

"There was—There was a woman there. Not there *really*," Lou quickly added. "But a memory of one. An echo just under the surface. And as the little girl stared down at her, the woman opened her eyes."

Rich had gone completely still. Even his breathing was hushed.

"The woman's eyes were full of tears—oceans of them—her hair the tangle of weeds that wrapped the girl's legs. She carried stones in the pockets of her cotton dress, the weight holding her down. *'I've been waiting for someone to see me,'* she said and she reached out her hand to—"

"Jesus, fuck!" Rich said with a high-pitched laugh. "What the hell?!"

His voice jerked Lou from her memory. She blinked and the dim bedroom returned. Outside the parted curtains, the inky surface of Bertha Bay lay silent. Above it ran a saw's blade of mountains. Beneath, Lou knew, but didn't dare say.

"What the hell kind of story is this, Lou?"

"It's just a story, Rich. A story about Waterton. Relax."

"So what happened then? What'd the girl do?"

"She stumbled back to shore, crying. All the way, the woman in the water kept whispering her secrets, until her voice became the sound of waves, her hair returned to weeds, and the stones in her pockets were only a scattering of rocks near the shore. It wasn't until the girl was home, safe in her bedroom, that she realized she knew who the woman in the water was."

Rich rolled over and propped himself up on one elbow. "She did?"

"The little girl lived in her books, remember? Well some of them were legends and one particular story talked of the Lady of the Lake. The girl realized that she'd seen her, only she'd been too frightened to listen to her words."

"I don't blame her," Rich said. "That's messed up."

Lou hummed but didn't reply. She wanted to tell Rich it had taken her weeks before she'd returned to her favorite piece of shoreline, that her father had blamed the vision on a 'wild imagination' and forbidden Lou from talking to anyone about it, that her mother had warned Lou of the dangers of shiryō, the souls of the uneasy dead, that young Louise had tried to forget it had even happened…But that if she listened closely—she could *still* hear the woman.

Outside the house, the wind had settled into shudders.

"I wanted something *real* about Waterton," Rich said. "That was a ghost story."

"Yes, it was. But that doesn't mean it's not true."

"So this happened? I mean, that kid was you? You saw something in the water?"

His hands were still, but he hadn't pulled away. *Not yet.*

"I was young, Rich. *Very* young, in fact." She forced a laugh she didn't feel. It was easier to pretend. "My parents always said I had an active imagination."

"That's an understatement."

Rich smothered laughter against the pillow. His fingers roved over her bare skin as his kisses dragged Lou's attention back to his body, warm and hard, in bed next to her. Lou thought he'd forgotten all about her story when he lifted his head and spoke.

"I used to freak myself out when I was a kid too, you know. There were times I swear I heard things in my grandparents' cellar. A voice in the shadows."

"Really? A voice saying what?"

"Someone calling to me. Saying my name. A woman, now that I think of it." He laughed. "Maybe all kids come up with shit like that."

"Maybe."

"Christ! I hate basements even now. The day of the break-in, I was down under the Whitewater. I couldn't see a thing—the power was out—but there was someone in the dark with me."

"Colton?"

"Police never were sure, but I think so. I swear I could feel him, even before he moved. It was like being back in my grandparents' cellar again. I was so glad when I got out of there. Sheesh! If I'd heard a voice in the dark that night I would've shit myself."

Lou smiled. "But wouldn't that depend what the voice was saying?"

"No! I'd freak out even if it was reading off lottery numbers."

"Really?" Lou giggled.

"Yeah. Wouldn't you?"

"I don't know," Lou said. "I always kind of felt sorry for the Lady in the Lake."

"But what if she was a ghost? Doesn't that bother you at all?"

"Why?"

"Jesus, Lou. Ghosts!" Rich laughed so hard the bed shook. "You can't be serious!"

"I can't see being scared of a ghost, if I wasn't scared of a person.

And, active imagination or not, the woman just seemed sad to me."

Rich rolled on top of her and pinned her to the bed. He smoothed the hair from her face. "That is messed up, Louise Newman," he said, though she could hear the smile in his tone. "You know that, right? It's seriously fucked."

He leaned in to nuzzle Lou's neck and her lashes fluttered closed. "This is why I don't talk about my past, you know. Active imagination sounds like 'crazy' in the right context."

"No, it doesn't."

"You sure about that?"

"I wouldn't change anything about you, crazy stories or not. I love you, Lou." He kissed her lightly. "Every creepy detail." And he broke into another gale of laughter.

CHAPTER FIVE

Wind howled, hurricane-like, outside the windows when Lou came out of the bathroom. It was a weekend, but it looked like Rich intended to spend his time at the cabin working. He sprawled across the unmade bed, a pencil tucked behind one ear, the coverlet covered in papers. Lou tossed the damp towel in the hamper and headed to the dresser.

Rich's gaze lifted. "Morning, Lou."

"G'morning to you, too, sleepy head." She tugged open the top drawer. "Feel good to be home?"

Rich grinned. "Lemme tell you, I've missed the view." His eyes lingered on her black panties and tank top. "That's a good look for you, by the way."

"You think so, hmm?"

Rich shuffled the papers together and set them on the bedside table while Lou rooted through the drawer. He came up behind her and put his hands on her hips.

"Yeah, I do. Or maybe it's just the person wearing the outfit."

Lou giggled as he nibbled her ear.

"Mmm…" Rich said. "You taste good too."

Lou twisted to face him. Rich tugged at her panties, his mouth moving over her shoulder and collarbone. "You're in a good mood this morning. I think you've missed—" She shrieked in sudden laughter as Rich slid his hands underneath her and lifted her up. "Stop!" she laughed as he tumbled them back onto the bed. "Seriously, Rich, I'll never get out of here at this rate."

"You're going somewhere?"

"Lethbridge," she said. "I'll be back this afternoon."

Rich's crestfallen expression was answer enough. "But I just got back to Waterton."

"I know, Rich, and I'm sorry, but I've got an order for supplies to fill, and I've got to pick up a few parts for the furnace. It's on its last leg."

She cupped her hand against his cheek and he kissed her palm.

"I could keep you warm," he said.

"I'm sure you could for now, but middle of winter, that'll be harder than you think. Got to replace that thermo-couple before the first hard frost."

"I can't convince you to just hang out all day? I could make it worth your while."

"I'd love to, but I've really got to go. Totally out of groceries."

"But the grocery store—"

"Is closed for the season like everything else."

"Please," he said. "Please, please, please stay home with me."

His face nuzzled lower and Lou's lashes fluttered closed.

She lay on a sun-warmed pile of hay, soft and pliant in the aftermath of desire, the wheat fields that needed reaping forgotten. She blinked, the lost memory warming her as much as Rich's tongue. Lou caught hold of his shoulders and tugged him to a stop. He glanced up.

"I have to go," she said. Rich flopped onto the bed with a groan. "But you could come along with me if you wanted," she added.

He looked up. "Like… *now?* I just got back."

"Yes, now. Lethbridge isn't that far."

He glanced at the papers and groaned. "I should probably finish going through these."

"What if I promise to get you back before dinner, huh? That way you could still do your work and we could spend the day together."

Rich chewed his lip for a few seconds and then a tentative smile broke across his face. "Yeah… yeah, that'd work. We could take my car if you want."

"We could, but then you'd end up holding a hell of a lot of boxes on the way back. My truck works just fine."

"As long as you're not in a rush. Now if we wanted to go for speed…" He gave her a wolfish grin.

"I'm not in a rush," Lou said. "And there are always things to see along the way." She stood from the bed. "You should come along; try enjoying the drive. Sometimes life slows us down to get us to see what's really there."

"Mmm…?" Rich watched her from under hooded eyes.

"There's a story I heard once about that."

"A story about a gorgeous woman who drove a beat-up old truck?"

"No, this story is about a man travelling through the jungle. He was in a great rush with little time to pause and see what was around him. As he ran, a tiger began to chase him. The man ran straight through the heavy brush, dodging and sprinting through the jungle, until he came to the top of a steep cliff."

Rich snorted, his smile widening.

"Now, the man couldn't stop," Lou said, "because he was going too fast, so he tumbled over the edge. Fortunately, the man caught onto a vine hanging down the cliff, and for a time, he was safe."

"Lucky."

"Maybe…" Lou winked. "You see when the man looked down, he discovered that a *second* tiger had heard his cries and was now waiting at the bottom of the cliff, pacing and snarling. Up above, the first tiger roared in frustration."

Rich reached out for her. "Feel kinda sorry for the guy."

"The man didn't know what to do. He hung there, terrified, until he felt the vine shudder. He looked over to the rocks to discover that two mice had begun to chew away at the vine." Rich laughed and pulled Lou down. She straddled his waist and smiled down at him. "The man searched for an escape, but there was nothing he could do. Then his eyes caught on a bright red strawberry, clinging to the cliff face. He held onto the vine with one hand." Lou ran her fingers along Rich's arm. "And with the other, he plucked the strawberry…" She leaned in and touched her lips to his, then pulled away. "It was the sweetest thing he'd ever tasted in his life."

"So where's my strawberry in all of this?"

Lou climbed off his lap. "It's a new day," she said with a smile, "and you're taking a drive in one of the most beautiful places on earth, and you get to enjoy *my company* the whole way."

"Now that *is* something worth savouring."

Lou turned away to hide her blush. "And that, Rich, is *exactly* the right answer."

* * *

Susan Varley glanced up from her dog-eared *Birds of Alberta* book as the latest occupant of the Bertha Mountain Bed and Breakfast, a Mr. Alistair Diarmuid, appeared at the top of the stairs. He gave her a too-wide smile and Susan's teeth clenched.

"Good morning, Ms. Varley," Alistair called down to her. "Glorious day, isn't it?"

She rolled her eyes and retreated behind the book's pages. The man irked her. "Glorious, huh?"

"The skies are fair, the sun is out—"

"And it's windy as hell."

"Wind aside, the Alberta weather has held steady for yet another day." He jumped down the last three stairs and landed with a clatter before her desk. "What could be better?"

She put her forefinger in the book to mark her place and glared at him over the top of her thick glasses. "Better? How about if I didn't have to worry you were going to break your neck every time you came down my stairs. Normal people *walk*, you know."

"Normal is overrated and I assure you, I could survive a fall of a mere three stairs."

The corners of her lips turned down. "It's not your survival that concerns me, Mr. Diarmuid. It's you *suing me* afterward."

Alistair tossed his head back and laughed. With his long hair and deep tan, the man looked more like a surfer than a filmmaker. Susan had no use for him. When she'd read his email message earlier this summer—that he was a filmmaker from Berkeley California, and quite happy to pay for the suite in advance—she'd thanked her lucky stars for a long-term guest. Money had been tight all summer. A month-long guest (with an inflated room rate) would help Susan survive the winter. And then Mr. Diarmuid showed up. While he looked good on paper, he wasn't at all what she'd expected.

Alistair set his satchel on the counter, and leaned in. She fought the urge to recoil.

"Now, Ms. Varley, could you tell me where…" He pulled a scribbled post-it note from his pocket. "Harebell Road is?"

Unspeaking, she lifted a map from the metal stand at her elbow and slid it across the desk to him.

Alistair picked it up. "Ah, there it is, right there. Tell me, Ms. Varley, do you happen to know Mrs. Darcelle at all?"

"Name's Parcelle," Susan said. "And no, I don't know her. Not really."

"Parcelle? Good thing you caught that." He picked a pen off the desk in front of the proprietor and stretched his "D" into a "P".

Susan glared at him. "You done?"

"Almost…" He bared his teeth in what could have been a smile, but wasn't—*not quite*—then placed the pen in front of her. "There's your pen back. Now, I had a few more questions for you, Ms. Varley, if you don't mind."

"I mind."

He stared at her, the insolent half-smile lingering.

"I-I'm busy right now," she said. "I don't have time."

Alistair glanced around the empty foyer. The only other guests at the B&B were a young couple from Montana who had left at dawn to hike the Wall Lake trail. Alistair looked back to her and his toothy smile grew a shade wider.

"I'm busy," she said, lifting her book. "Reading."

"It wouldn't take but a minute. I promise."

Susan let out an ill-tempered sigh. "Fine. What?!"

Alistair flipped open the tab on his leather bag and pulled a typed paper from the interior. Several pens and a gnawed pencil rolled onto the counter. "I have a few people I need to interview. I was wondering if you could give me some pointers since you live here and all?"

"Mr. Diarmuid, I really don't think—"

"I'm not asking you to say anything personal about them. Just tell me who they are, what they're like, so I don't walk into this blind."

"Mr. Diarmuid—"

"Tell me a little about Audrika and Vasur Kulkarni."

She didn't answer.

"Come on now, Ms. Varley. I'm not asking you to betray them or anything. I just want to know who the Kulkarnis are before I call."

"Fine. They own Fine and Fancy. And you'd *know* that if you actually read any of the pamphlets I gave you when you arrived."

"Perfect. And how about…" He ran his finger down a list of names. "Siobhan Andler."

"Manager of the Prince of Wales."

"But I couldn't find an address for her."

"Doesn't have one," Susan said. "She's an American. Lives up at the big hotel in the staff quarters through the season. Leaves for Montana as soon as it closes."

"Well, I'd better get hold of her before she does. How about Hunter Slate?"

"Runs Hunter's Coffee Shop."

"Margaret Lu?"

"Owns a t-shirt place on Main Street." Susan's voice dropped to a growl. "You're wasting my *time*, Mr. Diarmuid."

"Only a few more. Murray and Arnette Miles?"

"Murray runs the bookstore. Again, you could've found that in the pamphlets."

"And Arnette?"

"She's his wife, obviously."

"But could you tell me anything about her?"

"No, Mr. Diarmuid, I couldn't." Susan slapped her book down on the counter. "And even if I could, I wouldn't."

"But—"

"You want to meet these people? Get out and meet them. But don't go wasting my time by asking me to gossip about them behind their backs." She jabbed a stubby finger at the metal stand on the counter and it rocked precariously. "Read the damned pamphlets! All the information's in there."

"For the business owners who live here, yes."

Susan threw her hands in the air in exasperation. "Well, who else are you wondering about?!"

His hand snaked out and he caught her wrist, his dark eyes dancing with mischief. "Why, the *dead ones,* of course."

"Th-the what?!"

Alistair's fingers tightened on her wrist. "Your pamphlets have the living townspeople, but not the dead ones. Those are the people I *can't* talk to. But if you're not going to tell me about those who live here, perhaps you could tell me about the people who used to?"

Susan jerked free of him. "I-I don't think—"

"Let's start with Lou Newman." Alistair said. "Moved to the park and started Lou's Garage with his wife, Yuki. Now, I know that Yuki was born in Magrath, but not Mr. Newman. He immigrated to Alberta in the sixties, but my research shows his papers were checked twice by officials before they were finalized. Why? No one seems to know exactly. The archives hint that there was some question of who sponsored him. Some confusion about his birth name. But then Mr. Newman got married to Yuki, a Canadian by birth, and that was all set aside."

"This is all just gossip!"

"I'm not *trying* to anger you, Ms. Varley. I'm just trying to do my job. And that involves finding the truth."

"The truth?"

"Yes. As unpleasant as that might be. My film's about the conscientious objectors who left America during the Vietnam War. I think some of them came here to Waterton."

"I can't help you with that."

"Can't or won't?"

"Can't," she snapped. "I don't know any of the old-timers in the Park… Not well, at least. You'll have to talk to someone else."

Alistair smirked. "And who do you think I should talk to?"

Susan grabbed the list off the counter. She slid her glasses down, reading over the top of them as she went through the list of her names. Her lips were almost white, a blotchy rash of colour on her neck and cheeks.

"Him," she said.

"Levi Thompson?"

Susan nodded. "He's the oldest person alive in the park today. The last of the old-timers. If anyone will be able to help you, it's him. But don't expect him to be any more helpful than I was. People don't like being bothered, Mr. Diarmuid. Especially not by outsiders."

"Of course they don't. I'll be the very picture of politeness." With a cackle, Alistair gathered his paper and satchel. "Thank you, Ms. Varley. I know you didn't intend to, but you've been very, *very* helpful." And with a skip in his step, he headed out the door.

Susan massaged her wrist as she watched him climb into his car. *There's something wrong with that man… Very wrong.* She waited until Alistair revved the engine and drove down the street toward Harebell Road before she picked up the phone.

Audrika answered on the second ring. "Fine and Fancy. How may I help you?"

"It's Susan. You have a minute to talk?"

There was a slight pause and then Audrika's honeyed voice returned. "Susan, dear. What a surprise. Didn't expect to hear from *you* today."

"I'm not calling to chat," Susan said. "There's a man in town. He's from Hollywood."

"Ooh! You don't say."

"He's going to be trouble. I don't know how, exactly. I just do."

"Oh?"

"He's snooping around in things," Susan said. "He's- He's—"

"He's *what*, dear?"

"He's messing in business I'm sure we'd all like forgotten: immigration reports and the like."

"Oh my, well that *is* a problem, isn't it?"

"Can you get everyone together?"

"At Hunter's?"

"Of course."

"Good," Susan said. "Because Alistair Diarmuid's going to be a problem."

* * *

The door of the truck was the first warning that the drive would be interesting. It jerked in Rich's hand and banged against his knuckles.

He slammed it closed. "Nice day."

"Least it isn't winter," Lou said. "Then you'd really feel it."

She drove from Whispering Aspens down to the main road, and from there, toward the lower lake, leaving the town behind. The wind became a physical force. Each gust shuddered the windshield and threatened to take them off the road. Rich stared out his window to marvel at the white caps that scored the lake's surface. No one would be boating today.

As they mounted Knight's Hill, Lou reached out for the radio dial and the truck shimmied under another blast. The open slope loomed on the passenger side.

"Jesus!" Rich's foot jammed uselessly against the floor.

Lou giggled. "Trust me. I've driven in worse than this."

Rich let out a nervous laugh, his hand lowering from the panel of the door. The wind was too rough, the landscape, with its angled trees, fierce and forbidding. Lou tapped her fingers along to the music while Rich tightened his seat belt and locked his door.

"Feeling better now?"

"Yeah. Just nervous when I'm not driving."

"Thought so."

The song picked up its beat and soon Lou was singing along. The wind outside had reached a steady roar. The truck jerked under each blow, the music in the cab muffled and staticky. They reached the Park gates and Lou eased the truck onto the highway. The road skirted the boggy muskeg of Maskinonge Lake before the highway straightened out and headed due East onto the prairie.

At that point, the roar abruptly stopped.

Rich's brows knit together in confusion. They were driving away from the mountains, the wind inexplicably gone. He turned off the radio. There was the steady rumble of the well-tuned engine, the faint hiss of the air vents, but other than that, it was silent.

"What the...?" Rich looked around. The saplings on the hill next to him were angled to the side, the distant treetops bouncing. "What just happened?"

"We're driving with the wind. Happens here sometimes."

Rich looked out at the passing scenery, perplexed. He rolled the window down and waited for the gust of air.

Nothing changed.

The realization came to him in a rush. "It's because we're the same speed. That's it! That's why it's so quiet. The wind is going a hundred clicks too!"

He looked over to find Lou smiling to herself, eyes on the distant horizon.

"Pretty cool, huh?" she said.

"I'd say."

Rich stuck his hand out and twirled it up and down, waiting for the force he knew *should* be there, but wasn't. There was no wind at all. "Amazing…" he breathed, unexpected happiness spreading across his chest.

He turned back to discover that Lou had rolled down her window too. He hadn't even heard it. She began to sing again, her face content and easy, fingers tapping away. Rich realized that *this moment* was who Louise Newman was. This, right here, was how she lived her life.

"That's how you do it," Rich said. "You don't fight the push. You just move with whatever is happening around you. Ride it out."

Lou glanced over and the truck shimmied; the wind rose like the sound of a crashing wave, then dropped again. Her gaze went back to the highway, but he could see a faint blush on her cheeks. "Yeah, I suppose I do."

"How'd you learn to do that?"

"What do you mean?"

"How'd you learn to just go with life? Just trust that things are going to work out?"

"I—Well…" Lou sighed. "I don't exactly know."

"I always fight the push of things," Rich said. "I don't know how to go with the flow, to *trust*." He glanced over at her and smiled. "I wish I could learn how to do what you do, Lou."

She nodded, hands steady on the wheels. "You will. I know it."

He nodded and for a long time the two of them drove in silence, riding the wind together.

* * *

Hunter's Coffee Shop was almost empty. A trio of late-season hikers laughed together as they ate, while near the entrance, a handful of park locals chatted over coffee. A single waitress served them all.

Far in the back corner, two officers from the Waterton police force sat alone, separate from the rest. They were on their lunch break, but as so often happened, their work had spilled over into their personal hours.

"I've been thinking about the print we couldn't place," Sadie said. "The one from the top of the breaker box."

Jim raised a brow. "What about it?"

"We know the Zanesville police have a match to that print, so whoever made the print had to be in Ohio in 1970. It's not a lot to go on, but I feel like it's important. That it all fits together somehow."

"It's a match to a cold case, Sadie. A murder, too. Isn't that enough of 'how it fits' for you?"

"Don't be a smartass, Jimmy. I'm serious here."

He snorted with laughter.

"Ohio, 1970," Sadie said. "Police officer gets killed in the line of duty. Someone gets away and disappears."

"Uh-huh. But that's all stuff we know. Gotta be more than that."

"Agreed. And I think I figured out *how*."

Jim took another sip of coffee and waited for her to continue.

"We know that someone besides Calhoun was down in the Whitewater the night of the blackout," Sadie said. "Someone who tripped the breakers and left the print."

"Agreed."

"My gut feeling is that the same person was there the night the Whitewater burned, and Amanda Sloane died."

"Your gut?"

"Yes, my gut." Sadie bumped Jim's leg with her knee. "What's your gut tell you, huh? If you're so quick to dismiss mine."

"My feeling is that Rich Evans isn't the arsonist," Jim said. "No matter what Captain Nelson might think."

"Uh-huh. But I also think Colton Calhoun wasn't working alone. He had a friend—one who'd been in Ohio in 1970—who helped him break into the Whitewater. Maybe that same guy helped him torch the hotel."

"You think?"

"I'd bet my badge on it."

"Well, I wouldn't go quite that far," Jim said with a chuckle. "But I trust your gut."

Sadie blinked. "You—you do?"

"Of course I do. You're not a rookie anymore, Sadie. You've got good instincts. I trust you."

"Thanks, Jimmy. That… that means a lot to me."

He laughed. "You say it like you don't believe me!"

"No. I do," she said in a stilted voice. "I just—Thanks, alright?"

Jim laughed as the waitress refilled their coffee mugs. For a few minutes the two sat in contented silence as Jim watched the other people in the coffee shop. Old Ron Hamamoto peered through the glass front door. Cane in hand, he hobbled inside and went over to the group of locals. He whispered something to Susan and Margaret, then bustled out the door again. The two women collected their purses and followed.

"So if your gut's right," Jim said as the door closed behind the trio, "and what you said about the print being related to the arson follows through, then we've still got a murderer in town."

"Unless it's someone seasonal," Sadie said. "And we won't know that until we investigate, but I know for damned sure those are not

Rich Evans' fingerprints from the breaker box."

"The Lethbridge police are in charge of the arson investigation. Not us. Shouldn't we pass this info onto Nelson?"

"I already sent him an email," Sadie said. "Not that he's going to do anything about it. In the meantime, I say we keep moving forward with our investigation for the break-in. Those latent prints mean age is the key. And if it turns out we find the arsonist at the same time, well, I wouldn't be unhappy about it."

Jim chuckled. "Neither would Evans, I'd guess."

"Look there."

"Where?"

Sadie nodded to the door where Levi Thompson had appeared.

The old man ambled up to the counter, rapping his knuckles to get the waitress' attention. "Hunter around?" he asked.

Sadie dropped her voice. "You know as well as I do that most the people who live in Waterton come from somewhere else," she said. Jim nodded. "But only a handful are old enough to have committed a crime in 1970."

* * *

Four hours later, they were on their way back. The truck bed was packed full of supplies, a tarpaulin tied across it to keep lighter items from flying away. Gusts of wind popped and snapped the fabric like a sail as Rich drove.

His shoulders ached as the steering wheel jerked under his hands. Lou hadn't been joking about handling the vehicle; the truck was fighting him with every gust. A red car sped past and cut in front of Rich just as an SUV appeared in the oncoming lane. He slammed on the brakes. Somewhere in the supplies, a bag overturned, and cans rolled around the back of the pickup.

"Asshole," Rich muttered.

"In such a rush they'll miss everything," Lou said, her gaze on the blurred landscape.

"Miss what exactly? It's prairie as far as you can see."

"It's not!"

Lou glared and Rich snorted with laughter.

"I'm teasing you," he said. "You know that. Right?"

"Maybe."

He grinned and turned his attention back to driving. Next to him, Lou fiddled with the radio. Up ahead, a flashing series of signs announced that a section of highway was closed. On the side of the road the red sports car which had passed them minutes earlier appeared. It was parked in front of a police car, the officer leaning in the driver's side window.

"Guess he saw what he was supposed to," Rich said.

"Or he missed it."

They reached a row of pylons and highway signs, and rolled to a stop next to a sunburned man holding a stop sign. He stepped up to the passenger window.

"What's going on?" Lou asked him.

"They're moving a house across this stretch of highway," the man said. "You have to wait for the house to be moved, or take a detour, then get back to the highway on the other side."

Rich groaned.

"Any idea how long it'll take them to get the house off the road?" Lou said.

The young man wrinkled his sunburned nose. "Uh… maybe thirty minutes? Forty? They aren't going far. Just up to a secondary road near the St. Mary's reservoir. You can either take the detour or wait. Up to you."

Lou thanked him and rolled up the window.

"A house?" Rich chuckled. "Oh my God, Alberta is nuts."

"Could be worse. We could be stuck behind that house the whole way back."

Rich turned the truck and headed toward the Magrath exit. "So what do you want to do?"

"We're here," she said. "Might as well just hang out a bit."

Rich smothered his laughter. The place was a scattering of houses, a few shops, farmland and little else. "Are you serious, Lou? There's nothing *here!*"

"Stop it!" Lou said, poking him in the ribs. "My mom grew up here, alright? There's lots of things to see."

"Uh-huh…? Show me."

Lou pointed up the highway. "Head toward Del Bonita," she said. "Near the McIntyre ranch there's a beautiful bit of land. Hills and valleys, a little creek moving along the bottom… it's gorgeous. We could stop there."

Rich looked out at the bald prairie and grinned. "Hills around here?"

"Only if you know where to look."

CHAPTER SIX

They lay on the grass at the edge of the creek, insects pulsing in the air around them. Lou hadn't been south of Magrath since she'd visited her cousins in her teens, and the area was imbued with the kind of magic only childhood memories could create. Rich leaned in, his lips moving over hers. The heat of the day was a drug and his hands on her body heightened the sensation. All of the stresses of the last weeks disappeared and the two of them stood on equal footing once more. *In love.*

"This was a great idea," Rich said. "Glad we stopped."

She reached up, brushing her fingertips over the crinkles at the corner of his eyes. Memorizing them. "Me too. Just a perfect day."

Far above them, clouds bustled across the dome of sky, hurried on by the wind. At the top of the hill, the treetops danced and swirled, but in the hollow of the valley, the breeze was gentle and soft.

Without explanation, Rich rolled sideways and reached into his pocket. Lou giggled, the sound growing in fits until she was cackling.

"Something wrong?"

She shook her head, but laughter pushed past closed lips.

"Seriously, what?" Rich reached out, tapping her nose.

"Sorry," Lou said. "Only *you* would be checking your phone at a time like this."

He dropped down beside her and grinned. "I'm not."

"What're you doing then?"

He held a small silver camera out for her to see. "I *was* going to take a picture of us, but now I don't know…"

"Oh don't be like that, I just meant—"

Rich leaned in and kissed away her words. *Need to get back to town… Back to Waterton… to the house… to the bed…*

Lou smiled as she sat up and brushed her hands through her hair. "You could've picked a better time for a picture," she said. "I'm a mess."

"You're beautiful." Rich pulled a strand of grass from her hair. "I love your laugh. *That's* what I see right now: Beauty."

He lay back on the grass. They were side by side, Rich's face next to Lou's shoulder as he held the camera at arm's length. He felt so warm, *so right,* and Lou turned to glance over at him just as the shutter snapped. Rich turned the camera around and scrolled to the image he'd just taken. Lou's breath caught. They looked younger; the angle pulled them back a few years. Rich's worry lines were gone, his face in a lopsided grin. Lou's expression was blissful, her gaze on the man next to her rather than the camera, her hand against his chest. If there'd been a picture of *joy*, it was this.

Her throat tightened as she saw it. She wasn't sitting on the outside anymore. She was living this, *feeling this.*

"I want a copy of that," Lou said.

Rich put an arm behind his head and squinted at her. "What? Living in the moment's not good enough for you?"

She threw a leg over his hips and scrambled on top of him. "No, but it's a nice picture, and a good day. I want to remember it. That all right with *you*, Richard?"

As she leaned down to kiss him, he caught her shoulders. His smile wasn't bright any longer. Like a sunny morning with clouds on the horizon. *Poignant.*

"No matter what happens with the preliminary trial," he said. "I want you to know, I don't regret moving to Waterton. I'm glad it happened…because I got to meet you. I'm grateful for that. I—I wouldn't give it up for anything."

She nodded, wanting to answer, but the words wouldn't come.

"This was a good day," Rich said, "and I'm glad you let me come along."

"Me too."

* * *

Alistair scowled as he walked the lakeshore, his eyes on the trees. They listed drunkenly sideways, shaped by the relentless wind. This afternoon, he'd interviewed an octogenarian who'd lived in the hamlet of Waterton for decades. The old woman had signed the release forms without question and rambled through the two hour interview with the eagerness of someone starved for visitors.

Her words returned as Alistair walked the rocky beach.

"In the sixties and seventies, the town began to change. The locals didn't have much use for that," she said.

"Changed how?"

"New people coming in. Others leaving."

"Do you remember who?" Alistair asked.

"Who what, dear?"

He forced his voice to remain calm, though her wandering mind irritated him. "Who moved to Waterton in the sixties and seventies?"

"Oh goodness, who was it now? Mmm… the Kulkarnis for one. That Audrika—she ruffled a lot of feathers, I tell you! And then there

were the teachers at the school. Three or four of 'em, one after the other. They came and went. Can't recall their names."

"Who else, Mrs. Parcelle?"

"Well, there were the Newmans who started up the garage. Mind you, she was from Magrath and he came from Lethbridge, so that's not so far away. But there were others, too. Oh dear, my mind just isn't what it used to be."

Alistair scowled as he followed the trail out of the scrubby trees. Without their protection, the wind redoubled and his vision blurred with tears. He tucked his chin down. Mrs. Parcelle's memory had wandered, but there was enough in her interview to solidify what the previous clues had hinted at: draft dodgers *had* come here. He knew that he should be happy, but he wasn't. Anger rippled under his skin. He wished she'd given him more to go on. *Wish in one hand, piss in the other,* his father's voice mocked from distant memory. *See which fills up first.*

Alistair scowled and walked faster.

His father had never understood his drive for the truth, whereas Alistair was ignited by it. During the lengthy interview, he'd prodded Mrs. Parcelle, hoping to dislodge long-forgotten details.

"Don't worry if you can't remember the names. Anything at all will help."

"I'd help you if I could, but I really can't remember. Oh my. I used to be quicker than a whip, but not now. I can see their faces in my mind." She tapped the side of her wrinkled brow. "But the names are gone. I used to—"

"Do you know of anyone else who might know who moved here?" he interrupted.

"I'm sure if you talk to Old Levi, he'd remember."

"Levi Thompson? The man who owns the ranch just outside the

Park gates?" The name was already on his list of locals, alongside a scribbled note about 'oldest man in the Park', but Mr. Thompson hadn't answered any of Alistair's phone calls, nor replied to the form letter.

"Yes, that's the one. Levi's got a much better memory for those things than I do. I'm not a local, see? But Levi is. I moved here in '58 when I got married. The locals didn't mix too much with us new folks back in those days."

He laughed angrily. "Not sure that's changed."

Alistair kicked a stray rock off the path and watched as it skittered into the grass and disappeared. They'd been talking for more than an hour when the conversation had unexpectedly moved sideways.

"Waterton seems very separate from the rest of the world. Very self-contained," Alistair said. "Perhaps you could talk about the isolation of the community. Why do you think it's like that?"

"Oh-ho," she said. "Now I see what everyone's been saying about you!"

"Saying about me?"

"You're digging around where you shouldn't be. Trying to make mountains out of molehills."

Alistair's false smile faded away. He knew he should let it go, but found he couldn't. The anger was back.

"I know there's something going on in Waterton," he snapped. "I just don't know what."

"Some things are better left to rest, dear."

"What things?!"

"You think that you know our little backwoods town because you've come and stayed, and photographed the buildings, but you're just like everyone else. You're an outsider, Mr. Diarmuid. You don't

know what it's like to actually live here."

He leaned in and her eyes widened. "Then TELL me!" he barked.

"But I—"

"You say I'm an outsider. Then help me to understand!"

The old woman's face paled at his outburst. "I-I don't…"

"Come on, Mrs. Parcelle. Surely you can tell me what you mean."

She took a slow breath, then began. "Making a living off the land is hard, but the people who stay are harder. We stick together. Take care of our own. It's why locals have such a hard time with newcomers moving here."

"And if a draft dodger were to—"

"Stop."

"Or what?! I know there were illegal immigrants here. I—"

"That's quite enough!" She rose from the couch and pointed to the door with the end of her cane. "We're done here, Mr. Diarmuid."

"But—"

"Get out of my house!"

Alistair shook with rage. He gathered the tape recorder and permission forms, already signed, from the coffee table. Inside him, the fury fought for release.

"I know men like you." The old woman's voice trembled with indignation. "Saying you're looking to get the real story when the truth is, you've already decided what you believe."

"I didn't mean any disrespect," he said in a stiff voice.

She swung the door wide and the hinges squealed in protest. "I don't care what you meant by it. We're done."

Alistair backed out the doorway, seething. "If we could just talk for a moment longer, I want to—"

The door banged shut before he finished.

Walking along the beach hours later, Alistair let out a blast of swearing. If he wanted the truth, he needed to become a better liar.

* * *

The judge's decision had yet to be announced, but given how the preliminary hearing had gone, Stu Callaghan wanted to prepare in advance. He spent two days in Waterton before leaving for New York. He followed Rich around, laughing at the remoteness of the town, and checking his phone again and again without success. Rich smiled. At some point, he realized he'd grown to see this as normal. The barrier of the mountains was no longer a cage that kept him in, but a fence that kept the world out. Lou was here, and that was enough reason to stay.

While Rich worked at the garage, Stu talked to locals, built Rich's defense strategy, and filed subpoenas with the courthouse. The two men spent one interminable afternoon at the local pharmacy—the only place in Waterton with a photocopier—Xeroxing the box of files the police had returned to Rich's care.

"Do you want to take the papers to New York with you?" Rich offered. "I don't mind, man."

"Nah, I'll just get a copy," Stu said as he fed another pile of papers into the archaic machine. It came to life with the buzz of a nest of upturned hornets. "That way if anything gets misplaced, we've got a backup here with you."

"Right. That makes sense. But you don't think anything will—"

"Relax, buddy. It's gonna be fine."

"You say that like you're certain. Are you?"

"Not certain, no," Stu said. He pulled the warm copies from the bin, and tapped them. "But the police's case isn't air tight and that means I just need to poke a few holes to get it to sink."

"Easy as that?"

"Not easy, but predictable." He winked. "Done it a hundred

times before."

"Right."

With photocopies finished, Stu pulled them from the machine and double checked that none had been left behind. "Don't worry; just be ready. That's my motto."

"Should I be doing anything to prepare for the trial?"

"If you want."

Rich glanced down at the box. There were hundreds of files—both his and Chan's—that told the story of the Whitewater's short but dramatic existence in Waterton. His gaze caught on Chan's signature and he scowled. This was *his* fault.

"I do."

"Good." Stu laughed. "But don't think I'm gonna pay you as my assistant."

"Wouldn't think of it." And for the first time that day, Rich smiled. Money aside, Stu Callaghan was a good friend. Rich trusted him.

At the end of the week, Lou and Rich drove Stu to the Lethbridge airport. He hugged Rich, then turned to Lou. "It was great meeting you."

"You too."

"Never thought I'd see a woman make an honest man out of Rich here."

"Stu, please don't," Rich groaned.

Lou smiled, but the expression didn't make it to her eyes. "Rich *is* honest."

"Maybe," Stu said, "but I've known Rich a long time, and he always walks away..." He shook his head. "Let's just say the change *surprises* me. I like it." He pulled Rich into a one-sided hug and pounded him hard on the back. "Great to see you again, buddy. Try to stay out of trouble while I'm gone."

"I'll try."

Rich stepped back and Stu reached for Lou's hand to shake. She stared at him as if she wasn't certain of his motives. Stu did the same.

"It was good to meet you, Louise," he said.

"Goodbye, Stuart."

For the first time in the years they'd been friends, Rich realized that if needed, he'd side with someone other than Stu and the realization surprised him.

"See you in a couple weeks," Stu said. "Don't stress it, buddy. I've got your back."

In minutes he was on the other side of the security gate, behind the frosted glass. Rich turned to Lou. "What Stu said. It was never like that. I just—I hadn't met the right woman. You know?"

She tipped her head to the side. "Why are you telling me this?"

"I..."

Seconds passed. Lou stepped closer and stared up at him with piercing eyes. "I'd know if you didn't want to be here with me," she said. "But you should know that I *want* to be here with *you*, too. You're not the only one choosing to stay."

Despite the long weeks of tension, everything felt better in the wake of that admission.

* * *

Sadie stood next to the billboard. She clasped the end of her braid between tight fingers as her eyes moved over the details if the newly-opened investigation. They'd amassed a huge amount of information since the Zanesville police force message a week ago. Images of the Whitewater, which had only recently been filed away, had been disinterred from sagging boxes and pinned into position on the wall of Jim and Sadie's shared office. Another person needed to be accounted for the night of the break-in.

A person wanted for murder.

Looking at the pattern of yellow sticky notes, pictures, and photocopies, Sadie could see a shape emerging, though she couldn't yet tell what it was. It reminded her of a black and white photography course she'd taken one summer, shadowy images in the developer appearing by degrees. Investigation worked much the same way: bits of information pulled into focus, shading in an image she'd never imagined.

Her fingers tightened as her gaze caught on an enlarged photocopy of the two stray fingerprints from the top of the hotel's breaker box. She gave one sharp tug and let go of her braid.

"The guy's still in Waterton." Sadie wasn't sure *how* she knew that, but she did.

She stepped up to the complicated mesh of notes and photos. Faxed documents from the Zanesville Police filled an entire corner of the board; it included a grainy black-and-white picture of a freckled teen. She wore a headband and held a placard denouncing the Vietnam War. *Catherine LaVallee.* The girl's face was burned into Sadie's memory, along with the nameless other who had followed her into the forest that night. It wasn't Catherine's boyfriend, or brother—the original investigation had determined that—but it was someone important. Another hunch. That person had been with Colton Calhoun in the basement of the Whitewater the night the lights had been cut.

"Who are you?" she murmured.

"What's that?"

Sadie turned in surprise to see Jim in the doorway. He carried Hunter's heavy coffee mugs in both hands. Hunter didn't believe in disposable cups. When you ordered coffee to go, he gave you a mug and reminded you to bring it back.

"Just talking things through. Trying to put the case together in my head."

Jim offered her one of the cups and she took it. "Any new ideas?" he asked.

"I think we're closer to finding this guy than we realize."

Jim stepped up next to her. "I finished running the names of guests from all the hotels and bed and breakfasts in town the night of the break-in and the fire."

"And?"

"And nothing. Everyone's clear. Barring a few priors for illegal use of controlled substances and unpaid parking tickets, there weren't any priors. Waterton's guests were squeaky clean this summer."

Sadie made a sound of disapproval in the back of her throat. She was waiting for a lead. Like a candle, one part of her mental image guttered and went dark. "It worries me, Jimmy," she said. "Those extra prints match someone."

"I'm sure they do. But he didn't stay in one of the hotels. I'm going to check camp grounds next."

"Sounds good."

"Whoever he is, he's been lying pretty low since 1970," Jim said.

"Well, if you're gonna lie low, Waterton's the perfect hole-in-the-wall place to do it."

Jim choked with laughter. "Be nice, Sadie."

"I'm always nice."

"Be nicer," Jim said with a grin. "I grew up in a smaller town than this one."

Sadie shook her head and returned her attention to the board.

The feeling was back. *Who are you?* For some reason Lou's face rose in her mind.

Sadie's eyes widened. "I've got it!"

"Got what?"

"We almost caught this guy when we were looking into the break-in. I *knew* we were close! I just couldn't figure out *why*."

"I don't follow."

Sadie gestured to the crime scene photos from the basement of the lodge. One showed the open breaker box. Another showed an overturned crate and metal trays littering the floor.

"When we talked to Louise Newman after the break-in, she said she'd seen someone running away from the Whitewater that night," Sadie said. "She couldn't tell who it was. But the guy took off into the trees when Lou called out to him."

"Calhoun running away from the scene?"

"Could be," Sadie said. "But that still leaves one person down in the basement when Evans went downstairs. Lou said she saw someone running away at least *ten minutes* before they got the lights back on at the hotel, but Evans' report said that the person in the basement bumped into him and knocked him down less than a minute before Nando arrived to deal with the breakers. That's not someone who's *done* with what they're doing; *that's someone in the middle of it!*"

"Jesus. That's right!"

"I think Colt and this other guy came in together. One of them ran off—and that's who Lou Newman saw running away—but the other guy stayed to finish the job."

"The two of them were up to something worse than a power outage—gas lines or something else—"

"And Evans interrupted him partway through."

"Rich Evans has bad luck," Jim said. "Too bad he didn't interrupt them the night of the fire too."

"So we still have one known murderer, and one murder-suspect fooling around in the basement of the Whitewater the night of the blackout. That doesn't go away on its own." She examined the black and white photograph of the ruins of the Whitewater. "And with the hotel gone, it makes me wonder if these two finally succeeded in what they were trying to do, the second time they came back."

"You figure this perp was down there the night it burned?"

"Yeah, I do."

"The guy's gotta be in his fifties or older. That narrows the search. We can use Park gate information to track the people who bought park passes in the weeks before the break-in. Compare them with those who left before the fire and those who left after it. Narrow the search by age. It won't account for any travelers that came along with them, but it's a start."

Sadie's eyes fell on a photograph of a middle-aged man wearing a police uniform and horn-rimmed glasses. *Constable Randy Selburg, father of two, one gunshot wound to the chest, shot at close range.*

"That's a good idea," she said. "But first, let's draw up a list of locals."

"Locals? Why?"

"Cause there's a chance the guy from the basement's still here."

* * *

Levi Thompson climbed from his aging pickup truck, his gaze on the sign above the gas station door. Lou's Garage had been a Waterton landmark since the seventies, when the original Lou Newman had opened its doors. Levi had liked the man well enough, and that opinion hadn't changed, no matter what complaints he had with his daughter. The two of them had butted heads many times over the years. He wondered if that would happen again today.

Standing in the drizzling rain, Levi hooked his thumbs in his belt loops and leaned back as he waited for the tension across his lower back to ease. His ranch was a twenty minute drive away, but even that amount of sitting left him aching. Forty years ago, he could have given any hiker in town a run for their money. Twenty before that, he'd been quicker than a goat, and twice the daredevil.

I still feel like I'm eighteen. The mountains have just gotten steeper.

He squinted in the front window of the store, seeing young Mila at the counter. Figuring Lou had to be around, Levi ambled over to the open garage doors. He stepped inside and waited for his eyes to adjust to the darkness.

"Was wondering when you'd come by," Louise said.

His hands tightened into fists, irritated despite himself. She unnerved him, always had. "Yeah, well," he said. "The ranch's keeping me busy with all the blasted wind. Door on the barn blew in twice. Ain't had a minute's peace this week."

Louise nodded in agreement. With summer over and autumn begun, everyone in Waterton was waiting for the gusty west winds to slow. Houses bore dark patches of missing siding, lonely shingles pinwheeled down the streets. Lou stepped out from behind the hood of a car and wiped her hands on an oil-stained rag.

"I've got your dry goods," she said. "You want me to bring them around to the truck?"

"If you don't mind."

Lou nodded, but didn't move. She seemed to be waiting for him to say something—*She can wait all goddamned day!*—and that set another flame in the tinder of his aggravation. He didn't want to make small talk. Not with her.

"You know, Levi," Lou said, "I wanted to talk to you about the trouble Waterton had this past summer."

His white brows dropped over flinty eyes. "Trouble?"

"I know you haven't been in town much, but you must've heard what happened with Colton."

He grunted noncommittally. He'd helped pay for the boy's funeral. Of course, he'd heard about it!

"Hunter told me he was your cousin."

"Hunter should mind his business," Levi said.

"But Colt *was* your cousin, wasn't he?"

"Second cousin, once removed."

"And he worked as a ranch hand on your ranch after high school?"

"Reckon he might've." Levi sniffed. "Can't recall."

Lou's face shifted, the perplexed lines an echo of her mother's. That thought left the old man fighting a wave of deep-seated shame. There was too much history he'd like to forget, but his memories were on the surface today, closer even than the woman across from him. For a single heartbeat the shop faded and Slocan appeared: huts in rows, men and women like cattle within its fenced boundaries.

There were things you did, his mind argued, *when times were tough.* He'd had a family to support in those days, and the pay had been plenty good. It had been something he hadn't even questioned. Canada had been at war, after all.

"It was a prison," Yuki's voice chided from memory.

"Canada was at war, damnit!"

"Maybe so, but they took children to those camps too…"

Lou tipped her head and Levi stumbled backward. He didn't *want* to remember, but with Lou staring at him, he couldn't forget.

"Levi, are you alright? You look sick."

He ran a hand over his wrinkled face. "I'm fine," he said. "Just tired. Too much goddamned work, and too bloody old."

"I only asked about Colton, because Hunter said—"

The embers of frustration blazed to life. "Hunter says a lot of things he shouldn't!" Lou opened her mouth to answer, but he didn't give her room to speak. "Now, you either got those supplies I ordered, dammit, or I got no business with you!"

Lou turned away and disappeared between the shelves. Levi didn't follow. Yuki Nakagama had told him what her mother and father had gone through in the internment camps, had told him the story of a little boy—her uncle—four years old and dead of the flu in the grip of winter. Yuki's ghost, and that of a nameless child, waited for him in the shadows.

Swearing, Levi limped back outside.

* * *

The deliveryman waited for Rich to sign the forms, his eyes on the jagged teeth of the mountain range that surrounded them. The town was the centre of a bowl; the Rockies the rim. Nothing got in or out without effort.

The courier handed the package to Rich and smiled. "Hope it's good news, man."

"Yeah," Rich said. "Me too."

He waited until the van pulled from the curb before he walked into Lou's kitchen and pulled open the tab. He shook the papers out and scanned through legalese. The document was embossed with the Coldcreek Enterprises logo, a reminder of a promising career which had derailed. There were a few pages of details regarding his pension monies. Rich flicked past them. Stu's fees meant he'd need to cash those in. It wasn't until the last page that he stopped.

There, Prischka Archer had left a yellow sticky note:

Hope this letter finds you well, Richard. Call me when you decide to get back in the game.

Prischka

Rich pulled the note off the page and crumpled it. Underneath was a typed list of numbers. Seeing them, Rich's eyes widened.

"Jesus," he breathed. He scanned the list, counting zeros in growing surprise, then flipped the document closed. "My God," Rich laughed, the happy sound trapped by the empty kitchen. "What a payout!"

He wished Lou was here. He could imagine rushing over and kissing her, twirling her in his arms. He *needed* to share this with her. The settlement was far bigger than he'd let himself hope. Stu Callaghan had more than earned his wages on this one. And now Rich had the money to pay him if they went to trial. If they *didn't* go to trial, Rich had a nest egg he'd never expected. He could take a year off. Hell! He could take two.

"Good old Stu," he said with a smile.

Bankruptcy no longer loomed, but the rest of Rich's life hung in the balance. A hesitant smile played over his lips. The trial for arson wasn't a total certainty. Stu had done a good job. *Maybe this is it. The break. The do-over.* Rich laughed aloud. If anyone deserved one, it was him.

He had no job, no home, and no idea what he'd be doing a year from now. But he also had two years' salary, a monetary equivalent of unused vacation pay, a decade's worth of pension monies, and a one-time bonus payout for *"exceptional dedication and effort"* courtesy of Prischka Archer herself.

For the first time since the fire, he felt hope.

* * *

The coffee shop was buzzing with conversation when the door

opened and a frail-looking octogenarian appeared.

"Afternoon, Mrs. Parcelle," Hunter said. "It's good to see you."

Audrika Kulkarni had been the one to call today's meeting on 'a request from a concerned citizen'. Annie Parcelle wasn't a regular participant of their group. Her unexpected arrival took Hunter by surprise.

"It's good to be here, Hunter," she said. "Haven't been going out-side much these days."

"Can I get you a coffee or tea? A piece of pie, maybe." Hunter pulled out a chair for her. She didn't take it, though she put her bony hand on the back for support.

"No pie right now, thanks Hunter. This is a business call."

Hunter lowered the coffee pot he held. So Mrs. Parcelle *was* Audrika's so-called 'concerned citizen'. "Well, then," he said. "What can I do for you?"

"It's not you in particular. I need to talk to everyone." Her rheumy eyes drifted over the group. "I have some news," she said. "Something you'll all want to hear."

The chatter continued.

Mrs. Parcelle cleared her throat. "Listen up everyone. Audrika, I'm waiting. Grant, I need your attention, too. Arnette and Murray? Are you listening to—?"

"Just spit it out, woman!" Levi snarled. "Stop making such a damned show about it."

A few muffled snickers followed Levi's outburst.

"Fine then." Mrs. Parcelle said. "They found a print."

"A print?" one of the people at the back of the room said. "From what kind of animal?"

"Not an animal print. A human print, from down in the base-ment of the Whitewater."

"From the Whitewater fire?" Hunter said.

"No, dear. One from when the Whitewater was burgled in the summer, weeks before the fire."

Levi rolled his eyes. "And who'd you hear that from, huh? You hardly step out of that cottage o' yours."

"I heard it from the secretary who works down at the police station," Mrs. Parcelle said. "The girl stopped talking when she saw me, of course. My eyes might be weak, but my ears are as good as any. *There was a print on the breaker box* is what the girl said."

"Who cares?" Audrika said. "There's plenty of prints around, I'm sure. What difference does one or another make? The hotel's gone. Surely a burglar isn't of any concern."

"Ah, but it's not just *any* print," Mrs. Parcelle said. "See, it's not from around here. And whoever it is, has a shady background. The police are determined to find out who it is."

Audrika shook her head.

"Words to the wise, my friends," Mrs. Parcelle said. "They're looking for the match to those prints. And they're certain to find them."

"Well, whose prints are they?!"

Hunter peered to see who'd shouted, but there were too many locals in the way.

"That's what the police want to find out," Mrs. Parcelle said. "I tried sussing it out with that new officer: Jordan something-or-other, but he wasn't having any of it. But I know what I heard. '*The prints are key.*' That's what the girl at the counter said." Her voice dropped. "They've linked the prints to a *murderer.*"

"Murderer!" The word passed from mouth to mouth like a hiss of steam.

"And that's not all," Mrs. Parcelle said. "There was a strange young man who came by my house to ask questions the other morning. Wanted to talk to me about people in the park."

"That'd be Alistair Diarmuid," Susan grumbled. "He worries me."

"Worries me, too," Mrs. Parcelle said. "Seemed a bit… quarrelsome."

"Who's that?" a voice called.

"A man from California," Susan said. "He's staying at my Bed and Breakfast. Annoying fellow. Always twisting his words around to get his own way. I told Audrika—"

"Mr. Diarmuid was asking about people who moved to Waterton in the sixties and seventies," Mrs. Parcelle interrupted. "I told him I couldn't remember, but he's a hot head, that one. And he has the bit between his teeth. Be warned: he's digging. And he won't give up until he *knows*."

The room filled with uneasy whispers.

Mrs. Parcelle turned to Hunter. "Now, dear. What was that you were saying about pie?"

He nodded and handed her a menu, but walked away before she could order.

CHAPTER SEVEN

Prischka Archer,
Coldcreek Enterprises,
23rd Floor, Flatiron Building,
175 Fifth Avenue,
New York, New York
10010

June 19, 1998

Dear Ms. Archer,

It is with regret that I must write to request additional funds to assist with the completion of the East Wing. While my original plan had been to use the revenue from the West Wing of the Whitewater Lodge to finance the remaining section, my estimates for summer traffic to Waterton appear to have been overly optimistic. We have lost business consistently this quarter.

There are several reasons for the downward slump. For one, Waterton has recently experienced a rash of poaching. A cougar was discovered disemboweled by Cameron Falls, and a big horn sheep gutted near the marina off Main Street. Both were covered by local news agencies. Obviously, incidents of this nature are bad for tourism and while I have complete trust that the police force will take the matter in hand, it has affected summer travel to the area.

If Coldcreek Enterprises would be willing to co-sign an additional loan to accommodate the current deficits, I'm certain I could work within the constraints to bring this season to a successful close. The business community still appears willing to work with Coldcreek to bring an amicable resolution to the situation.

Please advise as to your intent.

Sincerely,

Jeffrey J. Chan, HRIM, Manager

Whitewater Lodge, Waterton Park, AB

Special instructions: CC

CHAPTER EIGHT

Rich was working the till of Lou's Garage when the phone rang. He picked it up, twisted the handset to untangle the spiralled cord, and brought it to his ear.

"Lou's Garage. How can I help you?"

"Rich? That you, buddy?" Stu's voice buzzed through the receiver.

"Yeah, it's me. Everything okay? Any news?"

"I'm doing alright," Stu said. "But I got official word about the trial this morning. It's… it's a go. Sorry, man."

Rich caught himself against the counter, breathing hard. This was it. The event he'd been dreading. There were no more do-overs. He'd go to trial for arson. And if he lost, he'd go to prison, guilty or not.

"Pretty sure that the police will be over to give you the official summons," Stu said, "but I wanted you to hear it from me first. It's not good news, but it's not the worst thing that could happen either. We know what we're facing. I still think you've got a good defense." Outside the large front window, a police cruiser rolled to a stop and Officer Jim Flagstone swung open the driver's seat door. "The trial starts October 25th," Stu said. "I'll fly into Lethbridge the weekend before then. In the meantime, I'll keep you updated with phone calls every few days."

"Calls. Right," Rich said.

Outside the window, he saw Officer Black Plume climb out of the passenger side of the cruiser. The two officers walked to the door.

"Thanks for telling me, Stu," Rich said. "I mean it."

"You okay, man? You don't sound so good."

The door to the garage swung open and the two police officers came inside. Jim nodded to Rich. "Mr. Evans, we need to talk to you when you have a moment."

"The police are here," Rich said. "I-I gotta go."

"Lou around?" Stu asked.

"Yes. I mean, no. Not right this minute. She's working in the back on a car." Rich cleared his throat. "Do you want to talk to her?"

"Not me," Stu said. "Just want to make sure you're not alone right now."

A smile ghosted over Rich's lips. "No. Lou's here with me."

"Good. Tell her I said 'hi.'"

"Will do. Talk to you later, Stu." Rich hung up the phone and straightened his shoulders. "What can I do for you?"

"Mr. Evans—" Jim placed an official-looking document on the counter. "We just received word from the court…"

* * *

Alistair Diarmuid had been searching for the truth his entire life. At one time he'd thought that meant priesthood. When that failed, he'd turned to the secular.

Today he stood on the porch of the ranch-house, his breath appearing in pale clouds. From his perspective, the Rocky Mountains were a wall, the prairie rushing up to crash in motionless waves against it. In the distance, an uneven gray line marked the two lane highway, a few farm houses scattered across the wide plain. It was beautiful but barren, the view barely touched after a hundred and fifty years of settlement. *Conscientious objectors would love a place like this. Half an hour from the border. No neighbours. No one to see.* Alistair grinned. *The closest place to the middle of nowhere you could find.*

He turned back to the door and rapped hard. He'd knocked once before and no one had answered. Still, the smell of breakfast—sausage, eggs and coffee—hung in the air, a hint that he wasn't alone. So he waited. He shoved his chilled hands deep into his pockets and rolled his shoulders to ease the strain of the satchel. It held a questionnaire assembled from the bits of information he'd gleaned in the Lethbridge archives. There were ghosts in the missing documents, the promise of an answer he was close enough to taste.

While other townspeople had delayed replying to Alistair's phone calls, or told him 'no' outright, Levi Thompson had been slippery. He'd ignored both his first and second request for an interview. This time, Alistair would make the request in person. As both Susan and Mrs. Parcelle had told him: Everyone knew Levi Thompson. And though the old man didn't live within the boundary of the park, his ranch was close enough to consider.

"C'mon, c'mon…" Alistair lifted his hand and knocked again. "I know you're in there."

Truth. That's all he wanted.

Decades earlier—when Alistair believed that priesthood would hold the answers—he'd struggled with a loss of faith. On the advice of the Cardinal, he prayed for guidance in the private chapel late that night. He'd had a vision just before dawn.

In it, he was lost and wounded on a battlefield, his right arm a bloodied, broken weight at his side. He stumbled his way over the no man's land between the two lines of trenches, blinded by mustard gas, chest heaving. He arrived at the wall of razor wire, sobbing for help, only to see that in the last hours he'd turned around and was staring into the raised rifles of the enemy lines.

Screaming, Alistair woke in the chapel, as the vision—like those he'd had as a boy—swirled around him. *Real.* He didn't know what it meant, but he knew it was a sign. Any plans for the priesthood ended that night. He left the seminary and began to travel. In those first years, he'd read everything and anything he could find: questioning all, growing more frustrated by the day. He moved from place to place… angrily searching. Always waiting for the truth that would set him free.

Documentary filmmaking had been a logical step in that quest. *The truth at any cost.* This was one of his crusades.

Alistair felt the low thud of footsteps moments before the muted sound. He stood taller, hoping that the ill-fitting suit jacket and tie he wore would do enough to dispel the uncertainty his appearance gave. The door opened and the weathered face of an elderly man appeared. A fringe of thinning white hair was combed back from a weathered face, the belt buckle, plaid shirt and faded jeans in contrast with the beaded moccasins he wore.

"Are you Mr. Thompson?" Alistair asked.

"I am. What're you selling?"

"Not selling anything, sir. Just here to talk."

"You that Hollywood guy who keeps calling?"

Alistair's mouth turned down at the edges. No matter how many contacts he made beforehand, as many doors were slammed shut in his face as were opened. "Yes, sir. The name's Alistair Diarmuid. We've spoken twice."

"Don't know what you expect to find out," Levi said. "I was born in Canada, grew up 'round here. I'm not the American you're looking for."

Annoyance rose inside Alistair, but he forced his voice to remain calm. "Of course you aren't, sir. Your grandfather, Ephraim Thompson, was one of the first settlers in Waterton. That's why I want to talk to you."

"And where'd you find that out?"

He was about to answer 'Susan,' but at the last second, he didn't. "The Historical Society, Mr. Thompson. They were the ones who suggested you might help me, seeing as you know everyone in the area."

The old man's lips twitched as if he found his words amusing. "You're a tricky one, aren't you?"

"I'm only looking for the truth."

"What for?"

Now *that* was a question Alistair hadn't expected. He was so close to securing an actual interview, but he could lose it just as fast.

"I want to share what happened during the Vietnam War," he said. "I want to tell the story of those men who escaped the draft, conscientious objectors who had no choice but to leave their homes in America rather than fight. Honestly? I just want the truth. Always have."

"Seems like you're stirring up trouble to me. What's done is done. Twenty-five years is a long time to hide."

"You can't find the needle without moving the haystack."

The old man snorted. "Figured you was a lawyer or something the way you talked on the phone."

"Law wouldn't work for me. I was never any good at following rules."

"Mmph. You're not the only one."

"So can I ask you a few questions, Mr. Thompson? It'd be a short interview. Twenty minutes at most."

The old man shook his head. "Not interested."

"But I thought—"

Levi swung the door half-shut, and Alistair caught it in the palm of his hand. He peeked around the edge to find the old man glowering.

"If I could just talk to you, sir, I'd—"

With surprising strength, Levi ripped the door from Alistair's grip and slammed it so hard the windows of the house rattled. "Go home, Mr. Diarmuid!" Levi shouted from the other side. "I said 'no', and I meant it."

Irritated, Alistair waited. A minute passed. *Not getting away from me this easy, old man.* Jaw clenched, he lifted his hand to knock again, but a flicker from the curtains of a nearby window caught his attention. Alistair froze.

Levi Thompson glared out the window at him, the barrel of a shotgun clutched in his bony hand. "You git, now! Get off my property 'fore I lose my temper with you, boy!"

Alistair backed off the porch with slow, cautious steps. When the curtain dropped back into place, he turned and ran.

* * *

With the announcement of the trial, Rich no longer had a way out. He'd either be acquitted, or he'd go to jail. It was terrifying in its simplicity, and it threw him into a rush of activity.

Jeff Chan, the absentee manager of the Whitewater Lodge, had disappeared the year prior, and any insights into who might've hated the Whitewater enough to torch it, were gone before they'd started. After a sleepless night, Rich knew he needed help.

He dialed Coldcreek's number from memory. There'd been a time not long ago when Prischka Archer had been the first and last person Rich had spoken to each day. He hoped she wouldn't hang up on him.

The ringing stopped, and Prischka's cultured voice appeared.

"Prischka speaking."

"Ms. Archer, this is Richard Evans."

There was a pause. "Well, well, Richard," she said. "Didn't expect to hear from *you* so soon."

He smiled despite himself. Prischka kept on top of things. Payout or not, she'd fortify her position. He just didn't want Prischka to decide *he* was one of her losses.

"I'm sorry for bothering you, but I need to ask for that favour you offered."

"When I said I'd help, I meant *after* things had settled," Prischka said. "You know as well as I do, I can't get involved in this whole arson mess. The trial's in less than two weeks, isn't it?"

"Yes, but I need to ask about one of Coldcreek's previous employees."

"There are employee policies, of course. I can't share private information with you. There'd be questions and—"

"I need to find out what went on with Jeff Chan last year."

There was an even longer pause. Rich had just begun to wonder if she'd hung up on him, when he heard Prischka clear her throat. "Jeffrey Chan," she said, rolling the 'r'. "That young man has been a thorn in my side since day one."

"He disappeared around American Thanksgiving last year," Rich said. "The police believe that he helped cover up a homicide in the Aspen Suite of the Whitewater Lodge before he left."

"Left? I thought he was dead."

"They have an open missing person's case on him. No leads."

"Mmm… well," Prischka said. "That's interesting. Chan's been quite the nuisance to me, you know."

"With the arson trial coming up, I was hoping you could help me locate him. I mean, if he's alive."

"That's a very big 'if', Richard." Prischka let out a long-suffering sigh. Rich could imagine her in her sun-filled office, her ebony skin and shantung suit a tall silhouette against the Manhattan skyline. He'd sat there more than once, pinned by her withering glare.

"The private investigator Coldcreek hired last year wasn't able to find anything about Chan's whereabouts," Prischka said, her words sharply enunciated. "I looked through the file myself. It was very thorough."

"But no one's been looking for him since last winter, right? There are more clues now. The new information from the police report might be what the investigator needs to find Chan." Rich forced the panic out of his voice. "Please, Ms. Archer. If you could just have the investigator contact the Waterton Police."

"Why?"

"To see if he could find Jeff Chan. I'd really appreciate it."

Prischka's laughter filled the phone. "Oh, I can look into it for you, Richard, but I want you to be aware that Coldcreek's interests may *not* be the same as yours."

"I need to know what happened with Chan last year," he said. "No matter what it is."

"Are you certain about that?"

"I am."

"Then I'll get in contact with the investigator about the wayward Mr. Chan," she said. "If he finds anything this time, I'll let you know. Of course, then if I need *your* help down the road, Richard, I'll expect you to be more than willing to play your part."

Rich's hand tightened on the receiver. "Of course, Ms. Archer.

And thank you."

"A pleasure," she said. "Anything for a friend."

* * *

Jim stared at the names on the computer screen, eyes swimming. For the last two hours, he and Sadie had checked an ever-widening list of people who resided both in town, and in a semi-circle surrounding the park. They'd narrowed it to a list of locals who'd been in town the night of the Whitewater break-in. None seemed likely.

"Old Levi's almost eighty," Jim said. "He's more than old enough to have been in Ohio in 1970."

Sadie's disembodied voice echoed from the other room. "Already got him. Who's next?"

"Sydney Roberts."

"Was he around that week?" Sadie asked from the doorway. "Thought his wife said he was visiting family in Montana."

"But she wasn't sure what day he got home. You want to keep or pull him?"

"Keep him if she isn't sure. Who else?"

"Hunter Slate. He was in Waterton that week. But I don't think—"

"If he was around, then he's in," Sadie interrupted.

Jim opened the driver's license file for the final name, S. Varley, and scanned until he reached her date of birth: *January 12, 1953.* "Susan Varley," Jim said. "She was seventeen in 1970. In or out?"

"Close enough; keep her in."

Jim exited the drivers' license database and picked up his list of handwritten notes, heading over to where Sadie was assembling the names on tags. He read through the final list.

Siobhan Andler
Sam Barton
Jeannine Barton

Elaine Decker

Ronald Hamamoto

Audrika Kulkarni

Vasur Kulkarni

Pete Long Time Squirrel

Margaret Lu

Grant McNealy

Murray Miles

Arnette Miles

Annie Parcelle

Walter Phillips

Sydney Roberts

Hunter Slate

Levi Thompson

Susan Varley

"So that's it then," Jim said, frowning.

Jim had grown up in the town of Mountain View, twenty minutes outside the Park. Many of the people on the list had children Jim had gone to school with. All of them were neighbours. Many, like Hunter Slate, were close friends.

Sadie left the billboard to come stand next to him. "That list's a lot shorter than I expected," she said.

"Don't jinx it. I'm sure there'll be something waiting just around the corner to screw it all to hell."

Sadie laughed. "Suppose so. But then again, it'd be boring if there weren't." The edges of her smile turned down. For a long moment neither spoke.

"I know these people, Sadie," Jim said quietly. "They're all good folks."

"I know. That's what bothers me."

* * *

Alistair's hands shook as he drove back to Waterton. He'd had close calls before: Once in Guatemala, Alistair had found himself on the wrong side of a knife-wielding grifter. Only the arrival of an American tourist had saved him. Another time in Portugal, a priest had hit him on the basilica steps of Santo Cristo.

Neither had angered him like today.

Levi Thompson hadn't shot at him. *But he could have.* And no one would have known. The ranch was isolated. There were no on-lookers. No witnesses. It struck Alistair that if Levi Thompson *had* killed him, he'd have the perfect place to dispose of the body. The thought was infuriating!

Reaching the park gates, Alistair headed straight to the police station. He parked the car, and put his hand on the handle. Unexpectedly, Susan's words returned.

"Levi's the oldest person alive in the park today. The last of the old-timers. If anyone will be able to help you, it's him. But don't expect him to be any more helpful than I was."

"Goddamnit!" Alistair banged his hand on the steering wheel. If he reported the old man, there was no way he'd stay anonymous. The locals were already talking.

"People don't like being bothered, Mr. Diarmuid. Especially not by outsiders."

Who was to say the police wouldn't be on Levi's side? It wouldn't take much to convince them he'd been the aggressor, not the eighty-year-old.

Nervous of small-town justice, Alistair parked the rental car and gathered his papers. He walked down Main Street. There were other things on his list. Other people who could help.

He paused mid-step. "The Historical Society has local files!" He was almost at the low, one-story building when he saw a hand-written note in the window.

Closed for lunch. Back in an hour or so.

Sydney

Alistair swore. He turned around to scan the barren street, temper prickling. He could feel people's eyes in windows as they watched him, and laughed at his efforts. He looked back the other direction, but before he reached his car, a brightly-painted sign caught his eye. *Fine and Fancy.* The shop was one of the few places he hadn't gone.

Alistair crossed the road, and headed to the door. Unlike most the other venues on Main Street who'd closed up for the season, the sign in the front window and open door declared the shop was open, but the interior was quiet.

Alistair ducked past dangling dream catchers and stepped inside. "Hello?" he called. "Anyone here?"

A flash of turquoise appeared behind a row of Waterton shirts as the owner came forward. Short and rotund, the woman had the look of a pampered Persian cat, her heavy makeup and long, painted nails at odds with the mountain locale. She carried a bundle of bear-bells in one hand, and they chimed in time to her dainty high-heeled steps.

"I'm so sorry!" she said warmly. "Didn't hear you come in." She moved behind the counter, set the bells aside, and unlocked the till with the key on her bracelet. She looked up at him expectantly. "Now then, what can I ring up for you?"

"Actually, I'm not here to buy anything."

The woman's expression dimmed. "Are you sure? It's end of the season, you know." She waggled bejeweled fingers toward the empty store. "Everything's on twenty percent off. Lovely choices."

"That's a wonderful offer, Mrs. Kulk..."

"Kulkarni," she said. "But do call me Audrika, dear." She ran her finger along the frayed edge of his windbreaker. "You certain I can't interest you in a jacket and hat? It's warm outside today, but the weather's already starting to change. Autumn's a tricky season in the Rockies."

"Thank you, Mrs.—"

"Audrika."

"Audrika, right. See, I'm not here to buy," Alistair said. "I'm working."

"Working?"

"Doing some research on the Waterton area."

"Whatever for?"

"For my next documentary. My name is Alistair Diarmuid. I'm a filmmaker."

She gave him a coy smile. "Oh! Well what kind of films do you make, Mr. Diarmuid?"

"Documentaries. I'm doing some research for my next one."

"About...?"

"The history of Waterton in the sixties and seventies," he lied. "Trying to get a flavour for the town before I decide whether or not I can make a go of it."

"Mmm... that's surprising."

"Why's that?"

"No reason, really. I figured you were here to snoop around about the infamous Mr. Calhoun like the *rest* of the reporters who showed up in the summer."

"No thank you. I'm sure someone else'll go after that angle, but I'm not interested in sensationalized stories; I'm interested in important ones. So can I talk to *you* for a few minutes? It'd be very helpful. I have a few questions to—"

"Questions about what?"

"About the town. About Waterton, the townspeople and their lives."

Audrika watched him for several seconds. Alistair had the distinct feeling she was measuring him up like a producer might.

He leaned closer. "I'd make it worth your while."

"And how might you do that?"

Alistair gave her a rakish grin. The hook was his forte. "Well, Audrika, a very *large* number of people will see my documentary, and I'd be happy to feature your delightful shop as a taste of the local flavour, in return for your time."

"I'm not sure… I mean, I've never even heard of you, Mr…"

"Diarmuid," he repeated, "Alistair Diarmuid. My last film— *Peligro*—placed at Sundance and Cannes. The documentary before that, *Spiritus Sanctum*, got an Oscar nomination for its expose of the Catholic Church."

"Oh?"

"You might not know my name, but then again, how many documentaries have you actually seen? The movie theatre here might have limited choices."

"I've seen a few," she said coolly. "But not yours."

"Look, I don't mind either way. But if you aren't willing to help me out, I'm certain one of the other business owners would be more than happy to. There was a woman the other day… now what was her name? Margaret something-or-other. She owns a shop too. I'm certain she'd give me an interview if I asked." He gestured to the door. "I can head over there and ask her now, if you like."

Audrika's gaze sharpened. "My name absolutely *cannot* be included as a source in your film."

"I use false names when I—"

"And I want you to include a shot or two of Fine and Fancy in your documentary. Make it look busy and bright. Full of customers. Sell it. I'm sure a man like you knows how to do that."

"Of course. Whatever you want."

"Good. As long as that's clear."

"Clear as crystal." Alistair reached into his jacket pocket and pulled out a release form and a handheld camcorder. "Now, if you could just sign this, we'll get started."

* * *

Rich was halfway through the Whitewater correspondence for 1998 when the argument started.

"All I'm saying," he said, "is that if you were there in Lethbridge for the trial, it'd make things easier."

"Easier for who?" she asked.

"For who? For me, Lou. For you. I don't know why you won't consider it."

"I have considered it, Rich. I really have." Lou tightened the lid on the canteen and headed to the door. "But I can't make it work. I'm sorry."

Rich was surrounded by papers: email print-offs, carbon copies, letters. A maelstrom of Jeff Chan's inefficiency. He pushed the pile aside. "God, Lou. I'm all alone here. I don't *know* anyone in Lethbridge. I just—I need some support."

"I *will* be supporting you. I'm just a phone call away, but I can't just drop everything and leave Waterton behind."

Frustrated, Rich gathered the papers and tossed them back into the box. *Chan could wait.* He came to Lou's side, waiting as she fiddled with the straps of the pack. "Can't or won't?" he said. "C'mon, Lou. You came before."

"Running into Lethbridge once in a while is fine, but I can't stay the entire time. I have the garage to run. People need gas for their vehicles. If I'm not there—"

"You're hiking today, aren't you? So who is running the garage? I mean, if you can't be away."

"Mila's there until five, but—"

"If she can handle things for an afternoon, why can't she cover for a couple days?"

"Rich, *please* don't do this."

"Come into Lethbridge with me," he pleaded. "I just… I need you there. It'll only be a couple days."

"Not a couple days. A couple weeks. Isn't that what Stu told you?"

"Yes… no." He shrugged. Stu had told him *"two weeks at the very least,"* but he didn't want to think about that now. "I'm not sure how long the trial will take. Won't know until it happens. Please come."

Lou reached up to the line of hooks next to the door, and pulled down her jacket. "Rich, you know I can't."

"Why not?"

"You know how I feel about conflict. It's just not my thing."

"You'd go if it was someone else."

"What do you mean?"

"If it was someone else," Rich said. "Someone from *Waterton*, you'd be there in an instant."

"That's not true," Lou said.

"It is!"

"Rich, the garage needs—"

"This isn't because of the fucking garage!"

"Yes, it is!"

"It's about me! About *us!*"

"This has nothing to do with you!" Lou said. "It's just how I am.

It's how I've *always* been."

"Not true!"

Lou opened her mouth to argue, but he wasn't finished. He wanted Louise to *feel* today. Wanted to shatter the calm he both loved and hated about her. To make her feel the things he did. *To hurt her.*

"If the trial was for Hunter Slate or Sam Barton," he said, "or anyone *else* from this goddamned hick town, can you tell me you wouldn't be there in a heartbeat?"

Lou's mouth snapped closed. He'd done what he wanted. She was close to tears now, but the victory left him feeling worse than ever. The last weeks had been a storm without end: his career was over, but he was still trapped in Waterton. The control Rich Evans had spent his entire life perfecting was gone. Louise was right: *It wasn't about her.*

"Lou, I'm sorry I shouldn't have said—"

"I'm going to go for a walk," she said. Her voice was different. *Empty.* He'd expected the pain he saw in her expression, but not the distrust.

"I didn't mean to yell at you," Rich said. "I've been under a lot of stress. I..."

His words faded as Lou lifted the backpack onto her shoulders. She stepped away from him, her posture a warning. He buried his hands in his pockets. Touching her would make this worse.

"Where are you going?" he asked quietly.

"Out. I need to think."

"I'm sorry, Lou."

"I am too."

And then she was gone, and all Rich had left were regrets.

CHAPTER NINE

Excited, Alistair watched Audrika signed the release form. The interviews had been dead ends, but Mrs. Kulkarni knew the town in which she lived. If there were secrets, she'd know those, too.

He cleared his throat. "Now, I wanted to start with a bit of—"

She pushed the camcorder back toward him and turned it off. "I don't think we'll be needing this," she said. "I do *not* want to be on camera. Is that clear?"

"No problem. But do you mind if I still use the camera to record our interview, so I can quote you correctly?"

He reached for the 'on' button.

"Don't you have a tape recorder to do that?"

Alistair sighed and exchanged the camera for the tape recorder in his bag. Mrs. Kulkarni was sharper than most. He fiddled with the 'record' button and popped in a new tape, glad he'd double checked the batteries this morning.

"This alright?" he asked.

"Fine, but no voiceover for your documentary either. You understand me? I want no one to know I talked to you."

Alistair's smile drooped. "Completely."

"Good. As long as that's clear."

"Perfectly." Alistair pulled a list of questions out of his bag and set them on the glass fronted desk next to the till. "I'd like to start by having you tell me about Waterton."

"Tell you what?"

"Something more than I'd get on the news programs that have been doing such good business this summer. Something different than—" He made air quotes. "—Serial killer in woods of border town."

"Paparazzi," she said. "I'll be glad when they're gone."

"The town's been caught up in of a lot of controversy, hasn't it?"

"Pfft! Colton was an aberration, nothing else. One bad apple, causing trouble for the rest."

"You didn't like the exposure?"

"Of course not! Who would?!"

He paused to see if Audrika would offer something unprompted—many people did—but she seemed content to watch him from her perch.

"Must've been difficult with all the news crews poking around," he said.

"A nuisance is what it was."

"There are a lot of people living here who'd rather things stayed quiet, aren't there?"

Audrika rolled her eyes. "Wouldn't *you*, Mr. Diarmuid? If your hometown had been overrun with the- the… dregs of society."

"Of course I would."

"The people from Waterton do, too."

"But it seems like the townsfolk are wary of people from other places. I've had a heck of a time trying to get people to agree to interviews. Almost everyone I've talked to has either declined, or told me outright to stop snooping."

"We're a tight knit group," she said. "That's true. But no more than any other small town."

"People from Waterton don't like outsiders, do they, Audrika?"

"Oh no, that's not it at all. Goodness! Everyone who lives here comes from somewhere else. Levi Thompson's one of the few old-timers left, but the rest of us moved here at some point."

"Were any of them Americans?"

She glared at him. "The park straddles the US / Canadian border. What do you think?"

"I think it'd be a pretty easy place to get to if you were an American looking to hide."

"We get our share of smugglers trying to cross the Chief Mountain border. That's no secret."

"Ah! But that's only if you go through customs. You could just come in from Glacier and walk into Waterton Park if you wanted."

"There are rangers on the border," she said. "The trails are crawling with them since the troubles with Calhoun this summer. Even he didn't walk the whole way. Read the papers. Colton had a whole system set up. One of his men would walk to the beach on the American side, and he'd pick them up. But those trails are being monitored now. You couldn't even get that far if you tried."

"The trails are, but you could go through the woods instead."

Audrika laughed. "Go ahead and try it. They have sensors in the trees. You'd be caught before you made it halfway to town, Mr. Diarmuid."

Alistair smiled. She still didn't understand what he was asking and he was happy to wait. That was part of the game he played, lure them in a little at a time, gain their trust. *Then attack.* He cleared his throat. "But they didn't have those sensors in the sixties, did they?"

Her expression lost all joking. "I-I don't know what you're getting at."

"Oh, I think you do."

"I—I—"

"You couldn't get across the border today, but people *might* have come in years ago. They wouldn't have even needed someone to pick them up on the beach."

Audrika's gaze darted to the empty store, then back to him. "Why would you say that?!"

"Because I think some people did that."

"Rumours!"

"Americans came to Waterton during the Vietnam war, didn't they?"

She glared at him, her long nails tapping a staccato beat against the glass counter. For a moment Alistair thought she wouldn't answer, but she lifted her chin, defiant. "Yes, there were some that did."

"Men avoiding the draft?" he said. "Conscientious objectors?"

"We called them 'draft dodgers' back in the day. And yes, I recall a few. Some immigrated here after they left the States. Others settled elsewhere."

"Did some of them hike their way into Waterton? Stay here... *illegally*?"

Audrika drew herself up. Her nails had stopped their drumming, but the silence was more oppressive without it. "My name *cannot* be anywhere in your documentary! Agreed?"

"Yes, yes! Of course," he said. "Now tell me—did they hike into the Park, Mrs. Kulkarni?"

"And this shop is to be featured glowingly?"

"Absolutely. But tell me, did some hike in? Is that how they arrived?"

"That's not what I heard," she said. "It was more organized than that."

"How?"

Audrika pointed to the Park map taped to the underside of the glass counter. It had a web of trails marked on it, the upper and lower lakes picked out in blue. She tapped the far end, beyond the American border. "You can take a boat from the lake-head, if you have someone waiting for you. It just means having someone who knows you're coming on this side of the line. If you have a friend waiting, all you have to do is show up on the trail and climb into a boat. Easy as pie. I'm not the only one who's heard that story. It's probably where Colton got his idea in the first place."

Alistair didn't care about the drug bust the prior summer. His motives were hidden decades earlier. He reached for a pad inside his pocket and scribbled a furious note: *Someone helping from this side of the border. WHO? A Canadian?*

"In Toronto, there was an exile community," Alistair said. "They were organized, had an office on Spadina Avenue to help American arrivals. They even published a manual for new immigrants. Gave legal advice for those who had difficulty getting immigrant status." He looked up, realizing he was speaking aloud. "What happened to the Waterton exiles once they arrived?" he asked. "What'd they do?"

"I've no idea."

"But where did they go after they arrived?"

"How should I know that?"

Alistair's fingers tightened around his pen. 'Not telling' was as good as 'telling' some of the time. "There are *still* exiles living in town today, aren't there Mrs. Kulkarni?"

"What?!" she yelped.

Alistair leaned forward and Audrika moved back in the same motion, almost falling from her stool in her haste. "Who are they?! I want their names. Tell me!"

"I-I can't!"

"Why not?! I won't use your name," he said. "They'll never know it came from you!" Alistair wanted to grab her, shake her, but he forced his hands to stay down. *He was so close!* "Just TELL me!"

"I-I really can't. I'm sorry."

"Why?!"

She scrambled out from behind the till. "Oh, Mr. Diarmuid. You have no idea what you're getting into, do you?"

"This all happened decades ago. You need to tell me!" He banged the pen down and it skittered across the counter. "People deserve to hear this story! People need to know the truth!"

She darted across the store and for a moment he thought she would run onto the street. Instead, she threw the door wide. "If it's a story you want, Mr. Diarmuid, you'll need to find it yourself."

"But I—"

"This interview is over!"

* * *

Eyes prickling with unshed tears, Lou hoisted the knapsack to her shoulders and headed away from the cabin without a clear direction in mind. She'd meant to ask Rich to go to Bertha Lake with her, but since the trial had been announced, they'd been fighting at every turn. Each morning she told herself she'd find a way *not* to argue with him.

It happened anyways.

He wants the truth. Lou knew that, but there was too much at stake, and too many things she couldn't say. *He'd never believe me.*

Everything in her life was coming apart at the seams. She dashed away tears with the back of her hand as she walked toward the lakeshore, one of the many haunts of her childhood. She bolted across the street, passing an aging hotel on the corner of Mount View road to reach the worn pebbles of the beach. The sound of the waves brought with it memories of childhood and the semi-wilderness surrounding the town. It had been her refuge.

Louise had been ten years old the last time she'd told her father about her hidden, inner life. Then, like now, the words had been hard to find.

She and her father were working on a truck, Louise handing her father tools as he rebuilt the engine. It was Louise's gift each day: helping him once she was home from school and her homework complete. She loved the hours at his side, the calm it brought her. Outside the garage, a heavy blanket of snow covered the ground and mountains, muffling sounds. The garage was full of wonder.

"How was school today?" her father said. "Quarter-inch ratchet," he added in the same breath.

She moved through the case, picked it up, and double checked the size. Her father's fingers waggled impatiently. "It was good, Daddy."

"Just good?" He peered at her over his shoulder for a moment before returning to the engine.

"Classes were fine."

"But?"

Louise's shoulders slumped. She didn't know how to explain this to him. He wasn't her, he'd never—

"Louise?"

Her father leaned against the front fender, his arms crossed on the soiled bib of his coveralls. "What happened, baby?"

She gave a one-shouldered shrug. "Stuff."

"Stuff meaning what?"

Her gaze dropped to the dusty floor. She loved the pitted concrete, loved sitting there, and listening to her father talk his way through engine issues, loved imagining the day she'd know enough to do it herself. "It was nothing," she said. "Just some kids bugging me."

Her father put a hand on her shoulder. "Doesn't sound like nothing to me."

Louise fought the urge to cry. The kids at school were right; she *was* a baby sometimes.

"You want to talk about it?" he asked.

"Not really."

"You sure? Sometimes it helps just to say it out loud."

Louise peered up at him through tear-spiked lashes. "You wouldn't get it, Daddy."

"Try me."

"Well, about two weeks ago I…" Her voice caught. "I told Jason Hansen something I shouldn't have."

"You call this boy a bad name?"

"No, not exactly."

"Then what happened?"

"I told him he should be nicer to his mom, 'cause if she died, he'd regret it."

Her father stared at her. "And…?"

"And that's it."

"But Louise, baby, that doesn't make sense. Why would Jason be upset if—?"

"Because his mom died last weekend," she choked, tears blurring the garage. "And today he came back to school, and told everyone what I'd said to him."

"Oh honey, his mom didn't die because of you."

"But I warned him about it," she said. "Daddy, I don't think you—" Her words disappeared into painful sobs.

"Louise, honey, people die all the time. That's a hard fact of life, but it doesn't mean—"

"But I told him how it'd happen!" she cried. "I- I- I *knew*."

There was a long, uneasy moment.

"You… *knew*?" Her father's face had lost its ruddy tone, his hands white-knuckled where they clutched the ratchet.

"I told him that his mom would leave for work, and she'd be rushing, and there'd be a stalled car on the road by the Leavitt turn-off. I told Jason she'd swerve to miss it, but that she'd lose control on the ice. She'd roll the car in the ditch, and be thrown out of the front window…" Louise's words tumbled out like an unstoppered bottle. "I saw it before it happened, Daddy. And I tried to warn, Jason. I did! But it still happened. I couldn't make it stop."

Her father stepped back and bumped against the truck's grill. "Louise," he said warily. "What'n the world are you talking about?"

"Don't you get it? I saw it before it happened! I knew she'd die!"

Her father shook his head, the old look of distrust Louise knew so well appearing. "You dreamed it. That's not the same as—"

"It wasn't a dream! I could see it happening. And it did!"

"Louise, listen, I don't—"

"And now I see her following Jason around. She's there, Daddy, watching him."

"Louise, stop this right now!"

"She keeps trying to talk to him! Telling him it'll be okay, and—"

"ENOUGH!" The roar of his voice shocked her into silence. She swallowed down hitched sobs as she waited under her father's steely gaze. He ran a calloused hand over his face. "We've been over this more than once," he said. "You can't go saying things like that."

"But what if they're true? What if—"

"They're not! Now go home to your mother, and don't you dare say a word of this to her." He glared at her. "Promise me!"

"Yes, Daddy. I promise. But what about the engine? Shouldn't we—?"

"Not today, Louise. Go home!" His turned back dismissed her.

Louise stepped away from the toolbox and pushed open the door of the garage, closing it quietly behind her. Snow crunched underfoot as she headed away from the garage. She paused at the end of the street. It was the lonely twilight hour between night and day, roads barren. She couldn't go back to the garage. But if she went home, Yuki would see she'd been crying, and then she'd have to lie. Either to her mother who'd want the truth, or to her father for breaking her word to him. If she stayed out, she'd be cold, but she could cry.

Louise hunched her shoulders and headed to the lakeshore.

Two decades later, the same beach was bright and bare: winter snow exchanged for autumn's golden colours. Lou wiped her eyes and walked faster. She'd learned long ago there were things in life you just didn't talk about.

Knowing was one of them.

* * *

Audrika watched Alistair Diarmuid head toward the path that traced the lakeshore. When he was almost at the beach, she lifted up the receiver and dialed. The phone rang twice, before it clicked through.

"Hello?"

"We have a bigger problem," she said.

"What kind of problem?"

Audrika stood on tiptoe, her nose almost touching the window. Mr. Diarmuid was almost out of sight. His head was down and shoulders hunched as he trudged along the shore. A small part of her felt guilty for the trouble she was about to unleash on the man. But not enough to stop it. Friends were friends, after all, and she knew other people in town would do the same for her.

"It's that filmmaker again," Audrika said. "The one Mrs. Parcelle warned us about."

"Oh? What about him?"

"He's snooping around again. Seems to know a little more than we thought he did."

The voice on the phone sharpened. "Meaning what, exactly?"

"Well, we already knew he was checking on the people who moved to the park in the sixties, but it's more than that. From the questions he was asking me, he seems interested in those whose immigration was a little… under the table, if you will."

There was a long pause.

"Do you know if he's after someone in particular?"

"He didn't say." Audrika reached up and flipped the 'open' sign to 'closed'. "But I'm guessing he's looking for *you*."

* * *

Lou's tears had dried, but she didn't go back to the cabin. *Rich is there. He'll want to talk.* The truth she carried was too difficult to explain, too strange to be understood, and she couldn't bear for Rich to hate her. She'd rather live a lie of normalcy with him than have nothing at all.

Bereft, she wove along the lakeshore. The trail switched from smooth asphalt to red shale, and Lou stumbled.

Her vision crackled like lightning, the mountainside disappearing between one breath and the next.

She and another man stood barefoot on rocky soil. They'd had shoes once, but the homemade leather had worn through on the march to the sea. Lou squinted into the distance where a bare stone wall met them against a blinding blue sky.

The man at her side spoke: "So this is it."

She nodded. There was no use worrying about the next weeks of siege. She was a part of the machine of death, as was her friend.

"It's smaller than I expected. Figured the papists would have a wall all the way to heaven."

Lou smiled but didn't answer. Those walls were plenty high enough to kill them when the snows came.

The unwanted vision recoiled with a jolt that left Louise shaking. The smell of grit and sweat lingered sharp in her nostrils. Ahead of her—at the point where trees the blocked the trail—a man's silhouette appeared as he moved from solid shadow into bright light. His hair, two shades lighter than her own blue-black, hung in waves, clothes loose on his muscled frame. Though she'd never met him before, the hair rose on her arms as he neared.

It was the man from her vision moments before.

CHAPTER TEN

For years Alistair Diarmuid had struggled to believe. All his life, he'd wondered if he was mentally ill (as he'd been accused of being more than once), or if there was another reason for his innate strangeness. Standing on the trail, the flat glitter of Waterton Lake on one side, mountains on the other, his doubt was abruptly gone.

The woman from his dream was *real*.

"I- I know you," he blurted.

The woman's eyes widened. "You do?"

Horrified at his own admission, Alistair winced. "I just—It *seems* like I know you."

She frowned.

"Let me start over." He reached out his hand. "My name's Alistair Diarmuid."

There was a long moment of hesitation when the nameless woman didn't speak. Alistair could barely breathe. *She's the one I dreamed of! She's the soldier at the wall.*

"Louise Newman," she said with a wary smile. "But people call me Lou." She shook his hand briskly and pulled back just as fast.

Alistair waited for Louise to say something—*anything!*—as the seconds dragged out.

"Diarmuid… I know that name," she finally said. "Are you that filmmaker everyone's been talking about?"

"You've heard of me?"

She nodded. "You've got everyone in town worked up over your documentary. Levi wants to run you out of town. Even old Mrs. Parcelle was worried." She laughed, though it was a tired sound. "You're *not* what I expected, Mr. Diarmuid."

"People rarely are."

Her smile faded. "I suppose that's true."

He opened his mouth and closed it again. There was so much *more* he wanted to say to her, but Alistair knew that he couldn't. He could remember her. He could remember *this:* the two of them standing side by side. Only it wasn't this moment, but another, centuries before. Two sides of the same coin. It made him want to shout in excitement; it made him want to hide in shame. *She doesn't remember.*

"Well, it's good to finally put a face to the name," Lou said with a nod. "I'm sure I'll see you around town then."

She turned to walk away, but Alistair followed. It felt like the only thing he *could* do. He needed to find out if the vision he'd had was real. "Wait!" he shouted.

She glanced up.

"Are you out for a walk today, too?" he asked.

She nodded and Alistair gestured to the lakeshore.

"You mind if I join you for a bit?"

Louise shrugged and continued walking. "If you want."

"Thank you. Waterton can be a bit lonely for an outsider."

She shrugged. "Only until people get to know you."

"Fair enough, fair enough." He glanced over at Louise who stared indifferently forward. "I… I don't want to be a bother to you, Lou."

"No bother. It's fine." She forced a smile. "Why don't you tell me about what brought you to Waterton, Mr. Diarmuid?"

He tipped his head, considering how much of the truth about his search for draft dodgers he could share. "Well, I was scouting locations for my documentary," he began. "Waterton seemed like the right fit…"

As they walked through the cool tunnel of trees that lined the beach, Alistair talked and Lou listened. He gave the benign version of his research endeavours, hoping against hope, that Louise would offer something. She didn't.

Eventually Alistair drew her into conversation with questions about the park. They shared bits of everyday life, trivial nonsense that made Alistair want to scream. The sense that he knew her was as strong as ever, but he didn't trust it. *What would it mean?* His uncertainty grew with each step. Finally, their words bled away and they walked in silence.

As they reached a small footbridge, Louise stopped walking and looked up at him. "What?"

Alistair belatedly realized he'd been staring. "I—It's nothing."

"No, it's not. What's going on, Mr. Diarmuid?"

"Going on?"

"With *this*. You…" She frowned. "You want to say something to me. So just say it."

"I—" He laughed. "Forget it. It'll sound crazy."

She took a half-step closer and Alistair's breath caught. *I know her!* The thought was so strange and certain, it terrified him.

"Something is bothering you. Tell me what it is."

Alistair took a slow breath and blew it out again. *She won't believe you*, a voice hissed inside him. *She'll think you're crazy, too.*

"Please…" she whispered.

It was the tone of her voice—patient and kind—that pushed him to speak the truth.

"I…I know it sounds crazy, Louise, but I… I think that I *remember* you."

Her brows rose.

"I had a dream the other night," Alistair explained. "*You* were in it."

"What kind of dream?"

"We were part of an army; we fought side by side. I can remember bits and pieces of it. Images mainly. There was a stone wall. Ladders."

Her eyes widened. "A siege," she said in a hoarse voice.

"Yes. At least that's what I think it was, but I—"

"We were in France," she interrupted. "Fighting for the king. We had no shoes. I…I saw your dream."

Alistair staggered. "You did?!"

She nodded. The air around them hummed with her admission. *I'm not crazy after all. She remembers!*

"No shoes," he repeated, "but winter was coming."

"I remember that, too."

"What does it mean, Lou?"

"I don't know."

"What do you *think* it means?"

Her brow creased as if in pain. "I…I think we knew one another *before*. In another time. Another life."

"Another life? But how?"

Louise shook her head. "I can't say. But you dreamed it, and I saw it, too. Seconds before I saw you on the trail, I saw *then*, and I knew you. I just didn't want to say."

"Me neither. What did you see in your vision?"

"A long march, and a voyage across the sea," she said, "and a stone wall that went all the way to heaven."

"I remember that part." Alistair waved between them. "This...
This thing—Has it... Happened to you before?"

"I've always remembered snippets of the past," she said. "But I've
never actually *met* someone from a vision."

She continued walking and Alistair jumped to follow. Now that
the truth was out there, he needed to know everything.

"I haven't either," he said. "I wasn't sure I hadn't imagined them.
In fact, I was almost certain I *had* imagined this until you spoke,
just now."

Lou gave him a gentle smile. "You've tried *not* to remember, haven't you?"

"I did."

"Me too, at first," she said. "But the visions wouldn't go away."

"I had strange dreams when I was a boy," he said. "Things I felt
strongly, but couldn't explain. It never meshed with my family's
faith. Even the priest was called in to talk to me, but he brushed it
off as an overactive imagination. And so I learned not to see those
things."

Lou winced. "My father wasn't a believer either."

"And your mother?"

"Her family was Buddhist. It was easier for her to accept I'd lived
before."

The admissions loosened both their tongues. As they walked,
they passed stories back and forth like a thread, one ending where
the other began. An hour passed. Alistair had never met anyone
like Louise Newman. He couldn't contain his glee.

When they passed the falls and started back toward the main
townsite, Alistair touched Lou's arm and she stopped walking. The
wind had lowered, but the excitement of his mind was the hum of

a thousand bees.

"What is it?" Lou asked.

"Is that what this *knowing* is? Memories of the past? Other lives that I'm dreaming about?"

"I don't know for sure, but sometimes for me, it's a warning of something to come. You've returned for a reason, Alistair. You need to find out why."

Alistair stared up at the vaulting peaks around them. He could feel some realization nearing. A truth—once held back—now burning like a torch inside him. *Like St. Paul on the road to Damascus.* The hum of his thoughts had grown into a deafening roar. His body and soul was awake. Aware.

"Perhaps I'm meant to teach," he said quietly. "To share my knowledge. Yes. Yes, that's it."

"What's it?"

He grinned. "You said your mother was Buddhist. Then it makes sense that she'd understand your gift. You would have had her to guide you. To send you on your way."

"I—I don't know what you mean."

He reached for her hands and pressed them between his own. "Don't you see? You're a Buddha," he said in a low voice. "We *both* are."

She jerked free of his grip. "No, I'm *not*, I'm just—"

"You *are*, Louise. And so am I. That's the reason we had to find one another. Here. Now. That's why I had to meet you. That's why we both remember." Thoughts tumbled one after the other, Alistair's memories surging. "There's a passage from the Buddha: *With the cognition of the recollection of past lives, the Bodhisattva remembers one birth, two births… up to one hundred thousand births.* We remember because *that* is who we are."

"Alistair, I don't think it's—"

"There's a plan to life—I've always believed that." His words were quietly emphatic. "We were meant to meet, and we did."

"I don't know, I just think—" She shook her head. "I don't know what I think."

"You told me you help those who need you, right?"

"Yes, but that's not the same."

"Forget what you know of Buddhas," Alistair said. "Just think of what you *do*."

She gnawed her lower lip. "I don't know..."

"What do you mean, you don't know? You've *always* known." He let out a sharp laugh that frightened the birds from the trees. "You live here. You help people. You change lives. What is that if not a calling?"

"I hope I help," she said as she walked away from him. "But that's not why I'm alive."

"Then why?" Alistair shouted.

Lou glanced back at him. "It's enough that I exist."

* * *

Constable Flagstone waited on the sagging step of the cabin's porch. He shifted the fingerprint box under his arm and knocked again. "Mr. Hamamoto? Are you there, sir?"

A short cough was his only answer.

"Mr. Hamamoto," Jim said, "I know you're in there."

No answer.

Jim knocked again. "Sir, I just need to—"

"Go 'way! I want no part of this!"

Jim smiled despite himself. "Look, if you'd just let me explain, sir, you'll see that—"

"Not a chance in hell! You want my prints, then you better be ready to take me out in handcuffs."

Jim fought the urge to swear. Old Ron Hamamoto had been a stalwart member of the Waterton community for decades, but he kept to himself, and always had. Still there was no question: Someone had tipped him off that Jim was coming for prints.

"It's not like that, sir," Jim said. "I'm asking for you to voluntarily—"

The door opened a crack and rheumy eyes appeared, blocked by the door's chain.

"Voluntary, my ass! You think I don't remember the camps?"

"The camps?"

"They came to get us, just like this. But I ain't going with you. Not this time."

"Mr. Hamamoto, you don't understand, sir. I need the prints so I can—"

"Then you bloody well get your warrant!"

The door slammed shut, and Jim took two steps back. The interviews weren't going well at all.

* * *

The path on which Lou and Alistair walked turned away from the shore at Cameron creek and led them back toward the embrace of the townsite. She took fleeting glances at him as they walked the trail: his long hair tied back, his clothes unkempt. He could have been a prophet… *or a madman,* a voice inside her whispered.

Alistair told her about his long years of wandering. How he'd tried and failed to follow his family's faith and eventually found his voice through film. It made Lou wonder about her winter in Edmonton, and the certainty that she needed to return home. *What would have happened if Mom hadn't died?* She had no answer. She hadn't understood who or *what* she was then. Even now, the word

Buddha left her cringing.

Absorbed in the stories of her companion, Lou barely noticed that they were approaching Whispering Aspens. Some part of her knew Rich would be worried, but she brushed the thought away. She'd lied about who she was for years, and now, for the first time since her mother's death, she didn't have to. Alistair felt like a brother she'd never known.

"Why did you want to be a priest?" Lou asked.

"It was my visions. The memories and dreams that were mine and yet …weren't."

"Your other lives."

"Yes, though I didn't know what they were," he said. "They worried me."

The vision of the man within the glade flickered once, and her chest tightened. *Something dark is coming…* Did she need to warn Alistair? Or was the warning about *him*? It bothered her that she couldn't tell the difference.

"Your visions," Lou said warily, "do they… do they ever come true?"

Alistair stopped. "Sometimes a little bit. At least they seem to hint at things. The other night I had a dream about the two of us, and today, here you are."

Lou looked up and her heart twisted. They'd arrived at the cabin; Rich's silver car waited a stone's throw away. For a moment she wanted to go inside and leave Alistair behind—his strangeness worried her—but another part of her wanted to stay. She'd never met anyone who shared her gift.

I'll be careful with him.

She turned away from the cabin and headed down the road. "Come with me," Lou said. "I have one more place I want to show you."

"Where's that?"

She smiled. "My garage."

* * *

It was late afternoon when the bell at the police station jangled. Before Sadie'd even reached the door, the customer bell on the front desk pinged a second time, then a third. "Just a minute," she said. "I'll be right—"

"Hello?!" an irascible voice called. "Anyone work around here?"

Levi Thompson. Sadie groaned. She plodded out the office door to discover the octogenarian waiting at the front counter; his fingers hovered over the bell, poised to ring it yet again.

"Afternoon, Mr. Thompson," Sadie said. "What can I do for you today?" The man had the shortest fuse of anyone she'd met.

"Was wonderin' what happened to everyone."

"Liz's daughter is down with the flu, so we don't have anyone out front today." Sadie gave him a tight smile. "I came as soon as I heard the bell, Mr. Thompson. Now what can I—?"

"What happened to the other one?"

"The other one?"

"That Gladstone boy," he said. "I want to talk to him, not you."

Sadie's hands tightened at her sides. She'd worked in Waterton for five years, but Levi still treated her like she'd just shown up. "Jim's working a case right now, sir. And like I said, Liz had to go home."

"Waste of taxpayers' money."

"I'm here," she said as she pulled the reports sheet from under the counter. "Not all of us have the privilege of being retired, you know."

"Yes, well, I just want to make a complaint."

"You don't say." Sadie forced a smile and pushed a pen and a sheet toward him. "More kids throwing rocks at your horses?"

Old Levi's temper had made him a target whether he liked it or not. Last Hallowe'en two boys from Mountain View had been chased off his property with a shotgun. When Jim and Sadie arrived, Levi explained that it'd been loaded with rock-salt. Sadie shook her head. The man was from another era entirely.

"Not the kids this time. Some hippie Hollywood type. Came onto my porch, and wouldn't leave when I told him to git."

"From Hollywood you say?"

"Told me he was makin' some kinda doc-u-mentary." Levi stretched the word out like a foreign language. "Mind you, I didn't believe him."

"Why not?"

"He was shifty-like. Trouble-maker, far as I could tell."

"Oh?"

"And he wouldn't leave when I said I didn't want to talk to him."

"You didn't... *do* anything to this man, did you, Mr. Thompson?"

"Didn't shoot him if that's what yer gettin' at."

Sadie nodded. That made this easier. "Well, that's good. Why don't you just fill out the forms then, and I'll add him to our watch-list."

With a dissatisfied grunt, Levi complied. Sadie watched him write out the complaint in his careful, grade-school handwriting. Her frown deepened. *Alistair Diarmuid stirring up trouble again.* More than one person in town had complained about him in the last week.

Finished, Levi tore off the sheet and handed it back to her. "So are you'n Jim gonna do something about my complaint, or just file it like all the others? Guy was up on my porch, y'know. He wouldn't leave. I know my rights!"

Sadie took it from his hand and scanned the form. "I'm going to look into this one personally."

"You are?"

She folded the paper. Levi's acerbic personality was enough to turn most people off, but he wasn't the only townsperson who'd complained. "I can't say it'll change anything, but yes, Mr. Thompson, it sounds a bit suspicious."

"'Tis," Levi agreed.

"You call me if you see him again, alright?"

Levi smirked as he headed for the door. "Oh, I'll do more'n that."

* * *

Lou lay on the backboard, her gaze on the engine above her, while Alistair's voice rose and fell in undulating waves. "...and my parents believed God was testing me, but I didn't believe there *was* a God. He was no longer real to me. I believed in nothing, so I left and never returned."

Lou dropped the ratchet to the floor with a clatter. She peeked over, Alistair's legs and torso half-hidden by the underside of the car. "You never saw them after you moved to California?"

"Not my mother. She died of a stroke while I was filming in India."

"Oh Alistair. I'm so sorry."

He shrugged. "I reconsidered things then, but I still couldn't face my father; couldn't explain to Da' who I really was."

The conversation with Rich returned to mind and guilt filled Lou's chest.

"If things are going to work, we've got to be able to talk."

"We do talk!"

She'd been aware, even then, it had been a lie.

"A few months later, my aunt contacted me to say that my father had been diagnosed with dementia and that I should come home. I… I didn't go back for months."

Lou frowned. She'd come home the moment she'd heard about her mother. How could someone leave a parent to die alone?

"Why didn't you go?" she asked.

"If you don't believe in God, does it matter if someone dies?"

Frowning, Lou slid out from under the car. "But it was your father."

"It was… but we hadn't been close for many years. Besides, all things die. Everything that's alive must experience death."

"But, how could you—?"

"I went eventually, Lou. But by then it was far too late. My father was dying, his life down to days. His memory already gone."

"I'm sorry, Alistair."

"Don't be. I'm not." He laughed, but it was an angry sound and Lou shivered. "Funny thing was, he and I could never talk in life, but when he was dying, it was the easiest thing in the world. He told me about his parents. About his childhood in Lincolnshire. Told me stories of my mother as a young girl. Things he'd never told me when I'd been at home. It was like a stranger wearing the skin of my father. Talking and talking. Always goddamned *talking!* He didn't know who I was anymore. Called me Aaron sometimes; that was his younger brother."

A circle of anxiety wrapped Lou's chest. She wanted to comfort Alistair, but his anger unsettled her. "But you were there," she said. "You came back."

"Near the end, Da' didn't know anyone. He was scared. Angry. But one morning—must've been the last—he sat up, like something had woken him. It was like Da' had returned. '*You're good to sit with me, Aaron,*' he said to me. '*I get so scared when I'm alone in the dark.*' Then he drifted again." Alistair snorted. "One last moment. A *good* moment. And all I could think was that those words were meant for someone else."

Alistair tipped his back and began to laugh, the sound ricocheting in the dim interior of the garage, making Lou cringe. There was something *wrong* with this story. Something he'd missed. For a brief moment, her mind was filled with thoughts of her mother's untimely death and the pain and peace that followed.

"I… I don't know what to say," Lou said. "That story's just so sad."

"Is it though? I found it strangely funny."

She stared at him. *That's just wrong.*

Alistair shrugged as if he'd heard her inner thoughts. "Perhaps that feeling of sadness we all get is just our human nature refusing to accept the way life needs to be. It wouldn't make sense otherwise."

"What do you mean?"

"Maybe my father's death was nothing more than that. Just an ending. A period on the end of a sentence. A finished thought."

"I don't think—"

"It's the same end we all get. *Death.* I've faced it a thousand times." Alistair gave her an enigmatic smile. "And you have too." And with that, he began to hum.

CHAPTER ELEVEN

Prischka Archer,
Coldcreek Enterprises,
23rd Floor, Flatiron Building,
175 Fifth Avenue,
New York, New York
10010

August 2, 1998

Dear Ms. Archer,

I am relieved to announce that the East Wing of the Whitewater Lodge is finally complete and finishing work is underway in the West Wing. There are serious issues, to be sure, but ones I feel confident handling. The ones I cannot handle are related to Waterton's isolation and lack of amenities.

As per my previous letter, there have been a number of poaching incidences recently, despite increased security. This continues to be a major concern. One guest ran across a bear eating the carcass of an illegally shot deer only yards from the main doors. If that guest had been attacked and something like that made it to press, the success of the Whitewater Lodge and that of Coldcreek itself would be compromised.

While I understand your reasons for selecting Alta-Force Security via your Coldcreek business partners, I feel that there may be better local choices. After the bear incident, I made an executive decision to sever the Whitewater's existing security contract. I feel, given the nature of Waterton's poaching, a park-based security detail will have a better chance at protecting the hotel.

I have forwarded the planned changes to the current contract to both you and the Coldcreek shareholders. If you have concerns about this decision, contact me and I'd be happy to explain.

Sincerely,
Jeffrey J. Chan, HRIM, Manager
Whitewater Lodge, Waterton Park, AB

Special instructions: CC

CHAPTER TWELVE

"I, um… yes, ma'am. He is. And I'm sorry to bother you, but Constable Flagstone asked me to tell you he has another meeting this afternoon."

"Mmm… how interesting. So do I."

"And since you were so very busy," Trent said, "Constable Flagstone offered to come talk while you worked." He stepped forward. "I'm so sorry. I couldn't delay him any longer! He's on his way up now, ma'am."

"He's what?!"

"I'm sorry, Ms. Andler."

She stood and straightened her jacket. There was a line of wrinkles across one side and that fanned her annoyance. Siobhan liked her clothes the way she liked everything else: orderly.

The thud of footsteps neared and the focus of her anger appeared in the doorway. Jim Flagstone's uniform was neatly pressed, and he carried a small box under one arm. He stepped straight past Trent to Siobhan's desk.

"Sorry to bother you, Mrs. Andler," he said. "But I promise I won't take more than ten minutes of your time. Thanks for seeing me."

"I am *very* busy."

"As am I, as am I." Jim reached down to fiddle with the walk-ie-talkie on his belt. "But this is police business, so I'm certain you understand the importance."

"Well, you've already interrupted my work, so we might as well do this. Have a seat if you'd like."

Jim took the proffered chair and she sat down at her desk. She knew why he was here; Jim had told Trent. But Siobhan had no intention of helping him, not after the issues she'd had with the Whitewater Lodge the last two years. First Jeffrey Chan and then Richard Evans. She swore Coldcreek Enterprises had selected managers purposefully to annoy her.

Jim set the box on the desk. "All I need is a sample of your fingerprints."

"I thought that Mr. Evans was going to trial for the arson," she said. "That's what the papers said."

"Yes, that's true, but this is to do with—"

"He should be in jail! Rich Evans said he was going to take that hotel down in front of a roomful of people. Has something changed? Has he already weaseled his way out of a conviction?"

"Ma'am, the arson trial doesn't start for another couple weeks. My visit has to do with a different case altogether."

"About what?"

"The Whitewater break-in."

Siobhan coughed. "From last summer?!"

"Yes, exactly."

"But-but what for? It was a worker, wasn't it? Lurking around in the basement? Turning off the lights, knocking things down?"

"That's never been proven," Jim said. "Now if I could get your prints."

"But the hotel burned down! There's nothing left of it. I hardly think it matters who broke into the basement—"

"There'll be justice, arson or not. And I find it interesting how much detail you recall about the break-in."

Siobhan's cheeks were white, eyes flashing. "You've got to be kidding. I had *nothing* to do with that!"

"I'm certain you didn't. Chances are, the person was a visitor, but just to be sure, Constable Black Plume and I are eliminating everyone else. I need a sample of your prints, Ms. Andler. Won't take but a minute."

"Am I being charged with something, Constable Flagstone?"

Jim sighed. "No, ma'am, you're not. At this point we're just asking people to voluntarily—"

"Then if it's voluntary, you can wait until *my convenience.*" Siobhan stood from her chair. "Now, if you don't mind, I have a meeting, and *you* have just made me late!"

* * *

Unsettled by Alistair's strange words, Louise stood from the floor and walked out of the car stall. She loved her garage, but today the room felt cloying.

"It's getting late," she said as she swung the door open. "I should get going. Rich will be wondering where I got to."

"Rich...?"

"Yes, Rich." She stepped back to wait for Alistair to leave. "He's at home, waiting for me. I should get back."

"Alright then." He stretched with catlike grace. "I'm sorry if I've upset you, Louise."

"You didn't," she lied. "I just need to go."

"Was it my view on death?"

"No. Not that."

"Then what?"

"Nothing. It's- it's fine, Alistair. Everyone *does* die. Like you said. I just—" She took another step back and waited for him to take the hint and leave. "I really *must* go home now."

He headed out the door. "It's been a strange day for me too," he said as he passed her. "I've never known anyone like me. *Ever.*"

She nodded.

"I spoke more fiercely than I should have," he said. "But that's only because you *understand* me. I've never had that before."

Lou cringed. *Who was she to judge Alistair's personal demons?* "I... I know."

"I do hope we can talk again, Lou."

"Of course we can. I'll catch up with you later. Okay?"

"Later," he said as he walked away.

She stared at him for a few short moments. The elation she'd felt when she'd first met him was gone, nervousness in its place. Although she felt she knew and understood Alistair... *did she really?* The man was an enigma. With a sigh, Lou locked the door and jogged down the road away from Lou's Garage towards home. Rich was upstairs, shuffling through papers when she came through the door. She peeked around the doorway.

"You're back," he said with a tired smile.

"I am."

"Did you have a good walk?"

Lou nodded, Alistair's name unspoken on her lips.

"I'm... I'm sorry about what I said," Rich said. "I shouldn't have pestered you about the trial."

"It's fine, Rich. I just... I needed some time to think about things."

Rich reached out his hand and she crossed the room to take it. "That's fair. And I'm sorry, Lou. I really am." He squeezed her fingers. "I'm letting things get to me. I shouldn't do that."

"You're allowed to vent. Everyone is."

"But you don't. You're always so pulled together, Lou. So calm."

She opened her mouth to disagree, then closed it instead. What could she say? The moment today was yet another piece that didn't fit. *I'll tell him about Alistair later.* Instead, she leaned in and kissed him.

* * *

Jim stalked out the front doors of the Prince of Wales hotel and headed toward the squad car, the skin of his cheeks prickling with heat. *Goddamned Siobhan Andler, and her goddamned stalling!* He was halfway across the lot when he heard the radio crackle in the police cruiser.

"…new report. I repeat, contact the station as soon as possible."

Jim glanced down at his belt to the hand-held. He'd turned it off in Siobhan's office so they weren't interrupted. He'd meant to turn it back on when he'd left.

"Goddamnit!"

Jim sprinted forward.

"…come in Constable Flagstone," a voice on the radio repeated. "Jim, are you there? Please answer."

He swung open the door, reached inside for the handset, and clicked the 'receive' button while he slid across the seat.

"Flagstone here," he panted.

"Jim, that you?"

Constable Jordan Wyatt was the newest of Waterton's police force. Though the kid meant well, he was still wet around the ears, and made Sadie—with her five years' experience—look like a seasoned pro.

"Yeah, it's Jim. What's up, Jordan?"

"Warden McNealy just called. Hunter Slate found something out by the fish hatcheries."

Jim's hand tightened on the receiver, remembering the murders of the previous summer. Colton Calhoun was dead, but his presence rested uneasy amongst the townsfolk. "*Something* meaning what exactly?"

"An animal of some kind. Deer, I think he said."

Jim let out a heavy breath. Dead animals he could deal with. It was dead bodies that bothered him.

"Warden McNealy figured the deer came in from outside the park," Jordan said. "McNealy and Slate are over by the hatchery right now. Need us to come by so we can do the official report."

"Official report for what?" Animal issues were the warden's side of things and he had work to do.

"McNealy seemed mighty worked up. Insisted you come."

"Fine. I'll swing by and pick up Sadie. Tell her—"

The crackle of the radio cut him off. "No can do. Sadie's working on her own reports for that break-in. She asked me to go out with you."

Jim gritted his teeth. *Great. Just great. Now I get to babysit, too.* "Alright," he said. "I'll swing by and pick you up and then we can head out."

Twenty minutes later, Jim and Jordan were on their way. The fish hatchery was located a quarter mile from the park entrance building, and hadn't been in use since the early sixties. One solitary building remained of what had once been a thriving operation, the area falling into disrepair. Jim slowed the squad car as three large dogs came bounding forward; they bayed at him as he drove down the overgrown road.

"Get your goddamned dogs off the road," Jim muttered.

"They Hunter's?" Jordan said.

"Yep." One of the younger dogs lunged at the car, and Jim swerved out of the animal's way. "He's got a pack of them." The dog came closer and Jim slammed the heel of his hand on the horn. Jordan jumped.

"Hunter needs to get his mutts under control!" Jim snapped.

A piercing whistle echoed and two of the dogs turned and disappeared up the road, kicking up dust. The third danced back and forth, undecided. Jim tapped the horn. The dog lifted his muzzle and howled.

Jim leaned out the window. "Get off the road, you stupid dog!"

Another sharp whistled echoed and the half-grown mutt turned tail and bounded up the road in front of them.

Jordan leaned forward, squinting. "There's Hunter now," he said as Jim drove forward. "His truck's pulled over to the side. He's got the dogs in now."

The warden's truck appeared. Grant McNealy and Hunter Slate stood next to it, staring into the underbrush.

"I, uh… I want you to tell me if I miss something," Jordan said.

"Miss something?"

"While we're tagging the crime scene," Jordan said. "Like… something I should see. A clue, you know? If I don't see it on my own, I mean."

Jim rolled his eyes. *Babysitting duty.* "Oh, I will," he said. "Don't worry about that."

"Thanks."

Jim eased the squad car onto the shoulder and parked, annoyed at the turn of events. He wished Sadie was here. They worked together well; he could rely on her, whereas having Jordan in tow felt like he was on his own.

He swung open the door. "Grab the kit. I'll take the camera and start documenting."

"Right, thanks."

Jim put the camera strap over his neck as he strode forward. Hunter and McNealy stood next to Hunter's rusted truck, and a trio of dogs barked and danced inside the cab. There was something about the set of McNealy's jaw that reminded Jim of the summer previous when the warden had found the body on the Lineham trail. *Just an animal,* he thought uneasily. *Nothing worse.*

McNealy looked up. "Jimmy. Glad you made it."

"Why'm I out here?"

The warden gestured to something in the trees. "That."

"If it's an animal," Jim said. "That's your business."

"This one's gonna affect you, too."

"Oh?" Jim reached the warden's side and nodded 'hello' to Hunter. "Why's that?"

"Well, it's kind of—"

"Why don't you look," Hunter said.

Jim followed Hunter and McNealy's line of sight down into the trees. His stomach turned at the sight. The animal's guts were spread in a bloody half-circle, the intestines lewd pink worms. That, Jim knew, was the carrion-eaters. But that detail wasn't what bothered him. One haunch of the deer had been cut off with medical precision, the hide flayed back with a butcher's care. The rest had been left to rot.

"Damnit," Jim said. "We've got a poacher."

Behind the three men, there was a grunting sound. Jim spun, his hand already on the handle of his handgun. A run-in with a pissed off bear would screw up this day even more.

It was only Jordan, whey-faced and heaving at the side of the squad car. *City kid,* Jim thought. Hunter snorted with half-suppressed laughter, and Jim glared at him before he turned back.

"Go on back to the squad car, Jordan," Jim said. "Give Sadie a call. Let her know what's happening."

Jordan wiped a line of drool from his chin and stood upright. He looked like he was about to faint. "B-but shouldn't I help you to—"

"Call Sadie. I've got this."

"I've already looked," Warden McNealy said. "There are footprints around the back side of the deer. Cowboy boots by the look of it. I left 'em as is. Figured you'd want to photograph them."

"Thanks."

"If you've got this under control, I'm gonna head off," the warden said. "That alright with you, Jim?"

"Yup. Just fine."

Jim started into the trees and peered through the bushes. A line of horseshoe prints led through the forest and Jim carefully picked his way forward, taking pictures as he went until they disappeared. He added flagging to a broken branch. Another piece to a scuff mark. Behind him, he heard McNealy bid farewell to Hunter and start the truck.

Jim searched the ground as he walked. Near the deer's crimson stomach, something gold glittered in the mulch. *A shell casing?* Before he'd taken another step, Hunter spoke.

"Wasn't there trouble with poaching when that Chan fellow was around last year?"

Jim looked up. "Yeah. I think so. Why?"

"Well, I'm no cop, but d'you think this is related?"

Jim lowered the camera. "Doubt it," he said. "This looks like someone was out hunting, and tracked it into the park. Probably got scared once they realized where they were."

"Shame," Hunter said.

"It is."

"Waste of an animal, taking the back leg and nothing else."

Jim nodded and looked out at the horizon. A lot of crown land abutted the park, but so did private ranch land. This particular stretch led directly to Levi Thompson's place. He didn't feel like a fight with the old man today. Not if he didn't have to.

The door of the squad car opened and Hunter's dogs burst into a renewed barrage of barking. "Sadie wants to know why you're telling her," Jordan shouted over the din.

Jim gritted his teeth. "I'll talk to Sadie," he said. "You go start the paperwork on this."

"Paperwork?"

"Mr. Slate, here, found the deer. We need his official statement."

"Right. Of course," Jordan said. "Mr. Slate, could you come with me a minute?"

Jim looked back to find Hunter still staring into the trees, his eyes on the mess of guts and the stiff-legged deer, his face pale. The sight of it sent a thrill of electricity up Jim's spine.

"Hunter? You okay?" Jim asked.

"Fine. Just thinking."

"About?"

"Chan came into my coffee shop last year. Went on about a dead animal he found on his porch. Said the guts were spread all over the place. Blood smeared from one end to the other." Hunter's throat bobbed. "Just like this."

Jim frowned. There *had* been a number of poaching incidents last year. Warden McNealy had said the dead animal at the manager's cottage had probably been killed by cougars. Jim hadn't been entirely certain. "I remember that," he said. "Chan filed a report about it. Thought it might be wolves."

"You think this has anything to do with that?"

"Doubt it. Like I said: probably just someone who wandered in past the boundary without knowing it."

Hunter's frown deepened until his entire face looked like it was going to fold in on itself. "Well, I guess there's nothing to do about it then."

Jim shrugged. "Probably not."

* * *

Rich's mouth moved over Lou's as he undressed her without breaking the kiss. They tumbled onto the bed and fell naked on the coverlet. In the band of light coming through the windows next to them, Lou's skin was golden, the dark 'v' of curls an arrow leading downward.

Beautiful.

Rich caressed her neck to her collarbone, tracing her skin. The frustration of the afternoon had turned to wildfire, their bodies aflame. This was right. *This made sense.* Any anger he'd felt disappeared in a wave of passion.

Lou moaned and Rich shifted sideways, nudging her thighs impatiently with his knee. "Oh Jesus, Lou!" he gasped as he slid home. In a flash of awareness, everything made sense. Louise Newman was light and love and life itself. He clung to her the way a drowning man might hold a life raft. "Love you. Love you so much."

The heat of the room redoubled and Lou's back arched and she shouted in release. Her supple exhaustion was twice the aphrodisiac her passion had been. Visions of Lou in this room—over the months of their courtship—played out over the film of here and now as he moved against her. Rich loved Lou and she loved him. *What did anything else in life matter?* And as he hit the moment of oblivion and fell, exhausted, into Lou's open arms, he had one final thought:

Louise Newman felt like coming home.

* * *

It was almost dawn, the end of Sadie's last night shift of the week, when Jim walked in the door of the police station. He stomped to his desk and dropped the print box with a clatter.

Sadie paused with her jacket half-on and smiled warily. "You doing okay, Jimmy?"

"It was a long goddamned day."

She glanced at the clock. *5:07 a.m.* "I thought you were done at eleven."

"I was, but I ended up driving into Pincher Creek to file some papers with the RCMP. Had some issues 'cause only the night staff was on." He rolled his eyes. "Been two steps behind myself all day."

"Sorry I couldn't get out to the hatchery this afternoon. I was swamped."

"No biggie," he said. "It was just a poacher. Already filed it with Fish and Wildlife."

"Then what's bugging you?"

Jim shook his head rather than answer.

"Did Jordan…?"

"Jordan's fine. Dumb as a post, but fine."

"Then what's wrong? You look ready to attack someone." Sadie hid her smile behind her hand. "I mean… other than being six hours late to get off work."

Jim threw himself down into a chair. "Goddamned locals are driving me nuts," he said. "Everybody's so angry about me poking around in their business. Nobody'll talk."

"Shit."

"Only got three people printed all day. Siobhan Andler and Ronald Hamamoto wouldn't let me take their prints at all."

Sadie pulled over her chair and sat down beside him. "They *refused*?"

"Voluntary only works if they're willing to let me print them. This case is gonna take us a long goddamned time, Sadie."

"No it won't," she said. "Not if we get the warrants right now."

"All of them?"

"Think about it. It'll take a while, but it'll be worth it in the end. That way we ask them for prints and they have no choice. No matter how they feel about it."

Jim's gaze went back to the line of suspects, untouched on the wall. The results of the three he'd printed wouldn't be back for days. And there'd been twice that who'd outright refused to cooperate. He cringed as he imagined asking a second time.

"The locals aren't going to like it, you know."

"No they won't," Sadie said with a hard laugh. "But I frankly don't give a shit. My gut says this guy's still in Waterton, and we're not stopping until we find him."

* * *

Susan walked up the sidewalk in the raw morning light, her ears attuned to the trill of the white-crested sparrows which filled the trees. She passed beneath the branches and another bird broke into song. Susan smiled. Sparrows were an interesting bird. They had dialects unique to each region they inhabited. If Waterton had a sound, it was the lonely sparrow, keening for its mate. The trill was peaceful, but melancholy.

Seconds before she reached the front steps of the bed and breakfast, a figure emerged from the bushes.

Susan yelped and stumbled backward. "Sweet Jesus, Mr. Diarmuid! You scared the living daylights out of me."

"So sorry, Ms. Varley," Alistair said.

"What the hell happened to you?" She gestured toward the leaves tangled in his hair, the twig caught in the pocket of his coat. "You're a mess."

He glanced down as if noticing the state of his clothes. "Nothing...Everything."

"Have you been out all night, Mr. Diarmuid?"

Alistair gave her a strange smile. "I was watching the stars," he said. "There were lights in the sky. Stars and galaxies glowing: light dead millions of years, so bright and—"

"Are you drunk?" she asked sharply.

"Not drunk; *changed*." His voice dropped to a low whisper. "I met someone. Someone like *me*."

"Like...you?"

"Yes, exactly." He leaned closer and Susan took a step back. "A woman walking along the lakeshore," Alistair said. "I *saw* things while I was with her."

"What kind of things?"

"Things about life. About me. Things I'd once wondered, but now *knew*. She was a stranger, you see, but not. Someone I already knew from before."

Susan crossed her arms. "That makes no sense."

"Ah, but it *does*. She understands me. She's shown me the way. I *know* what I need to do."

"Mr. Diarmuid," Susan warned. "If I find drugs in your room, so help me God, I *will* call the police."

Alistair broke into sudden laughter. "Oh, it's not drugs."

"Then what?"

He tipped his head, watching her for a long moment. Susan squirmed under his perusal.

"I'm alive," he answered. "For the first time in forever, I know my place. My purpose."

"Purpose?"

"Yes, exactly." Alistair's smile widened to show sharp white teeth. "Have a good day, Ms. Varley."

He waved once and disappeared around the corner of the bed and breakfast. With a shake of her head, Susan climbed the front steps, and pulled out her key. In the wake of Alistair's passing, the birdsong was gone. Only the wind in the trees remained.

"Goddamned city folk," she grumbled and headed inside to start her workday.

CHAPTER THIRTEEN

The morning coffee shop buzzed with excitement, the drama of months past returned. Amidst the shouting, it was all Hunter could do not to kick everyone out. He hadn't seen people riled this much since Colton Calhoun wrought havoc on the mountain town. Hunter moved between the tables as he refilled cups.

"…had some evidence of smugglers coming through," someone at the back growled.

"Drug runners again?"

"Not this time. From what Diarmuid said, he figured they were bringing *people* in. Crossing the border without permission."

"It's here-say, is all! Just talk. Nothing else."

"…but the guy says he's got proof."

"Bah! Just rumours."

"Rumours that'll tar and feather us all!"

Hunter paused next to Audrika and she covered her teacup so he wouldn't add coffee to her tea. (Distracted, he'd done that once already.)

"This Diarmuid fellow told me he *knew* there were illegal immigrants in Waterton," a voice said. "Who in their right mind would tell him that?"

Hunter cleared his throat. "Just leave the man alone," he said.

"Mr. Diarmuid will go away if no one gives him reason to stay."

"But he's already found something!" Susan said.

"He was talking about the Crypt Lake landing when he interviewed me…"

"…people bringing Americans into the Park."

"It's idle gossip. Let it be."

"Unless he decides to put it in his damned film."

"Oh Jesus! D'you think he would?"

"A documentary would affect us all!"

Hunter moved on with his coffee pot. The only one who seemed unperturbed today was Audrika. She sat at the table, listening without comment as she sipped her tea.

Hunter paused. "Has Alistair interviewed *you*, Mrs. Kulkarni?" he asked.

A flush rose to her cheeks. "Alistair who, dear?"

"Alistair Diar—"

"Diarmuid," Susan said. "The Hollywood fellow we've all been talking about."

Audrika wasn't looking at her, she wasn't looking at *anyone*.

"Oh, Audrika," Hunter groaned. "You *didn't* tell him something, did you?"

Before Audrika could answer, the door to the restaurant opened and a gust of wind blew the first autumn leaves in the door. Everyone turned. Jim Flagstone stood in the doorway.

"Coffee, Jim?" Hunter asked.

Jim shook his head. "Not today. Only have a minute to talk."

"Everything alright?"

"It will be. Can I talk to everyone a second?" Jim said. The chatter of the room dropped to a buzz. "I need to talk about an open investigation Sadie and I are working on."

"Which one?" Susan said. "I thought things were done now that Calhoun died."

"Yes, but this is to do with the Whitewater."

"Wasn't Evans charged with arson?" Susan said. "The trial starts in October, doesn't it?"

"He was and it does. But that's not what this is about."

Hunter set the coffee pot on a nearby tabletop. "It's not?"

"Nope. This is about the break-in from earlier this summer." The word *Whitewater* ran through the group like a hiss of steam. "I've cleared all the guests and employees," Jim said. "So the investigation will be expanding. Sadie will be interviewing people around town, and—"

"But I thought you were lookin' for the fool who tripped the breakers," Hunter interrupted.

"We are," Jim said. "But there's, uh… there's more to it, Hunter."

The chatter grew.

"You can't be serious!" Audrika snapped.

"…no way I'm doing this. I'm no criminal!"

"I know my rights!"

"You've no right to do this!"

"I can't go into the details of the case." Jim said. "I just wanted everyone to know beforehand that I'll be coming to get fingerprints from all of you." The buzz rose to a roar.

"But I thought you were checking tourists!"

"…this is ludicrous!"

"You can't think *we'd* be involved!"

"…no one would dare!"

"…trouble enough with the documentary!"

"This will make things worse!"

"Good lord, can you imagine if Mr. Diarmuid hears about *this!?*"

Jim pounded his fist on the table so hard the mugs jumped and spoons clattered. "Enough! I'm here to tell you I'll be taking prints from *everyone*, whether you think my decision makes sense or not. And yes," Jim said. "There *will* be warrants, if you are concerned about me infringing on your rights."

Shoulders slumped, Hunter turned away. This year would be the death of him.

* * *

Alistair hadn't slept last night or the night before that. In fact, he hadn't done anything more than doze since he'd met Louise Newman. Their meeting had altered him, and Alistair was still reeling from the change. There were things about Louise Newman that were strangely familiar; he knew the stirrings of her soul as he knew the color of his own eyes. He had too many memories to relive, too many ideas to discuss. His entire understanding of the universe had been reborn, and *she'd* been part of that.

It excited and infuriated him!

The first night, the sky had opened up as bright swirls of shooting stars marked his passage. The next morning, he'd tried hiking, but had been overwhelmed by thousands of wildflowers on the slope. Later, he'd attempted an interview, but he couldn't keep his mind on what the person said. Furious, he'd returned to the lakeshore in an attempt to calm himself, but echoes of other lives appeared, keeping time with the waves.

Now he sat across from Lou, a cup of coffee held in quaking fingers. "…and the universe is vibrations, and a vibration is just motion… not really form at all. So if you stop the movement, there's nothing there in the first place." Alistair gestured to the window and coffee sloshed over his hand. "That's it. Don't you see? The great *what* is not a person or a thing, but a sound, and the sound is made of vibrations and—"

"Alistair, you need to lay off the caffeine," Lou said.

"But I have so many thoughts. So many ideas to share! There are so many things I haven't considered, things I want to tell you." He reached for her hand but she pulled away before he caught her fingers.

"I don't think—"

"There was a *reason* behind our meeting, Lou. We have a *purpose* to fulfill!"

A grizzled man paused next to the table. "This guy bothering you, Louise?"

"It's fine, Hunter. We were just about to leave." She fished a twenty dollar bill out of her pocket and left it on the table, guiding Alistair from his chair by his elbow. "Please just *stop!*" she said under her breath.

Lou led him across the parking lot to her garage. Alistair sensed she was worried. The emotion draped Lou's shoulders like a cape but when Alistair reached for the vision, it dissipated with a shimmer.

Lou jerked when he touched her. "What?" she said warily.

"I-I'm sorry," he said. "I've never known the truth before. I need to talk it through to understand. It'll get better, I'm certain."

She shook her head. "I hope so. 'Cause I think Hunter's about ready to throw you into the back of his truck and drop you off outside the Park. C'mon to the garage and you can sit for a while. I'll even tell you a story or two."

Excitement welled inside him. "And I have one for you."

* * *

Sadie pulled open the door to the police station, the file folder with Rich's police report tucked under one arm. An old man's growling voice rolled forward to greet her:

"—a bloody nuisance is what it is! I ain't never had a bit of trouble 'til that feller came 'round."

Sadie's face fell. *Damnit!* Levi Thompson was back again. Any plans she had for working on the cold case were on hold.

"Just back up a bit," Sadie heard Jim say. "Who came onto your property, Mr. Thompson?"

Sadie pulled the door closed quietly behind her. She slid off her coat and hung it on the rack, hoping Levi wouldn't turn around.

"That Diarmuid feller. The Hollywood one I told you about."

Jim frowned. "I don't remember anything about a—"

"Well, you *should* remember!" Levi snapped. "I put in that report more'n a week ago!"

With a sigh, Sadie strode to the counter. *No escaping it now.*

"Mr. Thompson put in a complaint about a trespasser last week," Sadie said. "It's on file."

"Or at least it *should* be!" Levi pointed at Sadie with a gnarled finger. "This ain't the first time I've complained about prowlers, you know. Wouldn't surprise me in the least if you were ignoring my reports!"

"We're not, Mr. Thompson," Sadie said. "But we've got other things keeping us busy, too."

Jim cleared his throat. "Mr. Thompson told me he heard someone on his porch last night. He, um…" Jim bit back a smile. "He warned the trespasser he was armed, and by the time he opened the door, the intruder was gone."

"Was the person on foot?" Sadie asked.

"Nope. A car. Watched the taillights heading out to the highway." Levi lifted his chin smugly. "The guy headed into the park. That makes it *your* problem, you know."

"I know." Sadie tossed Rich's report aside and grabbed a pen. "Did you get the make of the vehicle, sir?"

"I er… I couldn't say."

"Was it a mid-size?" Sadie asked. "A sedan?"

"Don't rightly know."

"What color was it?"

"No idea."

"Light? Dark? If you can remember anything at all, Mr. Thompson, it'd help us to—"

"I said I don't know!" Levi snapped. Sadie's eyes widened at the vehemence of his words. "It was night, alright! And I've got cataracts. Eyes ain't what they used to be. It was a car. But more'n that I couldn't tell you."

Sadie nodded. "Understood."

"We'll get on that," Jim said. "I've got the report right here and—" He gestured to Sadie. "Officer Black Plume will fill me in on your earlier information."

"Fine." Levi grabbed his cowboy hat from the counter and set it on down-white hair. "I'll be waiting for you to do somethin' about it this time."

"Of course, sir."

Levi pushed open the door, and his flinty eyes flicked back one last time. "But if he comes back on my land again, well, I'm gonna protect what's mine."

"Mr. Thompson," Sadie said. "Your property is your property, but you can't go around saying you're going to shoot someone if—" The door cut off the rest of her warning.

Jim snorted with laughter.

Sadie frowned. "You find that attitude funny?"

He laughed harder.

"Seriously, Jim. The guy's a loose cannon. He'll shoot someone someday. It's *not* funny."

"Oh God," Jim wheezed, wiping tears from the corners of his eyes. "I know I shouldn't laugh, but seeing the two of you, toe-to-toe. It's like a standoff in an old Western movie. Levi's just so… so…"

"Nuts?"

Jim's laughter grew louder. Sadie couldn't help the smile as he wiped his eyes on the sleeve of his jacket.

"He could kill someone, you know," she said dryly.

"You're right," he said, wheezing. "It's wrong for him to say it, but that's just—" He smothered another laugh. "It's just how he is."

"Was he always so crabby?"

"Levi's just got character, is all."

"Character, huh?"

"He's alright once you get used to him," Jim said.

"You sure?"

"Levi's the last of a generation. He doesn't like change."

"Or people from other places," Sadie added. She'd grown up on the Blood Reserve, but it could have been on Mars as far as most of the townspeople were concerned.

"He's just… set in his ways."

"You think?"

"Levi was born in Waterton," Jim said. "Lived his whole life here. He's a rancher; grew up poor. His family'd almost lost everything by the time he took over the operation. Spent his summers breaking horses, spent his winters away, earning money to pay back a mortgage his father owed."

Sadie's gaze moved to the door, now closed, where Levi had passed minutes before. Something niggled at the back of her mind, a memory she couldn't quite set her finger on.

"That's a tough life," Jim said. "It'll wear you down after a while. Old Levi grew a thick skin to deal with it."

"He spent his winters away?"

"Uh-huh. Never had use for people who said they needed holidays. He figured he'd worked year-round, so should everyone else."

"Where'd he go in the winters?"

"I… I don't know for sure. Why?"

"He never told you?"

"I don't think so," Jim said. "You think he was doing something he shouldn't have been?"

"If you're not in Waterton, you've got to be somewhere else. Right? Maybe Levi was helping people come into Waterton from the States. Maybe he was in New Concord Ohio in 1970. Maybe," Sadie said, "*he's* the one we're looking for."

"Old Levi? Seems a bit of a stretch."

She shrugged. "So does everything else about the case."

* * *

Lou and Alistair sat on the grass outside the garage under the purple shadows of the trees. The branches had grown bare in the weeks since Alistair's arrival, the town changed. *Something dark is coming.* Lou glanced up at the ragged peaks that surrounded them. In the midafternoon light, their brooding bulk was flat grey and indifferent. She shivered.

With Alistair's arrival, the memories of Lou's other lives had risen to the surface, but their appearance disturbed her. *Broken bodies in a muddy field. A rag-covered stump where a man's arm had once been. Children's faces, skeletal from starvation.* The flashes left her nauseated as they receded.

Was he the cause or was it merely coincidence? Lou couldn't tell.

"Something's bothering you today," Alistair said.

She brought her gaze back down to the figure at her side. Alistair had plucked a late fall dandelion and he smiled as he twirled it.

"I keep trying to figure out what these visions mean. Why am I seeing all the death? Why not life?"

"Because life is as much about death as it is about living. Every death is the renewal."

He shook the dandelion and the seeds drifted up on the breeze, a memory moving forward in the same way. *She and her father stood side by side, her mother's ashes in an urn.* This wasn't an echo, but her current life. Lou'd told her father much the same thing as they'd spread Yuki's ashes: *"We're not alive unless we also die."* It didn't give her any consolation now.

"I know," Lou said, "but these visions usually hint at something about to occur, or something happening now. I can't understand these ones. I don't know what to do."

"You're a Buddha," Alistair said. "You should—"

"I'm not."

"Fine, then a bodhisattva," he said with a sharp laugh.

"Meaning what, exactly?"

"Meaning you've reached nirvana, but returned to existence to ease the suffering of others. A Buddha who—"

"Don't use that word."

"Why not? You know it, and so do I."

"It's just—" Lou's eyes moved up the alley, waiting for Rich. She could feel him today. His absence was the tug of a toothache. "I can't explain why," she said, "but that word…it *worries* me." She turned back to find his gaze needling her.

"That's your problem." His voice had a different tone, just slightly *not Alistair.* The hair on Lou's arms rose.

"What is?"

"You know what you are, but still you deny it."

"I-I don't. I know what I am. *Who* I am."

"Do you tell anyone? Do you take your rightful place?" Alistair smiled, but anger sharpened the edges of his mouth.

"No, but that's different."

"You say you want to *know* what's coming, but you won't take up the mantle, *be* what you're supposed to be. It makes no difference to you at all what life holds. You don't *do* anything, Lou. You're an outsider… a watcher. *A liar.*"

"That's not true. I talk to everyone, Alistair. I help them all. I share my stories to—"

"All from the outside. You never join in. You never let people know the real you. You stand on the edge, looking either way, but never choosing."

She took a slow breath, letting Alistair's words find their place inside her. There was truth in his accusation. "So what am I supposed to do?" she said.

"You *live,* Lou! You eat and sleep and breathe and DO instead of listen!" He gestured to the mountains around them. "Get out and live this life! This moment in time you've been given!"

"And if that's not the right path?"

"*All flesh is grass, and all the goodliness thereof is as the flower of the field,*" he said in a zealot's tone. "We all die, Lou, but do all of us live? Hardly! You need to do, *to be!*"

"Maybe, but I need to know what the memories mean. I feel like they're a warning…but I don't fully understand."

"I could tell you the secret of that…" Alistair said. "But it won't help you. You've got to discover it yourself."

A shiver ran up her spine. "What secret?"

"The one I've been looking for. The truth about Waterton and what it hides."

"Is this about the murders last summer?"

"No."

"About your film then? About the people here?"

"Yes and no... No and yes. I've found things in the time since I've been reborn. I understand it all, Lou. Every piece in the puzzle has a place. Even your memories play a part."

The hair crawled on Lou's scalp. "What *kind* of things have you found?"

"There's something dark here," he said. "Something you should be careful of."

Lou blinked. *She was in the glade again, watching the man with the shimmering sword. He swung it upward and—*

Lou jerked, her heart pounding like a trapped bird. "The slaver!" she gasped. "He's the danger!"

With the sun going down, Alistair was shrouded half in light, half in shadow. "People can do terrible things to one another in the name of God," he said. "And there's only one way to stop them once they start."

From the back of Lou's mind came another tug of attention. *Rich is heading this way.* She climbed to her feet and wiped sweaty palms against her jeans. "So what do I do?"

"If you want to change things, you need to grab hold and take a stand."

Lou wandered to the edge of the garage and squinted into the distance, waiting for Rich. The day was muggy and still. She ached for the calming chill of winter, many long weeks away. Lou's lashes fluttered closed and her breath slowed. Her thoughts spread outward until she could feel the shape of the wind that *could be...* Could trace it in her mind's eye. Feel it on her skin.

She waited.

An icy breeze appeared, licking over the edge of her collar and around her cheek.

"Another skill you've never told me about," Alistair said with a chuckle. "I didn't know you could do that."

Lou gave a bashful smile. "I don't talk about it. At least not since my mother died."

At the far end of the alley, a familiar figure appeared. Rich lifted his hand and she strode forward, leaving Alistair alone in shadow.

"Rich!" she called, a smile tugging up the corners of her mouth. "I thought you might be coming by."

Rich laughed, and with that happy sound, Alistair and his dangerous questions were forgotten.

* * *

With the preliminary hearing over and the trial about to begin, the seriousness of Rich's situation sank in. He spent one final afternoon in the Lethbridge courthouse filing paperwork, with Stu Callaghan piped in via conference call. Given the technical difficulties, the process dragged out for hours. Rich walked out the courthouse doors into the late-afternoon sunshine.

"Mr. Evans!" a woman shouted. "A word with you!"

He lifted his head as a crowd of reporters surged forward. The woman in front was Delia Rosings, a reporter Rich recognized from the Calgary Sun newspaper, whose face was plastered over several billboards in town. Rich stumbled to a stop as Delia and the others buzzed around him like a swarm of wasps.

"You've been charged with arson, Mr. Evans. How is your team preparing your defense?"

Rich stumbled back, overwhelmed by the cameras and microphones. Men and women bumped him from all sides.

"…heard you've been cooperating with police…"

"Is there a plea bargain being offered?"

"…trial is closed to the public. Any word on that?"

"…a source told our paper an unsolved homicide took place inside the Whitewater, months before it burned. Are you involved with that, too?"

Rich turned the other way, but reporters blocked his path. He squinted into the low slant of daylight. "Excuse me. I need to pass."

The shouts rose.

"…the fire may have been to cover up a murder…"

"Can you tell us more about the last manager of Whitewater Lodge?"

"…when Jeff Chan went missing last year."

"…a theory that Chan may have been Colton Calhoun's last victim…"

"Are you being investigated for homicide?"

Rich shoved past a heavy-set reporter. The man jerked backward and cameras flashed. "Hey, now!" the man bellowed. "You can't do that!"

Someone had Rich's arm, another his briefcase. "Move!" he said.

"…just a moment of your time!"

"Only a few questions!"

"…care to comment?"

"Mr. Evans! Are you—?"

"No comment!" Rich shouted. "NO COMMENT!"

In seconds, the crowd grew into a mob. Rich heard someone on a megaphone order the group to clear the steps, but he couldn't tell who it was. Police sirens broke through and the mob retracted, leaving a narrow eddy of empty sidewalk around him. Rich crashed through the wall of bodies and sprinted down the street past news vans and wide-eyed onlookers. Running track years earlier had honed his reactions and he didn't stop until he'd rounded the corner and reached his car. He fumbled with his keys, and climbed inside.

Two police cars sped past, but no one followed.

He'd seen the headline on the Lethbridge Herald newspaper this morning: *Manager to Stand Trial for Arson,* but he hadn't considered the firestorm that revelation would unleash. He slammed his palm against the steering wheel and the impact buzzed up his arm, leaving his hand throbbing. There was no way to hide what had happened. He'd already been branded a criminal by the media and the trial hadn't even begun. Rich's fingers tightened into claws.

His career was over.

Just need to talk to Lou. She was in Waterton, an hour and a half away. He reached into his coat pocket for his phone and dialed. It rang over and over. There was no answering machine; Lou didn't own one. He flicked through his contacts to find the number for Lou's Garage just as the same blonde woman with a microphone appeared on the empty street behind the vehicle. *Delia Rosings!* She waved to a cameraman behind her then sprinted forward.

Rich tore away from the curb, tires squealing. He headed straight for the highway. He passed a metal framed bridge which stitched the two sides of the city together, then down through the coulees to the south. Rich dropped the phone on the seat. There was no point in calling. If Lou was at work, she'd be alone, and if she wasn't, she was choosing not to answer. The road was long and lonely, and by the time the sports car reached the Park gates, night had arrived. Rich slowed as he entered the townsite; the 30 km speed limit felt like a crawl after the unfettered rush of the highway. Reaching Lou's cabin, Whispering Aspens, Rich turned into the driveway. The car's headlight's bounced across the yard, catching, for a moment, on something dark, standing on the step next to the door.

"What the hell…?"

Before he could say more, the figure bolted. Rich slammed on the brakes, the terror of last year alive in the darkness. The car lurched to a stop, half-in the driveway, half out, but the prowler was gone.

Pulse racing, Rich stepped from the vehicle. It wasn't yet nine, but every light was off, with no sign of Lou. He scanned the windows, but nothing seemed amiss. As he reached the porch, his stomach dropped.

The door hung ajar.

More disturbing than that, a glistening lump of raw flesh and brindle hair—a coyote or perhaps a dog—glistened in the moonlight. The pitiful lump was surrounded by a smear of entrails and blood that went from one side of the porch to the other.

"Lou!" Rich screamed and ran inside.

CHAPTER FOURTEEN

Prischka Archer,
Coldcreek Enterprises,
23rd Floor, Flatiron Building,
175 Fifth Avenue,
New York, New York
10010

September 12, 1998

Dear Ms. Archer,

I am writing to again request assistance with the continued financial challenges of the Whitewater Lodge. Given your lack of response to my previous query, I assume that my correspondence may have gone astray. Please allow me to restate.

The Waterton area is growing increasingly dangerous due to an increase in illegal activities in the area, in particular poaching of wildlife. While the first incidents appeared random, there have been a number of recent events that have given me serious concern. All of them, Ms. Archer, have occurred in a four block radius of the Whitewater Lodge! Guests are frightened. Staff refuse to stay late. And I'd be lying if it didn't occur to me that *I* may be a target. On the mornings of August 26th and September 7th, I discovered what can only be described as "bloody remains" on my front porch. I reported both incidences to local police.

I do realize that Coldcreek has many interests throughout the world, but Waterton's needs are unique, spanning from telecommunications issues, to simple safety requirements. If you are serious about maintaining a presence here in Alberta, I need additional funding.

Please contact me at your earliest convenience so we may discuss this.

Sincerely,
Jeffrey J. Chan, HRIM, Manager
Whitewater Lodge, Waterton Park, AB

Special instructions: CC

CHAPTER FIFTEEN

Lou stood at Rich's side as Officer Black Plume wrote down the details of what Rich had seen. Rich's arm was tight around her shoulders, his fear palpable despite the hours that had passed since he'd arrived home to discover the disturbing tableau.

"The figure was on the porch when you returned?" Sadie asked.

"Yes," Rich said. "He was at the door. I think he was leaving that *thing* on the porch."

"Warden McNealy is dealing with the poaching of the coyote. Let's focus on the break-in," Sadie said. "Did you get a good look at the perpetrator?"

Rich's fingers tightened on Lou's shoulder and she glanced up, willing him to be calm. Nothing changed. Rich's emotions were a swirl, too overwhelmed to manage. Lou needed time alone with him to sort through what had happened, but every second since he'd called her at the garage—shouting about someone breaking into the cabin—had been filled.

"No. He was in front of the light. I couldn't see."

"Tall? Short?"

"I don't know. An adult. Average size, I guess."

"Fat? Thin? Muscular?"

"Not sure," Rich said. "Look. I wasn't even sure it *was* a person on the step, and then he moved—"

"So it could have been anyone. You have no description. No details."

"He was standing at the door," Rich snapped. "It was open. I saw him take off at the same time I saw the blood on the porch. When I looked back, he was gone. It all happened too fast to see anything else!"

"I'm just trying to get facts, Mr. Evans."

Lou leaned into Rich's shoulder. The house seemed to be fine, but the door *had* been wide open. Problem was, Lou couldn't remember whether she'd locked it or not and the wind in Waterton was always an issue. The figure might have been a passerby. *Or Rich's imagination.* The dead coyote, a cougar's kill as McNealy seemed to think.

"Anything missing from the house, Lou?" Sadie asked.

"Not so far as I can tell. I was working at the garage when Rich got home."

"Hmm…" Sadie flicked the report shut. "It's probably nothing, but I still want you to call the station if anything else happens. There've been a few reports about a guy coming onto people's property and harassing them. Can't talk about that case, but given that it's happened, you should be extra cautious."

"What are you doing about it?" Rich snapped.

Both women turned to look at him.

"About the person you saw on the porch?" Sadie asked.

"No, about the prowler harassing people around town."

Rich's tone was sharper than it needed to be, and Lou felt her uneasiness return. She wanted calm, but she couldn't separate her roles when she was caught in the middle.

"Constable Flagstone and I are looking into the complaints," Sadie said coolly. "I doubt that case has anything to do with this one."

"So what, you're just gonna—!"

"Rich and I will keep an eye out for anything strange," Lou said. "And thank you for coming by so quickly, Sadie. I appreciate it."

Constable Black Plume smiled, and Lou felt the tightness in her chest ease. "Not a problem, Lou. Just doing my job." She turned to Rich and the smile faded. "Now, Mr. Evans, if I could get you to read through your statement, I'll be on my way. Warden McNealy will deal with the animal remains."

There were papers to sign—a final rush of documents—and in minutes, Rich and Lou were alone. The kitchen was dim, the single light above the stove on. Rich stared down at his copy of the police report. Lou slid her arms over his shoulders and leaned into him. He was leanly muscled, rather than bulky, but she liked the feel of his hard angles under her fingers. He was still upset, but alone, she could deal with those emotions.

"I was worried about you," Rich said. "When I saw that door open, I kept thinking of what happened in the summer. How different things could have been."

"It's fine… I'm fine."

"You sure?"

She nodded.

Rich's expression was sharp, more like the almost-memory of the future she'd seen and less like the man she knew. Things were changing between them, and not necessarily for the better. She wanted to smooth things out, but didn't know how.

"Rich, are you okay?"

"No, I'm not," he said thickly. "I had a hell of a day."

"Nothing was stolen. No one—"

"The break-in was just one part of an all-around shitty day."

"Oh?" Guilt rose inside her. Lou'd spent the day talking to Alistair about life and philosophy. She'd had no sense that anything was wrong. *No inclination.* "What happened?"

"There were reporters waiting for me outside the courthouse," he said. "They came after me. Chased me down the street. I tried to call you—"

"I was at the garage."

"—but you didn't answer. And then to come home to find some-one standing in the yard, a dead animal on the porch, the door open and- and—" His breath came in gasps. "Fuck! I'm just so—"

Lou reached out as Rich spun back around. His face was tracked with tears, the lines of his face incised with a sculptor's precision.

"Oh Rich, sweetie. I'm so sorry—"

His hand caught on her shoulders and he burrowed his face into her hair. Sobs tore through him. He hadn't cried like this since the night the Whitewater Lodge had burned to the ground, killing Amanda Sloane, and it struck Lou that he had that same terror of losing *her*. She waited out his sobs, the two of them clinging togeth-er in the dim light of the kitchen.

Without warning, Alistair's voice filled her mind: *"You're an out-sider... You never join in... You stand on the edge, looking either way, but never choosing."* Her heart contracted. It hurt to be in the chaos with Rich, but more telling, she *wanted* to be there.

Eventually, Rich's sobs faded and he looked up. Lou smiled.

"When the trial starts," she said. "I'll come to Lethbridge with you."

* * *

Lou sat against the wall of the garage, a wrench forgotten in her lap. Outside, the day was bright and cloudless, the beauty of late-September no balm for Lou's heartache. Her mind was torn in ten different directions. Grief was everywhere today; flares of Rich's panic arrived like discordant shouts in the back of her mind. He was having another phone meeting with Stu Callaghan. It *wasn't* going well.

Lou frowned, wishing she could bring Rich here, but his free time was completely taken up by preparations for the trial. Whatever newfound understanding had sparked between them on the night he'd returned to find someone on the porch was still there, but it was tempered by not quite being in the same place at the same time. They spent hours in one another's company, but they weren't together the way they'd been earlier that summer. If they'd still had a vehicle to work on, that might have helped, but Rich's every minute was eaten up by the upcoming arson trial. A twang of fear arrived from far away, and Lou winced.

If Rich was found guilty, he'd be tried for Amanda Sloane's murder next.

A knock at the open door of the garage drew her from her thoughts. She looked up to discover Alistair watching her.

"Alistair," she said uneasily. "What are you doing here?"

"I thought I was needed."

"Needed?"

"I sensed something was wrong. I thought I'd come by and see why." He walked into the garage as if he owned it, and took a seat at her side. Irritation pricked Lou's calm façade. Her interactions with Alistair had grown tense, especially since his fables drew out her own hidden worries. *What was she to do about the town's conflict? What would happen when Rich went to trial? Was she on the right path anymore? And why couldn't she imagine a future that involved him?* Alistair had a constant refrain: *"Live the truth."* But she had no idea what that meant.

"What're you thinking of, Lou?" he asked. "You're frowning."

"Amanda Sloane—the woman who died in the fire—used to work here," she said, grasping at the first thing that came to mind. "When Amanda first came to Waterton, she worked in my father's garage. We used to talk in the mornings. I miss her."

"Can I tell you a story?"

Lou nodded.

"The story is an old one," he said. "It's the story of a young monk and his master. They would sit together each day and have tea. One day, as the young monk prepared for the tea ceremony, he broke his master's favourite cup. He picked up the pieces and hid them under a mat. When his master came into the room, the young monk asked him—"

"Why do people die," Lou finished, with a half-hearted laugh.

"I *knew* you'd know this one."

"It's fine," she said. "I like the story."

"The master went on to tell his apprentice that all things must die. It is the way of life, and he should not worry about it. At that point, the young monk pulled out the broken pieces of the cup and showed his master. *'You see,'* the young monk said, *'it was time for your cup to die. Do not grieve for it'*…"

"A thing, easily replaced."

"People die every day," Alistair said, "and it isn't easy, but you know as well as I do that it needs to happen."

Lou frowned. She knew that too well. "I could feel it coming last summer, but couldn't stop it. And Amanda died. What's the use of a vision if you can't tell what it means? If you can't prevent it."

A smile flitted over his mouth. "Perhaps you weren't *supposed* to stop it, Lou. We *all die*. It's a matter of *when*, not if. Even *you* cannot change something like that. Death simply *is*."

"I was given a warning. I should have known." Lou shivered as she said the words. *I've been given another one, too...*

"Sometimes you need to embrace the chaos. Sometimes that's the only way to move forward."

"But I don't believe that. There are other ways to change things."

"Like what?"

Lou struggled to form words. Unsettled as she was now, it felt like shaping wet clay; each thought spilling into the next. "I try, if I can, to take the middle way," she said, "to take no side and to let people discover their own path."

Alistair leaned closer, (far closer, Lou thought afterward, than she should have let him get.) "But can you really help them that way?" He reached out and pressed his finger to the center of her forehead. "Or do you just *think* you can?"

A voice interrupted before she could answer.

"What the fuck?!"

Rich stood in the doorway, his hands clenched in fists. Backlit by the yellow blaze of sunlight through the autumn leaves, he looked like an angry god. Rage came off him like heat waves. She climbed to her feet and stumbled. Alistair caught her hand.

Rich stepped closer, ready to attack. "What the hell is going on here?!"

Lou jerked her hand away from Alistair. "Nothing."

"Nothing?! I KNOW what I saw!"

Lou could see the weight of exhaustion mixed with too many stresses to count. This wasn't *about* her, and yet it was. "Rich, I can explain—"

"That- that GUY was touching you!" Rich turned on Alistair. "I don't know what the fuck you think you're doing, asshole, but I am *not* in the mood for it!"

"Apologies," Alistair said. "But I should go." He took two dancing steps away from them, a wry grin spreading across his face. "Chaos, Lou... Remember what I said."

Rich tried to intercept him but Alistair was too fast. He jogged to the far end of the garage and disappeared out of one of the open stalls.

Lou turned back to find Rich glaring. "Rich, listen. I can expl—"

"What the hell did I just walk in on?!"

"Nothing. I just—"

"Like HELL that was nothing! You were almost kissing that guy."

"No, I wasn't. We were just talking—"

"I know what I saw!" Rich yelled. "That asshole—"

"His name is Alistair. And he's my... my friend."

"Since when do you have friends like that?! The guy looks like a goddamned hobo!"

"I'm friends with *everyone*, Rich. You know that. But there's nothing between the two of us."

"Then why was he in here?"

"He had a feeling I was upset, so he came to talk to me." She lifted her chin. "I was glad he did. I'm not even sure where this is all coming from. The two of us were just talking."

Rich stepped toward her. They were now closer than they needed to be to talk and Lou felt him struggle with that uncertainty, his anger spreading outward, looking for a target. *Finding her.*

"You know," he said through clenched teeth, "if it was the other way around—you walking in on me and some girl touching me— you'd be just as pissed off as I am!"

"No, I wouldn't."

"I don't get you! You said you'd come to the trial, and I thought things were finally changing. I thought we were going somewhere!"

"Things with us have been good lately," Lou said. "But Alistair's a friend."

"Bullshit!"

"Rich, listen… you're angry—"

"You're damn right, I'm angry! And I want this to stop!"

Lou felt her irritation growing. "Stop, what? Stop hanging out with Alistair? Stop talking to him? Or do you mean the other people in town, too? I'll talk to whomever I want!"

"Fine!"

"Look, Rich, this whole month—no, this whole summer before this—has been awful, and I think if we just let things settle down, you'll see—"

"Why?" Rich interrupted. "Why can't you just stop talking to him? The prick pisses me off and I don't *know* why, but he does!"

"I don't think any of this has to do with Alistair."

"It has *everything* to do with him! I saw how he looked at you!"

"You see what you *want* to see. Hear what you *want* to hear."

"Hardly!"

"It's true. You're always looking, and what you see is that I'm not enough." Lou's arms crossed, and she forced them down. "I'll *never* be enough for you."

"What?!"

"This isn't about *you*, Rich. It's about what's going on with me."

"What does that even *mean*?"

She swallowed painfully, the last of her peace disappearing like smoke. "I-it means I don't know what's going to happen with us," she said. "It means, that I can't just drop everything—"

"What *everything*?" Rich bellowed. "You keep telling me to 'live in the moment' and now *you're* the one who's scared of us? What *us*, Lou! We haven't even started!"

Behind them, the door to the front of the garage opened and Mila appeared. "Lou…? Is everything okay in here?"

"Fine," Lou said. "We're fine, Mila. Just talking."

Mila glowered at Rich before retreating.

"I'm not saying I don't love you, Rich," Lou said. "I do. And I'm not saying I don't *want* to be with you… because I do. But there are things I've never told you about myself. Things that Alistair has helped me to underst—"

"Stop," he interrupted. "I don't want to hear about that asshole!"

"Rich, please."

"No." He turned away and stumbled out of the garage. "I deserve better than this."

In seconds he was gone.

* * *

When Alistair left Lou's Garage, the afternoon light was starry with dust motes, the autumn sunshine a gentle warmth on his shoulders. Every detail drew his attention, from the lines of tree rings on the top of a wooden post, to the skiff of clouds that moved across the skies, to yellow-gold leaves, painted by the changing seasons. Alistair's mind buzzed as he stumbled down the street, pausing here and there, absorbed in the mysteries of life. His hands drifted to touch each item he encountered: the ragged stucco of buildings, peeling birch bark, the smooth curve of a truck's hood, a soft flannel jacket that—

A sinewy hand against his chest tore him from his musings.

"Thought you woulda run off by now!"

He lifted his chin to discover Levi Thompson. The man's anger was a splash of vitriol, jarring Alistair from his thoughts. He struggled to focus, but it felt like resurfacing after diving too deep beneath the waves.

"Wh-what did you say?" Alistair said.

Levi shoved Alistair away and he stumbled. "I *said,* I figured you woulda left."

"Oh no," he laughed, "I can't leave yet. I'm not finished playing my part."

"Your part?"

"Yes, I have things to do. Things to—"

"Why're you stickin' your nose into everyone's business?" Levi said. "No one wants a greenhorn like you 'round here."

Annoyance rippled through Alistair like wind through the trees. "You don't want to cross me, Levi Thompson. That would be… foolish."

"I seen a mess lot scarier men than you in my time!"

"Stop it," Alistair said quietly.

"I won't!"

"I'm warning you."

"You get outta here!" Levi yelled. "Go on! Go back where you came from!"

Alistair narrowed his eyes; a rush of memory and emotion funneled into the sudden urge to punish. "No!" His words emerged far lower than his regular speaking voice, drawn from another source entirely. Levi didn't hear.

"No one wants you makin' your damned movie. No one! So pack your bags and—"

"You have no idea what I am," Alistair said. "No idea at all."

"City slicker's what I see! Foolish, no-good, yellow bellied—"

Alistair's talonlike fingers grabbed hold of Levi's shoulders. "I can see *inside* you, old man! I can see ALL of you! EVERYTHING!"

Levi jerked away. "What the hell'r you going on about?"

A feeling of power wrapped around Alistair, drawn from places he'd never known existed. Every black thought he'd pushed away in his life was back. He could remember countless lives, but the ones that surfaced in this moment were the darkest.

"That boy you killed," Alistair said, dragging in details like rope. "The little one with black hair and pink cheeks. That's who I see watching you."

Blood drained from Levi's face. "Wh-what did you say?"

"I know about the boy at Slocan. I know about your secrets… I know *him*. I know everything about you, Levi."

"Liar!"

"You carry that boy's death with you. I see him there in the shadows, watching. Don't tell me you can't remember his face. You should. You took it from his family."

Levi took a step back. "I- I don't know what you mean."

Alistair followed. "You think Yuki ever forgave you? You think Lou has? You killed that little boy as real as if you'd stuck a knife up under his ribs." Alistair cackled. "That would've been kinder, actually."

"Stoppit! Stop it, NOW!"

Memories appeared in the rush of fear. "A blanket," Alistair said. "Isn't that what he asked you for? And you told him 'no'!"

"Please! I don't—"

"You think about that at nights sometimes, when it's forty below and the wind's whistling under the eaves. You think about that while you're in your warm bed and the snow is falling: How that little boy suffered through the coldest winter Alberta had ever seen when—"

"ENOUGH!"

A woman on the street turned and stared.

"No more of this!" Levi cried. "I… I don't want to remember."

Alistair smiled, but his eyes were flat, cold stones. "Don't you be telling me what I know," he said. "*You* are the child, old man. And you know nothing about me at all."

* * *

It was almost midnight and Jim and Sadie sat in the Watering Hole Saloon, a half-empty jug of beer between them. The bar was almost empty and the music from the jukebox echoed hollowly. Jim had been ready to call it quits an hour ago, but Sadie was riled about something, and there was no way he'd let her go home in that state. She'd just phone him an hour later. It had happened more than once.

"Audrika said this Diarmuid fellow was over asking her questions, too." Sadie lifted her glass and took a sip. "She didn't want to talk to him, but he wouldn't stop pestering her."

"Likely story," Jim snorted.

"Why's that?"

"I mean, come on… this is Mrs. Kulkarni, right?" He laughed. "That woman would stop a watch just so she could tell it the time of day. She wouldn't hold back on a little gossip for some Hollywood reporter."

"He's a filmmaker not a reporter," she said. "And Susan told me he was bothering her too."

Jim lifted the jug, refilling Sadie's glass before topping up his own. "Susan Varley hates everyone. You know that."

"Seems to like *you* well enough."

"That's just 'cause I've got a way with the ladies."

Sadie erupted into laughter and her beer sloshed. She set the glass down, swearing as beer trickled down over the edge of the table onto her lap. "Goddamnit, Jimmy. You're a bad influence."

"Hardly. You're just easy to tease."

"Bloody beer everywhere. Shit! I'm soaked through."

Jim grabbed a wad of paper napkins from the next table and dropped them onto her lap. "Easy now, or I'll have to get you to walk the line."

Sadie swore as she sopped up the last of the moisture.

"Better?" he said.

"A little. Gotta wait for it to dry though." She shook her head. "Lost my train of thought."

"The charms of the delightful Miss Varley."

Sadie's mouth twitched in an unwilling smile. "Yes, well, this Diarmuid guy is staying at Susan's B & B, but she doesn't like him at all."

"He been harassing her?"

"Susan never liked him to begin with." Sadie wadded up the wet napkins and tossed them into the center of the table. "But she says he's gotten worse the last few weeks."

"Worse than *what?*"

"Than what he was like when he'd arrived. She thinks he's on drugs now."

"Is he?"

"Maybe… Or he's just some asshole, snooping around and riling everyone up. Playing games. Heard from one of the girls at the Park office that he was screeching at Levi yesterday."

"Mr. Thompson come in and file a report about it?"

"No. Don't think so."

"I wonder why."

The music changed and the moment stretched out.

"What if it's more than that?" Jim said.

"More than what?"

"What if there's more to why Diarmuid is picking at things," Jim said. "I mean, why's he here now? Why all this interest at this moment?"

"You think he's up to something?"

Jim stared out at the empty bar. Waterton was a ghost town by this time of year, the tourist trade dwindling to nothing in the weeks since summer had ended.

"I'd say we have a stranger in town, causing trouble with any number of people. Levi Thompson was ready to shoot the guy. Add to it that Rich Evans saw someone standing on Lou's porch in the middle of the night, the door wide open... and we've still got an unsolved break-and-enter to the Whitewater from last summer."

Sadie smiled, her dark eyes sparkling. "A new person of interest?"

"Only one way to find out for sure."

"I'll get a warrant for Alistair Diarmuid tomorrow," she said.

CHAPTER SIXTEEN

Rich came up the front steps of the cabin slowly, unsure whether to hope Lou was asleep or, as the light in the window had suggested, she was still awake. He unlocked the door, and left his shoes on the mat. The light above the stove was on. *Left for me.* For some reason, that insight made his guilt worse. He'd driven the twisted roads of Waterton for hours after their fight. The high peaks of the mountains were a barrier again, a ragged obstruction that pressed down on him from all sides. Only a low fuel gauge had driven him back to town. It was too late to find another place to stay; half the hotels were closed for the season, the other half B & B's which closed each night. Heartsick, Rich had returned to Lou's cabin.

The house was quiet, the ticking of the clock above the mantle in the living room and the faint buzz of the furnace the solitary interruption. Rich hung up his coat and crossed the kitchen to the stove to turn off the light. Upstairs, he heard the mattress move. His chest tightened. He tiptoed up the risers and put his hand on the door, undecided whether to go in or not.

"I'm still awake," Lou said.

Rich jerked. Sometimes it was like she read his mind. He pushed open the door to find her sitting up in bed, book in hand.

"Hey," Rich said.

She closed the book without looking at the page, and set it to the side. "Hey."

Lou's hair was a black swirl against the headboard, dark rings under her eyes. It reminded him of how she'd looked the night the Whitewater had burned, and she'd cared for him, taking him away from the death and destruction, holding him near. Rich's brow crumpled. She deserved better than him. Better than—

"I'm glad you came back," she said. "I thought you wouldn't."

"I, um…I just needed a little time to think about things."

"And…?"

"And I thought about what you said and I want you to know I know what you were saying about Alistair. He's your friend, and I get that." His throat bobbed. "I'm sorry. I was wrong to yell."

Lou climbed out of bed and crossed the room to hug him. He slumped against her, breathing in the warm smell of her skin, and the faint hint of perfume.

"I love you, Rich," she said. "So much."

"Love you, too."

* * *

Susan was locking up the front door of the bed and breakfast for the night when a shadow moved in the darkness. Heart pounding, she jumped back before she was even aware of what it was. Two more steps took her into the street lamp's light, ready to make a run for her car.

The shadow rippled and a silhouette appeared. Seeing it was a person not an animal, Susan let out a relieved breath, anger replacing her fear. In shades of grey, a ghost emerged; it grew clearer until Alistair Diarmuid stood before her.

Susan drew herself up to her full height. "You're coming back pretty late tonight, Mr. Diarmuid."

In the last week and a half, Alistair's appearance had grown increasingly eccentric. He wore a suit jacket atop a soiled t-shirt. His hair was lank and unwashed, his chin unshaven.

"I had an interview," he said breathlessly. "Another person telling me secrets through the voice of their lies."

"Seems a bit late for an interview."

"I went walking by the lake after we finished. There's a trail by the water. Wave after wave, like years passing, repeating the same mistakes all over—"

"Is there something *wrong* with you, Mr. Diarmuid?"

He laughed. "Not at all."

"This here… this thing you've been doing the last few days, it's not *normal*."

Alistair smiled. "But I understand now. The connections are all there. The war. The people who left, they—"

"You're bothering the other guests."

"Bothering? How could I be bothering them? I'm just talking to them."

"That's not what they tell me."

"But don't you see? It all makes sense." Alistair reached out for her and Susan slapped his fingers away. "The truth I've been looking for is everywhere. I understand it!"

"Understand *what*, exactly?"

"The trouble. The danger. Waterton Park—lost and lonely. The fear and joy it holds, the darkness and light, like life itself. I *know* what's happening here, Ms. Varley. I understand it all. We're all connected. We're all playing parts in a film, but the film is life itself. Each one of us, part of the bigger story that—"

"I've got no time for this!" Susan snapped. "Should've known better than to let you stay here. Old Levi was right, you've been trouble from the start. I think you should go."

Alistair looked at her for a long moment. The night sounds had begun and they filled the air around them with the chirps of crickets and nighttime wings. In the distance, a dog howled.

"I can't leave Waterton," he said quietly. "I have things to do here. Everyone has a role to play…" His eyes narrowed. "Even *you*."

"Then you best leave my other guests alone. If I hear another complaint, you're out." She slid the key into the lock and swung the door open. "Go on then. Get inside."

Alistair smiled at her, but the glitter in his eyes was unnerving. "No more troubling the guests. I understand."

She rolled her eyes. "I doubt it, but at least now you've been warned."

* * *

Hunter plodded down the nighttime street, a headache pulsing behind his eyes. He knew it wasn't the dog's fault, but he was furious all the same. He'd been trying to train the pup since he'd gotten him the summer before, but Duke seemed determined to defy his best attempts. Tonight's escapade was one in a line of many.

"Goddamned dog!" Hunter said. "Runnin' off again."

To say Duke was high strung was an understatement. The cougar hound dug under fences, wriggled out of his collar, and wrought havoc among Hunter's other dogs. Walking the dog alone after nightfall when the streets were empty seemed to help. But then there were times like tonight, when Hunter opened the door to the cabin and Duke ran off before he could stop him. Hunter had done two circuits of the townsite, searching for the wayward mutt without success.

Legs aching, Hunter turned off Windflower Avenue and headed back toward his cabin. Near the line of houses where Duke often played, Hunter whistled again, but there was no answering howl. The night was quiet, the town asleep and dreaming, but Hunter was oblivious to the calm that filled the air.

As he reached his street, Hunter's ears picked up the sound of his other dogs baying in panic. He increased his pace despite the protest of his calves. The chorus of dogs barking from inside the house was audible all the way to the road and as he came up the cabin's driveway, Hunter discovered why.

A figure waited in the shadows next to his house.

The man was a black cut-out, his body backlit by the light on the porch. Duke taking off tonight had lit a fire under Hunter's temper and the person on the porch fanned that into wildfire. *Too bloody old for this nonsense!* When he was halfway to the door, the shadow turned, his wrinkled face bathed in light.

"Jesus Christ, Levi. Wasn't expecting you to come by tonight."

"You seemed a little worked up at the coffee shop," Levi said. "Figured I'd stop by and check on you."

"Mmph." Hunter stepped onto the porch and headed to the door. "You coming in?"

"Just for a minute. Can't stay long."

Inside, the dogs' barking rose to panicked howls. "Settle down!" Hunter ordered. Happy whines replaced the barking. "Go on now," he said, as two auburn muzzles appeared in the narrow band between door and door frame. "Inside you go."

Hunter stepped inside, Levi following, and the dogs danced around the two men.

"So what's bothering you?" Levi asked.

"I'm fine."

"Hardly. Can see it in your face. Looks like you been rode hard and put away wet. And that ain't no compliment."

"It's nothing. Just got a lot on my mind."

"You was never any good at lying, so you might as well spit it out. Something's botherin' you, and I ain't leaving 'til I know what it is."

"It's what's been happening 'round town," Hunter said. "All the troubles this year."

Levi gave him an impish smile. "Trouble? Things seem just fine to me now that the dust's settled from the summer."

"Don't play the fool. You know as well as I do, what's happening goes way beyond the murders."

"Colton's dead, and his group's gone too. They ain't bothering anyone anymore."

"I'm not just talking about that," Hunter said. One of the older dogs sat down at his feet and he reached down to rub the loose skin on the dog's head. "Sadie and Jim are looking for the person that helped Colton. The *other* person down in the basement."

"Mmph. They know about that, huh?"

"They do."

"It's not your issue though. Things'll settle down. They always do."

"They won't this time. Things are gonna get bad, Levi. Real bad."

For the first time, Levi's smile wavered. "What d'you mean?"

"Jim's taking prints."

"Well, then. I suppose that does change things, don't it?"

Somewhere outside a dog howled, and Hunter turned toward the sound. "Duke," he said absently.

"What're you going to do about the prints?"

"Not sure... But you *know* I can't let him take mine."

Levi reached out and patted Hunter's shoulder. "Don't let the bastards get you down. Isn't that what you used to tell me?"

"Yeah."

Levi's fingers tightened. "If it comes to it, Hunter, I'll help you deal with things. You know that, right?"

Hunter nodded. This wasn't the first time Levi had come to his aid. "You got time to have a drink?"

Levi nodded. "Make it a tall one. It's gonna take a bit to figure this one out."

* * *

The last weeks had changed many things about Alistair Diarmuid. For one, the life he'd left behind felt more like a dream than the reality he lived now. The present was the only thing that intrigued him. Waterton was no longer just a venue, it was a purpose, and he liked being here. The orange-leaved trees were a constant reminder to him of the changing seasons, and of the rebirth he could feel in the air. There was an ebb and flow to the lives that coalesced in the border town: the ranks of tourists that dwindled with each passing day and the locals at the heart of the tiny community.

"Do you want to play a game?" he asked Audrika Kulkarni the first time he saw her after their interview. She turned in surprise, then glanced up and down Main Street, but besides a few window shoppers, the sidewalks were bare.

"No, thank you, Mr. Diarmuid," she said. "I'm much too busy to—"

"I'll tell you a secret and you tell me one in return."

"I said no thank you, I've—"

"My secret," Alistair said, "is that there's darkness here. Everyone thinks it was Calhoun, but they're only half right."

"What?"

He laughed. "You've only scratched the surface. There's so much more to it, don't you see? It's starting."

"What in heaven's name are you talking about?"

"Calhoun wasn't the only danger. You thought he was, but he wasn't!" Alistair leaned closer, and Audrika's hands rose to her throat. "And now you tell *me* a secret."

"Mr. Diarmuid, please. I don't think I—"

He grabbed her by the shoulders. "Why did you tell people about me?!"

"Help!" she screamed.

"Why did you do it?!"

"HELP! I'm being ATTACKED!"

Two people on the street—Susan Varley and a nameless companion—turned at the sound of her cries. Susan and Alistair's eyes met for a heartbeat.

"Mr. Diarmuid! STOP!" Susan shouted.

Alistair let go of Audrika and she fell to the ground. "Susan, please HELP ME!" Audrika screeched.

Susan sprinted toward the duo. "You get AWAY from her!"

Alistair danced backwards. "It'll come home to roost!" he cackled. "You think it's over, but it's NOT!" He headed up the street and disappeared around the corner just as Susan reached Audrika's side.

Susan pulled Audrika from the ground and hugged her. "It's okay now," she said. "He's gone. You're fine."

Hidden from them, Alistair slumped against the stucco wall as a dark smile played over his thin lips. Deep in his chest he could feel Susan's panic at what she'd seen, and Audrika's brightly-faceted fear, now fading. He liked the play of their emotions over his own. *He wanted more of it.*

When no sirens began, Alistair left the alley and walked toward the lakeshore. He felt things moving together in the little town, fragments of his visions mingling with the now. Like so many other lives that crawled under his skin, this too had its place in the great arc of life. Alistair grinned.

Sometimes, his mind whispered. *The only way to move forward is to cut the past away.*

*   *   *

Jim was already in the squad car when Sadie pulled open the door. Her grin was so wide, she looked younger than she was. She climbed into the car and slid the seatbelt on in the same motion.

"What're you waiting for," she said. "Let's get going!"

Jim popped the car into gear and eased it away from the curb. "I take it you've got it?"

Sadie pulled the paper from her pocket, dangling it in front of him. "Susan and Audrika's police report about Diarmuid gave us just cause. Warrant's signed and ready. Let's go get him!"

Jim smirked. "You sure you want to come along? I could ask Jordan, if you're busy."

"Not on your life!" She punched his shoulder and the car swerved.

"Ow! Stop!" Jim laughed. "That hurts."

"Then go. I want to take him in today."

Jim grinned. "You got it, Sadie."

*   *   *

Alistair Diarmuid was sitting in the shade of a grove of pine trees when he felt a sudden tug of awareness. The feeling rippled and flowed, sharpening with his intent. It was one of the officers he'd seen at Fine and Fancy with Audrika: the woman who wore two long braids. She was, even now, starting to look for him.

Need to leave.

With a calm born from a hundred memories of struggle and escape, Alistair walked back to the Bertha Mountain Bed and Breakfast. He didn't take his clothes or books. He could get others. He didn't bother with the recorded interviews or notes about the conscientious objectors which had consumed him for the last years. He didn't need them. Alistair knew the truth.

Instead, Alistair dropped the key into the mailbox, climbed into his Volkswagen and started the engine. As he crested the top of Knight's hill, he began to hum. His part in Waterton was done.

* * *

Constable Black Plume stood next to the counter, the warrant laid, upside-down, so that Susan could read it. The older woman glared down at it through her reading glasses, checking the points off with her nail as she went. For someone who seemed so determined to get Mr. Diarmuid off the streets, Ms. Varley was fussy about paperwork. Reaching the end, she looked up.

"Alright then." Susan lifted a skeleton key from the hooks behind the counter. "There you go. Last door on the left."

"Is Mr. Diarmuid in his room now?" Jim asked. "We didn't see the car in the lot when we drove up."

"Don't know. Haven't seen him since he went after Audrika on the street."

"Thanks for telling us about that," Sadie said.

"Had to. Guy's loony as a March hare."

Jim smothered a smile behind his hand.

"All the same," Sadie said. "Your report was very helpful." Sadie passed the key to Jim. "We won't take long, Ms. Varley."

"Just don't be bothering the other guests when you take him in."

"We'll talk to him first." Jim said as he headed for the stairs.

"Suit yourself," Susan answered. "I'm glad to be rid of him."

"Has Mr. Diarmuid caused trouble for you?" Sadie asked.

"You ever meet the man?" Susan said. "Strange, I tell you."

"Yes, that's what I'd heard."

Jim's quiet footsteps moved up the stairwell, but his subterfuge was for nothing. "Don't go getting any mud on my carpets!" Susan called shrilly. "I just had 'em washed!"

Sadie clenched her teeth. *So much for nabbing him unawares.*

"Has Mr. Diarmuid ever done anything dangerous?" Sadie asked.

"Not too much, no."

"But you called him 'loony', didn't you?"

"Oh yes. An odd bird, that one."

"What do you mean?"

"Kept strange hours. Would show up out of nowhere when I was just closing up for the night." Susan crossed her arms. "That's a real nuisance for a B & B, you know."

"I imagine it would be." Upstairs, Sadie heard Jim knock on Diarmuid's door. "Now, Ms. Varley, do you think you could remember if he ever—"

"Sadie?!" Jim's voice interrupted.

"One second, Ms. Varley. I'll be right back." Sadie jogged the stairs two at a time, excitement rushing through her. The Bertha Mountain Bed and Breakfast had once been a large home, and the second floor had a line of bedroom doors. "Jim?"

"Over here!"

Sadie turned to find Jim at the far end of the hallway. "Take a look at this, would you?" he said.

Alistair's room was tucked in the far corner of the house. The door to the suite hung open, an unkempt room visible beyond. She stepped inside, glancing around at what seemed to be the aftermath of a windstorm: papers cluttered every surface, a box of files atop the dresser had tipped over to cascade to the floor.

"What did you find?"

"It's all research," Jim said. "I haven't touched anything yet, but at first glance, we've got a mess of documents here. Birth certificates, land titles and the like." He pointed to a handwritten piece of paper taped to the mirror. "Diarmuid had a list."

"A list? For what?"

"It's people in town," Jim said. "But that's not the weird part."

A frisson electricity ran up Sadie's spine. "It isn't…?"

"Nope. Strange part is that it's almost exactly the same list as *ours*."

CHAPTER SEVENTEEN

Rich and Lou were restocking shelves during the mid-afternoon lull when Levi drove up to the pump. "I'll grab that," Rich said, "you've got your hands full."

Lou smiled up at him from her position on the floor, surrounded by boxes of candy bars and gum. "Do you mind?"

"Not at all."

"Just give me a shout if you need some help," she said. "If it's someone for the garage, send them around back."

"You got it."

Outside, the truck's engine idled then fell silent and Rich strode forward. Levi rolled down the window. The old man's wrinkled face rippled as he took in Rich's 'Lou's Garage' shirt and blue jeans. Hunter, sitting in the passenger side of the truck, nodded.

"Fill'er up, Mr. Thompson?" Rich asked, fighting unexpected laughter. Levi looked like he'd seen a ghost.

"I, er… yes. Right up. Lou not around?"

Rich clicked on the pump, put the nozzle into the truck's tank, and locked the valve open. He wandered back to the window. "Lou's around. Want me to get her for you?"

"No. It's fine. Just didn't expect to see you."

"Not much else to do until the trial starts," Rich said. "Figured I might as well keep busy."

Levi stared at Rich as he pulled out the squeegee from the water can and wiped down the windows of the truck. Incredulity had replaced his annoyance. The gas pump stopped, and Rich added in the last few ounces by hand to get it to the nearest dollar.

"Thirty-seven even," Rich said.

"Goddamned train robbery is what *that* is."

On the other side of the cab, Hunter pulled out his wallet. "Levi, I'm happy to—"

Levi swatted it away. "I got it." He pulled open the truck door with an ear-splitting squeal. "Gonna put this one on the card."

Rich jogged ahead, pulled open the door to the garage and stepped back.

The old man scowled. "Surprised you're not too good to get your hands dirty."

Lou stood up from the behind the shelf, hissing: "Levi!"

Rich chuckled. "My hands have been dirtier than this." He pulled out the credit card machine from under the counter.

"I find that a bit of a stretch," Levi said. "You don't strike me as someone who knows hard work." The old man reached into his coat pocket for a leather billfold and pulled out a shiny new credit card.

"My grandparents were immigrants," Rich said. "They had a farm in Minnesota and I used to live there in the summer. Hard work, but good memories." Rich slammed the credit card panel back and forth, then wrote in the numbers. When he looked back up, both Levi and Lou were staring at him. "What?" Rich laughed, holding out the transfer and pen toward Levi. "You don't believe me?"

Levi eyed him uncertainly before he signed the paper. "I believe you. Just didn't expect it."

Rich tore off the top sheet and handed it back to Levi. "You never know until you ask."

"No," Levi said, "I suppose you don't." His wrinkled mouth tightened, and then he pulled out a dollar coin. He dropped it on the counter, turned and pushed the door open with his shoulder. "See you both later then."

Hunter waved once as the truck drove away.

Rich stared at the dollar on the counter. "What's this?"

"I'd say it's a tip." Lou giggled. "Don't tell Brendan. He still hasn't got one from Levi."

Rich opened the till and dropped it inside. "He reminds me of my Gido," he said. "God, but the man could curse. I couldn't understand the half of it, but I knew when I was in trouble." When he looked back up, Lou was still watching him, her lips curled in amusement. "Sorry," he said, "is that extra dollar going to mess with the float?"

Lou shook her head. "I never knew that your grandparents were immigrants. Evans sounds very... American."

"I think that's the point. Dad was just a boy when his family emigrated, but he left home and changed his last name as soon as he could." His smile faded. "He wanted to forget where he came from... wanted his kids to have the best opportunity. We were supposed to be the perfect American family. Two parents. Two kids. Church each Sunday. No dirt under our nails. My grandparents' farm was never good enough for him."

"What was his name before he changed it?"

"My father was named Mikhail Yevtushenko by his parents, but he's been Mike Evans since the day he turned eighteen."

Lou smiled, her expression soft and sad. "Richard Yev-tush-en..."

"Yevtushenko," Rich repeated. "It's a family full of poets and rebels. Let's just say my father never wanted to be associated with that. He wanted to start fresh; leave it all behind." He gave a bitter laugh. "Wanted us to forget where we'd come from."

"That's why he told you being a mechanic wasn't a good enough career."

"Exactly."

Lou put a hesitant hand on his arm. "My father's last name wasn't actually Newman. He changed it when he moved to Waterton in the seventies."

"Really? Why'd he change his name?"

But before she could answer, the bell for the pump rang and the story that had waited for so long was put aside yet again.

* * *

Jim sat at the table, his fingers drumming on the checkered cloth. It bothered him that Diarmuid's research intersected the names of so many townspeople who'd been flagged in the ongoing investigation of the Whitewater break-in. He knew it meant something. *But what?* He frowned down at the handwritten list of names, measuring his years growing up in Mountain View against his decade on the force in Waterton.

"All good folks," he muttered.

"What's that?" Hunter asked as he came forward, coffee pot in hand.

Jim covered the list with his hand and smiled. "Just the guy I wanted to see."

Hunter set a cup in front of Jim and filled it without asking. "What can I help you with, Jimmy? Everything alright?"

"Just fine, just fine. I just need a little advice."

Hunter sat down across from him. "Well, why didn't you say so?"

"You've lived here for decades, Hunter. You know everyone, right?"

"I s'pose so. Why?"

Jim pushed the paper forward. Hunter dug through his pocket for his reading glasses, and perched them on his nose as he scanned through the list. "What's all this?"

"It's some of the people Alistair Diarmuid was looking into," Jim said. "I put the list together with…" He trailed off, wondering how vague he could be and still get an answer. "…some other things Sadie and I've been looking into."

"That right? Looks like the Chamber of Commerce listing to me."

Jim frowned. Each person on that list *was* on the Chamber. How had he missed that?

"I was wondering if you could tell me where they came from," Jim said.

"Where *who* came from?"

"The people on the list. Where'd they move here from? Where were they born?"

There was a long pause before he answered: "No."

Jim frowned. "No…?"

Hunter was on friendly terms with just about every person in town, and was always quick with a joke or a smile. Today he stared, steely-eyed at Jim. "No, I can't help you."

"But why not?"

Hunter grabbed hold of the pot and pushed back from the table. "You want to know where people are from? Then go talk to 'em yourself."

"I will if I have to, but I figured you could save me some time."

"You figured wrong." All good humour was gone from Hunter's

face.

"C'mon, Hunter. Help me out here."

Hunter shook his head. "I'm not talking behind anyone's back. These are my friends."

Jim stood from the table as the older man walked up the aisle. Unlike Sadie, Jim didn't work on gut feelings—he liked things black and white, clean cut facts, solid evidence—but today something felt off.

"You know who Diarmuid was looking for, don't you?" Jim said loudly.

Hunter spun back around. "I never met that Diarmuid fellow in my life."

"That's not what I asked. I think Mr. Diarmuid knew something about—"

"Jimmy Gladstone, I've known you my entire life! You worked for me. And I don't know what you're suggesting but you're wrong!"

"You know what I remember about working for you? That you were quick to tell stories about everyone but you never said a damned thing about yourself."

"Hardly! Everyone knows me. Christ! I hired you as a dishwasher when you were a kid straight off the farm. You forgetting that?"

"I haven't forgotten, Hunter, but you're still not answering my question." He reached down and picked up the list. "Where're these people from? You've lived here for decades. You know them better'n me. I grew up outside Mountain View."

The restaurant was practically empty, but Hunter stepped close and dropped his voice. "You can't think any of those people on your list had anything to do with the troubles this summer, can you?"

"Truthfully, I just don't know. I mean, we all thought we knew Colton Calhoun and look how that turned out."

"Right."

"Now, before I go," Jim said, "I need to get your prints."

The explosion into motion was violent and unexpected. Hunter slammed the pot down on the nearest table—coffee sloshing over the side—and stormed past him. Their shoulders slammed together as Hunter headed into the back room.

"Hunter!" Jim shouted. "Wait! It'll only take a second."

"Get your goddamned warrant first!"

* * *

Lou was puttering in the kitchen, putting together a quick dinner of spaghetti when the phone rang. The room was heavy with the scent of pasta, a faint pallor of mist over the windows from the boiling water as she flicked off the burner under the sauce and stepped over to pick up the receiver. She stretched the cord out as far as it would go, a thin line between stove and wall.

"Hello?"

"Lou," Hunter breathed. "Thank goodness."

Lou's breath caught at the sharp sound of his voice. "Hunter, you alright?"

"Been trying all day to get hold of you. Where've you been?"

The sauce began to boil, heat transferring through still-hot coils. Lou stretched further, the receiver pressed tight to her ear.

"I was in and out all day," she said, reaching out with the spoon and tugging the pot sideways. "Rich and I are heading into Lethbridge for the trial. I wanted to—"

"Jim Flagstone came by the coffee shop today."

"Jim Flagstone? What'd he want?"

"Sadie and Jim have been asking about things. Snooping around. Wanting to get prints."

"What do you mean, prints?"

"Fingerprints, Lou. They're trying to match them to the break-in at the Whitewater. You, uh… You haven't told anyone about…" His words trailed off.

Lou glanced at the ceiling. Rich couldn't hear her, but she still dropped her voice. "No, I haven't said anything to anyone."

"Your father was my best friend. I hope that with this Evans fellow around, you didn't go talking about—"

"I didn't say anything, Hunter."

"Sorry, hon. I've just been… well, worrying about things."

"Hunter, please," Lou said. "What's going on with you?"

"Nothing."

"You keep saying it, but I don't believe it." She pressed her fingers to her temple and closed her eyes. "I can hear it in your voice. You're hiding something."

"I'm just protecting the town."

Upstairs, footsteps crossed the floor from the bedroom to the bathroom. Lou dropped her voice even lower. "And who's going to protect Rich, huh?"

Hunter made a sound somewhere between a cough and a growl. "Seems you're doing a good enough job for all of us."

* * *

Siobhan Andler had never been so happy to close the Prince of Wales hotel as she was this year. She walked through the empty third floor, clipboard in hand, checking off details. Outside, plywood sheets covered the first floor windows. Tomorrow, plumbers from Cardston would arrive and the water would be turned off as the pipes were drained in preparation for winter. In a few days she'd be home again and her real life would start up once more.

Unless…

Her lips twitched. There had been gossip about the Whitewater investigation for weeks, though Siobhan knew it was unlikely that anything would happen before she left for Montana. Her divorce had taught her that refusing to do something was sometimes twice as effective as a fight. Now, as she was about to leave, it appeared her stonewalling had worked. As she headed down to the second floor, footsteps alerted her to someone nearby.

Siobhan stopped in her tracks as he turned the corner. "Constable Flagstone," she said in an icy voice. "It's rather late for a visit. What can I do for you?"

Jim smiled, but it didn't reach his eyes. "Glad I caught you, Ms. Andler." He held out a piece of paper. "I have a warrant to get a copy of your fingerprints before you leave town."

* * *

Constable Black Plume waited as the computer struggled to life. Like everything else in the office, it was too old to be effective and too young to be replaced. The lagging internet connection appeared and she clicked open her email, waiting as the hourglass icon turned over and over.

Five minutes in, the system launched with a flash of colour, two unread items appearing in her inbox.

A thrill of excitement ran through her as she read the subject lines. Perhaps *today* things would start to move.

Subject: Request for criminal record check on Alistair James Diarmuid. Sender: Captain M. Lau, Police Department for Los Angeles, California

Subject: Results for print sample M15: 081903 Sender: RCMP Fingerprinting Service Dept.

Sadie clicked on the first and leaned back in her chair. *Loading… Loading…* Alistair Diarmuid might have gone off the radar, but she had been able to track him down.

Constable Black Plume,

I've attached both the driver's license information for Alistair James Diarmuid and the criminal record check you requested. I'm afraid they won't be much help to your case. Mr. Diarmuid's files are clear. He has had two criminal record checks done in the last eight years: one for an application for employment, the other for an application for out-of-country film work. So far as his records show, he has never been involved in a crime.

If there is anything else I can do to help, please let me know.

Regards,

Captain M. Lau

Sadie's smile faded. She paused on Diarmuid's driver's license and scanned for the birth date: October 9, 1964.

"Damnit!"

Despite her suspicion that Alistair might be involved in the break-in, he was far too young to match the prints from the Ohio case. With a resigned sigh, she clicked open the second email.

Loading... Loading...

Sadie and Jim had attempted, without success, to locate Alistair Diarmuid after his disappearance. They'd sent away his prints to see if they were on any criminal database. With a silent prayer, Sadie clicked open the second email.

We regret to inform you that the prints you have forwarded are not flagged in either the Canadian or U.S. criminal databases. If you would like to include these prints as part of an ongoing criminal investigation, please contact the RCMP Fingerprinting Service, or the Canadian Criminal Database for submission details...

"Goddammit!"

She reread the two emails, disappointed. A new thought occurred to her and she forwarded each before opening a new email.

To: Captain S. Nelson, Lethbridge Arson Squad
Subject: Possible Suspect for Whitewater Arson Investigation
Captain Nelson,
I have forwarded you two emails which may be related to the arson investigation for the Whitewater Lodge.

She stared at the blinking cursor as she composed her words. Alistair Diarmuid could not have been involved in the Whitewater break in, but he'd still been reported by three separate townspeople for strange, unsettling behaviour in the last weeks. Given that Diarmuid had been in Southern Alberta for several months prior to the fire, there was still a possibility he'd been involved in the arson. That case was still open.

She began to type.

While I realize you have identified Richard Evans as a suspect, I'd like to offer some details regarding a person of interest by the name of Alistair James Diarmuid. Though his whereabouts are currently unknown, he appears to have been around the Waterton area near the time of the fire, and possibly before. His particular interest in people in town has unnerved a number of townsfolk. He may be of interest to your ongoing arson investigation…

With a nod, Sadie hit send.

* * *

The house was quiet, the autumn chill passing from the windows to the air inside. Beyond the glass, the world loomed purple as day bled into night, but Lou's eyes rested on the man next to her. Rich's chest rose and fell, exhaustion etched into every debauched line of his body. He looked, for all intents, as if he'd fallen asleep mid-act. *And he almost had,* Lou thought smugly. His chest was half covered by the sheet, one hand open on the white cotton of the pillowcase, a wrinkle of blankets tangled across his narrow hips.

The wind rose, reminding Lou of the nights when she'd been a child, certain she could hear voices in the breeze outside the cabin walls. She smiled as her eyes drifted down Rich's body and the musculature which had become so familiar. In the last months she had discovered the intensity of her connection to him. His emotions were linked to her own. Even now, she could feel him settling into a fitful sleep, the tensions of the last week played out behind his closed lids. *Not taking the middle road now,* an inner voice chided. Louise knew she should stay neutral, but with Rich this near, it was hard to remember why she needed to keep him at arm's length. She *wanted* to tell him the truth about herself.

And that, Lou decided, *was the problem.*

She traced over the lines of Rich's palm as he dreamed. A dissonant note twanged inside her chest and his face tightened in concern. She wondered what he was seeing; it couldn't be good. Rich's eyes flickered behind closed lids. His hand clenched and legs jerked. Lou could feel desperation and panic rise inside him like flood waters.

"Shh…" she said. "It's just a dream, Rich."

He turned toward the sound of her voice and moaned. His emotions loomed in the bedroom, swirling. There was a flash, and Lou saw a photograph of a burned remains amidst a group of photographs spread on a table. *They showed him the picture of Amanda's body at the preliminary hearing,* she realized in horror. Anxiety rising, Lou reached out and stroked his blond brows, pausing between them. Her will rose, enveloping him, forcing his thoughts to comply.

"Peace," she whispered. "Feel it."

She could sense him fighting her intention, moving against the pull. It surprised her; most people didn't push back, even when awake. Gradually, however, his thoughts eased. Rich sighed and went still, the nightmare over. Lou placed her hand against his chest. After a time, she laid her head next to his shoulder and waited for sleep to come.

Today, Constable Black Plume had contacted Lou about Alistair Diarmuid's disappearance and Lou'd given her what little information she had. There was still trouble in town, and no matter how she tried, Lou couldn't see it clearly. She sighed, her mind drifting to other issues.

The arson trial started Monday.

Lou sighed and Rich's eyes fluttered open, the blue dark and half-lost in sleep. "Lou," he mumbled, then fell asleep once more. Outside, night darkened from indigo to black as the mountain ridge merged with the sky. Rich's breath was soft on her forehead, his arms a comforting weight over her. Worry meshed with fatigue and her lids closed. Rich was warm and he was here.

That was enough.

The wind moved around the windows and doors, chilling the room. Lou burrowed closer, her limbs entwined with his until she could no longer tell when she ended and he began. *Sometimes,* a voice from the darkness whispered, *you need to embrace the chaos.* Half-awake, Lou barely noticed where the thought came from, or that it wasn't her own thought at all.

Content in the circle of Rich's arms, she slept.

CHAPTER EIGHTEEN

Prischka Archer,
Coldcreek Enterprises,
23rd Floor, Flatiron Building,
175 Fifth Avenue,
New York, New York
10010

October 8, 1998

Dear Ms. Archer,

It is with sincere regret that I must request a transfer from my position as Manager of the Whitewater Lodge. This decision has been many months in coming, and while I fear finding a replacement may put you in a difficult position, I see no other way. When I accepted this position at the Whitewater Lodge, I was certain that there were no positions within Coldcreek's holdings that I could not manage, no task too difficult to tame. I was eager for the challenge of working in a national park.

I have, in the last months, been forced to reconsider my optimism.

Waterton is too primitive, and I don't feel I'm adequately prepared to manage a hotel in the area. There is dangerous wildlife in the townsite. My dog was killed by a cougar while chained in my yard. Although I've made concerted efforts to establish a positive, working relationship with the townspeople, there are serious issues. I simply do not have the skills to manage this situation.

Consider this my official request for transfer. If you need further details, please do not hesitate to contact me and I'd be happy to provide them.

Sincerely,
Jeffrey J. Chan, HRIM, Manager
Whitewater Lodge, Waterton Park, AB

CHAPTER NINETEEN

Alistair headed west first.

He drove toward the setting sun, following the path of shadows into the bared teeth of the continental divide. There were places where the road became a line of thread, looped by a careless seamstress, other times it was the needle itself, notching holes through barren rock.

Still he drove. Through rainstorms, and down windswept slopes, across the narrow fruit-bearing valleys and the hidden, secret mountain paths where the rusted carcasses of abandoned cars appeared at the bottom of deep ravines. *West. West...* the thought spurred him forward. He slept when his eyes wouldn't stay open, and woke, shivering, in the blue-white morning light.

Louise Newman never left his thoughts.

Eventually, the need for distance eased. The western coastline lay out before him, a tattered ribbon on the hem of the ocean's dress. The majesty held him close and spoke to him in the secret voices of wind and surf: different than the low voices of Waterton's peaks, but sympathetic. Alistair found a room in a faded, backwoods town, and settled in to wait.

The storm he'd seeded drew nearer.

* * *

The trial commenced on a blustery day in early October. The opening arguments were slated to begin at 9:00 a.m., so with this in mind, Lou and Rich came into Lethbridge the night before. They drove Rich's sports car, the ninety minute ride quiet as both of them mulled over an uncertain future. Rich's phone buzzed as they left the Park's borders. He dug through his pocket and tossed the phone into Lou's lap.

"You want to get that for me?"

"It's a voice message," Lou said.

"From?"

"P. Archer."

"Shit," Rich said. "That's Prischka."

"You want to pull over so you can listen to it?"

"No, you go ahead."

Lou lifted the phone and pressed play. The phone beeped twice and a woman's educated voice appeared on the other end. "Hello, Richard, this is Prischka calling. Give me a call when you get this message. It's very important."

Lou relayed the message. "I think you should call her, Rich. She sounded worried."

Rich shook his head. "No. Let's get to Lethbridge and talk to Stu first. We've got to get ready for tomorrow."

The feeling of uneasiness rose inside her until it was in her throat. "Are you sure?" she said. "I think you should—"

"I'll call Prischka when we get back to the hotel tonight."

Lou opened her mouth to argue, then closed it again. There was no way to explain her anxiety without revealing more about herself than she wanted, so she turned and stared out at the barren fields instead.

* * *

Hunter was at the post office when Sadie Black Plume walked in. He stepped away from the bank of postal boxes. "Just finishing up," he said. "I'll get out of your way, Sadie."

She didn't move.

"I don't mean to bother you, Hunter." She held out a sealed envelope. "But this came from the courthouse in Lethbridge. It's important."

"What the hell?" His anger rekindled like wildfire through dry grass. "I told Jim I'm not letting him take my prints without a warrant!"

The constable's face darkened. "Jim told me you refused to be printed, but this has nothing to do with our ongoing investigation."

Hunter held the envelope at arm's length and squinted. "What is it?"

"It's an official summons," Sadie said. "You've been subpoenaed to appear in court for the arson trial of Richard Evans."

* * *

Stu stayed at a four star hotel downtown, while Rich and Lou opted for a less extravagant place a block away. The three of them met for dinner when they arrived and talked through plans.

Stu flashed Lou a knowing smile. "It'll be you they'll go after, since you're the only one who can corroborate Rich's story."

"I didn't lie to the police," Lou said. "And I don't think there'll be an issue."

Stu steepled his fingers. His eyes were hard and inquisitive. *His lawyer look*. "Mmm… I'm glad you're confident, but there are always issues. No worries, I've already got that contingency covered."

Rich leaned his elbows on the table. "What do you mean?"

"I talked to a number of townspeople last month," Stu said. "A town as small as Waterton…" He gave Lou a once-over. "A new romance is gossip. It always has onlookers." Rich chuckled, but Lou stared at Stu with trepidation. "I've filed subpoenas for a number of them."

"Who?" Lou asked.

Stu rifled through his notes. "Audrika Kulkarni was *more* than happy to talk about you two. Mila St. Jean, lots of opinions. Grant McNealy, Sam Barton… neither likes Rich, but they had lots to say when I asked about when you'd gotten together, and one last-second addition to the list…" Lou's fingers tightened on the chair's arm. "Hunter Slate—"

"No!" Lou yelped.

Both men looked up in surprise.

"He won't come," she said, her voice brittle with urgency. "Don't call on him."

"And why *wouldn't* I?" Stu said. The tension that had been building between them was back, Rich caught in the centre.

"H-He's very private."

"Really?" Rich said. "'I've always found Hunter to be—"

"Call the others first, leave Hunter until last." Lou leaned toward Stu, her voice persuasive. "*Please*, Stuart. This is very important to me."

"I don't know," he said. "I thought he'd be a good witness to start with."

"Just think about it," Lou said.

"I…" It seemed like Stu was going to say something else, but his expression softened. He dropped his hands to the armrests and settled back against the seat.

"He's not that important," Lou said. "He's only one out of all the rest."

"I, um… yeah, I guess so." Stu nodded, as if this had been his idea. "Yeah, I suppose I could call the others first, and leave Hunter Slate out unless I really need him."

"You might not need him at all," she said in a voice so low Rich struggled to hear it.

"Yeah," Stu said. "Might not even need him at all."

Rich eyed the two of them. Something strange was going on, but he wasn't quite sure what. It was like he'd been pushed to the side and the conversation was flowing on without him. His body tensed, a fear which he didn't understand rising in reaction to… *something*.

"You know, I don't see it as an issue," Rich said. "Hunter *does* know everyone in town. Stu will do what he needs to do. You get that, right, Lou?"

She reached out across the table for his hand, but he didn't take it. "I'm sure it'll be fine," Lou said.

"Sure it'll be fine," Stu echoed.

Rich's scalp crawled. "Look, I've never liked Hunter Slate, but if he can help us win, then I think we should use him."

As Stu nodded, Lou pulled her chair closer to the table, positioning herself between the two men. "You know," she said, "this reminds me of a story I once heard."

"Lou, I don't want to hear a story," Rich snapped, "I want to talk about—"

"There were two monks travelling along a mountain road after a storm," she continued. "They came to a portion of the road covered in rain water. Next to this spot stood a beautiful young woman. She was waiting, unable to get across."

Stu's eyes were heavy-lidded. Rich felt the tug to listen, but he fought against it. "Lou," he said, his irritation growing, "I'd rather talk about what's going on with the trial and—"

"The two monks stopped, uncertain what to do." Lou's words

washed over the two men like a stream. Her gaze was intent on Rich and he found himself drawn to the colours in her eyes, dark brown and gold flecks mixing together in a swirl of amber. "The older monk offered to carry the young woman across. When she was safely on the other side, the two monks continued on their journey."

"Lou, I don't…" Rich's words faded in bewilderment. He tried to pull back his earlier indignation, but the story begged for him to listen.

"As they neared the road to the monastery, the younger monk turned to the older one, and asked *'Master, is it true that, as monks, we are forbidden to touch women?'…*" Lou's voice was low and soothing. She held out her open palm, and Rich took her hand. A sense of calm rose inside him. He turned to her in confusion and she smiled, emanating peace.

"The other monk agreed that it was forbidden, and for a time the two travelled in silence. When they reached the gates to the monastery, the younger monk spoke: *'Master,'* he said, *'if that teaching is true, then why did you carry that woman across the road?'* The older monk turned to his apprentice with a smile. *'Ah,'* he said, *'but you see, I left that woman at the side of the road hours ago, whereas you, my child, are carrying her even now.'*"

Lou's voice disappeared, and Rich sighed as a sense of well-being settled over him like a warm blanket.

Stuart nodded, his eyes hazy and soft. "That makes sense," he said. "Just let it go."

Rich lifted Lou's fingers and pressed a kiss to the back of her hand. Everything seemed easier when Lou was there. She turned to him as if he'd said the words aloud. Her face was pale, eyes sad.

"Let's try to get some sleep," she said. "We all have to be up early tomorrow."

"Sleep," Stu murmured. "Good idea." For whatever reason, Lou had grown quiet, and Rich found himself struggling to remember why.

They walked to their hotel in silence, the peace of the night matching how Rich felt. Once in their room, he opened his briefcase and pulled out an envelope.

"I printed this when Stu and I were downtown," he said. "It's not much but…"

It was the photograph from the afternoon by the river weeks earlier. The two of them were laughing into the camera. He watched Lou's face as she pulled it open, expecting her to smile.

Her face crumpled. "Oh Rich," she said in a broken voice. "This is lovely."

Lou was breathing hard. Something *else* was going on, but imbued with peacefulness, Rich struggled to understand what. He reached out to touch Lou's face and she pulled away.

"What's wrong?" he asked her.

"I- I can't—"

"Can't what, Lou? What's going on?"

"Rich, I'm sorry. I shouldn't be doing this with you."

He took a step closer, but she moved back. The serenity he'd been feeling disappeared, leaving him cold. "Shouldn't be doing *what* with me?"

Lou looked like she was about to cry. "This… *Us.*"

"What just happened? One minute we're talking, and the next minute you're having second thoughts."

"It's too hard to explain. I can't. I… it'll sound crazy."

Irritation prickled under his calm. "Try me."

"Rich, please—"

"Whatever it is, I *deserve* to know."

"I… I…"

"What?!"

"I-I'm a Buddha," Lou whispered.

He frowned. "A Buddhist?"

"No. I'm a bodhisattva: a *tathagata*… an enlightened being."

Rich jerked away from her like he'd been burned. "You're a *what*?!"

"Alistair helped me to see it, but I always knew. Even as a child, I knew."

"Lou, stop—"

"I'm a Buddha. I'm here to help others. And I shouldn't be doing this with you, Rich. I shouldn't be following this path, pretending we're going to be together. I shouldn't—"

"No. That's nuts, Lou." His expression twisted into a sneer. "This isn't *funny*! I mean it!"

"I'm not joking," she said. "I know I should have tried to explain earlier, but…"

"But *what*?!? But it was never the right time? Maybe it's that you know how fucking CRAZY it sounds!"

"Please listen. I—"

"Fuck you!" Rich shouted. "What the hell am I supposed to do with this, huh? Goddammit! It makes no fucking sense! It's insane!"

"I'm sorry," Lou whispered as a tear rolled down her cheek. "I should have told you before, but I—"

Rich stormed out of the room before she finished.

CHAPTER TWENTY

The pictures on the wall shook as the door banged closed. Lou took a heaving gasp. A thin layer of disbelief hovered around the edges of the room, ragged flashes of doubt unravelling away as she watched; prickly spines of betrayal lurked under that, the anguish so deep it pulsed like a heart.

"I'm sorry," Lou choked.

She'd told a handful of people in her life about her visions. Only Alistair Diarmuid had ever understood what that meant. Her mother's warning waited in the shadows: *"Be sure you follow the right path. You've come back for a reason."* Lou no longer knew what that path was, or how to get back to it. She was too entwined in the chaos that had engulfed Rich's life to be an unbiased adviser.

I can't fix this.

Trembling, Lou turned away from the door and stumbled into the shadows. Rich's suitcase sat against the wall, the briefcase open where he'd left it, papers neatly stacked inside. Heartsick, Lou stared at the photograph in her hand, where Rich smiled at her from the surface, his arm wrapped around her. *Things were so good then.*

Blinking back tears, she tucked the image inside the envelope and set it on the bedside table. She fumbled for the lamp cord and pulled it on with a click. Light flooded the room and—

The forest thinned to let in the midday sun. Half-blinded by sunlight, Lou sprinted forward and tripped on an exposed root. When she staggered upright, she was no longer alone. Another person had reached the glade: Death in human form.

Winded, she faced him.

Lou's ebony hands tightened on the spear. The stranger bared his teeth as he stalked closer, his silver blade dancing with points of light. Lou knew better than to plea for mercy. Men like this were demons. Soulless. Her attacker swung his sword in an arc, and Lou gave a battle cry to rally the spirits of her ancestors. She stepped forward, bringing up her wooden spear to block the attack. The single blow fragmented half of it into splinters.

The attacker laughed.

His stance widened. It was time to run... to escape now or face a certain death. Lou knew this, but she lifted the broken shaft of her spear and prepared for one last attack. Her children were in the fields at home. If she fled, this man and the others would follow and—

Lou jerked her hand from the lamp. Her arm ached where she'd held the remembered spear, her hand clenched so tight it throbbed. She sank down onto the bed, the past life pulsing with remembered horror. She could almost hear Alistair's laughter.

"Something dark is coming," she whispered.

* * *

Rich rolled over in the unfamiliar bed and squinted at the clock. *4:42 a.m.*

He groaned and tossed an arm over his eyes. After the fight with Lou, he'd booked a room at the overpriced hotel where Stu was staying, but he hadn't slept. There were too many questions that made no sense. Worse than that, there were some things that *did* make sense... and Rich no longer knew how to fit them into the linear structure of his life.

I'm a Buddha.

Rich jammed his elbow into the soft mattress and rolled to his side. Lou's claim was ludicrous! No one said things like that. No one *believed* that about themselves. *Did they?* His hands clenched into fists and he forced them to release, concentrating on slow, even breathing. *Sleep!* his mind ordered, but his body wouldn't listen. An image of Lou crying in the hotel room resurfaced. After an interminable amount of time, he peered at the blue numbers once more.

4:51 a.m.

He groaned in defeat. He'd be getting up in an hour and a half so he could meet Stu for breakfast. He'd tried to call his friend when he'd booked into the hotel, but for whatever reason, Stuart wasn't answering his phone. *Probably sleeping.* Rich didn't know how he was going to explain the sudden change of sleeping arrangements with Lou, or if he even wanted to.

"I'm a tathagata... an enlightened being."

Rich swore under his breath. He didn't want to think about Lou right now! Instead, his mind returned to the trial like a mouse on a wheel. It all hinged on one pissed-off comment that anyone could have said. *Anyone who knew what running Whitewater was like would've said the same.* The problem was, no one did. They all assumed that it went like clockwork, but the truth was, the lodge had been dogged by problems from day one. In fact, the only one who could possibly know what Rich was going through was—

Rich's eyes snapped open. "Jeff Chan!"

He clambered out of bed and rifled through his jacket pockets to locate his cell phone. Prischka Archer worked in the main Coldcreek Enterprises office in New York and Rich knew from experience that she was always first in, last to leave. He dialled her private number, breath held. Amid the preparations for the trial, and the conflict with Lou, he'd forgotten Prischka's message. The phone rang once and her voice was there.

"Prischka speaking."

"Ms. Archer, so glad I caught you."

"Richard? Is that you?" she said tartly.

"Yes, it's me."

"This is a bit early for Alberta, isn't it?"

"Yeah. Couldn't sleep, but figured you'd probably be in the office."

Prischka clucked her tongue. "Well, yes. You know me."

He smiled. Some things never changed.

"Prischka," Rich said. "I got your message yesterday. Is this about Jeff Chan?"

"Yes, it is." Her voice faded for a second, then returned with a snap. She'd just turned him off speaker phone. "I have some new information about him. Our investigator found the wayward Mr. Chan yesterday," she said. "I thought, given your interest in his whereabouts, you should hear that directly."

Rich couldn't breathe. His chest was too tight, the hotel room stuffy. "Found him *alive*? How? Where?!"

"The usual methods. He was located in Pittsburgh and turned in to the police. They had him in custody for a few hours yesterday while they took his information. Your lawyer, Mr. Callaghan, had a video-conference with him late last night, I believe." Rich blinked in surprise. So *that's* why Stu hadn't answered his phone. "I thought you should know before the trial started, in case it affects things."

"But they'll go after Chan, right?"

"From what Coldcreek's legal team has told me, Mr. Chan hasn't been charged with anything yet, though I'm certain he will be.

Coldcreek's team of lawyers will be pressing charges regarding the apparent embezzlement. I've been told your lawyer is going to request a delay in the arson trial. But then you'd know more about that than me." She cleared her throat. "Now, Richard, I'm rather busy this morning and—"

"Wait! Prischka, you made me an offer to help me when we last talked."

"I did, but I meant once the trial was *over*, of course."

"Yes, I know. But I want to talk to you about something that might affect the trial right now."

"Oh?" Distrust dripped through the single syllable. Rich took a steadying breath, his hand a claw around the receiver. He needed her to say yes.

"I know Coldcreek's relationship with Jeff Chan is tenuous."

Prischka made an unladylike snort. "At best, the fool was incompetent, at worst, a complete criminal. I'd say that's more than tenuous."

"I know that's an issue, Prischka, but I was wondering if you could give me Mr. Chan's contact information."

There was a long pause.

"To what end?"

"To help me fight the arson charges. To give me a chance to figure out my own situation. Mr. Chan is the only person who knows what Waterton is like. And if I could talk to him. If you could give me his number..." Rich closed his eyes, praying for the first time in years. "It would really help."

Somewhere on the floor above him, a shower turned on. The hotel's other guests were starting to wake up, the day beginning. The trial would begin in a few short hours and unless Stu Callaghan could convince the judge to delay litigation, Rich needed this information *now*.

Prischka's voice brought him from his thoughts. "I'll give you Chan's number, but only because *you're* the one on trial, Richard," she said. "But if anyone asks, you found the number yourself."

* * *

Hunter woke half an hour before his alarm. Two of his dogs were atop the covers, sleeping at his feet, but the third, Duke, had wheedled his way up to the pillows and his paws twitched in some imagined chase. Hunter didn't have the heart to chide him. He wished he shared the pup's peacefulness, but Sadie's subpoena had torn that away.

The windows beyond his second floor bedroom were a dull gray, the pale gleam of the streetlamps on the street beyond. Hunter rolled to his side. All three dogs awoke in a jangle of tags and flapping ears. Duke barked and jumped to the floor with a clatter, then danced circles around Hunter as he made his way down the stairs. Reaching the kitchen, Hunter pushed open the back door. He watched the dogs head into the shadows. It was a habit—deer hated dogs—and Duke had narrowly escaped being stomped when he was a pup. But today the yard was empty. In minutes they were back in the kitchen.

On most days, Hunter would have started his day with bacon and eggs—half for him, half for them. The three mutts waited patiently on the floor beside him, lines of drool announcing their anticipation. Rather than reaching for the frying pan, Hunter tucked a granola bar in his pocket, and headed for the front door. Three sets of drooping ears perked up in surprise. Duke whined.

"Not makin' breakfast today," Hunter said. "C'mon then." The second he touched the lock, they were off in a rush: bounding, barking, whining in the backs of their throats.

"Enough, enough," Hunter said. "Nobody's leavin' you behind."

The truck was already packed. A bagged lunch and a canteen of water sat on the front seat. Hunter slid his feet into his hiking boots and picked up the rifle case from beside the door, then took one last look back into the cabin. It wasn't the first time he'd had to step out of the way of approaching danger and he suspected it wouldn't be the last. Still, it bothered him.

"Stop thinkin' about it and get doin' it."

Duke's barks revived him. Hunter gave a wan smile, and tugged open the door amid a cacophony of howling. In minutes, two of his dogs were in the cab of the truck. Hunter glanced behind him at the empty porch. The youngest was nowhere to be seen.

"Goddamnit, Duke!"

Hunter turned in a circle as he searched the bushes for the way-ward hound. With the tourists gone, the streets were bare. Cabins empty. "Duke!" Hunter shouted. "Duke, you git over here!" He lift-ed his fingers to his mouth and whistled shrilly.

A dog barked in the distance. Hunter squinted. The cougar hound had run over to the Old Pattison place yet again, his usual haunt. Hunter swore under his breath as he climbed into the cab of the truck. He rolled down the window, shouting as the vehicle ambled down the street. "C'mon, Duke! Let's go!"

The dog waited on the porch next to the 'for sale' sign. He barked happily and pawed at the closed door.

"Stupid dog," Hunter said with a smile. He popped the truck into park and opened the door wide. Duke scratched frantically at the cabin door. "C'mon, Duke," Hunter said, walking across the lot. "It's time to go. He's not here."

Duke turned back around, looking longingly from Hunter, to the house, and back again.

"Gotta go, boy," Hunter said. "It's time for a drive."

The words were magic. Duke tore off the empty porch in a skittering rush. He bounded across the lawn and launched himself through the open door of the vehicle. By the time Hunter got back inside, Duke was jumping from floor to seat with an energy Hunter admired.

"You're a good dog," Hunter said and Duke barked in reply. "Thick as a post some days, but a good dog all the same."

The other dogs leaned in, and Hunter patted them each in turn. Outside, the horizon had begun to bruise purple with the first hint of coming dawn.

It was time to run.

* * *

Jeff Chan didn't answer his phone the first time Rich called. It went to a busy signal the second and the third. Frustrated, Rich programmed the number into his cell phone and jogged down to the main entrance to meet Stu. The lawyer was already on the phone when Rich reached his side. Stu's expression told Rich what he already feared: there would be no delay to the arson trial.

Opening statements began at nine o'clock, and the prosecution's lawyer, Glen Asharif, launched immediately into his case. "Your jobs, ladies and gentlemen, is to consider this evidence and decide whether or not Mr. Evans is, indeed, guilty of the crime of arson."

According to Asharif's timeline, Rich planned the arson after two wings of the Whitewater were closed down by the building inspector. Unable to deal with the fallout from the murder scene and the potential ruin of the hotel, Rich had supposedly committed arson in order to claim insurance monies to rebuild. Rich, according to the lawyer, had pulled the fire alarms to get all the guests out, not expecting Amanda Sloane to stay inside. He'd then gone downstairs to tamper with the gas lines under the hotel's main building. The arson investigation showed that a pilot light had likely been the source of ignition. It had caused a chain reaction as the gas lines ignited. With the exception of the digital alerts of the fire alarms set *prior* to the explosion, all evidence had been destroyed.

Rich scowled. The problem was that Glen Asharif made it sound entirely plausible. Rich *had* made the half-hearted joke about razing the Whitewater to the ground, and the server, Grace Blessington, had reported that to the police. Rich caught sight of her sitting with the other witnesses. Feeling Rich's attention on her, Grace lifted her eyes, then quickly looked away. Rich scanned through the rest of the group, finding, not surprisingly, Hunter Slate missing.

Asshole decided not to show up!

Audrika Kulkarni sat next to Mila; Grant McNealy and Sam Barton on either side. Susan Varley was there too. *A witness for the prosecution!* She glowered at him from across the room. Next to her were two unfamiliar men and at the very end of the group sat Lou. Rich's chest tightened as their eyes met. Her face was pale, eyes bloodshot, as if the pain she felt had taken root in her body.

Rich brought his attention back to the front. He didn't have time for this—*for her!*—right now.

Three hours passed before the judge called an end to the morning session. Rich strode into the hallway, intending to call Chan's phone number. A voice shouted out from the other end of the corridor: "Rich! Can we talk?"

He peered over his shoulder to see Lou approaching. He turned his back on her and dialled. The phone rang and Rich held his breath.

It connected.

"Hello?"

"Hi," Rich said. "Can I speak with Jeffrey Chan?"

"You've got him."

Rich looked back over his shoulder. Lou was gone.

"Mr. Chan, this is Richard Evans, from the Whitewater Lodge... or at least I *was* from the Whitewater. Coldcreek released me from my position a couple weeks ago."

The phone filled with unexpected laughter. "Released... fired," Jeff said. "Good to know I'm not the only one they screwed over."

"I'm actually calling about the Whitewater..." Rich provided the ex-manager with an abbreviated summary of events. "And I was wondering if you could tell me anything that happened while you were there: about Borderline and Colton Calhoun, or the troubles around town. Anything that might have *worried you* during your tenure."

"I told your lawyer yesterday," Chan said. "The thing with the loan was Whitewater's issue, not mine. I'm not being the fall guy for that."

Up the hallway, Rich could see Stu looking for him, but he stepped into an alcove, unwilling to end the conversation. "I've got a roomful of people ready to put me in jail for something I didn't do," Rich said. "I know it's a long shot, but I thought maybe you'd be able to help."

"Not gonna testify," Jeff said shrilly. "No fucking way! Coldcreek is already after me. You can talk to my lawyer, you can—"

"I'm not asking you to testify. I just want to know what happened when you were there. I mean, why co-sign that loan with Borderline? Why leave with no word to anyone? It was the middle of winter, you hadn't—"

"The place was a money pit!" Chan said. "Everything I tried to finish ended up costing more. And then there was Archer breathing down my neck. God! I couldn't stand it!"

"Know what you mean."

"Not just her, I mean the townspeople too. They were fucking crazy!"

"They don't care for outsiders."

"That's putting it lightly," Jeff said. "I mean they *did things!* There was an animal… found it dead on my porch! Ripped right open, throat slashed. And footprints in the snow!" Rich's eyes widened. *There had been footprints around the cabin when he had been there too.* "And then my dog disappeared!" His voice had reached a fever pitch. "Motherfuckers just wanted me out. They *loved* every setback to the hotel."

"They tried to push you out of town?"

"More than that. I was *warned* that I needed to leave. Get out or else!"

Rich's hands were clammy. "Who?! Who warned you?"

"Hunter Slate," Jeff said bitterly. "Showed up on my fucking porch in the middle of the night. Told me he just wanted to talk. Said there were people who wanted me gone. That if I knew what was good for me, I'd listen to him… that I was in danger." His voice broke. "They took my fucking *dog*, Rich! Do you get that?! Took Tucker right off his chain in my yard! I loved that dog!"

The hallway started to empty. Rich could see Stu at the far side of the corridor, but he didn't put down the phone.

"Hunter said you were in danger. Danger from what?"

"Not what… *Who.*"

"Colton Calhoun," Rich breathed.

"Him too, but not *just* Colt. It was *all* of them. The locals hated me! Every goddamned one."

Stuart caught sight of Rich and waved. "Calhoun owned Borderline, but why would the others want you out?"

"Jesus, man! Haven't you figured it out yet?" Chan laughed. It was an eerie sound, high-pitched and unnerving. "Waterton's full of people from other places, and a lot of them don't want to be found. You mess with them, they're going to bring you down. Place as barren as the Rocky Mountains? There's a hell of a lot of places to hide a body."

Stu strode forward, his face flushed. "Rich!" he bellowed. "We've got to meet before the afternoon session begins. Get moving!"

"So what do I do?" Rich asked.

"If I were you, I'd take off and not look back."

* * *

Sadie stood at the billboard with a black marker in hand, her face grim as she examined the list of names. The door to the office swung inward with a squeal and she looked over her shoulder to see Jim Flagstone balancing a pile of envelopes.

"More warrants today," Jim said. "Looks like we've got…" He rifled through them. "Peter Long Time Squirrel, Hunter Slate, Mrs. Lu and the Mileses."

"Not sure Hunter's in town right now."

"Why's that?"

Sadie tapped the marker against her pants in irritation. The first results for prints had arrived that morning. A black line now cut through the names of Walter Phillips, Elaine Decker and Sam Barton, their prints cleared of any connection to the Whitewater break-in.

"I served him a subpoena the other day," she answered distractedly. "He's a witness in the arson trial. Hunter probably headed into Lethbridge last night."

"You certain? I'm pretty sure I saw his truck in town this morning."

Sadie's head jerked up. "You saw *what?!*"

"He was in his truck. Had a bunch of dogs in the cab, gear in the back. Looked like he might have been headed out of town for a while."

"That *bastard!* He's not going to respond to the subpoena!"

Jim handed her the warrant. "Then let's get him before he leaves."

CHAPTER TWENTY-ONE

When Hunter reached the ranch, Levi was loading the last horse into the trailer. Guilt rose inside him. Levi Thompson was past eighty, but he put men half his age to shame for a day's work.

The Thompson ranch was neat and tidy despite its advanced age. Like a faded photograph, it hinted at another era. Once, long ago, Levi'd been a young man with a wife, a handful of daughters and one, much-loved son. All of that had disappeared in the intervening years: the girls married and moved far away, his wife was buried in the family plot near Glenwood, and his son, taken by the hand of fate before he'd reached adulthood.

The dogs whined as Hunter drove across the graveled drive toward the barn. He eased to a stop by the doors and climbed out. The paint on the building was peeling, but otherwise it looked much the same as the day Hunter had first visited the ranch decades earlier, when he'd been a green kid, straight out of college. Hunter had worked with Levi that long-ago summer, mucking out the stables without complaint while he earned the seed money for Hunter's Coffee Shop. Hunter was known for his good temperament and easy way with people, but his expression today was anything but.

"You're right on time!" Levi said, grinning. "Ready to go?"

Hunter lifted his eyes to the horizon. Grey clouds skudded the sky to the north, but otherwise the day was bright and clear. He was on the run again, but this time he was grateful to have Levi at his side.

"Ready as I'll ever be."

* * *

Constable Flagstone knocked on the cabin door a third time, his ears attuned for sound. The house was silent. With a sigh, he dropped his hand and headed down the stairs.

It had been a morning of disappointments, Flagstone's bad mood rising with each one. They'd started at Hunter's Coffee Shop, but the windows had been boarded up, the requisite "closed for the winter" sign in place. They'd hoped to find Hunter at home, but his cabin was equally barren.

Reaching the police car, Jim saw that the cab was empty. "Sadie?" he called.

"Over here!"

He followed her voice around the side of the house where she stood next to the gate.

"Hunter's not at home," Jim said. "His truck's gone."

"So are his dogs."

Jim swore under his breath. The warrants were supposed to make things easier, but that only worked if they had the people to talk to.

Sadie drummed her fingers along the fencepost. "Jim, you like to hunt, right?"

"Yeah."

"When does hunting season start?"

"Moose and whitetail are open now, the season for bighorn sheep is just beginning."

"That's it!" She sprinted toward the police cruiser. "I know where he is."

"Where?"

Sadie pointed to the horizon. "Levi Thompson's ranch. I'm willing to bet my next paycheque the two of them are headed into the mountains to hunt."

* * *

Susan Varley and Audrika Kulkarni waited on the higher level of the two storey corridor which stretched from one side of the Lethbridge courthouse to the other. As opposite as night and day, there was an unspoken intimacy between the pair, but it was born out of decades of familiarity rather than goodwill. Audrika peered down with sharp eyes as yet another Waterton businessman came through the security gates. She leaned toward Susan as the queue ended.

"Told you he wouldn't show up," Audrika said.

"I'm sure Hunter's got a good reason for not coming. He always does."

"Mmph… Maybe so, but the judge isn't going to see it that way."

Susan's expression darkened.

"What?" Audrika laughed. "It's the truth, dear."

"The truth is that Rich Evans burned that building to the ground. Hunter or no Hunter, Evans'll get exactly what he deserves."

"Yes, he likely will."

"No thanks to you," Susan said.

"What's that supposed to mean?"

Susan put her hands on her hips as she loomed over the other woman. "What goes around comes around."

"Pfft! You're just mad I sided with Evans last summer."

"Of course I am!"

"What difference is it to you?"

"The difference is the town," Susan said. "Hunter's not here because he sees it too. A change is coming to Waterton and Richard Evans' trial's not going to stop the progress."

Audrika gave her a cat's smile. "Maybe. Maybe not. Change isn't always bad. I've been thinking of bringing a motion for a new business lease myself."

"You wouldn't!"

"Oh, but I would. With the Whitewater gone, there's room for the town to grow."

Susan paled. "But…but you fought against building the Whitewater as much as anyone else. I remember you and Chan going at it during the Chamber of Commerce meetings."

"Mmm… yes. But Richard Evans is a very different sort of man than Chan was. I'm not foolish enough to ignore that. If the trial goes in his favour, I might see if he wants to go in with me on my new project."

"You're the only one who ever liked Rich Evans!"

"I don't like him. I just respect a good businessman when I see one. Even *you* must understand that," Audrika said. Louise Newman appeared at the far end of the corridor and she narrowed her gaze. "My… my… Now that I did *not* expect."

Susan tipped her glasses up to increase their power and searched the hallway for the object of Audrika's attention. "Who is it? Who's here?"

"Louise just arrived…" Audrika's smile widened hungrily. "But she came in alone."

* * *

Jim followed the perimeter of the ranch house all the way around, meeting up with Sadie on the other side.

"Front's shuttered," she panted. "And the gate to the paddock's locked."

"Windows on the back have the shutters up, too," Jim said. "Some fresh tire tracks in the mud near the Texas gate. A truck pulling a trailer if I had to guess."

"That bastard!"

Jim gestured up the road toward the hamlet of Mountain View. "You want to see if any of the neighbours know where—"

"They're already gone! No use wasting more time here."

She stalked back into the police cruiser and slammed the door with a ferocious bang. Jim could hear her shouting into the car's CB receiver, the Pincher Creek dispatcher answering in crackling tones. He waited outside. Sadie was in a mood today, and in their years of working together, he'd learned that at times like this, staying out of range was the best policy. After a few minutes, she clicked off the radio and returned the receiver to its mount.

"Done," she said.

Jim pulled open the door and climbed inside. "Everything okay?"

"Getting better and better."

"Oh?"

"I contacted the RCMP. Levi and Hunter are gone for now, but they'll have to come back sometime, and when they do, the entire Pincher Creek police force will be watching for them."

* * *

The two men left the courthouse side by side. Rich stared into the street as Stu reached into his pocket, pulled out a crumpled pack of cigarettes and tapped one into his palm.

"Pretty good day," he said, lifting the cigarette to his mouth and cupping the end so he could light it in the wind. "Susan Varley's testimony didn't help, but the cross examination smoothed most of that out." Stu took a long drag, the ember flaring bright. "By the time I'm done, the prosecution isn't going to have a leg to stand on."

Rich nodded. He didn't have the lawyer's confidence, but it wasn't that; it was everything else that left him unsettled.

"Do you and Lou want to do something for dinner tonight?" Stu said. "I have a few things I want to prepare for tomorrow, but I could spare an hour or two."

"I um… I dunno."

"You sure? I mean you gotta eat, right?"

"Maybe."

"Or maybe you just want to keep Louise all to yourself," Stu said. "You've got it bad, my friend. Real bad."

Rich squinted into the afternoon sunlight. Lou appeared at the main courthouse doors and she lifted her head as she caught sight of them.

"If it's okay with you, I'll just head off tonight." Rich said. "And thanks for everything, Stu. Seriously, man. I owe you one."

Stu slapped him on the back. "No worries. You'll get my bill, but in the meantime, relax, Rich. I've got this covered."

"Thanks. I appreciate it."

Stu headed to his rental car and Rich made a beeline to Lou's side. "The private eye for Coldcreek found Jeff Chan," he said. "That's why Prischka called."

Lou's eyes widened.

"I talked to Mr. Chan today," Rich said. "He told me things about Hunter Slate."

"Hunter?"

"Yeah, Hunter. Chan told me that Hunter warned him to leave last fall. Told him it was dangerous to stay in town."

Lou's expression was aghast, her lips parted in horror. Rich's hand lifted, as if on its own, and he forced his fists deep into his pockets.

"Hunter's the arsonist, isn't he?" he said. "That's why you didn't want him here. That's why you're protecting him."

"He's not," Lou said. "I promise you he's not."

"Then why didn't you want him coming to court? Why ask Stu to leave Hunter out? You're protecting him and I want to know why!"

"I could tell you, but it's a long, long story."

"Lucky for you, I've got nothing but time."

* * *

Rich hadn't known what Lou meant when she'd asked the server for a traditional room at O'Sho's. The back section of the sushi restaurant was arranged to create private eating cubicles complete with low tables and tatami mats; they sat cross-legged on the floor, the voices of the other patrons muffled by dividers. She seemed at ease, her legs crossed neatly under her, whereas Rich felt out of place. He peeked up at her between bites and wondered how much of Lou's calm was an act. Rich was no longer angry, but the thing she'd claimed was huge. It *changed* things.

"You said you'd explain," he said.

"I don't know where to start."

"Just tell it like it is," Rich said. "I'm listening."

Lou sighed. "It's not that easy. It's… it's complicated."

Rich's annoyance slipped down a notch. She looked fragile tonight, and that just wasn't *Lou*. "So tell me a story instead."

"What do you mean?"

"Just make it into one of your stories. Tell it to me like that."

Lou took a slow breath; lines of concentration marred her forehead. After a long moment, she began. "Once, many years ago, there was a great war. It raged for years, becoming bigger than anyone had ever imagined, until the war itself became a god, a great death machine, eating all the children of the lands which fought."

"What war?" Rich asked, but her story flowed over his words like a stream.

"Now as the war dragged on, the God of Death grew stronger and began demanding sacrifice. None of the people who lived in the land wanted their children to die, so a lottery was developed. Letters would appear in mailboxes, demanding certain children be given." Louise dropped her voice. "And whether or not those children wished to go to war—*whether they believed in death or not*—they had to go. It was the law of the land."

"The letters," Rich said. "You mean like a draft?"

Lou's words stumbled. "My father and his best friend were children when the war began. They grew up under the shadow of the death machine and its tithe. They knew the stories of those who'd been called to serve and never returned, and they decided to serve life instead. To work against the God of Death. The two of them joined with others, arguing against the war. They came of age in that time, teaching friends and neighbours, siblings and school friends, that there were other ways to fight. That everyone had the choice to decide whether they'd serve Death or Life."

"Your father was an American... Vietnam?"

Lou gave a barely perceptible nod. "And then one day, my father received his own letter. He was twenty years old, and scared, but he knew that he'd never fight. It was never in his nature to kill, but that's what the God of Death demanded... and so he did the only thing he could think of." Lou's voice broke. "He left his home and never returned."

"A draft dodger," Rich breathed. It was a term he'd heard used in American politics, but never really thought about. He certainly didn't know anyone who'd done it.

"My father came to Canada in the sixties," Lou said. "He moved around a bit, attended the University of Lethbridge for a time and applied for immigrant status. He was one of the lucky ones who was granted it. He came to Waterton in the seventies with a new history and a new name…" She smiled. "A new man."

"Your name."

Lou brushed his palm with her fingers and Rich looked down at their hands as if they held some secret he couldn't quite understand.

"Your father's friend," Rich said. "That was Hunter Slate, wasn't it?"

Lou moved her hand, but Rich caught hold of her before she could pull away. He looked at her, his gaze hardening.

"Yes."

"What's Hunter hiding, Lou?"

"Rich, please. That part isn't my story to—"

"I deserve to *know.*" Rich's fingers tightened around Lou's hand. "Tell me. Please."

"Not everyone was granted immigration status. Hunter moved to Lethbridge and worked odd jobs while he waited for his application to go through. He waited months and months. But two years after my father became a Canadian, Hunter's application was denied."

Rich sat up straighter. "So Hunter's an undocumented immigrant?" The man was so well known, such an edifice in the Waterton community, Rich hadn't even considered it.

Lou shrugged. "Everyone in Waterton comes from somewhere. He's not the only one with secrets."

Rich's fingers relaxed and he released her hand, but Lou didn't pull away. "So how do you know he's not involved in the Whitewater break-in or the arson? He warned Jeff Chan to get out last year."

"Hunter wouldn't break into a hotel. And he'd certainly never start a fire."

"I'm not so sure."

Lou squeezed his fingers gently. "I *know* him, Rich. He was a draft dodger, a pacifist willing to give up everything. He'd never do something like that. Not at the risk of people's lives."

"Maybe."

"Think about it. Hunter's whole life is here in Canada. If he were to be dragged into something like this—if he was exposed, taken to court or sent away, it would destroy him."

Rich weighed what she'd said. He believed Lou, but he wasn't certain about Hunter. People were capable of crazy things, and Chan had been convinced enough to throw away a high-paying and prestigious career based on Hunter's warning.

"Do you believe me?" Lou asked.

She watched him, her eyes dark and uncertain. Rich knew there was more in her question than this story. She wanted to know the rest of what they'd become, and whether he could accept her claim. Rich knew this, but he didn't have an answer yet.

He let go of her hand and reached for his wallet. "I need some time to think about things."

CHAPTER TWENTY-TWO

Days passed. The trial unfolded in a series of flashes, the arguments and counter-arguments blurring one into the other. From her position at the side of the room, Lou could see it unfold and her mind broke it into an intricate dance. The emotions of the jurors swayed back and forth, their decision too unsettled to call as the outcome neared.

Stu Callaghan was a better lawyer than Lou had given him credit for. He was thorough in his cross-examination of the prosecution witnesses, but focused on facts rather than trying to discredit them as people. When it came Lou's turn to present her information, Stu was polite and studious. He wove a clear line of events from the moment Rich left the Whitewater, to his arrival at Lou's garage, and his decision to spend the night at her cabin.

Then the cross-examination began.

Lou Newman had spent her life trying to see the good in all people, but Glen Asharif pushed her to her limit. She'd been answering incessant, accusatory questions for an interminable amount of time when the lawyer abruptly changed tack. Unable to pin down any difference in her timeline, he moved into her romance with Rich.

"You told the court that the two of you have been in a long-term relationship," the prosecution lawyer said. "Is this true?"

"Yes."

"How would you define 'long-term,' Ms. Newman?"

"Objection!" Stu shouted. "This has nothing to do with the whereabouts of Mr. Evans the night of the Whitewater fire."

The judge glared over the top of her glasses. "Explain your purpose, Mr. Asharif. "You're testing my patience."

"Of course," he said. "I'm just trying to determine whether the court might trust Ms. Newman's defense of Mr. Evans. She claims to be in a long-term relationship with the defendant, and I'd like to determine whether that description of long-term—" He turned to the jury. "Of which we *all* have our own definitions, might vary enough to impact her credibility."

The judge tapped her pen. "I'll let it stand... For now."

Mr. Asharif turned back to the stand and Lou felt his attention hone in on her. "Now, Ms. Newman, how would you define 'long-term relationship'?"

Lou glanced over at Rich. His eyes were angry. Next to him, Stu Callaghan whispered something and he nodded in reply.

"Ms. Newman?" Asharif said. "The court is waiting."

Lou cleared her throat. "I'd say a long-term relationship is one where both people commit equally to one another. It's one where the couple addresses each other's needs. Where they love one another, and make a—" Lou stumbled on the word. "Permanent bond."

"And you might live together?"

"Yes. That's right."

"And yet, if that's true," the lawyer said. "Why is Mr. Evans staying in a separate hotel room from you?"

The accusation hit Lou like a splash of icy water. *Now* she could see where he was going. The dance shifted steps as the jurors' intentions moved sideways.

"Objection!" Stu bellowed. "This has no connection to the trial whatsoever!"

"Objection denied," the judge said. "I'd like the witness to answer."

Lou frowned. "Could you repeat the question?"

"Of course," he said. "I want you to tell the court why Mr. Evans is staying in a separate hotel room from you, if, as you have claimed, the two of you are in a long-term relationship."

Lou forced every bit of serenity to flow into her voice. "I'm staying in a separate hotel because I didn't want to unduly influence Rich during the trial. I wanted it to be fair. To be just."

Asharif opened his mouth to argue and Lou's hand clenched shut. His mouth closed, too.

"I'm here as a witness," she said. "If I was near to Rich... staying with him, for instance, he wouldn't be able to focus on showing he's not guilty. He'd be concerned about me and my needs. It would divide his attention in two and I knew I couldn't do that."

Her fist released and Asharif spoke, his voice less certain than before.

"I-If... if that's the case," he said. "Then how can you..." He paused. The seconds dragged on.

"Mr. Asharif," Judge Pelletier said. "We're waiting."

His head bobbed. "Y-Yes, yes, of course. Sorry, let me rephrase the question." Lou smiled, and Asharif echoed her expression. "Tell me, Ms. Newman, how would you describe your relationship with Mr. Evans?"

"To put it simply, I love him." Lou turned her attention on Rich as she spoke. "When I met him, I never assumed that we'd end up together, but sometimes things in life don't work out as planned. He's a good man, and innocent of this charge. The two of us are happy… happier than I expected we would be." Her smile faded. "And yes, sometimes things aren't perfect, but real life never is. If I said things were perfect, you'd know it wasn't true. But I can honestly say that I'm closer to Rich Evans than any person I've been in a relationship with in my entire life."

Asharif nodded to himself as Lou's words faded away.

"Mr. Asharif?" Judge Pelletier said.

He didn't answer.

"Mr. Asharif," the judge repeated. "Do you have any more questions for the witness?"

The lawyer frowned in confusion. "I, um… no. That's all."

"Ms. Newman," the judge said, "you may return to your seat."

* * *

The first night, Hunter and Levi made camp near Beaver Mines, but the deer they were tracking disappeared before morning. The next day they moved to a forested borderland where Levi had connections with another rancher. The hunting would have been good if they were tracking elk. The whitetail, however, had moved on days before. After a disappointing afternoon of searching, they moved yet again.

Levi drove the truck and horse-trailer at a steady pace, ten kilometres under the speed limit, up the range road to Blue Lake. The area was tucked into the curved shoulder of the mountains between Pincher Creek and Waterton. Secluded enough to be difficult to access, but low enough that animals often over-wintered there; it was a place the two men had hunted before.

Hunter tapped his fingers on the armrest as he stared out the passenger side window. When the truck rolled to a stop, he lifted his gaze to the 'v' of brush-covered foothills on either side and the slope of misty mountains rising up in the distance. The landscape looked the same as in 1970. *Doesn't feel like thirty years have gone by.*

"There we are," Levi said. "Can't take the truck any further, but the horse trails are good."

Hunter nodded. They had reached the fence that marked the end of the Durnerin ranch. Levi pulled the vehicle to a stop and reached behind the seat for the two gun cases. From this point on, they were on Crown land which abutted the Park boundaries. Hunter climbed out and whistled for the three dogs in the back. They tumbled over from the side, yipping and barking. The youngest, Duke, took off up the road.

"Honest to Pete!" Hunter growled as Levi opened the heavy door of the horse trailer. "Duke!" he shouted. "Duke, you get back here, Goddamnit! DUKE!"

Behind him, Levi chuckled as he led the horses to the fence. He pulled a saddle from the back of the truck, smiling to himself. Hunter watched the dog recede until he disappeared over a hill, then turned back around.

"Bloody dog's gonna be the death of me."

Levi laughed as he lifted out the second saddle and handed it to Hunter. "That one's got more sand than sense."

Hunter swore under his breath. He lifted his saddle onto the first mount and helped Levi put his saddle on the other. The older man worked with an agility that surprised Hunter: tightening the straps before attaching the gun holster, canteen and packs.

"Not to worry," Levi said. "We'll find 'em once we hit the upper trail."

Hunter finished with the clasps on his saddle, and reached for the holster, attaching it securely. "Hope so... Or the damned mutt'll keep running until he gets to Waterton."

"Your fool dog," Levi said. "Where'd you get him?"

"A stray. Just like the others."

"Really? Looks purebred to me."

"Might be. Not sure." Hunter shrugged. "Problem with Duke is he likes to run. Can't stop himself."

Hunter slid his left foot into the stirrup and paused. *Not getting any younger.* With a grunt, he pulled hard on the pommel, swinging his right leg over and onto the other side of the saddle. Levi, twenty years older, was already on his mount. He clicked his heels against his horse's side and led him toward the trail.

"But you kept him anyway," Levi said.

"'Course I kept him. Had no other choice. Found him wandering around town last fall."

"You don't say," Levi snorted. "Might try callin' Duke the right name. Maybe then he'd listen to you."

Hunter harrumphed.

"Jesus H. Christ!" Levi laughed, slapping his thigh, "I knew it was you, you ol' coot!"

"Chan had no right to a dog like that!"

"That right? How d'you figure it? He sure was lookin' for that dog for weeks afterwards."

Hunter scowled. "Damned fool had that poor dog tied up in the yard day in, day out. I didn't take the dog off the chain, but when he ran off, well… I didn't return him, neither."

Levi's laughter rose into hoots.

"You wonder why Duke runs now?" Hunter said. "It's 'cause he never was allowed to run for all those long months when he was a pup. Chan mistreated that puppy! Damned right, I wasn't bringing him back."

"You dirty bastard," Levi said. "I told Chan I figured a cougar got his dog. You jus' made a liar outta me."

"Good. And I hope Chan believed you, too." Hunter kneed the horse, moving in closer to Levi. "Animals, they *feel* things, you know? Some people don't deserve to have 'em."

"Indeed, indeed."

"Anyways, Duke's happier now. He's just a little wild."

"We were all wild at one time. Even you, Hunter."

"I guess so."

Levi slapped his shoulder just as something reddish-brown appeared in the distance. Hunter lifted his field glasses to his eyes. Duke ran toward them, his tongue lolling out the side of his mouth, dust rising on the road behind him.

Hunter whistled through his teeth. "Well, colour me surprised," he said. "Duke's coming back."

"That dog better not have rustled up a bear," Levi said, his hand going to the gun at his side.

Hunter laughed. "Never know with him. Duke's been trouble since day one."

* * *

The jury had been out less than an hour when they walked back into the room.

Rich sat up as they headed to their seats. "That seems… fast."

Stu nodded, but didn't smile. "Don't worry, if this plays out badly, you can still go through with an appeal. Chan's reappearance should give you cause."

"You don't think—" Rich couldn't even say the words.

The next minutes stretched out for a lifetime. He turned to look at Lou and she smiled, but when he tried to return it, he found he couldn't. Everything balanced on a knife's edge.

"Your honour, we've come to a decision," the jury foreman said. Judge Pelletier nodded to him to continue, and Rich stopped breathing. "In the case of the Crown against Richard Evans, on one count of arson, we find Mr. Evans *not* guilty."

Rich took a ragged gasp, his head spinning.

Stu slapped him hard on the shoulder. "I knew it!" he crowed. "You're free!"

Across from them, Glen Asharif stared down at his notes in confusion. Rich stood up too fast and stumbled with light-headedness as he and Stu exited the courtroom. It felt like college again, the two of them against the world. Rich laughed as they hit the street. It was over. He was free to go!

"Congratulations," a voice said.

Rich turned. "Lou."

"I'm glad for you," she said. "Really glad, Rich."

"Thanks."

They stood too far apart, as if the bubble of space between them couldn't be breached. Seconds passed.

Stu glanced from one to the other, then frowned. "Do you need a ride back to Waterton, Lou?"

"Audrika already offered," she said. "But thanks anyhow. You did a great job today, Stu. I was impressed."

"Thanks. You too. You handled that asshole Asharif perfectly."

Lou's smile wavered. "Yeah, um… thanks, I guess." She lifted her gaze to Rich. "I'll see you around then."

She turned away without waiting for a reply and headed toward the line of vehicles that waited by the curb. Rich watched her until she reached Audrika's sedan. When he turned back around, Stuart was staring at him. *Furious.*

"What the hell are you doing?!" Stu hissed.

"What?"

"I've known you since we were freshmen, Rich. And in that time

I've seen you screw up every shitty relationship you've ever had." Stu shook his head. "Don't make me watch you fuck up the good one too!"

* * *

Lou walked away from the courthouse on wobbly legs. She'd been left before, but not like this. *Rich knew her.* There was nothing to hide behind when it came to him, no shade to protect her from burning.

"Are you alright, dear?" Audrika asked as she reached her vehicle. "You look positively ill."

Lou swallowed a stone of grief. "I'm fine," she lied. "Just tired."

Audrika smothered a smile behind her hand as she pulled out her car keys. Lou swallowed again and again. She wouldn't cry—*Not here!*—not where Audrika would revel in it. Lou wouldn't let anyone else know how she felt. No, she'd go home first, close the door of her cabin, and climb the stairs to her room.

Then she'd fall apart.

The sedan's lock clicked open and Lou fumbled for the door.

"Wait!" Rich shouted. "Lou, WAIT!"

She turned to see Rich sprint down the stairs of the courthouse toward her, a grin on his face.

"Well, now," Audrika said. "Mr. Evans looks like he's in quite the hurry."

"Yes. I, um… I don't think I need the ride after all," Lou said. "Thank you for offering."

Audrika muttered something that sounded like *"ungrateful"* but Lou was already in motion. She ran forward to meet Rich halfway. Lou laughed, her nose knocking against Rich's as they both moved in for a kiss at the same time. She could feel relief blur away the last of his uncertainty, his joy and confusion all twisted together. Underneath it was a deep well of love. It struck Lou that she no longer knew where her feelings for *him* started and Rich's for *her* began.

Rich pulled back, panting. "Let me drive you," he said. "I… I should have offered before. I'm sorry. I didn't think—"

"It's okay."

"It's not, Lou. I should've offered right away." His forehead wrinkled and he reached out, pressing her hands between his own. "Drive back to Waterton with me, *please*."

"You sure?"

He nodded, and Lou felt the last of his doubt shimmer once and then fade away. "Absolutely."

A news van drove up to the curb and a neatly-dressed reporter stepped out.

"We should probably get going," Lou said.

Rich nodded. "God, it feels good to be heading home."

Lou was comforted by his words as much as by the feel of him next to her. They walked down the street, arm in arm. "I'm glad you came after me."

"I had to." He leaned in, but Lou spoke before he could reach her lips. If they did this, it was going to be as equals. Truth was part of that.

"I didn't know if you were going to get past this," she said. "Not the trial, but with me and who I am… What I told you at the hotel."

"I know who you are. You're Louise Newman and I love you." Rich's hands tightened around her. "Whatever else you might be doesn't change it. And sometime I want to know the rest, but for now, this is enough. I love you, Lou. Start to finish."

She gave him a watery smile. "Thank you for that."

She was part of Rich's chaos now, and there was no way she was going to let it go.

* * *

Constable Black Plume sat at her computer, clicking through the inbox responses one by one. They'd received the last of the warrants this morning and the identification of prints was rolling in at a steady pace. With each passing hour, the list of suspects grew shorter, the answer nearer. Sadie clicked open an email and her face fell in disappointment.

"Andler's cleared," she said.

At the bulletin board, Jim scratched a line through her name. "Gotcha."

~~Siobhan Andler~~

Sadie scanned the rest of the emails as she chewed the side of her nail. "Margaret Lu's cleared too," she said. "Same with Ron Hamamoto, Murray and Arnette Miles, and Peter Long Time Squirrel."

Jim crossed off the names one by one.

~~Siobhan Andler~~
~~Sam Barton~~
~~Jeannine Barton~~
~~Elaine Decker~~
~~Ronald Hamamoto~~
Audrika Kulkarni
Vasur Kulkarni
~~Pete Long Time Squirrel~~
~~Margaret Lu~~
Grant McNealy
~~Murray Miles~~
~~Arnette Miles~~
~~Annie Parcelle~~
Walter Phillips
Sydney Roberts

Hunter Slate

Levi Thompson

Susan Varley

Eight people remained on the list, all of them friends and neighbours. Jim took in the grainy photograph of the Muskingum college protests, the picture of Randy Selburg in uniform, and the school picture of Catherine LaVallee smiling at him from the faded past. He forced himself to look at the last photograph of Amanda Sloane, her body a dark shape curled on a stretcher. Jim didn't like looking at it, but today he made himself see her. Disgust unravelled inside his chest.

Friends or not, one of the eight had done that to her.

"We've gotta get the rest of these prints," Jim said. "Any luck with Hunter and Levi?"

"Just checked. Pincher Creek dispatch hasn't seen any sign of them yet."

"So we wait for them to come back into town," he said. "But we get the rest of the suspects printed in the meantime."

"Audrika and the others won't be back until tonight. The trial just ended. Evans walked."

"Yes!" Jim said. "Knew it."

Sadie pushed back from the computer. "Oh, and Captain Nelson just emailed me for a complete description of Alistair Diarmuid," she said dryly. "He's *very* interested in anything I can remember about him."

"Finally realized they didn't have the right guy?"

Sadie stood and reached for her coat. "Nelson's not going to find the arsonist," she said. "It's not Diarmuid. I know it."

She stepped up to the board next to Jim. He gave her a sideways glance, bumping against her shoulder. "You *know* that, do you?"

"I've got a hunch."

"Uh-huh. And that is?"

She nodded toward the bulletin board. "The arsonist is the same person who broke into the hotel. I've thought that since the very beginning. We're close, Jimmy. I can feel it in my gut."

Jim's eyes drifted back to the fetal shape of the charred body and his smile disappeared.

"I feel it too."

CHAPTER TWENTY-THREE

Lou and Rich drove into the early evening light, admiring the bands of pink and gold that marked the outline of Chief Mountain and fanned the edge of the Rockies. They'd just passed the Lethbridge airport when conversation strayed into the territory Lou dreaded.

"So you always knew you were a… a Buddha?" The word tripped on his tongue.

"Not exactly. That was the word Alistair used. I just knew I was different."

Rich's face tightened at the mention of the man's name. "Different how?"

"I knew things," Lou said. "*Saw* things. It wasn't a question of trying… I just *was*."

"How'd your parents take it?"

Lou frowned as memories of her father pushed to mind. *"You've got a goddamned active imagination is what YOU'VE got, Louise!"*

"My mother was open to the idea of past lives," she said, "but my dad just… wasn't. I learned not to talk about it with him. With *anyone*, really. I learned to keep that side of myself apart. To close it up and put it away." She peeked over at him. "Until I met Alistair, that is. He understood me."

A muscle flickered in Rich's cheek. "That's why you two spent so much time together."

"Most people just don't get it. I haven't told many people about myself. Those who I did never understood."

He reached across the seat for her hand. "You told me."

"I did, but it took a long time to get up the nerve," Lou said with a weary laugh. "I've been keeping people out for a long time. It's how I cope with it… How I manage."

His fingers tightened. "I don't want you to do that with me. Not now. Not anymore."

"I'll try, Rich," she said through a yawn, "but there are things that make it hard… things other people have trouble understanding."

"Like what?"

"Little things I can push into being… or nudge the right way. Other things I just know, somehow, deep inside me, but can't explain. Neither happens very often." Lou smothered another yawn behind her hand. "I knew the year I went to University that I shouldn't be going, but I went anyhow. And all that fall I waited—waited every day, knowing something was coming, but not sure what."

"What happened?"

"My mother got cancer, but by the time it was diagnosed, it was too late to change it." Lou's lashes fluttered closed as the car's engine lulled her into a hazy stupor. "I hated myself for not coming home earlier."

"I'm sorry."

"It's okay." Lou's mind flickered between this time and that as her emotions ran like old photographs in the background. Her head bobbed and stretches of landscape disappeared. Her father's face flashed to mind, then her mother, Yuki, and then, strangely enough, Hunter Slate.

Where are you, Hunter?

"You can sleep if you want," Rich said quietly, "I don't mind."

Lou sighed, her mind drawn back to a memory that waited just below the surface. This was her life, years earlier. She yawned as her eyelids fluttered closed, two dark shadows against the white snow of her cheek.

"Just let me close my eyes for a bit," she murmured. "Then we'll talk…"

* * *

When the child awoke, her bedroom was heavy with the salt-tang of the sea. Loose tendrils of thought clung to her. Louise had been *someone* in the dream, but not the same someone she was now.

The idea scared her.

She rolled to her side and her lashes fluttered open to discover a tilted world: the dormer window of her second floor bedroom and the familiar bump of mountains beyond the glass.

"Home," she whispered.

In the fading echo of slumber, this place made sense where the dream did not. Her bed was warm, the sighing of the wind around the eaves a comforting rustle. Or maybe, Louise thought, it's not the wind at all. Under the breeze, there were *other* sounds.

Downstairs, her parents' voices rose and fell like the rumble of an approaching storm. Louise sat up. Her feet dangled over the edge of the bed for one second, two, before she dropped catlike to the floor and padded to the hall.

Their voices snapped into hard-edged clarity.

"He can't stay here, Lou. They'll come for him."

"They won't."

"His application was denied, wasn't it?"

"It… yes."

"*The RCMP will know that.*" Her mother's voice broke. "*I'm sorry, but he needs to leave. Tonight.*"

"*And go where?*"

"*I don't know. Just not here.*"

"*Yuki…*"

"*Where's the first place they'll look when he doesn't show up?*"

Louise tiptoed down the stairs, careful to stay to the side of the risers where the wood didn't squeak. She could see her parents through the triangular cut-out that led to the living room.

"*You're overreacting,*" her father said. "*It's just a few days until this blows over.*"

"*Not this time.*"

"*Why not? He's your friend as much as mine. If it was me—*"

"*Because we have a child now. A life!*"

Louise's father came to stand in front of his wife, the two of them shifting into a single silhouette. "*I could've been the one turned down. Surely you understand that.*"

"*Oh Lou, please don't say that.*"

"*It's true.*"

Their silence released Louise from her trance and she crept to the kitchen, then stumbled to a stop in the doorway.

A man sat at the table. He held one of Yuki's delicate china cups in his calloused hands, like a gemstone in the wrong setting. The stranger's head was turned to the side, eyes closed. Though the argument had returned, here in the kitchen, her parents' voices were barely audible. The stranger was listening to them, just as she was.

"Who're you?" Louise asked.

His head bobbed and his eyes opened in shock. "I… I'm a friend of your father's."

"Oh."

After a moment, she crossed the room, pulled a metal bucket out from underneath the sink and climbed on top. On tiptoes, she reached for a cup.

"You need a hand, short stuff?"

"Nope." She fought with the knob until a trickle of water flowed. "D'you?"

He laughed. "You could say that, I s'pose."

Louise filled her cup and stepped off the bucket. She took a sip of water. "Mama's mad at you. I heard her."

The man's smile faded. "Then you prob'ly shouldn't be down here talking to me."

"Maybe… but I like you."

"You do, do you?"

"Mm-hmm."

The certainty was a warm ember in the center of her chest. From the other room, the sound of her father's voice returned, a crack of thunder in the quiet, her mother's whispers following like rain.

"*I can't say no!*"

"*Why not?*"

"*Because I owe him!*"

"*Please, Lou. Take him somewhere else.*"

Louise dropped the plastic cup into the sink and toddled to the stranger's side. Much like her father, the man's face was both young and old at once.

"*Where?!*"

"*I don't know. But he can't stay.*"

"*I can't kick him out, Yuki. He's been friends with both of us too long.*"

"Daddy's not really mad," Louise said. "He's only yelling 'cause he's scared."

"Yes, he is." The man ruffled her hair. "Now, you should head on back to bed before they know you're down. G'night, Louise. It was good to finally meet you."

Louise smiled shyly. *He knew her name already.* "You, too," she said.

She tiptoed to the doorway to the living room, then paused. There were rare times that she could feel things caught and undecided. And there were other times (even less often than that) when Louise could nudge them into place.

"Please, Lou. I-I can't—This is hard for me, too."

Tonight Louise could feel her mother's terror. The man's whole life waited on Yuki's next words. Louise closed her eyes and the world winked into darkness. *Oh please, let Mama help. Let the man stay.*

Out in the hinterland beyond the living room and the house, beyond the tiny mountain town and the forest dark and quiet, Louise felt something click. She opened her eyes to discover her mother watching.

"Louise! What are you doing up?"

"I—I heard you and Daddy yelling. It scared me."

Yuki's brows drew together. "You should be in bed," she said, then turned to her husband. "Take him over to Levi's place."

"Do what?"

"Go to Levi's. He'll hide him until we can get the rest in order."

Her father's face rippled in confusion. "But I thought—"

"Do it now before I change my mind."

"Why in the world would Levi help us?"

Yuki's gaze caught on her daughter and the hair rose on Louise's arms. There was no doubt in her mind: Tonight she'd *caused* this choice. It frightened her.

"Levi Thompson owes me a debt," Yuki said.

* * *

When Lou awoke, it was night. The car engine alerted her to a change of place as the smooth highway switched to grittier pavement.

"Where are we..?" she asked groggily.

"Home."

She blinked in surprise. The mountains around them glowed ghostly white, the tires crunching on a layer of frost. From the peak of Knight's hill, the lake shimmered along the bottom of the mountain range, the Prince of Wales hotel like a doll's house, impossibly small by comparison.

"The first snow," she breathed.

* * *

Levi squinted up at the dark sky. "Storm's rollin' in. Tonight, most likely. We should head back to the truck 'n trailer."

Hunter turned the collar of his jacket up against the wind and glowered at the black line of cloud that marked the horizon. The horse underneath him danced nervously, its nose bouncing up and down in the cool air.

"Wasn't so bad the last couple nights."

"No," Levi said, "but the wind's changed. Coming from the north now."

"We could wait it out," Hunter suggested. "Move the camp into the trees. See if it leaves off."

Levi gave him a perplexed look. "You ever slept outdoors in a snowstorm?"

Hunter shook his head.

"Well, I have," Levi said, "and my bones're too old for it nowadays."

He tapped the horse with his stirrups and led him down the trail. Hunter waited for a long moment before he nudged his horse to follow.

"We'll get out hunting again," Levi said. "You just watch. Give the storm a day or so, it'll blow itself out."

Hunter didn't answer. For a time the dogs' barks and the horses' nickering were the only sounds. As they reached the treeline, fat flakes began to swirl from the sky. Hunter swore under his breath and hunkered down in the saddle. He shivered as a memory surfaced...

* * *

Hunter stood in the darkness beyond the glimmer of porchlight. His best friend since childhood, Lou Newman, stood on one side, Lou's young bride, Yuki, on the other. Their daughter, Louise, was fast asleep in the backseat of the car.

Backlit, a man appeared on the porch. He strode forward, a rifle in one hand. "What do you want?"

Lou cleared his throat. "I need your help, Levi."

"Help with what?"

"With my friend here." Lou gestured to Hunter and he stepped forward. Levi was tall and lean, like the imagined cowboys of Hunter's childhood matinees. He scowled down at the trio from his perch on the porch. The gun in his hand didn't drop.

"Hunter needs a job for a while," Lou said. "One that would keep him out of sight for a bit."

Levi's mouth twisted. "Why's that?"

"Well... you could say he's in a bit of trouble."

"With the law?"

"No," Lou said. "Just needs some time to get his papers in order."

"Likely story," Levi snorted before turning his attention on

Hunter. "You ever work on a farm, boy?"

"No, sir," Hunter said. "But I know hard work."

"Ever mucked out a barn?"

"No, sir."

"Ridden a horse?"

"No, but—"

"Don't need no city slicker wasting my time," Levi snapped. "Horses get spooked easy. Greenhorn like him—" He nodded to Hunter. "Wouldn't be much use to me at all."

"Hunter just needs a place to live for a while," Lou said. "Nothing fancy. Your ranch is out of the way. Safe."

"Safe for who? Not me."

"For Hunter," Lou said. "There'll be people looking for him until he gets his papers."

"Then keep him at your place."

"Can't do that. I grew up with him. Canadian Immigration knows that."

Levi crossed his arms. "He's not my problem, Lou. Don't owe him nothing."

"Levi, please," Lou pleaded, but Hunter knew it was useless.

For a few seconds the only sound was the wind blowing through the overgrown caragana bushes, the whine of an uneasy ghost. And then Yuki stepped into the light.

She was tiny, bird-like and Hunter had the sudden urge to step between her and the stone-faced rancher.

"I know a few things about debts," she said, her voice bolder than either of the men. "You want to talk about that, Levi?" Hunter felt a surge of love for her in that moment. The world might change, but Yuki never would. She was stronger than him and Lou combined. Stronger than any person he'd met. Stronger even than the love he had for her.

"I don't know what you're going on about, Yuki, but—"

"You know *exactly* what I'm talking about," she interrupted. "And that debt's not paid."

Above them, a cloud drifted across the moon's disk and the world grew darker. Hunter couldn't breathe. And then the cloud moved and half-light returned.

"Fine," Levi said. "But it can only be for a few weeks."

"Thank you," Lou said. "We appreciate it."

Yuki turned to Hunter and clasped his hand in hers. "I'm sorry I couldn't do more," she whispered, her fingers tight around his, "but I couldn't risk her." Yuki's eyes flickered to the car where the little girl slept, and then back to him. "You understand that, don't you, Hunter? I have to think of Louise's future, too."

"Of course I understand. It'd be the same if she was mine."

Yuki released Hunter's fingers as her husband stepped near. "Thank you."

Lou pulled Hunter into a bear hug, pounding him on the back. "Don't be a stranger," he said. "We're only twenty minutes away. Call if you need anything."

Hunter's eyes stayed on Yuki. *Twenty minutes.* An impossible distance with Lou standing between them. She smiled and turned away, heading to the car without looking back.

"Just sit this out. Let things simmer down," Lou said. He hugged Hunter once more. "Take care of yourself, man."

"I will."

"This'll blow over. Just give it some time."

"Right."

Lou turned and followed his wife across the yard; her frame was childlike against the giant canvas of night and prairie. "Thank you,"

Hunter called. "Thank you both!"

Lou turned back and waved.

Yuki didn't.

* * *

Hunter's memory flickered, summer night reversing into the sharpness of autumn. *Nothing's changed in all these years.*

Levi tugged his reins to slow his mount until the two men sat side by side. "Well, spit it out. You've got a burr under your saddle and I wanna know why."

Hunter gave him a half-hearted laugh. "Just don't want to head back into town," he said. "We have our deer tags. I was set on bringing down a buck."

"Liar. Don't think you can lay that one on me."

"What?"

"You put this trip off all goddamned week, then called me up on the spur o' the moment, saying it had to be right away. Don't try pullin' the wool over my eyes, boy. There's more to it."

"Haven't been called a boy in a long, long time," Hunter said, the first hint of a smile bracketing his mouth.

"You keep actin' like one, I'm gonna call you on it!"

"Thanks."

"Whatev'r it is," Levi said, "it ain't worth worryin' about."

"Sometimes things aren't that simple."

Levi waited for more, but Hunter's gaze had moved to the range of mountains where Waterton lay. If he ran this time, he couldn't go back.

"Can't be that bad. You're prob'ly buildin' it up in your head."

"Just something I should've dealt with a long time ago," Hunter sighed.

There was a deep sadness to his tone that reminded Levi of himself. He knew a bit about old grief, and the pain it caused. A memory of a child's face flickered like a candle in the darkness and Levi snuffed it out just as quickly. He patted Hunter's arm.

"C'mon," he said. "We've got warm beds and a bottle of rum at the end of the trail." Levi winked. "What could be better?"

Hunter whistled, and the dogs came tumbling out of the nearby brush. The young one, Levi saw in relief, was still with the others.

"Home by nightfall," Levi said with a nod. "And a good thing too. Bet the snow's already coming down in the park."

Hunter forced a smile and followed.

* * *

Arriving at Whispering Aspens, Rich and Lou stepped out into a magical landscape, the world reborn in white. Lou expected Rich would rush inside, but he stood in the darkened yard, closing his eyes and breathing. White clouds rose from his mouth and hovered in the air before disappearing.

"That *is* a great smell," he said. "Fresh air and water and pine."

"And snow," Lou said, grinning.

They dragged the suitcases inside with numbed fingers. The house was frigid, the windowpanes icy with cold.

"I'll bring in the rest of our stuff," Rich said through chattering teeth, "if you can get us some heat."

Lou headed upstairs. She cranked up the thermostat on the newly-repaired furnace and pulled an extra blanket from the hallway linen closet. When she got back to the bedroom, heat had begun to blow through the wrought-iron grate over the vents. Lou giggled as she caught sight of Rich. He was crouched on the floor next to the heat vent, holding his hands out as if next to a campfire.

He gave her a rueful grin. "Back to winter already?"

"Probably not for a bit," she said. "Autumn's... interesting in Waterton." Rich stood, coming toward her. "You watch," Lou said, "it'll be freezing for a week and then we'll get a chinook, and it'll be as warm as summer again."

"A chinook?"

"A warm wind that comes over the mountains. It takes away the snow, brings the temperature back up again."

Rich laughed. "The weather here is crazy."

Lou grinned as his hands spanned her waist. "I dunno. I kind of like it." Rich worked his way around to the buttons of her shirt and pants, undoing them one by one. "It's part of the wild," she said. "Unpredictable sometimes, but beautiful in ways you never expect."

"Like you."

Rich's mouth dropped to her shoulder, sliding down to her breast. Lou shuddered at the sensation, her hands in his hair, holding him against her. His caresses had begun to overlap with the emotions in the room, desire mingling with feelings of love and relief. The unexpected mixture left Lou fighting for breath.

"Love you," she said.

"Love you too."

Rich dropped his hand under her knees and lifted her into his arms, then crossed the room in easy strides. If it had been another day, another person, Lou would have laughed at the gesture, but not now. Things had changed between them, and for the first time, Lou let herself be carried, engulfed by him, rather than watching from the outside.

Rich lay her gently on the coverlet and his mouth grazed her lips, cheek, and neck. Fire spread across Lou's skin wherever he touched. Tonight, her whole body and soul felt connected to him, a growing ache yearning to be quenched. Lou fought to keep up with the newness of her emotions. The sensation of being loved for *who she actually was* was so raw and intense, it left her reeling. Tears of joy prickled behind her closed eyes.

Lou whimpered and Rich broke the kiss, staring down at her in the darkened room.

"You okay?"

"Yes. I just… I-I love you."

Rich smiled. "I love you too, Lou. And I have faith in you." She took a sobbing breath. "And I trust you, too. I believe in… in *whatever* you say you are. Okay? I believe in you."

Lou opened her mouth to answer, but Rich kissed her, his attentions driving her fears away. With each second, the connection sharpened, sensations rising until Lou felt herself near the peak. The room and the sky full of snowflakes and the wintery chill of Waterton faded until it was only the two of them, the love they shared a bright swirl of flame in which they burned.

Lost in the riot of her emotions, Rich's voice filled her thoughts. "Love you, Lou. Love you so very much." His words were a cord and they dragged her back, tethering her to this spot, this time, *this man.*

For a long while they lay tangled together in the darkened bedroom. Outside, the moon rose, the mountains unnaturally bright in the reflection of newly-fallen snow. Rich's body was tucked around hers, his lips against her ear, his hand against her heart. And for the first time since her mother's long-ago warning, Lou knew that this was *exactly* where she needed to be.

* * *

Rich awoke under an oppressive blanket of heat, his back against the mattress slick with sweat. He opened one eye and took in the familiar bedroom with its framed pictures and patterned curtains. There were suitcases against the wall, clothing strewn on the floor.

Rich rolled to his side and caught sight of Lou. She was asleep, but she'd kicked off all of her blankets during the night. She had a sheet tangled over one leg and under the other. Save for that, she was naked, and the curve of her breast and the skin of her stomach glowed golden in the morning light.

Rich smiled and reached out to touch her, then changed his mind. Instead, he climbed out of bed, tiptoed into the hallway and lowered the thermostat. The furnace had been doing double-time all night. The window at the end of the hall was beaded with moisture and lines of it ran down the inside to reveal the world beyond. Rich wiped his forearm across the surface and his breath caught in surprise. A thick layer of snow covered everything like a frothy topping of whipped cream. The car in the yard had transformed and disappeared under its weight. Parked next to it, the fender of Lou's truck was bedecked with toothy icicles.

The window fogged as Rich took in the scene beyond the glass: the white mountains shaded with blue, bowed trees sagging under the snow's weight, the glittering lake reflecting a brilliant blue sky. Last spring, the late snows had been something to rage against, but this morning, looking at the scene from the second floor, the snow felt like a sign. A blank sheet of paper waiting for the first drop of a pen.

The rest of my life.

He smiled at the thought. He still had no idea what the future would bring, but today it felt closer than ever.

CHAPTER TWENTY-FOUR

Constable Black Plume strode into the police station and stomped the slush from her boots. "He's back!"

Jim glanced up from his desk. "Who's back?"

He'd just finished printing Grant McNealy and Walter Phillips. The cardboard forms with the blue fingerprints sat on the computer scanner, waiting to be sent for analysis.

"Levi Thompson," Sadie said. "His hunting trip got snowed out. Levi's at home now and none too happy that the RCMP just showed up on his doorstep."

"He wouldn't be."

Sadie grinned. "So are you ready to go?"

Jim flicked the fingerprint forms with his fingernail. "Still got to get a few more prints," he said. "Sydney and Susan, and both the Kulkarnis."

Sadie let out a heavy sigh and Jim frowned. "You need me to come along?"

"No, it's fine."

"If you wait, we could head out to Levi's together."

"Constable Ramirez is already out at the ranch," she said. "Levi's pissed, but he's not going anywhere. I'm after Hunter."

"He out there too?"

Sadie shook her head. "He wasn't with Levi when Ramirez got there, but I think I know where he went."

"Came back into town?"

"Bingo!"

"I could go past his house before I get the rest of the prints," Jim said.

Sadie headed to the lobby. "Nah, I've got Jordan for backup. I'm sure we can handle Hunter Slate." She glanced back at him and grinned. "Almost there, Jimmy. You know that, right?"

"I do."

She pushed open the door. Outside, the sun on the snow was painfully bright. "See you later!"

"Be safe, Sadie," Jim shouted, "call me if you need anything!"

The door banged shut before she answered.

* * *

The morning passed by slowly since the fresh snow kept most people off the streets. Lou puttered around the front of the shop as she found excuses to stay with Rich. She reorganized the candy first, explaining how in the fall she only bought the chocolate bars she liked.

"Why would you do that?" Rich laughed.

"Because they're the ones I'm going to eat over the winter. Food doesn't last forever. I keep what I can use and donate the rest to the food bank."

Rich went back to sweeping. Lou brushed her hands off on her jeans and walked toward him. "How about you? What're you doing this winter?"

He paused and his gaze moved to the window, then the shop and then her. *Waterton. Garage. Me.* The pattern felt important and she bit the inside of her cheek to keep from grinning.

"I dunno," he said. "I've been so wrapped up in the trial I haven't thought about it." Dressed in his *Lou's Garage* shirt, his hair unkempt and jaw stubbled, Rich Evans looked like he belonged here, and Lou wondered how she could have ever thought he didn't.

"I have a story, if you want," she said.

Rich's grin spread from his mouth upward until even his eyes were dancing. "Sure. I'd like a story."

Lou leaned against the counter and let her mind filter through the endless tales that would fit. She considered telling him about her failed year at university and how that had all led to this moment, but another tale appeared in her mind's eye.

"This one's an old one, not a story from Waterton, but a parable from many years ago," she said. "It tells of an old man who was walking along a river when a piece of the bank fell away. He tumbled into the water, the current carrying him downstream."

Rich reached out, and Lou put her fingers into his. He stroked the centre of her palm with his thumb.

"Now, the people who saw him fall were certain he was going to drown," Lou said. "The river was deep and wide, and there were rapids that led to a waterfall. People ran after him until the old man disappeared around the bend of the river."

"He drowned?" Rich asked.

Outside, a police cruiser drove past, the wheels spraying a layer of slush out to each side like wings.

"No, he didn't. By the time the villagers walked down below the waterfall," Lou said, "he was lying on the banks, his clothes drying under the warm sun. The people said it was a miracle, but the old man disagreed. *'I adapted myself to the water,'* he explained. *'I flowed with it, rather than against it. I didn't think; I just did. By moving like a drop of water, I was shaped and altered by the river, rather than bro-*

ken against the rocks like a wooden boat. By diving into the whirlpool, I was able to come out of it again, unhurt..." Lou squeezed Rich's hand, her smile softer than before. "Whatever you do," she said. "Whatever you decide, it'll be fine. You've already made it through the worst."

"It's been a crazy year." He laughed.

"It really has."

* * *

Constable Flagstone knocked on Susan's front door and shuffled uncomfortably in the ankle-deep snow. He could hear a country song playing, and the smell of cooking bacon wafted from the interior. It was a comforting smell that did nothing to put Jim at ease. His thoughts were on Sadie. She had Jordan on call with her, but it still bothered Jim to see her off without him at her side. He liked Hunter Slate, but lately—

Footsteps interrupted his reverie.

Susan's face appeared in the window of the door. She pulled it wide and wiped her hands on a dishtowel. "Morning, Jim," she grumbled. "You're up early."

Jim gave her a patient smile. Susan Varley was prickly; there was no other way to describe it.

"Sorry to bother you, Susan, but I'm trying to get the last of these prints done for the Whitewater break-in."

Her lips pursed. "Thought you and Sadie were done with that."

"We're almost there," he said. "Just a few more." She opened her mouth to argue, but Jim was faster. "I've got the warrant here with me. I'd be happy to show it to you if you'd like."

Susan rolled her eyes and stepped backward. "Don't bother; it's fine. C'mon in. I've got eggs on the stove, but I can pull 'em off."

Jim smothered a smile as he followed her into the foyer. Pebbles of snow dropped from his pant legs to the floor and he winced. "Want me to leave my shoes here, Sue?"

"Leave them on," she said impatiently. "I'll wipe up the water afterwards."

In the kitchen, the eggs had begun to smoke and Susan flipped them with a spatula. Jim waited for her to finish. He glanced around the room, taking in the flowered wallpaper dotted with framed photos, the small cabinet of silver spoons, and the Audubon Birds calendar hanging on the wall.

"Burned 'em," Susan grumbled. The spatula rasped against the bottom of the cast iron skillet as she scraped the blackened eggs onto a plate.

"Sorry, Susan. Didn't mean to be a bother."

She scowled.

"It's just a formality," Jim added. "You know how it is. Gotta know for sure."

Jim stepped closer to the wall and his eyes focused on a single photograph. It was an image of Susan Varley, decades earlier, a young woman at her side. Susan was grinning at the camera, her arm slung over her friend's shoulders. She looked… *happy*. Jim realized he'd never seen her like this before.

"I always figured it was Evans, you know," Susan said. "But I suppose you'll never know with the hotel gone."

Jim frowned, his eyes resting on the lone image. There was something gnawing at his gut. "Couldn't be him," he mumbled absently, "Rich Evans is too young."

Susan looked up. "What do you mean?"

* * *

Jordan stood in Hunter's kitchen, listening to the rising argument with growing anxiety. He was new to the force and had only been in Waterton for the last year. Conflict resolution wasn't high on his skill-set.

"...and if you *don't* let me take the prints," Sadie said angrily, "then I have a legal right to arrest you!"

"Arrest me for what?!" Hunter yelled. "I didn't DO anything!"

Out in the yard, Hunter's dogs howled in panic. Jordan's eyes moved from the man who paced the kitchen floor, to Sadie, and back again. Jordan hated confrontation. Hated being forced into the middle even more. Sadie and Jim usually went out together, but Constable Flagstone was tied up with fingerprinting and paperwork today. That left Jordan, as the third officer on duty, as backup.

"Look, Hunter," Sadie said. "You're NOT getting out of this! So either sit down and do it, or I get my cuffs and—" With a blast of swearing, Hunter stormed past Jordan, slamming hard against his shoulder. "Stop him, Jordan!" Sadie shouted.

Panicked, Jordan's fingers moved to the butt of his gun and then away again. He'd worked in Hunter's Coffee Shop when he'd been a teen. He knew him, *trusted him*! The sound of the front door banging shut broke through Jordan's panic.

"Stop!" he shouted. "Hunter STOP!"

Hunter's truck roared to life. The vehicle screeched past and fishtailed on the slushy street. Jordan turned to see Sadie on the porch, her weapon out and raised. Her eyebrows were pulled together as if in pain.

"Goddamnit!"

"I- I'm sorry," Jordan stammered. "It's Hunter. I-I couldn't..." His words faded and he stared at the tire tracks that led up the street. Sadie holstered her gun and checked the safety.

"Sadie, please. I—"

"That's it!" Her eyes widened and she jogged back into the house.

"What's it?"

Jordan followed her into a kitchen that echoed with the sound of frantic baying. He leaned a hand against the wall, adrenaline leaving him shaky. Sadie rifled through drawers until she found a long-handled wooden spoon, then turned back to the table. Hunter's breakfast plate was empty, bits and pieces of bacon and toast dirtying the surface. A chipped mug, half full of coffee, was at one side, an empty water glass and a fork next to it. Sadie put the handle of the spoon into the tumbler and slowly tipped it sideways until she was holding it without touching the surface. She walked to the window and peered at the smudged glass through the hazy light.

"You got the warrant there, Jordan?"

"Yes, ma'am."

"Good thing," she said with an angry smile. "'Cause we just got Hunter's prints."

* * *

Rich sat at the counter, leafing through a magazine, his attention only half on the pages. Lou was in the back room, putting winter tires on Walter's truck, a tinny radio echoing in the background. Outside the window, an engine's growl rose. Rich lifted his eyes and watched as Hunter's truck sped past.

The truck turned the corner and he looked back to the magazine. His fingers had paused on an article in the finance section: *Investing in Your Future.*

Rich smiled and began to read.

* * *

"He's too young?" Susan repeated.

Jim nodded, his eyes caught on the picture on her kitchen wall. It was a black-and-white photo, but he could make out a line of brick buildings in the background, a central quad laid out below the women's feet.

"Yes," Jim said, distracted. "That's why all the hubbub with the locals." His brow puckered in concentration as a burr of awareness tickled his mind. He *knew* this picture for some reason.

"But why locals?"

"There's a prior case linked to the prints, but the person who left them is older." Jim's gaze moved from young Susan to the girl next to her. His eyes flared wide.

It was Catherine LaVallee!

He reached for his walkie-talkie and flicked it on with his thumb at the same moment he turned. Susan stood behind him. The cast iron skillet slammed into his temple with a force that crushed the side of his skull, blood spraying across the wall and the photograph, the force taking him to his knees.

On the walkie-talkie, the voice of the dispatcher crackled. *"Constable Flagstone, that you?"* Jim crumpled to the floor, groaning. Susan lifted the skillet above her head and swung it down crosswise once and then again, destroying the remains of his face. *"Constable Flagstone, I can't make out what you're saying. Could you come in, please? Jim, are you there?"*

Susan slammed the pan down one last time and Jim jerked like a fish on a wire. A frothy pile of red bubbles surged up from the hollow dent where his nose and mouth had been, his features reduced to a smear of torn skin, broken bone and blood.

The walkie-talkie crackled. *"Constable Flagstone,"* the dispatcher said. *"I'm sending backup. Please copy."*

Jim's foot twitched and went still.

CHAPTER TWENTY-FIVE

Susan Varley didn't cry. Her panic was beyond that. She stumbled off Jim like a drunkard, the frying pan in hand. One foot slid in the pool of blood, painting a calligrapher's 'C' across the floor as she caught herself against the chair.

Susan's eyes were trapped on Jim's body. (She wouldn't look at his face. Not yet.) Jim's fingers twitched and Susan yelped.

"Oh sweet Jesus!"

She clambered to her feet, tremours rattling through her. She was light-headed. Terrified. Susan had felt much the same that night. *That night! That awful night!* For a heartbeat she was there again, the woodland of Ohio, dark and looming, a man's body beneath her. She remembered the unnatural silence after the deafening crack of gunshot. How the woods seemed to contract, grow still. Even the birds had been silenced. There'd been so much blood. Both the officer's...*and Cathy's.* With that thought, Susan's vision swam.

She dropped the frying pan on the floor with a clatter. Flecks of blood and brain clung to her and they dried in small black dots that tugged at the hairs of her arm. Her gaze lifted to Jim Flagstone, seeing what she'd done to him. His face was gone, a lumpy blood pudding in its place. *Jim was my friend.* Nausea took hold of Susan's gut, and she turned away, dry-heaving.

Susan ran a wrinkled hand across her mouth. She took a slow breath, throat catching at the warm smell of blood mingling with burnt eggs. *Gotta keep it together. Be smart. Keep going.* She turned back to Jim and forced herself to see what was left: Not him. Not a person. Just a problem to deal with.

The walkie-talkie buzzed.

"Constable Flagstone," the dispatcher said. *"If you're there, please copy."*

With trembling hands, Susan reached down for the holster on Jim's belt and took out his gun. She stepped gingerly around the spreading pool of blood. The floor was awash with it.

"Backup's on its way. If you can hear this, Jim, please copy."

"They're coming," Susan said.

She spun into motion, a blind need for survival taking over. She rushed from room to room, seeing things in flashes of understanding: too big to take, no time to pack, useless on the road. *Go! Take what you can, and get out!* She grabbed her purse, a pile of clothes, her medications, and the small stack of bills she kept hidden in her sock drawer. She flicked through it, wincing. With the stress of the previous summer, she'd begun to borrow from the pile. Now there was no time to regain her losses.

Swearing, she headed for the door. Snow had melted into water where Jim had come inside the porch and the sight of it stopped her in her tracks. Susan stared down at the water, throat tight.

"Jesus." The unbridled fear clawed its way back to the surface. *How much time had passed since Jim had arrived? Five minutes? Ten?* Susan didn't know, but everything had changed since then. "My God," she whimpered. "I killed him."

Outside the faint sound of a siren broke her reverie.

She banged open the door and stumbled down the steps on

trembling legs. The air was sharp, snow heavy on everything. Susan shifted the clothing to her left arm and fought to pull the keys from her purse. A pair of pants dropped to the ground, but she didn't retrieve them. She had no time.

Go!

The car door swung open with an ear-splitting screech and Susan threw the clothes over the back of the seat. She clambered into the driver's seat and turned the ignition. It started with a roar. Susan slammed the car into drive and shimmied as she pulled onto the snowy street.

Run!

Yes, she could do that. She'd done it before. Susan's mind flicked through the growing list of things she needed to survive. Reaching the turnoff for Windflower Avenue, her gaze dropped to the car's gas meter.

"Damnit!"

She had less than an eighth of a tank.

* * *

The first customer of the day arrived just after noon. At the ding of the pump's bell, Rich pulled on his jacket and headed outside. It was Susan Varley, her window already rolled down, face white and pinched.

"Fill 'er up?" Rich asked as he neared the vehicle.

"Yes," she hissed, "and hurry!"

Rich flicked on the gas meter, lifted the nozzle and opened the gas tank cover. He put the nozzle into the car and picked up the squeegee. Eyes narrowed against the bright sun, he moved around the car and cleaned the windows. The backseat was strewn with clothing, a number of prescription bottles tossed on the floor. The pump clicked off. Rich added the last bit of gas by hand, and replaced the nozzle on the pump.

He stepped up to the window and smiled. "That'll be twenty-four…"

His words drifted off as a whiff of perfume hit him. He wasn't sure why it affected him—the cold air, or the faint odour of gas, or the nearness of Susan at the open window—but Rich was suddenly back in the basement of the Whitewater.

He searched for the breakers, the flashlight in hand. The panel box was on the wall ahead of him, the door inexplicably open. "What the…?"

Something moved behind him in the shadows, and he spun, swinging the flashlight back and forth as he searched. "Who's there?!?" he shouted.

Something shoved against him, knocking him down, a crate overturning. There was a smell in the darkness: the faint odour of perfume.

In his panic, Rich had missed it. Today it was unmistakable. He took a step backward. "It was you," he choked.

Susan's chin jerked up. "What?!"

"In the basement of the hotel. It was you—you all along."

Susan's face twisted in rage; she reached across the passenger seat and popped open the glove box. A handgun tumbled to the floor.

Panic arrived in a flash of adrenaline. Rich sprinted into the garage and grabbed for the phone next to the counter. Susan stepped out of the car, gun in hand. Rich dialed. She raised the weapon and Rich dropped below the counter just as the front window exploded in a shower of glass.

"Waterton Police department, how may I direct your—"

"Susan Varley's got a gun!" Rich yelled. "She's at Lou's garage! She's trying to kill—"

A second gunshot echoed, another window bursting, and Rich rolled sideways, leaving the phone behind. Susan stormed through the door and the bell jingled merrily. Rich lunged for the far shelves. The door to the garage was there. He needed out!

She shot a third time. The hollow boom—trapped inside the garage—left Rich's ears ringing. He'd made it halfway to the door, but could go no further. Susan would see him if he stepped into the middle aisle. He looked around, searching for something to make a distraction. Somewhere, far away, sirens rose. He heard footsteps crunch on the broken glass as she headed toward his hiding place.

The interior door to the garage opened and Lou stepped inside. "STOP!" Rich screamed, as an explosion echoed through the room.

Lou slammed against the door, her blue shirt blossoming crimson as she fell to the floor.

"Lou?!" Susan shrieked. "No!"

Lou lay on her back, the smear of blood on the door obscenely bright. Rich was in motion even before the bell on the door chimed as Susan fled. Rich crouched over Lou and fought to stem the flow of blood.

"No! No! NO!!!"

Sirens rose alongside Rich's screams.

* * *

There were sirens somewhere in the distance, but Sadie was so happy she barely noticed. She strode into the brisk air, keeping the glass aloft with the spoon handle. In the cruiser, the CB radio buzzed. Jordan jogged forward, grabbed the receiver and clicked it on.

"Constable Wyatt," he answered.

Grinning, Sadie headed around to the far side of the cruiser, her prize in the air. She and Jim would laugh about this one, that was for sure. She reached out for the door handle just as Jordan turned toward her. He looked, Sadie thought in that split-second before he spoke, like a little kid. *Scared.*

"Officer down," he said hollowly. "We… we've gotta respond."

A shiver ran the length of Sadie's spine. "Who?"

"Constable Flagstone. H-he's dead. He's…"

Sadie's hand dropped. The glass fell off the spoon and splintered into a thousand pieces at her feet.

* * *

Susan sobbed as she drove, the road a slippery haze of white and blue. They hadn't plowed it yet, and the tires caught and slid on the melting snow. She could see Lou's face, her eyes wide in surprise. *That's what Cathy looked like.* Hot tears ran down her face and blurred the tire tracks she was following. The car shimmied.

"Oh God, Lou," Susan choked, "I'm sorry."

There were sirens in the distance and she cringed at the sound. The car's engine protested as she raced toward Knight's Hill, her foot pressing the gas pedal to the floor. She was aiming for the highway, and from there, for the U.S. border. She didn't have any family left alive, no friends to help her along the way.

Not like last time.

In 1970, she'd returned to freshman classes at Ohio State, certain that someone would find out. She'd stayed there for weeks, terrified, her grades dwindling. The day that she'd seen the police officers interviewing students on campus, Susan had walked to the Registrar's office, and withdrawn from school. With nowhere to go, and too scared to return home, she'd turned to other war protesters for help. A friend of a friend had given her a ride to Boston, and Susan had spent a year sleeping on couches, panhandling for money when things were good, stealing when they weren't. She grew up fast, the happy teen ground out under the heel of necessity, emerging harder and wiser. She'd learned how to disappear. Any time the police neared, Susan ran. Each time she went further, until she made it to the Canadian border with a work visa in one hand and an immigration application in the other.

When she'd arrived in Alberta, Susan had contacted the only person she'd known. A rally organizer she'd met once, years earlier: Hunter Slate.

No one will help me this time. This time I can't stop running.

The sirens grew in volume, and Susan glanced in the rear-view mirror. The road behind her was oddly empty. The car swerved and Susan's hands tightened on the wheel. Looking forward, she was momentarily snow-blind. Bright rays of light danced over the snowy hill. She was going too fast for the conditions, but she couldn't stop. Susan needed to get as far away as she could before the truth came out. She'd killed two people today. She'd go to prison forever for that.

The car's engine rose to a whine as it launched up the final stretch of the incline. Susan took a sobbing breath, the memory of Catherine LaVallee's bloody corpse on the forest floor appearing in her vision rather than the road. She blinked, and the memory rippled into the image of Jim dead on her kitchen floor. She blinked again, and this time it twisted into Lou on the floor of the garage, blood spreading in a crimson pool. Susan had killed the man who'd shot Cathy. She'd done it for the right reasons, and she'd never regretted it. But Jim and Lou were different.

"Why?!" she cried. "Why did you have to walk in, Lou?!"

As she crested Knight's Hill, Susan reached up to rub her tears away. When she pulled her hand away, the scene had changed inexplicably from white to blue-black, the sun-blocked out by an unexpected sight. *Time slowed.* Two vehicles blocked the road: a snow plow and an ambulance. The ambulance was directly ahead of her—in the wrong lane—as it attempted to pass the plow that was coming due west. The driver slammed on the brakes, sliding.

Susan didn't have time to think.

She jerked hard on the wheel and swerved toward the narrow shoulder of the road. A half-kilometre before or after this spot, there would have been a ditch to coast into, but here there was only the narrow band of asphalt, and then... *nothing.* The car hit a patch of ice as it reached the shoulder and it spun sideways. Susan slammed on the brakes and grabbed desperately for the wheel. The vehicle swung around in a circle, narrowly missing the ambulance. It hit a post. It hit a second. And then it launched over the edge of the steep hill.

The clothing, the gun, and the hastily-packed luggage tumbled from the shattered windows as the car went down. When it came to a stop, the only things left inside were the broken body of Susan Varley and a single photograph. It was of two girls who'd met at a Vietnam War protest on the grounds of Muskingum College in November 1970.

Both those girls were dead.

* * *

Alistair stared at the broken cup on the floor of the diner, his heart pounding. His mind was trapped in the space between the vision and the now. *Lost.*

"Sir," the server said, "did you cut yourself?"

Alistair blinked back tears, unable to speak.

"Sir? Are you okay?"

"I... I'm alright," he said brokenly.

She'd done it. Lou had embraced the moment, becoming one

with the chaos. Moving into it rather than away.

"Sir, can I help you?"

Alistair stood. "I need my bill," he said. "It's time to go."

* * *

Lou took a gurgling breath, her chest aflame. In the distance, she could hear the keen of sirens, but she couldn't understand why. She stared upward, blinded by the bright shimmer of light through the broken windows of the garage.

A bomb? No. That didn't make sense.

Gunfire, her mother's calm voice replied. *You stepped in the way to protect Rich.*

It seemed like she should be concerned by that, but she wasn't. Rich appeared and he spoke to her in words she couldn't understand. He leaned closer and placed his hands against the middle of her chest. The pressure sent a jolt of white-hot pain through her, another life appearing like an overdeveloped photograph in her mind.

Lou stood, broken spear in hand. It was time to run, but she didn't.

The attacker pulled back the silver blade and Lou ran forward, putting herself directly into the path. The sword slammed into her chest. Before he could pull it from her ribs, she jammed the splintered spear upward. The point dug through the soft underside of his chin and into the demon's brain.

The two of them slumped to the ground. The man was dead, but Lou lingered, her eyes on the brilliant sky as her life's blood fed the soil. She smiled to herself as the words of the village medicine man came to mind:

"Sometimes only death can stop death."

Lou coughed, her throat thick with blood. "Can't breathe."

Rich leaned over her, his hands pressed to her chest. "Gotta stop the bleeding," he panted. "The ambulance is coming. Hold on, Lou!

They're coming for you!"

"Can't—" she gasped, "-breathe…"

"I've got to stop the bleeding," Rich said as Lou gagged on a coppery swell of blood. "You're going to be okay. Just hold on!"

"No… I'm not."

Rich roared, his face twisting in rage-filled grief. His emotions were everywhere, shattering and refracting like the bounce of light through broken glass. She smiled up at him, her hand moving to cover his, where he held them over the wound in her chest. She could feel her heartbeat through his fingers as the blood welled between them.

"Love you," she whispered.

Rich's face was ravaged by tears, bloodshot eyes impossibly blue. "Love you too." His anguish drowned Lou like the liquid filling her lungs. "Please, Lou. Just hold on."

"I'll try."

At the edge of her memory, a lesson Alistair once tried to teach her pressed to be heard, but she forced it away. Lou didn't need it or him. She understood now. She knew the secret. By loving Rich, she'd finally joined into the turmoil that was life, learning by doing, *by living*. Her own words echoed in each fading beat of her heart, her love reflected in the eyes of the man who struggled desperately to save her.

"What's the point?" her father had asked her once, years before.

"The point is that we're not alive unless we also die."

Lou smiled. "I understand now," she said as the light from the window grew softly hallowed.

"What? Understand what?!"

She wanted to touch him, but the effort was too much. Her hand slipped to her side and fell limply to the floor. "I want to tell you a story," she said, forcing the words to come. "It's about two monks. A… a master and apprentice." She took a rattling breath and swallowed a mouthful of blood. "Each day they would have tea. And one day… One day… the apprentice went… to get their cups, but…"

Her chest rattled and went still.

CHAPTER TWENTY-SIX

The dream started with a sound: A heartbeat, going slower and slower. Louise sat in her mother's bedroom, Yuki on the bed next to her.

"Mom?"

Yuki touched Lou's cheek and smiled. *"You need to make sure you walk the right path, sweetheart."*

"Which path is that?"

Outside her mother's window, a cloud pushed impatiently in front of the sun, and the room grew dark.

"Whatever one you choose."

Her mother's words were interrupted by a sudden blare of sound. Footsteps pounded along beside Lou; lights pulsed overhead.

"Lou? Can you hear me?! The ambulance is here. Hold on!"

She felt herself stretch out like a fine piece of wool, each thread thinning until it could go no further. Brightness swirled in her thoughts like autumn leaves. One flickered and Lou fell into the colour, finding herself in another time, another place.

It was dim in the basement, the air filled with the musky scent of dying vegetation. A blond-haired boy crouched over a wood bin filled with potatoes. He clutched the hem of his shirt to make a bag, and as Lou watched, he pulled the potatoes out and set them in his shirt. "One, two, three, four—"

"Rich? Is that you?"

He spun around, his face bright with fear. "Five," he said in a shaky voice.

Lou watched, amazed, as he strode back to the wooden stairs and jogged up, two at a time. The cellar door slammed shut and another flicker of colour appeared.

This time she found herself in the dim confines of a shed, lines of narrow beds on either side. Outside the thin walls, a winter storm howled. But Lou's eyes were drawn to a woman who had Yuki's frame, but her grandmother's features. She leaned over a little dark-haired boy.

The boy turned his head and looked at Lou with wide, owl-like eyes. "Shiryō," he whispered.

Lou's vision contracted.

"Blood pressure ninety over fifty-six and falling."

One final flicker rose, a single yellow spark from a dying fire. She stood in a nighttime forest and the sound of children's voices echoed hollowly through the trees.

"Where's the path?" a boy asked.

"It's gone," his brother answered.

"But it can't be!" the third said. "I can see the lights of Waterton right over there, between the trees."

We're in the dark divide, Lou thought. *And we need to find our way home.*

CHAPTER TWENTY-SEVEN

For the first days after Lou was shot, Rich felt like he was living a nightmare. Any moment he'd wake up. He'd tell Lou about the dream he'd had and they'd laugh at the idea that Susan Varley could *ever* do something as crazy as that.

"Her condition is stable, Mr. Evans," a nurse told him by phone. "The surgery was a success."

"Stable," he repeated. "Right." Nothing made sense.

"They stopped the internal bleeding," she explained, her voice buzzing in the receiver, "but Ms. Newman hasn't regained consciousness."

"When can I see her?"

"As soon as you'd like. Are you in town?"

He didn't remember anything about the drive. He blinked on the snowy outskirts of Cardston, and when his eyes reopened, he was at the hospital. He left Lou's truck parked in a 'loading zone' and stumbled his way to the intensive care unit.

Lou was covered in bandages, her body a broken butterfly in a spider's web of tubes and wiring. Rich fell down at her bedside, sobbing. "Lou…? Lou can you hear me?" The machines hummed and whirred. Lou didn't answer.

Days passed. A week.

"It's too early to say whether or not she'll ever regain consciousness," a stern-faced doctor told Rich. "You need to prepare yourself." The words cut through skin and sinew, lodging deep in his bones.

"Prepare myself for *what*?!"

"For whatever happens."

"But Lou's getting better, right? She's improving."

The doctor tapped the chart. "Ms. Newman's body is healing, but we don't know what the outcome will be. The blood loss alone was a massive trauma. We are *cautiously* optimistic that she'll regain consciousness, but need to be prepared if she takes a turn for the worse. We're transferring her to a unit where she can be cared for long term."

A new pattern began.

Rich drove to Lethbridge every day and ran the garage each night. Without Lou, his life was torn in half. He fumbled through her house in a daze, spent sleepless hours in her bed, staring at the wall where her pictures hung. A tiny version of Lou grinned out at him from her father's shoulders. Rich wanted to warn her but couldn't. He dreamed of her each night. In them, he chased Lou through the darkened basement of the Whitewater hotel, the labyrinth of corridors morphing into his grandparents' root cellar. Lou would run further and further ahead until she was just a speck in the shadows, and then, in her passing, the last bit of light would wink out.

After yet another sleepless night, Rich rose and dressed in a daze. The dresser drawer had no clean shirts. He scanned the discarded layer of clothes which covered the floor like an archeologist's dig: before and after. He nudged dirty shirts and socks aside with his toes, frowning. Finding nothing clean, he turned to the suitcases, still packed from the trial, a week and a half—*or was it a century?*—

earlier. He shook them onto the bed in hopes of something clean.

An envelope fell from Lou's bag.

Rich opened it to discover the photograph he'd printed. Sometime since he'd given it to her, she'd written a note along the bottom. *A perfect day.* Sobbing, Rich crushed the paper against his chest as the truth settled inside him: The attack had broken him, and he'd never be whole again.

* * *

It was Sadie's first day of work since Jim's death and she was supposed to be filing the report on Susan Varley's fatality, but her mind was too heavy to write effectively. The Whitewater Lodge break-in and arson were officially solved. A floorplan of the Whitewater, including the identification of gas lines and the tools used for severing them, had been located in Susan's garage. There had even been a cryptic note from Colton Calhoun, agreeing to help her with her "project" the night the building burned. Captain Nelson was thrilled, but for Sadie, it was a pyrrhic victory. She massaged her temple, her eyes smarting after hours at the computer.

There was a nervous tap at the door. "You have a minute, Sadie?" the receptionist asked.

"Sure, Liz."

"I wouldn't usually bother you," Liz said, "but there's a couple people asking for you in particular."

"Who?"

"It's Hunter Slate and Levi Thompson."

Sadie's mouth twisted. "What do they want?"

Liz looked over her shoulder, took two steps into the office and half-closed the door. "Mr. Slate says he wants to turn himself in to you. He mentioned something about running off on you when you were trying to get prints from him."

Sadie gave Liz a half-hearted smile. She didn't want to relive that moment, but everyone kept bringing it back up. She took a slow breath as she remembered Jim's words from weeks before: *"I know these people, Sadie. They're all good folks."*

Sadie turned back to her computer. "Tell Hunter to go home. The case is closed."

* * *

Hunter's Coffee Shop was closed for the season, but a murmur of laughter and low voices echoed from the industrial kitchen. The back door was propped open with a dustpan and a line of cars and trucks cluttered the alley behind Main Street. In light of recent events, informal breakfast meetings had resumed. Some of the members who attended had changed in the last weeks. Old Ronald Hamamoto now sat in Susan's usual spot while young Jordan Wyatt took the place where Jim Flagstone used to be.

Rich Evans had a standing invitation but never came.

The meetings had once been used to prepare for the Chamber of Commerce, but that mandate had changed as much as the people who attended. Without Lou's calming presence, her legacy of compassion had been re-established in the actions of her friends. Today, they sat in the coffee shop's kitchen. They perched on high stools, mugs balanced on knees or set on empty counters. Two pots of coffee waited on the warmers at the side.

"We have to do something for Rich," Audrika said.

"Why?" Levi grumbled.

"Because he's wearing himself down to nothing," she said. "Driving to Lethbridge each day to be with Lou. He turns sideways, you can practically see through the man."

"Now, now," Sam said. "He's got Lou's Garage open a couple hours a night. That's a good start."

"Hadn't heard that," Hunter said.

"Sam Barton, you *know* what I mean!" Audrika snapped. "Richard Evans is *not* doing alright. Far from it! And I'm not the only one who can see it."

"Well, yes, I suppose not." Sam added cream to his coffee rather than meet her gaze.

"Driving into town to see Lou each day, then back each night to run the garage," Audrika said. "Never smiling. Never talking. If he doesn't start taking care of himself, he'll take ill. You mark my words!"

Levi put his mug down on the counter with a thud. "And so what if he does?! He's a grown man. How's he any of *your* business, woman?"

Margaret leaned forward. "I think what Audrika's trying to say is that she's worried about Rich… We *all* are."

Hunter nodded, but Levi just grimaced. "A man has the right to deal with things in the way he sees fit," Levi said. "He's an outsider. Not our concern."

"This isn't coping," Hunter said. "This is something else. Rich is angry. He's hurting."

Levi stood. "Rich Evans is NOT my problem!"

The rest of the group—Sam and Sydney, Jordan and the others—stared at him. Levi headed for the door but Hunter blocked his way.

"He's *everyone's* problem," Hunter said.

Levi raised his chin. "How d'you figure that? Man hasn't even been here a year!"

"Levi, please," Audrika hissed.

Neither man moved.

"You tell me why I should give a damn about him!" Levi said. "Man's been trouble since day one! The satellite dish last spring, the fire this summer, the arson trial. Christ! The whole damned mess with Lou was his fault. The way I see it, Rich Evans *breeds* troubles!" Levi jabbed a finger at Hunter's chest. "Let him dig his own grave if he wants to. Why should I care?!"

Hunter's face crumpled. "Because that boy is *Lou's*! And she might not be able to tell us to help him, but you *know* she'd want us to!"

The accusation hung in the air. The hush of the restaurant broke as a chair squeaked on the floor and Audrika moved to Hunter's side. "Hunter's right," she said. "Lou would."

Levi swore under his breath.

"We have to do something to help Rich," Audrika continued. "Closing himself away… never talking. This can't go on forever."

Levi's face darkened. "I don't owe Rich Evans a goddamned thing!"

It was Ronald Hamamoto, surprisingly, who answered. "Maybe so, but how much did you owe Yuki Nakagama, huh?"

Levi spun on him, ready to attack. Old Ron leaned heavily on his cane. The two men were matched in age though one was bowed and frail, the other lean and leathered. "You leave her out of this!" Levi yelled.

"Yuki never forgot what you did to her family," Ron said, "and neither have I."

Levi shoved past Hunter and Audrika and slammed his hand onto the door. Ron's words followed him.

"You ever pay her back? Or is this just another debt you won't—"

The door banged shut, cutting him off.

* * *

As Lou had predicted, the snow faded as fast as it had appeared. Autumn's gilded beauty returned to Waterton, but Rich remained swaddled in his cocoon of sorrow. He followed a cyclical pattern—wake, drive, visit with Lou, drive, work, sleep, and wake again—blind to the beauty around him.

The day that Sam Barton showed up at Lou's Garage, asking in hitched phrases, if there was "anything he could do to help out," Rich decided he needed a better excuse than: "I'm busy."

"You could come on by for dinner after you close up," Sam said. "Doesn't matter how late. We'd be glad to have you."

"I, um… I'm in the middle of reading a book."

"Alrighty then," Sam said with an awkward wave, "but the offer is open anytime, you know."

That night, Rich picked up one of the books from Lou's bedside table and flipped through it. Once he started reading, he couldn't stop; Lou's remembered voice was hidden in the words. After a sleepless night, Rich drove into Lethbridge with the book on the passenger seat in Lou's place. He carried it to the hospital room and read aloud while she slept.

"Long ago, there lived a farmer and his son. They were very poor and owned only one horse. One day that horse ran away. "What bad luck," the neighbours said when they heard what had happened. "Maybe," he replied…"

Exhausted, Rich fell asleep with the book on his chest. Louise dreamed of a cabin ringing with the laughter of children who had her black hair and Rich's blue eyes, and Rich dreamed of losing Lou in the basement of the Whitewater yet again.

* * *

It took Alistair a week and a half to drive back down the west coast of BC and along the highway's ribbon that wove through the Rocky Mountains. One week after the vision of Lou's sacrifice he reached the rippling foothills that spread east like a wrinkled carpet to the wide, flat sheet of the prairie. Alistair parked his car on the edge of the road and breathed in the scene before him. He wasn't in a rush, there was no need. She'd die, and his task would be done. It was just a matter of time.

Alistair shop-lifted food when he remembered to eat. He washed in irrigation ditches and slept in his vehicle. He moved whenever the whispering voice inside him warned that danger was near. They were looking for him. Alistair knew this as clearly as he knew that Lou would die. *She had to.* That was the end of her story. Alistair expected as he woke each day that *this* day would be the one when he finally felt the thread of connection break.

It never did.

Days stretched on. One week blurred into two and the weed of frustration took root inside the confines of his mind. As long as Louise Newman hovered on the edge of life, his journey wasn't complete either. Realizing this, the answer became clear.

With pious intent, Alistair drove the range roads back to Lethbridge, and brought his rattling car to a stop outside the red brick hospital. Avoiding eye-contact, he walked inside. His inner voice guided him to the elevator and down the hall. He'd made it all the way to the door, when his gaze lifted. He stumbled to a stop. Rich Evans dozed in the recliner next to her, his eyes closed, a book open on his chest. Fury burned under Alistair's skin. He understood now.

Lou was staying for him.

Alistair moved like a wraith back through the warren of corridors and waited outside the building under a cloud of discontent. Rich didn't leave for lunch. He didn't leave for dinner either. In fact, he only walked outside when visiting hours were over and the hospital closed for the night. Alistair's expression tightened into a mask of discontent.

He couldn't get to Lou today, but someday Rich would leave her side. Alistair smiled darkly. Then he'd return.

CHAPTER TWENTY-EIGHT

Sadie wasn't exactly sure when she stopped thinking of Rich Evans as an outsider, but once she had, she couldn't go back. *Might have been after Lou went into the hospital* she thought as she added the final details on her current report. *Nah,* a voice in the back of her mind answered. *Happened earlier than that.*

She winced, her face pained for a second, then icily controlled. If Jim Flagstone had been Sadie's right hand in life, he was almost more than that in death. She couldn't stop thinking about him.

Around the office everything else was the same. Liz stood at the front desk as she filed papers into the upright cabinet. Jordan sat across from Sadie, squinting at his computer screen. *Where Jim used to sit...* She took a slow breath and choked on the lump in her throat. Jordan looked up.

"You okay, Sadie?" he asked.

She lifted her chin, her eyes bright and glittering. "I'm fine."

"You, um..." Jordan cleared his throat. "You seen Jim's plaque yet? I was down at the graveyard yesterday and—"

"Why are you telling me this?!"

"I-I don't know. I just thought you might want to go out to see it sometime."

"Well I *don't!*" Sadie hit the 'save' button at the same time she pushed back from the computer desk. "I've gotta go."

Jordan's gaze scurried away. "Alright then. Give me a shout if you need anything."

"Doubt it." Sadie grabbed her jacket and strode to the door. She slammed it behind her.

Jordan turned to Liz. "Why does she hate me?"

She shook her head. "She doesn't. Sadie's just hurting. She's dealing with things in her own way. And she's not quite through the darkness yet."

* * *

Audrika was the first to show up at the cabin. Rich didn't quite know what to make of Mrs. Kulkarni in her bright purple track suit, as she stood on his porch in the dark. She held a tray covered in tin foil, her cheeks and nose pink with the late-evening cold. Autumn was here, but winter nipped at its heels.

"I was baking," she said. "And I had too much so I brought you some."

"I'm fine, but thanks anyhow."

"You're not," Audrika said. "You're a skinny as a scarecrow." She shoved the tray into his hands. "Now, take it and don't argue with me. I'm coming back for that tray tomorrow, but in the meantime, you are going to eat."

Rich smiled. She reminded him of his grandmother. "Yes, ma'am."

Hunter drove up next evening with a trio of dogs in his truck. He and Rich stood on the porch and talked about small things while the dogs howled inside the cab. Rich could tell that Hunter wanted to say something. He shifted in place, his hands clenched behind him and then in front. Finally, he cleared his throat.

"People tell you that if you just pray hard enough, you'll get your miracle," Hunter said, "but I don't think that's true."

Rich's stomach contracted like he'd been punched. "Wh-what?"

"When someone's sick and not getting better, people give you all types of crap. They tell you things'll be fine because they want to believe it themselves. But the truth I've found is that you just have to learn to keep going despite the pain."

Rich tried to answer, but his throat was too tight. He wanted back in the house, back into the safety of his sorrow.

"I, um… I lost someone once," Hunter said, looking out at the mountains. "Not right away, mind you, but years after we'd met."

Rich nodded. He wanted this conversation over.

"I was in love with her years before," Hunter said. "But I… I waited too long before realizing it, and she went off and married my best friend."

"Wow, that… sucks."

Hunter snorted. "Well, yes and no," he said with a wry grin. "I mean, Yuki and Old Lou were good together. They really were." He shook his head. "She never gave me the time of day back then, but her and Lou, well… they had something special."

"You and Yuki?"

"Were never anything more than good friends," Hunter said, blushing under his stubble. "I waited too damned long to do anything about it, and by the time I had the nerve to ask her out, she was already dating Lou. And then they ran off and got married, and life just sort of moved on without me."

"I-I never knew that."

"Not many do. Still, I had to smile and talk to her for the rest of her life. Just about killed me, all that pretending." He cleared his throat. "Yuki died of cancer years ago. I had to watch that too. I prayed for her to be okay. Thought if I could just find the right words for God, she'd be alright. Even went to church. Didn't help."

"God, that's—that's awful."

"And then Old Lou—my best friend—well, he never got over her death. He died a few years later."

"Jesus."

"And then there was Young Louise," Hunter sighed. "I couldn't really tell *her* what'd happened with the three of us. Not with Yuki being her mother and all."

"Christ, Hunter." Rich said with a bitter laugh. "Aren't these stories supposed to make me feel better?"

"They are." The older man chuckled. "At any rate, they're *supposed* to."

Rich smiled, but the expression felt like a shirt that didn't fit. "Well, you're doing a crap job of it."

Hunter reached out and put a heavy hand on Rich's shoulder. "At least you didn't wait too long," he said. "Even if Lou never gets better, you had *some* time. There's comfort in that."

Rich's smile faded as the ache returned. The silence dragged on between them, pressing to be released. In the truck, the dogs lunged and barked, the rest of the world silent by comparison.

"I-I tried," Rich said.

"What?"

"The day Lou was shot—I—I was on the floor," he said. "And Susan was shooting—and Lou… she—" Rich's voice broke. "She came out of the back room. And I—I didn't have time to—to stop it—I—"

Hunter's fingers clamped tight on Rich's shoulder. "You can't blame yourself."

"But I should've stepped in the way. It should be *me* in the hospital. It should be me! It should—"

Hunter leaned closer, his faded eyes wild with pain. "Stop it!"

"But Lou—"

"I *knew* Susan Varley hated everything the Whitewater stood for! I warned Jeff Chan about her last year. And I figured, maybe, Sue and Colt were the ones who'd broken in that first night, but I just— Well, let's just say I knew why Sue wouldn't want to be caught." His wrinkled face fell. "I could've stopped this whole mess long before she walked into Lou's garage. If anyone is guilty of letting it happen, it's me."

This time it was Rich who reached out and he patted the old man's shoulder. "It's okay, Hunter."

"No, it's not. But that's life, and at some point you just gotta get on with it, no matter what you done."

The youngest of the three dogs had worked his way up to the truck window. As the two men watched, the dog wiggled through the narrow opening, nails scraping down the side of the door as he fell. He sprinted forward and ran happy circles around them. It was, Rich realized, the howling dog who'd terrified him the summer before.

Hunter chased after the cougar-hound. "Damned dog," he grumbled when he got hold of his collar. "Drives me nuts."

Rich gave a half-smile. "But you love him anyways."

"'Course I do." Hunter laughed. "He's just young is all. Inexperienced." He rubbed a hand over the loose skin of the dog's ears. "You're a good dog, aren't you, Duke?" The dog barked happily. Hunter nodded to the truck where the other dogs bayed. "Alrighty then, I should get moving. But try to come by for coffee sometime."

"I'll try."

Rich watched as Hunter dragged the dog back to the vehicle, his smile slowly disappearing. In minutes he was back in the cabin, finding another book for his continued vigil at Lou's side.

* * *

The first Monday night in November, Margaret Lu and Audrika Kulkarni showed up on Rich's porch like mother hens to escort him to Hunter's Coffee Shop. There, Rich sat brooding. He gazed out the window into the dark, wishing for an excuse to leave. The group argued about the plaque that had been installed to commemorate the life of Constable Jim Flagstone. Some thought it too simple. Others complained that cultured granite could have shaved off at least a thousand dollars from the cost.

"Sadie hasn't gone to see it yet," Hunter said. "Too busy is what she told me."

"She's *always* too busy," Audrika said. "I waited half an hour at the station, trying to talk to her." She sniffed. "Never came out."

"Maybe it'd help if someone else tried," a voice from the back offered. "Someone who *hasn't* been out to the plaque yet. Someone like…" Audrika glared and the voice died away.

Rich blinked gritty eyes and sighed. He wanted out of the restaurant so he could drive back to Lethbridge. He'd sit outside the hospital in the dark, and be there when visiting hours began. Distance hurt him.

"How about if you ask Sadie about it, Rich?" Hunter said. When Rich didn't answer, Hunter spoke again. "Rich?"

Rich blinked. "Sorry. What's that?"

"We were wondering if you'd take Sadie up to see Jim's plaque," Hunter said. "She hasn't gone yet. Neither have you."

"I—I don't think that's any of my business."

"It's everyone's business," Audrika said. "And you knew Jim and Sadie as well as anyone else."

"I don't think—"

"Have you been out to the plaque?" she asked.

"No, but—"

"Then it's settled!" Audrika said. "You get Sadie to go with you. We're all very worried about her, you know. The way she's closed herself off since Jim died." Her dark eyes pinned Rich down. *Was she talking about Sadie or him?*

"I, um… I don't know if… Look, I'm just a little busy."

"Now Rich, we'd do it if it were you and Lou." She nodded to Hunter. "Wouldn't we, Hunter?"

"Of course we would."

"Look, I'll think about it," Rich said. "But I'm not promising anything. With all the driving to Lethbridge, I—"

"You know, if *Lou* was here," Audrika said. "I'm sure *she'd* be the first one to talk to Sadie—"

Rich stood from his chair. "I've got to go." And before anyone could interrupt him, he walked out.

* * *

Rich sat at Lou's side, his fingers wrapped around her limp hand.

"I'm taking Sadie to see Jim Flagstone's plaque today," he said. "She doesn't want to go, but everyone in town thinks she should." He laughed tiredly. "And I somehow got roped into taking her."

His words trailed off. The room was quiet. Calm. Lou's face turned to the side on the pillow, as if in sleep. Rich leaned forward and touched her cheek.

"I miss you, you know?"

The machines continued their steady pace. The autumn light outside the window bright. On another day, Rich would have stayed until visiting hours were over, but the unwanted task was a weight he didn't want. *Sooner I do it, the sooner it's done.*

Rich leaned in and pressed a gentle kiss against Lou's lips. She stirred as if waking, and his heart lifted then fell as the movement stilled. "Well, I should probably go," he said, and let go of her hand. "I'll be back tomorrow."

For a full minute after he left, the only movement or sound was the steady thrum of machines, and then, like a sleepwalker, Lou turned her head toward the west window. Her brow creased, as if seeing something worrisome behind closed lids.

* * *

Sadie hunched on the grass next to Jim's grave marker, her face clutched in her hands. Ragged sobs emerged through her fingers as the sound of unbridled heartache filled the glade of trees. Rich waited a few steps away. Unlike the grassy plot with neat lines of tombstones where his grandparents were buried, the Waterton cemetery was hatched out of the wilderness, a square of grass stolen back from the forest. Tall trees surrounded Rich on all sides, the mountain peaks visible beyond. Above Sadie's weeping, birdsong filled the air.

Jim's plaque was understated in its simplicity. There was an engraving of a mountain range and then Jim's full name, James Harker Gladstone, followed by his birth and death dates. Beneath it was a single phrase: *A good friend.*

"Miss you so much, Jimmy," Sadie choked. "So goddamned much."

Rich took a step away from her. "I'm just going to go for a little walk," he said over his shoulder.

He took a few steps back to the parking lot, and paused, undecided. Sadie needed a drive back. She could be minutes or hours. How long did it take to say goodbye? Rich couldn't fathom it. *It could have been Lou buried here.* The thought terrified him almost as much as the doctor's warning to 'prepare'. With fear's arrival, the need to move rippled through his limbs. He couldn't endure the thought of Lou torn from him. Couldn't find his way back to his calm misery.

Without plan or direction, Rich walked straight into the trees. He started slow, but his pace picked up and in moments he was jogging. Sadie's raw grief had unsettled a new fear, deep inside him: *What if Lou doesn't wake up?* The thought propelled him forward. His legs pumped against the uneven ground, knees lifting the way he'd been trained when he'd run track, only this time he never slowed to find his pace. Today he sprinted full out, with the sole aim of escape.

Sweat trickled into his eyes and blinded him; his chest burned like fire. Brambles tore at his arms and twigs tangled his legs. Still Rich didn't slow. *What if Lou never recovers? What if she lives the rest of her life like this?* The trees thickened, and he tripped over a half-submerged stump. His feet squelched in horse manure. When he stood up, he saw a trail marred with horseshoe prints visible in the trees. There he could run without pause. Rich moved deeper and deeper into the forest as he followed the trail. *What if she never wakes up? My God—what if she dies?!* Branches whipped past and slashed his face and neck. Blood from a nick trickled down his cheek. His coat was torn by a ragged branch, and his shoes sullied and slippery.

Still he ran.

Ahead was a bright patch of sunshine where the path opened into a clearing. Rich forced his shaking calves and thighs to work harder, and pushed off the rocky ground the way he'd done years before. He was lightheaded with exertion, his tongue thick, mouth dry. He pressed forward and stumbled into the light. Beyond him lay a small, boggy lake, a few patches of brush along its edge. There was the scent of decay, and Rich's nostrils flared in disgust. His feet slowed just as one of the bushes moved. He jerked to a stop and his knee twisted in his haste. A stone's throw away, a grizzly bear, interrupted from its feast of carrion, stood up on hind legs.

Rich Evans was about to die.

CHAPTER TWENTY-NINE

The bear took a step forward and Rich's eyes widened in terror. He was going to die. Today. *Now!* That single thought cut through layers of pain.

"My God, no!"

A thousand details appeared at once: the diamonds' glitter of the lake's surface, the clouds overhead, the tang of carrion that hung in the air like soured perfume, and the car key that stabbed into his leg where it had lodged in the bottom of his pocket. Everything in that moment shone with crystalline perfection.

Rich stumbled backward. His knee throbbed and his footsteps were awkward and jerky. The grizzly took a step closer.

Lou's face appeared in Rich's mind. It was a random moment from one morning in the bedroom: Lou grinned at him, one hand held in the air as she told him a story.

"The man looked around, searching for escape, but there was nothing he could do. Then his eyes caught on a bright red strawberry, clinging to the cliff face. The man held onto the vine with one hand, and with the other, he plucked the strawberry... It was the sweetest thing he'd ever tasted in his life."

Rich gasped and Lou was gone.

The grizzly roared and shook its head, the scruff of its neck rolling back and forth with the motion. Rich cringed.

Time's up.

Something broke through the trees behind him and he half-turned. There was an explosion, louder than any thunder Rich had ever heard. He fell to his knees as the bear tumbled backward and its roar changed into a bellow of rage. Before Rich could move, the glade resounded with another ear-splitting clap of gunfire, and he hunkered down in fear.

The grizzly lay on the trail a few feet away, perfectly still, its muzzle blown half-off. He couldn't hear for the ringing of his ears, his mind shell-shocked. He blinked, the bedroom and Lou appearing once more.

"So where's my strawberry in all of this?"

"It's a new day..."

Rich lifted his head. His body trembled like a leaf; his heart thundered in his chest, but he was alive. *Alive!* He clambered upright on shaking legs and turned around.

A man on a horse came out of the shadows into the light.

* * *

Alistair had checked in at the hospital in the morning, but finding Rich's vehicle parked in its usual spot, he'd left. He drove to Medicine Hat and explored the city with a tourist's eyes. The city was small for Alistair's tastes, but it had an eclectic variety of shops and galleries. He wandered through the river bottom, comparing its lushness to Lethbridge's dryer climate. Both had beauty, though one was more—

Alistair's body went rigid, his vision doused in a vision so bright and real his eyes were alive with it. *A bear rushed forward in rage, its roar echoing through the valley. A person half its size waited for the attack as—*The vision released him and Alistair stumbled sideways, catching himself against a tree trunk. He struggled back to the present, confused by the sight. It wasn't Lou he'd seen standing in the mountain glade. It couldn't be Lou! She was trapped in Lethbridge, asleep and dreaming.

"Rich Evans!" Alistair gasped. "He's in Waterton today!"

Sometime in the hours since Alistair had left the hospital and driven the almost two hours to Medicine Hat, Rich had left Lou's side. *Alistair hadn't been there to see it.* With a howl of rage, Alistair sprinted through the trees to where his car waited. It was time to do his part. Louise Newman was a tathagata and he would set her free.

* * *

Levi nudged his horse forward and headed from the cover of trees into the meadow beyond. On the trail lay the grizzly, Rich Evans crouched near its feet. A short distance away, a half-eaten elk carcass lay on its side, stiff-legged and bloated. Behind the carnage, the scene was calm. Lonesome Lake was still as glass, the forest silent in the wake of the gunfire. Levi stared down at Rich, waiting for him to react.

"Wh- why?" Rich said.

"Bear was gonna kill you. You'd be dead if I hadn't."

"But… but why did you save me?"

Levi stared at Rich Evans. He tottered on his feet, his face ashen. Gone was the confident man he'd been months before, a broken shell in his place. For a split-second, a memory of another face appeared: this one was a four-year-old boy and he grinned at Levi from behind his father's knees.

"I owed Yuki Newman a debt," Levi said. "Always meant to pay it back to Louise, but never had the chance." He jerked hard on the reins and guided the horse onto the trail. "And now I have."

Rich followed. "But—But I don't understand. You love the Park.

Why would you…?"

"Now there you're wrong," he said. "I love *the land*, boy. That's what you're missing."

"But the park—"

Levi threw his head back and laughed. The park was as abstract to him as the new-fangled computers that everyone kept going on about. He nodded toward Bellevue Hill and the valley where his grandfather, Ephraim Thompson, had settled a century before. "I'd kill more'n my share of animals if it meant protecting this place."

Rich looked at the bear and then back to Levi. His mouth fell open in astonishment. "You're the one who put the dead animals on Jeff Chan's porch last summer. Not Susan. Not Colt. It was *you*… you all along. You chased Jeff Chan out of town!"

Levi's mouth twitched mischievously. "I just helped Mr. Chan come to his own decision with a little bit of… *decorating*, you might say. Tried it with you, too, but it seems you've got gumption." He touched the brim of his hat. "Guess I'll see you 'round then."

In seconds he disappeared back into the trees.

* * *

Rich walked through the forest on watery limbs, his knee pulsing in time to his footsteps. His breath was ragged and his head swirled with vertigo. Behind him, the forest closed in. The canopy of leaves swayed and sunbeams danced in time to the motion as lines of light passed through the shadows. Rich stared at them in awe. Even the breeze was different. It brushed over his sweaty neck and face, soothing him in the jittery aftermath of near-death.

The trail took him to the graveyard where Sadie waited next to the truck. Rich cut through the bushes to reach the open ground, his eyes on the great sea of sky and clouds that skidded over its surface like boats. His heart slowed as peace filled his limbs. For the first time since Lou had been shot, Rich felt completely alive.

Sadie called out to him as he approached. "Thought you'd gone and taken off on me. Was going to give you five more minutes, then walk back to town."

Sobbing laughter bubbled from Rich's chest.

"What?" Sadie asked.

"I wouldn't leave," Rich said, wiping tears from his eyes. "I can't."

Sadie tugged open the door of the truck. "Why's that?"

He gestured to the splash of autumn coloured trees, and the purple-grey mountains beyond. "Because Waterton is my home."

* * *

Visiting hours ended at seven, but Rich didn't care. He drove to Lethbridge with the windows down, the rush of wind through his hair as invigorating as the blood red bands of sunset that painted the prairie. He needed to share his revelation, to tell Lou that he understood what she'd meant that day.

The hospital's parking lot was mostly empty by the time he arrived. Rich took a spot near the door, glancing in surprise at a mud-splattered car with California plates. It struck him, as he jogged into the fishtank-like interior, that everyone in the world had their own story: The woman at the elevator who was carrying two paper coffee cups, and the young couple struggling with a baby's carrier and bags. Bits of people's stories were everywhere, and Lou knew how to read them. Reaching the unit, Rich began to jog.

"Mr. Evans," the nurse at the desk said as she looked up from her paperwork. "Visiting hours are ending in ten minutes. You—"

"I'll only be a second. I was away. I just need a minute!"

"Did your friend find you?"

Rich paused. "Friend?"

"An American," she said. "He came in a minute ago. Asked if you were around. Seemed in a real rush to get in before visiting hours ended."

"What friend?" Rich asked, dry-mouthed. Details interrupted his thoughts. *The car outside had California plates.*

"Thought you would've seen him at the elevators. He was only—"

"What was his name?!"

"Hmmm… It was odd. I can't quite remember…" Rich bolted up the hallway before she finished, already knowing the answer. The nurse stepped out to follow him. "I think the name was Al or something… No wait! It was Alistair."

"NO!" he roared.

"Wait! What's happened?"

"Call security!" Rich yelled. "Call them NOW!"

* * *

Lou's nightmare began with an image: She floated above the bed, looking down at herself. Her limbs were looser than they'd been in the last weeks, tiny twitches uncurling them like a flower about to bloom. She dropped lower.

There was a man at her side.

"Rich?"

He turned and the dream changed. It wasn't Rich, but Alistair Diarmuid, a small pillow clutched in his hands like a present. He smiled, but the look in his eyes scared her.

"If you want to change things," Alistair said, "you need to finish what you started. I'm here to help you."

Lou dropped lower yet again. Now she stared up at him with half-shut eyes.

Alistair reached out with the pillow. "Don't be afraid, Lou. I'm here to help you. Your journey isn't over. It's time to move on." He pushed the pillow down on her face and the nightmare changed again.

Lou sat on the dock and stared into the blue depths of Waterton Lake to where a figure floated under the surface. It was the woman who'd walked into Emerald Bay, her pockets full of stones, but in the dream, the woman's face was a mirror of Lou's own. Alistair clasped the back of Lou's neck and pushed her off the dock into the water. Lou twisted and turned, choking as she tried to get away.

"No, Alistair! I've chosen! I can't—"

With a splash, she slipped under the surface.

* * *

Rich slammed the hospital door open.

Two things came to him at once. First, that the room was too dark. Second, that Alistair had a pillow against Lou's face.

"STOP!"

He crossed the room in two steps and slammed headlong into Alistair's side. The narrow hospital bed screeched against the floor and slid sideways as the two men tumbled to the floor.

Rich came down hard on top of Alistair. "You BASTARD!"

"She's supposed to die! Louise sacrificed herself for—"

A fist to the mouth stopped Alistair's words. The two of them rolled together as Rich's knuckles flayed him again and again. The door swung open. A woman screamed. She rushed to Lou's bedside.

Rich didn't stop his attack. *Couldn't!* All the rage, all the disappointment, all the fury over Lou's loss coalesced in the violence of a prairie storm, unleashed with brutal intensity. Lightning flashed in the darkness of Rich's mind: *Alistair killed Lou.* Rich's fist slammed down and Alistair's nose gave way in a spray of blood. Another flash of lightning: *Lou's gone. Gone!* He slammed his fist into Alistair's teeth, tearing a ragged line into the corner of his mouth like a macabre smile.

"Mr. Evans!" the woman shouted. "Stop! Please!"

Rich's body was the storm, his fists hail as they pummeled the prairie grass down to the ground it had sprung from. Under him, Alistair writhed, a bloody grin on his face.

"She's dead!" Rich cried. "DEAD!"

He pulled his hand back once more and the physics of the room abruptly changed. Rich jerked and struggled as two security officers caught him in an iron grip.

"The other one too!" someone ordered.

Two men dragged Alistair away. His weird sing-song voice rose as he disappeared out the door: "She was never supposed to live. She stepped in front of you, Rich! She wanted to die! She wanted—"

The door slammed, and Rich turned to see two nurses working frantically over Lou. Her lips were blue, face ashen.

"Lou, please!" he begged. "Breathe!"

Hearing his voice, Louise Newman took her first full breath in weeks.

"She's breathing!" the nurse said to someone. *Who?* Lou wondered. It seemed like she ought to know.

"Lou!" Rich's sobbing voice broke through her confusion.

She rolled her head to the side, letting momentum move her. She was exhausted, every limb filled with lead. Two men held Rich by each arm, but he jumped and struggled like a fish on a line.

"Lou!" he cried. "You're alive!"

"Love you, Rich."

She lifted her fingers to reach for him. The motion seemed to be the sign the others in the room were waiting for. The uniformed men released Rich and he stumbled, fell, stood again, and threw himself against Lou, sobbing into her chest. Lou put her hand against the back of his head. Just that motion sapped her strength, but she held him against her heart.

"I had a dream," Lou said. "The strangest dream."

Rich lifted his head and smiled down at her from a tear-ravaged face. "What was it?"

"You were sitting beside me in our cabin and you were telling me stories."

CHAPTER THIRTY

It was late spring, and Lou's Garage had only been open for two weekends, since the winter everyone at Hunter's Coffee Shop had declared "the worst winter since '69". That was the year the mercury dropped until it bottomed out at -46 degrees, and then the wind—*the blasted wind!*"—rushed down from the North, forcing the windchill into the -60s. Rich grinned as old-timers, Levi and Hunter, and Old Ron Hamamoto, argued about what was worse: the dump of almost a foot of snow in September, and the steadily increasing drifts throughout the last winter of the twentieth century, or thirty years prior. Rich smiled and nodded, and let them talk. He didn't really care. He'd cheered the arrival of the new millennium in a tiny cabin in the Canadian Rockies, the woman he loved at his side, and a grin on his face. It was a far cry from where he'd expected to be, but sometimes you just had to enjoy the journey.

He'd been thinking that a lot these days.

The spring of the new millennium had arrived late, but Mother Nature seemed to be in a rush to make up for lost time. Mid-June, the summer was already shaping up to be a scorcher. Rich was working in the garage today, moving between the blistering sunshine and the blessedly cool shadows of the interior. He heard the grinding sound of the car's engine long before it arrived. Mila was working the front, but she popped her head through the interior door and rapped twice on the frame.

"Rich! There's a guy with car trouble," she shouted. "Gonna send him around to you, okay?"

"Gotcha."

Rich slid the backboard out from under Sadie's truck and wiped his hands along his overalls as the car pulled up. There was a middle-aged man inside, his face sullen with frustration. Next to him, a woman with bottle-blonde hair and dark sunglasses stared out the window. They both looked up as he approached.

"Can I help you?"

"Engine's giving me trouble," the man said. "Would you mind looking at it?"

"C'mon into the first stall. I'll see what I can do."

"We're kind of in a hurry," the passenger said irritably. "I hope you work fast."

Rich chuckled. Tourists were always in a rush.

"Leave it running for just a sec," Rich said, opening the hood. As the rasping grew exponentially louder, Rich's ears honed in on the hidden details of the sound. He lifted his head. "Turn it off," he shouted. "Think I have an idea of what it is."

The man stepped out of the vehicle and came to Rich's side. "What's the problem?"

"I'm guessing it's your engine mount," Rich said. "Of course I won't know for sure until I take a good look."

"Can you fix it?"

"Probably. Give me a bit and I'll know for sure."

The man nodded. The woman clicked on the radio and a repetitive techno beat filled the garage.

"So are you Lou?" the man asked.

"No, I'm Rich, but this is Lou's garage." He gestured to the line of tools on the wall. Pinned in place next to the clamps was the photograph of Rich and Lou, side by side. They were laughing, Rich's eyes on the camera, Lou's on him. At the bottom was a scribble of handwriting. "That's Lou over there. This is her place."

"Oh," the man said in surprise, "I just figured with the name and everything, it was you."

"Lots of people think that."

He moved his attention to the silent vehicle and his mind took on the calm he always found in engine repair. After a few minutes of tinkering, Rich glanced up. The stranger stood watching him work.

"Lou your wife?" the man asked.

Rich grinned as he thought of the small blue box he had hidden in the bottom of the bedroom closet. "Haven't quite convinced her yet," he said with a wink, "but I'm working on it."

The man's expression soured. His gaze flitted over to the woman filing her nails in the car, then back again. "Well, don't go rushing into anything," he said in a low voice. "What I wouldn't give to be back in your shoes."

His tone rubbed like grit over sunburned skin, and Rich bit back a sharp retort. Instead he forced a smile. "It's Lou who doesn't want to rush into things. I already brought it up with her twice. She keeps saying she'll know when it's time."

"Oh? That's… surprising."

"No. That's just Lou." Rich leaned in to peer at the engine. "She's the best mechanic I've ever met. And she has a story for everything."

"Did she ever have a story about cars breaking down in the middle of a road trip?"

Rich loosened a bolt. "Not exactly, but I remember her telling me a story about a settler named Ephraim Thompson…"

* * *

In the shade of the porch, Lou dozed in the Muskoka chair, her legs kicked up on its mate, a book half-forgotten in one hand. The two chairs were a remnant of Lou's childhood. Her father had built them decades ago and Yuki had painted them a verdant green, her favourite colour. Lou had all but forgotten the two chairs until Rich had pulled them out of the recesses of the garage earlier this spring, determined to "put them to good use".

"Rich." The sound of his name brought a half-smile to her lips. He had settled into her home and life with a solidness she'd never known before. Each day brought new joys. Whispering Aspens hummed with his continued presence.

Lou's eyelids drooped and the book slipped lower and lower until it rested against her lap. In the distance, a fat-bellied mountain bumble bee moved from bee balm to columbines, ignoring the shredded annuals that filled the flowerbeds. Rich had insisted on planting them despite Lou's warning that the deer would eat them. (They had.) She smiled as she remembered Rich's frustration the morning he'd looked down from their bedroom window to discover a doe nibbling his newly-planted seedlings. The appearance of two spindly legged fawns had silenced him.

The afternoon air was warm, Lou's body wrapped in it. The bee buzzed nearer and she sighed, the memory of spring blending into other thoughts: dinner with Hunter and Levi two nights ago, her daily walks to rebuild her strength, the nights in Rich's arms. A blush rose up her chest to her cheeks as the memory grew bolder. She wished Rich was home now too, but someone had to keep the garage open. Lou knew she *should* be there, but her recovery had been slower than she'd expected. It felt as if the winter in the cabin had been a chrysalis and she was only now beginning to emerge.

Her lashes fluttered and the first whisper of a vision flickered behind closed lids.

Lou waited on the crest of a hill, the wind ruffling over her hair, and cooling her neck. She turned in surprise.

It was the Crypt Lake trail, but more than that, it was the Crypt Lake trail from her vision of Rich, months before. The clouds, the sun, and even the swirl of foliage under the hand of the wind were the same... only she was here in it. Not above.

Lou's breath caught, as Rich broke through the trees. He lifted his eyes to the sky, wrinkles fanning his cheeks as he smiled, and then his gaze dropped.

"There you are, Lou," he laughed. "Thought we'd lost you for a minute."

Lou opened her mouth to answer him, but movement in the trees drew her gaze. A boy of perhaps four passed through the dark screen of trees and walked into the light. He smiled at her and she knew somehow—in the way she always knew—that he was the boy who'd once been lost. The child Yuki had pined for and Levi Thompson remembered even today. His hair was black, but his eyes were blue. Lou felt her heart swell in a wave of love so intense, her chest ached. He ran forward, passing Rich to—

"Lou?"

The vision recoiled with a snap. Lou lurched forward and her forehead bumped into Rich's chin. He stumbled back, laughing.

"Sorry, Lou. I shouldn't have bugged you. You were asleep, sweetheart."

"I was," she said with a smile. "But I'm glad you woke me."

ACKNOWLEDGEMENTS

The writing of a book is a lengthy process, but I could not re-lease *The Dark Divide* without expressing my sincere gratitude to the many people who have shaped it along the way:

Thank you to my husband, my most enthusiastic collaborator, for reading every iteration of this project from beginning to end, so that I could make sure the language sounded 'just right'. Thank you also to my children, for tolerating long periods when I couldn't play, as I wrote, rewrote, and rewrote again. I owe you one.

A grateful shout-out to my fellow writers—far too many to name—who kept me going when my spark for writing was low. Thanks to Morty Mint, my agent, for his unwavering support and level-headed advice. An enthusiastic thank you to Dinah Forbes, my editor, for her incomparable guidance; her counsel shaped this mystery into something worth reading. My sincere gratitude and affection to the Stonehouse publishing team, especially Netta John-son and Julie Yerex, for their tireless efforts in bringing this project together. *The Dark Divide* is yours as much as mine.

Finally, two special notes of appreciation. For my father, who inspired my love of the written word, but never lived to see the Wa-terton series published. And to you, the reader, for joining me on this journey. No book is truly 'finished' without your participation.

Danika Stone is an author, artist, and educator who discovered a passion for writing fiction while in the throes of her master's thesis. A self-declared bibliophile, Danika now writes novels for both adults (*Edge of Wild*, *The Dark Divide*, the *Intaglio* series, and *Ctrl Z*) and teens (*All the Feels*, *Internet Famous*, and *Icarus*). When not writing, Danika can be found hiking in the Rockies, planning grand adventures, and spending far too much time online. She lives with her husband, three sons, and a houseful of imaginary characters in a windy corner of Alberta, Canada.